THE
GOLDEN
CHALICE

Book #2 of the Guardian Keeps Series

The Congruent Mage Series

The Xenotech Support Series

The Guardian Keeps Series

Dedication

To my amazing daughter who has always inspired my writing!

Cover design and Guardian Keeps illustration
by Dave Schroeder

ISBN-13: 978-0-9978319-9-3

Spiral Arm Press
1725 Carlington Court
Grayson, GA 30017
www.SpiralArmPress.com

A Poem of the Sixteen Keeps

North Keep's for the Mages, famed for scroll and spell.
East Keep's for the Healers, ones who make us well.
South Keep's for the Fighters, trained in sword and shield.
West Keep's for the Scholars, wise in every field.

Rose Keep is for flowers,
Gold Keep stores up riches,
Herb Keep grows ingredients
For potions and for dishes.

Yew Keep is for bowyers,
Horse Keep is for horses,
Forge Keep is for smithing steel
To arm the South Keep's forces.

Iron Keep digs for good red ore,
Dragon Keep trains dragons,
Gem Keep knows all fine gems' lore,
And also—they make wagons.

Quill Keep is for copyists,
Silver Keep is hidden,
Ice Keep's full of frigid mists,
Where none may go unbidden.

Sixteen Keeps are built of stone,
Sixteen Keeps are standing,
Guarding from the Deeps below,
Tall and proud, commanding.

The Guardian Keeps

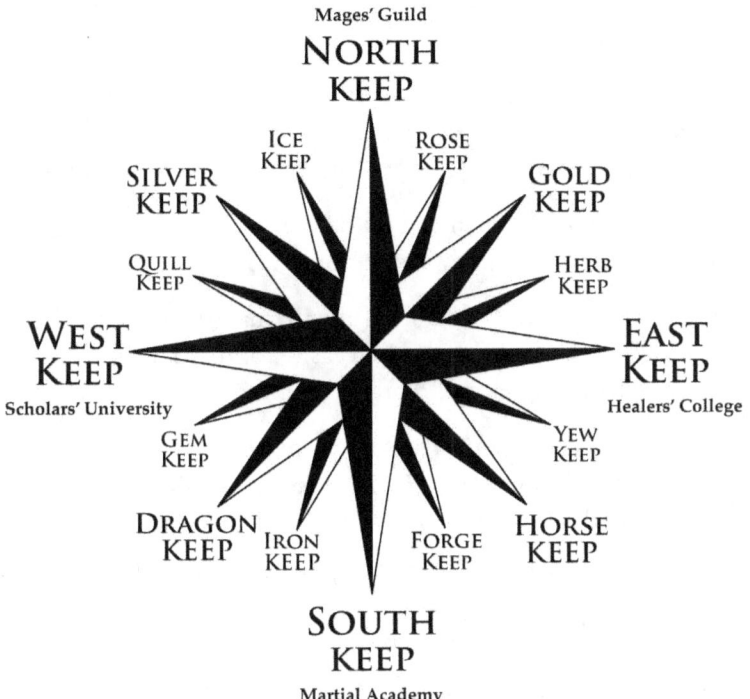

Mages' Guild
NORTH KEEP

ICE KEEP

ROSE KEEP

SILVER KEEP

GOLD KEEP

QUILL KEEP

HERB KEEP

WEST KEEP
Scholars' University

EAST KEEP
Healers' College

GEM KEEP

YEW KEEP

DRAGON KEEP

IRON KEEP

FORGE KEEP

HORSE KEEP

SOUTH KEEP
Martial Academy

Dramatis Personae
The New Golden Company

Garum: a halfling chief cook and slinger with military experience in love with Sweetie

Sweetie: a very short human woman and former server at the Green Doors Inn and Tavern. Granddaughter of Sir Donal. She carries the wand of illusion formerly owned by Céptianne.

Drain: a dwarvish woman and trained sewer mason. Sensible, even by high dwarvish standards.

Sir Donal Tilter: a tall, older human with many years of military command leadership but is often easily confused. Has bracers of strength. Sweetie's grandfather.

Prestyn: a young human mage, son of Prestio and Cadabryn, senior mages in the Mages' Guild. Has a many-limbed Cloak of Arms and dozens of spell scrolls from his parents.

Flisk: a young elvish archer with poor vision that's now improved.

Arrex: a young healer just out of the College of Healers. Fond of Lark.

Xarra and *Yarra:* young human farm girls who want to be adventurers. Becoming good with blades. Fond of almost everybody.

Crank: a young human man and former kitchen drudge at the Green Doors Inn and Tavern. A decent cook whose skills are improving. Mysterious connections to the Scholars' University. Carries a staff. Friends with Jelly.

Jelly: a blob of sentient protoplasm cut from a Jelly of the Deeps. Usually rides on Crank's shoulder.

Vip-vip: a vixer, one of the denizens of the Deeps that fixes things and keeps everything running. Has decided that traveling with the new Golden Company is more fun. Hard to understand.

Lark: a young human woman and healer who is better at making healing potions than most of the faculty at the College of Healers. Had been held back because the College didn't want to lose her skills when she graduated. Quite smart and fond of Arrex. He will eventually figure that out.

The Black Company

Görthang: a very tall and muscular orc fighter with huge fangs. Carries two swords *and* a shield. Fond of Blōgot.

Hrefna: a huge troll and powerful mage. Not wise to get on her bad side.

Blōgot: an orc and a skilled archer. She's fond of Görthang.

Kléppri: a gnomish fighter who carries an enchanted spear that can extend and retract at his command.

Gêrdun: one of the only ogres to attend the College of Healers. Expelled before he could graduate.

Chophorn: a sylviant and ranger who wears ironwood treebark armor and carries an axe.

Púki: a shortorc acrobat plus a trap and lock specialist. He's about the same height as Garum but has a much less pleasant personality. Shortorcs are the orc equivalents of halflings for humans.

The Original Golden Company

Aubericht the Magnificent: a very tall and muscular human fighter with a huge ego and little respect for women. Wears shiny gold-washed armor. Carries two swords *and* a shield. Fond of himself.

The Stone Prince: a supercilious 'royal' dwarf with an enchanted hammer-axe and helm.

Khrusósha the Archmage: a powerful mage with a Cloak of Arms.

Barton DeClāre: an older human healer.

Galingálë the Archer: a lithe elf of indeterminate age.

Céptianne the Exceptional: appears to be a beautiful young human illusionist, though her true age and appearance are unknown. Reputed to be quite lusty with indescriminate and wide-ranging tastes in her amorous partners. Carries a wand of illusion.

Alderōn the Ranger: a sylviant and ranger. Short for one of his kind, he wears grey-white red alder bark armor.

Chapter 1

On the Road

"Why do we have to *walk* to Gold Keep?" asked Xarra.

"Why can't we take a magecoach and *ride*?" chimed in Yarra.

"Aren't we rich now?" whined both twins.

Four six-legged kittens, who weren't walking, but were riding on Xarra and Yarra's left and right shoulders, meowed their agreement.

"According to my inventory, we have a sizable number of gold pieces and a substantial collection of valuable gems," said Prestyn.

Garum shook his head and exchanged a look with Sweetie, walking beside him. *At least Prestyn had the good sense not to detail just how much portable wealth they were carrying,* thought Garum.

"Yes, but all those gems and gold pieces aren't ours," said Sweetie. "They belong to the Golden Company."

"Possession is ninety-nine out of a hundred parts of the law," muttered Drain under her breath.

"Aren't *we* the Golden Company now?" asked Crank.

Jelly, the pyramid of protoplasm recently adopted by Crank and riding on top of Crank's backpack, started glowing with a bright golden-yellow light to reinforce Crank's assertion.

"We're just borrowing the name," said Garum.

"Can't we borrow the gold pieces, too?" asked Arrex.

"And the gems?" said Flisk.

"I haven't even *tried* to put a value on all our magical arms, armor, and artifacts," said Prestyn as the extensions of his Cloak of Arms, a truly impressive enchanted object, waved vigorously to emphasize his words.

"Those are priceless, aren't they, Your Majesty," said Sir Donal, Sweetie's grandfather.

"Yes," Garum replied. "And they're not really *ours,* either."

"But they might as well be," said Drain.

"The whole point of us going to East Keep," said Sweetie, "is to see if anyone at the College of Healers can figure out how to restore Aubericht, Khrusósha, and the other members of the Golden Company."

"The original Golden Company," said Xarra.

"We're the *new* Golden Company," said Yarra.

"Then why are we stopping at Gold Keep first?" asked Crank.

"Because Gold Keep is where the biggest banks are located and we may need more funds to pay the College of Healers for their help," replied Garum. *And because if we're going to restore the original Golden Company,* he considered, *I want more of their treasure in our hands in case the healers expect a huge amount of compensation for their assistance. I also want to see what I can get for a heartstone in Gold Keep.* Garum smiled, remembering the beauty of the small, transparent, robin's-egg-sized gem with a ruby-colored crystalline heart inside it that rested at the bottom of his belt pouch.

Sweetie gave Garum a knowing smile and a slight nod. He immediately returned both, still feeling the glow of last night, when the two of them had spent time together in a featherbed at the Rose and Crown inn. The only reason Garum was confident he could access the original Golden Company's funds on deposit with banks in Gold Keep was because of what Sweetie had told him between sessions of intimate connection.

"I found a note written in Aubericht's hand when I was cleaning his rooms upstairs at the Green Doors," Sweetie had said. "It was a list of the banks, account numbers, and pass phrases for all the Golden Company's treasure stored in Gold Keep vaults. I made a copy of it." She'd shaken her head, then continued. "Aubericht had a very poor memory and was more interested in wine, women, and killing monsters of the Deeps than in memorizing minutiae."

Garum had levered himself up on one elbow. "Why didn't the Stone Prince or someone with more business sense manage the Golden Company's finances?" he'd asked.

"Trust," said Sweetie after she'd reached down to give Garum's buns an affectionate squeeze. "The Stone Prince would have siphoned off all their shared treasure into his private accounts. Everyone knew Aubericht was more into girls and glory than gold, so they went along with him controlling their joint funds."

Aubericht's poor memory and Sweetie's resourcefulness mean we should soon have access to the Golden Company's accumulated treasure, Garum mused. *I expect there will be a lot of it, given their reputation as the most successful band of adventurers in the lands protected by the Guardian Keeps.*

"Why are you smiling?" asked Sweetie when she glanced down at Garum.

"I think you can guess," said Garum.

Sweetie touched a finger to her nose and Garum did likewise. It was wise to keep any discussion regarding the details of the original Golden Company's treasure under the rose, at least for now.

Garum decided to focus on his surroundings. It was mid-afternoon. They'd gotten a late start leaving Rose Keep after long goodbyes to Rose the innkeeper and promises from Rose that she'd care for Wuid's pods and melons. Garum and his fellow adventurers were headed clockwise along the main ring road that circled all sixteen Guardian Keeps. It was two wagons wide and paved with cobbles that had been smoothed down by mason's magic to a flat, seamless surface. To Garum's right was a three-and-a-half-foot stone wall providing a small measure of protection, so travelers didn't inadvertently fall over the steep cliffs above the Deeps. Narrow strips of vibrantly green grass bracketed the road, and every half mile or so a stand of hardwood trees indicated sources of water and shade for weary travelers.

The party was spaced out along the road in much the same order of march they'd used in the Deeps. Drain and Vip-vip led the way, though there was no danger of taking a wrong turn on their trek to Gold Keep. Garum and Sweetie trailed the dwarf and vixer, with the twins behind them. Prestyn came next, by himself since his Cloak of Arms took up a lot of space. Flisk and Arrex followed the young wizard, while Crank and Sir Donal formed their rearguard, not that such a function was necessary. Walking the ring road was not considered particularly perilous. There was too much traffic.

As if to emphasize that point, a magecoach driver shouted at Garum and his party as he directed his near-silent high-wheeled carriage down the center of the ring road, forcing the new Golden Company to scramble over onto the grass beside the wall. The twins berated the driver at high volume, using words that Garum had only heard before from grizzled sailors on the Inland Seas.

"I like horse-drawn carriages better," said Drain when she'd resumed her former position on the road. "You can hear them coming."

"They should have bells or something," said Arrex. "I've had to treat too many of my fellow students at the College of Healers who didn't hear approaching magecoaches and were clipped by them."

"I prefer horses myself," said Flisk. "They have a lot of sense."

"Horse sense?" asked Prestyn.

"I don't think that phrase is meant to apply to horses," said Crank.

"Well, *I* still think we should have taken magecoaches to Gold Keep," said Xarra.

"Görthang and the Black Company took magecoaches," said Yarra.

"They were spending their own money," said Sweetie.

"I don't think Aubericht and Khrusósha would begrudge us the gold pieces for taking magecoaches if it meant we could restore them sooner," said Prestyn. "My parents always took magecoaches..." His voice trailed off when he realized he was reverting back to his old habit of mentioning his famous parents, the esteemed mages Prestio and Cadabryn, in every other sentence.

"It's too late for that now," said Garum. "And after the Black Company chartered *their* magecoaches, there weren't enough left at Rose Keep for all of us to ride anyway. Besides, we need to work off our big breakfast, and it's only another hour's worth of walking to Gold Keep."

"But my legs are sore," said Xarra.

"So are mine," said Yarra. "And not just my legs. But it's a *nice* sort of soreness." She looked over her shoulder and smiled at Prestyn, Arrex, and Crank.

Garum didn't need to turn *his* head to know the trio of teenaged men were blushing.

"You're young," Sweetie told the twins. "I'm older than you are and feeling a *nice* sort of sore myself. If I can walk, so can the two of you."

"Yes, ma'am," said Xarra, surprising Sweetie.

Yarra just frowned and focused on petting her six-legged kittens, Vi and Matty. Soon, Xarra was doing likewise with her pair, Amy and Tori.

Prestyn's face and cheeks were still as red as ripe cherries. He diverted the others' attention by holding his kitten, Trisk, with two arms of his cloak while dangling the end of a third arm in front of Trisk's nose. The cuteness of a kitten at play was irresistible, and soon all eyes were on the kitten, not on Prestyn.

Arrex didn't have such a convenient distraction. He pulled up the hood of his healer's robes to hide his face and let his kitten, Willie, walk from the interior of his voluminous left sleeve to his right sleeve and back, out of sight of any onlookers. Flisk, who hadn't been part of the festivities hosted last night by Xarra and Yarra, held *his* kitten, Star, in his arms and played don't-bite-my-finger games with him unselfconsciously.

Jelly flowed around in front of Crank, revised his shape to look like a semi-transparent six-legged kitten, then generated an extended pseudopod that looked like one of the arms of Prestyn's cloak and batted it around like a feather on a string.

For a quarter mile, the party walked in relative silence, except for brief exclamations at odd intervals when tiny kitten claws pierced flesh. Vip-vip was the first to notice a series of signs nailed to posts every twenty feet along the wall side of the road ahead. "CH-CHINE!" shouted the vixer.

Drain, beside Vip-vip at the front of their columns, read the yellow text on black of the first one. "WHEN NEAR AND FAR YOU PLAN TO ROAM," said the dwarf in a voice loud enough for Sir Donal and Crank to hear in the rear.

"I see the next one," said Xarra.

"So do I," said Yarra as both of them ran ahead.

Xarra called back. "AND WANT THE BEST."

Yarra kept running until she got to the third sign. "AVOID THE REST."

Flisk, with his extraordinary elf vision, read the fourth sign. "AND MAKE THE GOLDEN DOME YOUR HOME."

"Isn't the Golden Dome the inn and tavern and gambling hall where the original Golden Company is supposed to stay at Gold Keep?" asked Prestyn.

"It's also a brothel," said Sir Donal.

Sweetie smiled at Garum and shook her head. Apparently, her grandfather, the old soldier, had heard plenty about the Golden Dome and might have experienced at least some of its pleasures firsthand. Garum lifted an eyebrow. He'd heard other slingers and cooks talk about the inns at Gold Keep, but they'd never shared any specifics. Before signing on as a retainer for the original Golden Company at North Keep and leaving the Deeps at Rose Keep, his only experience with the Keep Lands was visiting Forge Keep in the southeast many years ago. His memory was that the accommodations at *that* keep were far from sybaritic.

Flisk continued speaking. "There's a fifth sign," he told them. "It has smaller print."

"What does it say?" asked Drain.

"The first line reads 'BEDS. BETS. BEER. BEAUTIES. BANKING,'" said the elf.

"That implies a *second* line," said Garum, trying to keep exasperation from his tone.

"Sorry," said Flisk. "The second line says, 'ONE MILE AHEAD.'"

By this time the rest of the party had caught up to Xarra and Yarra.

"Only a mile!" shouted Xarra.

"We're almost there!" exclaimed Yarra.

"Can we stay there? Can we? Can we? Can we?" the twins burbled in unison, sounding almost as annoying as they did when repeating, "Are we there yet?"

"That's the plan," said Garum.

"Görthang said he'd reserve rooms for us," said Sweetie.

"And you didn't *tell* us?" said the twins at double volume.

"We don't know if they have space for us yet," said Sweetie.

The twins' excitement dimmed somewhat, but it was clear they had high hopes.

"It's hard to say no to Görthang," Garum whispered to Sweetie. "I expect the Golden Dome will find rooms for us one way or another."

"I think you're right," said Sweetie, equally soft. "Just don't get any ideas about indulging in *all* of the Golden Dome's pleasures."

"Why would I need to when I have you?" said Garum.

"Good answer," said Sweetie. She gave Garum a big smile and said, "Let's walk faster."

Chapter 2
Gold Keep

They walked by several dozen more signs on the ring road to Gold Keep. Most advertised establishments with *gold* in their name. The Golden Horseshoe had a racetrack as well as an inn, bar, and gambling. The Golden Nugget was both a bank and an assay office for prospectors, while the Golden Rod was a bar, inn, and brothel featuring handsome males of multiple subspecies, according to a painting displaying shirtless human, elf, orc, and ogre chests on a sign big enough to serve as a banquet table if turned horizontally.

"Want to stay at the Golden Rod instead?" Garum heard Yarra ask Xarra.

"Maybe we can just pop in for a visit," Xarra replied.

"I can guess what *you* want to pop in you," teased Yarra.

Garum shook his head and squeezed Sweetie's hand instead of continuing to listen to the twins' banter. "Have you ever been to Gold Keep before?" he asked her.

"I haven't," Sweetie replied. "But I've heard enough guests at the Green Doors talk about it that it almost feels like I've been there myself."

"Any advice on how to navigate the place?" asked Garum.

"Count your fingers and toes after every transaction," said Sweetie.

"There are a lot of cutpurses?" asked Garum.

"No," said Sweetie. "From what I hear, you're safer on the streets of Gold Keep Town than you are here on the ring road. It's the legitimate businesses that will take you for every gold piece, what with high prices for rooms, games of chance, fortified beers, winter-distilled wines, and upstairs rooms for entrepreneurs delivering their traditional services."

"I don't need to ask you to elaborate, do I?"

"I shouldn't think so," said Sweetie. "The twins figured it out fast enough."

"What's the first bank on your list?" Garum whispered.

"The Golden Dome Bank," said Sweetie. "That should be convenient. Everything under one roof."

"It must be a big roof," said Garum.

"I guess we'll find out soon," said Sweetie.

Find out they did, and well before they reached the outer wall of Gold Keep Town. The central tower at Gold Keep was tall, quite a bit taller than the more stolid one at North Keep, and painted with what Garum assumed was gold leaf that made it reflect the red-gold rays of the waning afternoon sun. A dark-green pennant charged with the circular image of a single large gold piece fluttered from the central tower's conical tip.

If the tower is gold plated instead of gold painted, thought Garum, *I'll have to revise my estimate of the keep's wealth substantially upward.*

The keep's outer walls were also covered with the same paint and continued the reflective theme of the central tower. In front of the outer walls, however, was a truly massive edifice, a huge, whitewashed cube of stone surmounted by a golden hemisphere that seemed to not only reflect sunlight but emit a glow of its own. Two long three-story wings of the same whitewashed stone stretched out left and right from the central cube. The window frames on the wings were traced in gold as well and the window glass was almost black.

Garum had seen similar panes of glass in the ruins of one of the ancient cities near the Inland Seas. *It must have been a lot of work to salvage that much glass,* he thought. *Though the toppled ancient towers had been tall.*

"The dome shines at night," said Prestyn. "My parents helped renew its enchantment." This time, none of his companions minded Prestyn's reference to his parents. "It's supposed to soak up sunlight during the day and release it when it's dark," the young mage continued. His tone shifted to something close to awe. "The Golden Dome has the best counting house and the best mathematicians of all the sixteen keeps."

"Better than the scholars at West Keep?" asked Crank.

"From what I hear," replied Prestyn.

"Maybe the best *applied* mathematicians," said Crank.

Garum filed that comment away as yet another potential connection between Crank and the Scholars' University. He made a mental note to try to draw out more details about the former kitchen drudge's early life when he could.

As they drew closer to the gates of Gold Keep Town, they saw more dark-green and gold pennants flying from tall poles atop of the town's crenelated walls. Similar rows of pennants on poles lined the spur road leading to the gates. Vip-vip, in his borrowed healer's robes, raised his hood to hide his round head and moved back to stand next to Arrex while Flisk stepped up beside Prestyn to give him room. Jelly hid himself under Crank's tunic, making the thin young man look somewhat potbellied. All seven six-legged kittens were stowed in packs or sleeves in hopes they wouldn't be identified as contraband taken from the Deeps. If they meowed, it was hoped they'd be taken to be sounds from kittens with only four legs.

Garum and Sweetie stepped up beside Drain and led their party up to the open gate, where they were met by a pair of guards—one human, one orc. Before Garum could speak, the orc waved them through.

"You must be the new Golden Company," said the orc guard. "Görthang told us to expect you. Enter freely and spend as you will."

"Thank you," said Garum. He bowed and nodded to Sweetie, who gave both guards a gold piece.

The guards smiled and bowed back. The human one, a well-muscled woman about Garum's age with a gold-hilted blade in a dark-green scabbard, spoke this time. "Görthang said he reserved rooms for you and your party at the Golden Dome," she said. "You're to go to the front desk to collect your keys and are invited to join him and the Black Company for dinner at the Golden Carp at eight."

"Very good," said Garum. Sweetie gave both guards another gold piece each and the party passed the walls and onto the high street of Gold Keep Town. To Garum's amazement, the cobble-stones were all painted gold. The curbs were covered in words and pictograms advertising bars, inns, gambling houses, theatre companies, and other services with far-older histories. A large, dark-green arrow in the middle of the street with the legend *This way to the Golden Dome* pointed straight ahead, not that it was necessary. The central cube and the dome atop it were clearly visible ahead.

The high street was busy as they tried to make their way to the Golden Dome. Street merchants were trying to sell jewelry—most of it of low quality—and varied types of street food from sausages in bread rolls to fruit with clotted cream and dough rings topped with sesame seeds and filled with soft cheese. The twins wanted to look at the jewelry and Crank was particularly intrigued by the dough rings, but their interest in the Golden Dome was strong enough that they kept advancing, even as the crowds grew larger the closer they got to the Dome's shimmering promise of every comfort and vice anyone might desire.

The buildings that lined the high street were three or four stories tall and so narrow a giant would barely have room to sleep in a bed that went across their width. Most had some sort of shop on the first floor, and from the window treatments on the upper stories, Garum guessed the store owners' families or tenants lived above the shops. He noted that several shops had signs with three gold balls hanging above their doors and paid particular attention to the locations of what he guessed were high-end jewelry shops with their names painted in small gold letters on their doors. *Perhaps one of them will give me a good price for my heartstone,* he considered.

Too late, Garum noticed that Sweetie was dealing with a man who was taking advantage of the crowded conditions to catch hold of her arm and try to convince her to patronize one or more of the individuals he represented. His hair was long and dyed a shade of gold never found in nature. Looking even more closely, Garum saw the man's hair sparkled, as if small flecks of gold had been shaken on it like flakes of pepper. He wore a goatee, but only on the left side of his chin, complemented, if that was the right term, by a neatly trimmed mustache that only covered the right side of his upper lip. *That's a style I've never seen before,* thought Garum. *I wonder if it's unique to Gold Keep?*

"No, thank you," said Sweetie in a reasonable tone, which soon switched to add a tinge of menace. "Now take your hand off me on your own or my friend will separate it from your wrist and feed it to you."

"This little fellow?" said the man with the odd facial hair as he used his free hand to indicate Garum. "How is *he* going to make me do *anything?*"

"Not the halfling," said Sweetie. "My very *large* friend."

A bearded, red-headed giant with hands the size of hams—one of Sweetie's illusions—appeared behind the annoying man, who turned, went white, and began to tremble. Dozens of passersby paused to watch as Sweetie made parts of her giant illusion solid. The giant's palms pressed down on the man's shoulders until his knees started to bend. He removed his hand from Sweetie's arm. Sweetie kept pushing until the man was on his knees, then flat on his face, the flecks of gold in his hair sifting off onto the cobblestones like so many sparkling raindrops.

"Mercy," called the man.

Some of the people watching began to clap. Others heckled. "Not that you've ever shown any mercy to your victims," said one woman.

"Leave him alone," called a person of indeterminate gender from a third story window in a nearby narrow building. The person seemed human but had an almost elfin beauty that transcended simple boundaries of male and female. A small rock sailed down from the window and struck the left side of Sweetie's forehead, breaking the skin and leaving a hen's egg if not a goose egg. The red-headed giant vanished like a popped soap bubble and the man with the odd facial hair promptly became arrogant once again.

"An illusionist, eh?" said the man as he returned to his feet. "I'll show you how we treat anyone who tries to stop someone from practicing his trade in the streets of Gold Keep Town." The man slid a small sap from his sleeve and was about to add a matching bruise to the right side of Sweetie's forehead when he felt the pointed tip of Garum's sword-dagger cut through the fabric of his robe and pierce the tender flesh of his back just over his left kidney.

"If I give this blade a good shove, do you think you can find a concerned citizen willing to fetch you a healing potion before you bleed out?" asked Garum.

"Uhhh…" said the man. Garum pushed a bit harder the man changed his monosyllable to "Owww!"

"You haven't answered my question," said Garum.

"Ummm, maybe?" said the man. He looked left and right, trying to catch the eye of any of the onlookers. The ones who responded did so with head shakes.

"What goes around, comes around, Prink," said a woman in the crowd.

Garum saw that Arrex was standing next to Sweetie, handing her a healing potion. Once she'd swallowed, he put an ointment on her bruised forehead. The double action of the potion and ointment soon made the swelling go down and the broken skin heal. Arrex gave Garum a thumbs up. "No lasting harm done," he told Garum and Sweetie.

"Would your healer's oath require you to give *this* man a healing potion if I lacerated his left kidney?" Garum asked Arrex.

"Only if I saw you do it," Arrex replied, promptly turning his back on Garum and the man.

The man—Prink, if that was really his name—began to tremble even more violently.

"I wouldn't do that if I were you," said Garum. "You might make me slide my blade in farther by accident."

"S-s-s-sorry," said Prink.

"Tell me, Drain," said Garum, getting the dwarf's attention. "How sharp is the Stone Prince's hammer-axe?"

"Which side?" answered Drain, following Garum's lead.

"The *axe* side," said Garum.

"Sharp enough to separate a man's head from his shoulders with one blow," said Drain. "Sharp enough I could shave with it—if I needed to shave."

"Good to know," said Garum. He spoke to the Prink like a sergeant questioning a new recruit. "Would you prefer to lose your head or half the hair on it?"

"Th-th-the hair?" said Prink.

"Was that a question or an answer?"

"An answer," said Prink, still wincing from the point of a blade in his back.

Garum beckoned Drain over with his free hand. The twins, Flisk, Crank, and Sir Donal were now enjoying the way Garum was giving the man a taste of the same attitude he'd shown to Sweetie.

Prestyn was using the tentacles from his Coat of Arms to keep members of the growing crowd at bay. When the person in the third-floor window threw another rock, one of the tentacles intercepted it and sent it back in the opposite direction at a more than equal velocity. The rock embedded itself into the tough salvaged glass above the head of the person who'd thrown it, leaving a star pattern of cracks radiating out around it.

"Don't hurt my uncle!" called the person at the window.

"Please don't hurt me," said Prink. "I'm just doing what I have to do to get by. Do you have any idea what it costs to live and do business in Gold Keep?"

"I don't, yet," said Garum. "And I won't have Drain cut off your head, though I do think I'll have her shave off some of your hair as a temporary reminder to be more polite."

Some of the onlookers laughed when they heard Garum. Even with Garum sliding his blade out half an inch, the man seemed even more tense.

"What will it be?" asked Garum. "Should Drain cut off all the hair on the left side of your scalp or the right?"

"If you want to show me mercy, while still teaching me a lesson, you could cut off all the hair on the left *and* right sides of my head, leaving a four-inch strip down the center," said Prink, his earlier arrogance returning. "That would be impressive."

"Should we be merciful?" Garum asked Drain.

"In a way," said Drain. "Don't move," she told Prink. "I wouldn't want my axe blade to slip and slice an artery."

"I wouldn't, either," said Prink. "May I kneel to make it easier for you?"

"I like it when a man is willing to accept his punishment," said Garum. He removed the tip of his dagger-sword from Prink's back and helped steady him as he went to his knees and bowed his head to make it easier for Drain to shave. A few minutes later, with only a few nicks to show for it, Drain was finished.

"There you go," said Drain. "I shaved a four-inch strip along the middle of your scalp."

"No!" said Prink. "I wanted you to *leave* a four-inch strip there. Now I'm going to look like a first-year novice healer."

"There's nothing wrong with that," said Arrex, who had turned around to watch Drain in action, in case his services turned out to be necessary—which they hadn't.

"Now," Garum told the man, "I never want to see you again. Get lost."

"But," cried Prink. "How can I earn a living?"

"Can you cook?" asked Garum.

"I can't, but my sister's child can."

"The one in the window?"

"Yes," said Prink. "And I'm not a bad handyman."

"Good," said Garum. "Pack up and find Rose at the Rose and Crown inn at Rose Keep. Tell her Garum sent the two of you."

"Y-y-y-yes, sir," said Prink. "Tell Rose, 'Garum sent us.'"

"And tell her Sir Donal sends his affections," added Sweetie's grandfather.

"I can do that," said Prink. His expression looked like a cornered fox trying to avoid a pack of hounds and he eyed Drain's hammer-axe warily.

"You should start packing right away," said Prestyn. "And leave first thing in the morning." Two thick tentacles extruded themselves from his Cloak of Arms, lifted Prink off the high street's cobbles, and stretched out to leave him perched on the windowsill next to the person who'd thrown the rocks. The man moved inside and closed the window—*with* the rock in it—firmly shut.

"Do you think anything good will come of that?" asked Sweetie when Garum had stepped over to confirm the bruise on her forehead had healed.

"I don't know," said Garum. "But I hope so."

Ahead of them along the high street, the Golden Dome's impressive gilded hemisphere was turning almost orange in the late afternoon light.

Chapter 3
The Golden Dome

Garum sighed when he saw all the steps leading up to the Golden Dome's pillar-flanked entrance.

"Maybe a porter can carry you up," offered Sweetie. "If it's a giant or a troll we could both ride."

"With my luck, our porter will be another halfling or a shortorc," said Garum.

As it turned out, they hadn't needed to worry. A six-foot-wide section of stairs in the middle was enchanted and moved continuously, with steps magically disappearing at the top and reappearing at the bottom. Garum, Drain, and Sweetie put their feet on the lowest step and were effortlessly raised to the portico in seconds. The only challenging part was remembering to step off at the top.

Drain was so caught up in trying to understand how the enchanted stairs moved that she almost lost her balance when the ascent was over.

Crank wanted to walk back down and ride up again, but the twins were too eager to go inside and convinced him he could do that later after they'd been assigned their rooms.

The members of the new Golden Company paused for a few moments to get their bearings. A man in a dark green tunic covered in large gold polka-dots was walking toward them from the shadows under the pillars, but he was still some distance away.

"Why couldn't they have enchanted stairs like these leading up to Rose Keep?" Garum asked Sweetie while they waited for the man to arrive.

"You know why," Sweetie replied. "The guardians don't want to make it easy for denizens of the Deeps to get to the surface."

"I just hope our rooms don't turn out to be on a high floor," said Garum.

"I'd heard halfling prefer single story structures," said Sweetie.

"You heard correctly," said Garum. "We tend to build out, not up, when we can."

"I can see the value in that," said Sweetie. "I have short legs, too. I never liked climbing stairs to clean the Golden Company's rooms upstairs at the Green Doors."

"Your legs aren't short," said Garum. "They're perfectly proportioned to the rest of your body. You're only short compared to most humans, just like most humans are short compared to giants and sylviants. From my perspective, you're delightfully tall."

"Keep saying nice things like that and I'll make it worth your while later," said Sweetie. She grinned at Garum, and he grinned back. Garum was spared the need for a witty reply by the arrival of the man in the dark green tunic.

"Welcome to the Golden Dome," said the man. A few years younger than Sweetie's grandfather, he was of medium height with a medium build, plus medium brown hair and eyes—a perfect example of someone easily forgotten. "You must be the new Golden Company. My name is Domo, and I'm chief of security for the Golden Dome. Görthang told us all about you and your rooms are ready for you upstairs, once you sign our guest book."

"That's what the gate guards told us," said Drain.

"How *many* stairs?" asked Garum.

"You must be Garum," said Domo. "A room for you and your lady friend is waiting for you on the fifth floor of the central block, right under the dome itself."

"Four flights of stairs to climb," muttered Garum.

Sweetie didn't look particularly pleased about the prospect either.

"Once you sign in, I can show you the lift," said Domo.

"Lift?" asked Sweetie.

"Like the moving stairs out front," said Domo. "It's a small chamber that's raised and lowered by magic. We don't expect our guests to *walk* up four floors."

"Good," said Garum, looking as pleased as if someone had just handed him a mug of hard cider.

"Of course," said Domo, "if you're uncomfortable trusting enchantments, one of our porters can carry you up four floors…"

"The lift will be fine," said Sweetie.

Garum nodded his agreement. "Duly noted," he said. "Now, where do we get our room keys?"

"Inside," said Domo, waving his arm toward the cavernous interior beyond the pillars.

Sir Donal stepped up to stand beside his granddaughter and looked Domo over. "I know you," he said. "You were an officer in the service of the Kingdom of the Ford."

Garum had heard of the Kingdom of the Ford. It was across a river just west of the Sleeve where two of the Inland Seas almost joined.

"You have me there, good knight," said Domo. "I had that honor, many years ago."

"You were a colonel—no, a major—and a spy," Sir Donal continued.

"I *was,* once," said Domo. "But no longer." He smiled at Sweetie's grandfather. "Most people can't remember me. I'm impressed you can."

"My grandfather's memory for things that happened when he was a lancer back in the Sleeve is often better than his recollection of what he had for breakfast this morning," said Sweetie.

"Pancakes," said Sir Donal.

"That's right, grandfather," said Sweetie. "Garum and I made lots of pancakes."

"I remember *him,*" said Domo. "Back in the day, he was an excellent diplomat, as well as a skilled warrior." Domo noticed Sir Donal's vambraces. "He still has those, I see," Domo continued. "I was on a hill, observing, when he killed a battle mage to claim them."

"I never heard that story," said Sweetie. "I'll have to treat you to a meal later and learn more about that incident."

"It would be my pleasure," said Domo.

"I'll join you," said Garum, clearly making it a statement, not a question.

"I shouldn't be keeping you out here," said Domo. "The sun will be going down soon, and you'll want to rest up before dinner at eight sharp. The Golden Carp is in the west wing, just off the central block. I recommend the fried fish. Görthang and the rest of the Black Company will meet you there."

"Very good," said Sweetie.

"May I also say," Domo told her over his shoulder as they walked inside, "I look forward to getting to know the *new* Golden Company and expect you to be an improvement over the original."

"Oh?" said Sweetie.

Garum focused on Domo, waiting to hear more. The others were paying more attention to the decorative stonework gracing the portico.

"Yes," said Domo. "Not to say anything bad about our guests, but Aubericht and his associates often posed certain, um, challenges for the staff."

"I'm not surprised," said Sweetie. "We all worked as retainers for the original Golden Company on a recent trip through the Deeps and I was a server and chambermaid at an inn at North Keep Town where Aubericht's Golden Company holds a part interest."

"A fellow hospitality professional," beamed Domo. "How delightful. I will not only look forward to having a meal with you and sharing more of my memories of your grandfather's exploits but would take great pleasure in showing you the inner workings of the Golden Dome, if you'd find that of interest."

"I certainly would," said Sweetie.

"Can we see the kitchens?" asked Garum.

"Of course," said Domo.

Further conversations were interrupted when they emerged into the central block's atrium and were under the dome. Ambitious flies would have found eleven open mouths to investigate when the members of the new Golden Company looked up and beheld the splendor of the dome's inner surface.

To Garum's surprise, it was *not* painted solid gold. Instead, it was covered in thousands of hexagons traced out in red and purple and green and blue as well as gold and silver. Each hexagon held a line-drawing of a plant or animal that could be found within a day's ride of the Keeps Lands. Some hexagons also held depictions of monsters from the Deeps. Garum recognized the simple geometry of a globe-shaped Argus Sphere and the sharp cubic corners of a Jelly of the Deeps. Other hexagons were filled with helmeted militiapedes, ratroaches, shovel snakes, bat-winged cats, and even red-throated Stinking Screamers.

The colorful lines that formed the designs on the dome's inner surface all seemed to glow, as if they were drawn on the inside of a thin-walled silk tent pitched beside a bonfire. As Garum took in more details, he saw that many of the hexagons held golden circles on dark green backgrounds, like the polka-dots on the robe Domo was wearing and the pennants flying on poles as they approached Gold Keep Town.

Gold pieces on green, thought Garum. *The wealth of the land. It seems a fitting symbol for the one keep out of the sixteen reputed to have the greatest concentration of riches.*

Garum reluctantly shifted his gaze from the dome to the square construction of the central block on which the dome rested. Corridors ran along the sides of the square on four levels, separated from the vast space below the dome by a short wooden barrier to keep guests from falling. They reminded Garum of the stone wall filling the same role for the cliffs around the Deeps. Doors lined the outer edge of the corridors, leading to guest rooms, Garum supposed.

Before him, around what must be the floor of the central block, were hundreds of chairs and small tables, most with wizard globes above them for proximate illumination, though Garum didn't think he could possibly read or focus on a conversation with the compelling distraction of the ceiling above.

Bars were parallel to three sides of the central cube. Garum could see that one was sized for trolls, giants, and sylviants, while a second was sized for humans, orcs, and ogres, and a third for dwarves, halflings, and shortorcs. *Not a bad solution to the challenge of serving guests of varying heights,* thought Garum. *But I like the way Veridan Green handled things at the Green Doors better. It keeps small folk from being inadvertently squashed by big folk.*

Domo led them to a counter on the side of the central block's atrium that wasn't a bar. Instead of the counter being at graduated heights to accommodate differing subspecies of guests, the counter stayed a uniform height, but the floor in front of it sloped from a low point that would be effective for the tallest sylviant up to a high point that would make a halfling child feel comfortable. The security chief led them to the center of the counter and Garum was surprised to feel the square of floor he was standing on rise until Garum was at a perfect height to converse with one of the Golden Dome's reception clerks. *I'll have to see if Hrefna knows how they do that,* thought Garum. *It's a lot like the chairs and tables we found in the refreshment rooms down in the Deeps.*

"You must be Garum," said an elf woman of indeterminate age, which most elf women were, at least in Garum's estimation. Once an elf—male or female—turned fifty or so, they seemed locked into an ageless physical beauty that didn't fade for more than two hundred years. "Here are keys for you and Sweetie. Your room is on the fifth level. The lift is in the corner to my right."

"Thank you," said Garum.

"No, thank *you,*" said the clerk. "Görthang told us you replaced Aubericht and the original Golden Company and even though it's against the Gold Dome's policy to say anything negative about current or previous guests, on behalf of the entire staff, I want to say we're glad you did."

"Aubericht, the Stone Prince, Khrusósha, Céptianne, and even Galingálë, who's my third cousin, treated us like carpet sweepings," the clerk continued. "Barton DeCláre and Alderōn were at least polite to us, but the others—good riddance." The clerk sniffed, which had to be an affectation, since elves seldom suffered from respiratory ailments. "I'm sorry to say so, but your *new* Golden Company *has* to be an improvement."

"We'll do our best," said Garum.

"Indeed we will," added Sweetie. "I've worked for Aubericht and the others and know their thoughtless words and whims can sting like whips across the backs of the people who serve them."

"Just for that, I'll have a bottle of aged sparkling cider sent to your room," said the elf-woman behind the counter.

"There's no need for such a kindness," Sweetie protested.

"See!" said the elf-woman. "You're already proving you're much more considerate. Céptianne would have demanded *two* bottles and would have considered it only fitting for someone with her impressive personal reputation."

"I've had to deal with her myself," said Sweetie. "Do you have rooms ready for the rest of our company?"

"We do," said the elf-woman. "Görthang himself gave us the relevant details. I've booked the young women and young men into a series of interconnected suites on the third floor and put Flisk in a room of his own on the ground floor next to the garden. Flisk is my second cousin once removed, you know," the clerk added. "His mother and I were close as children. Too bad about him sometimes seeing double."

"I'm improving now, Cousin Floria," said Flisk as he stepped close to the counter. "Mother sends you her best." He let his voice drop to a whisper. "And I would appreciate it if you didn't spread the details of my vision problems to anyone close enough to overhear you."

"Sorry," said Floria the clerk. "My mouth runs on like a human's sometimes, especially when I'm excited—and I *am* excited, as well as being quite happy to see you, cousin."

Garum's mind went to an old halfling ribald joke about a woman asking a man if that was a cucumber in his pocket, or was he just happy to see her, but he kept it to himself. He didn't want Sweetie to think he had *no* sense of decorum, after all. He also wasn't sure the joke worked as well between relatives.

"We have a room in the second subbasement for Drain, unless she'd prefer one that isn't underground?" said Floria.

"Underground is fine," said Drain. "It should be quiet, at least."

"I'm afraid it *is* near the sewage pumps," said Floria. "Some guests, even our dwarves, find their rhythmic pumping annoying."

Xarra and Yarra snickered when Floria said *rhythmic pumping*, and Prestyn's cheeks turned red, but Garum ignored them.

"I'm a sewer mason," Drain told Floria. "It will be like listening to my mother's heartbeat."

"Fine, then," said Floria. "We have a room for you near Hrefna, Sir Donal," she continued. "Hrefna was insistent on wanting to arm wrestle later this evening and we thought it would be convenient to have the two of you close by."

"A contest of arms!" said Sir Donal, his face lighting up like a wizard globe. "That would be splendid."

"Go easy on her, grandfather," said Sweetie.

"I'm always a gentleman," replied Sir Donal.

Domo raised an eyebrow, then winked at Sweetie. Garum could tell she was looking forward to hearing Domo's stories.

"What about our small ogre healer?" asked Garum.

"The vixer?" said Floria. "Görthang told us about him and the clock at the Rose and Crown. We have a room for him in the clock tower at the far end of the west wing. Our clock stopped last year and no one has been able to get it working again."

"You don't mind having a being from the Deeps above ground and staying at the hotel?" asked Sweetie.

"You've worked at an inn," said Floria. "You know that if we told the guardians at Gold Keep everything that goes on under the Golden Dome, we would have been shut down years ago."

"True enough," said Sweetie.

"Don't ask," said Floria.

"Don't tell the guardians," Sweetie completed.

Both women smiled.

"We would have asked your vixer to fix the mechanical dishwasher in the kitchen, but it's too useful to stick guests who try to walk away without paying for their rooms or meals with washing dishes that it hasn't been a priority," said Floria.

"What do you do with the people who can't pay the debts they run up in your gambling halls?" asked Garum.

"Do you plan to risk something like that?" asked Floria.

"Not at all," said Garum. "I'm just curious."

"Garbage duty," said Floria.

"That seems fitting," said Garum. "Good to know."

"Run along now," said Floria. "You'll need time to wash up, change, and relax before dinner with the Black Company."

"I think we might try relaxing, then washing up and changing for dinner," said Sweetie.

Floria smiled at Garum, then at Sweetie. "Don't wear him out, dear," said the elf-woman. "Görthang said he had a lot to talk about."

Chapter 4
The Golden Carp

The attached bath for the room Floria had assigned to Garum and Sweetie made the one they'd enjoyed at the Rose and Crown look like a portable metal tub filled with pots of water heated by coals in a hearth. Its tub was carved from a single block of marble and jets could be directed down on their separate and conjoined bodies from six different directions simultaneously.

They never even made it into bed—a pillow-covered extravagance big enough for a pair of mating giants—before they had to dry off and dress for dinner.

"What do you think Görthang wants to discuss?" Sweetie asked Garum. She was wearing Céptianne the Exceptional's elaborate illusionist's robes, which a team of Floria's fellow Golden Dome employees had managed to launder and alter while she and Garum were otherwise occupied.

"You look wonderful," said Garum, who was wearing a fancy new tunic himself, delivered from one of the tailor's shops in the east wing. *It's a good thing I can wear human boys' clothes,* he thought. *Especially if they're not tight-fitting.*

"You're looking sharp yourself," said Sweetie. "But you haven't answered my question."

"That's because I'm still thinking about it," said Garum. "Görthang and the rest of the Black Company agreed that we should take the chest to the healers at East Keep. I have no idea what he might want to do instead."

"Perhaps he doesn't want to talk about the chest and potentially restoring Aubericht and the others," Sweetie suggested as she brushed her long hair. "He could want to propose a longer-term alliance between our two companies."

"How would you feel about that?" asked Garum.

"I'm not sure," said Sweetie. "There could be quite a few benefits to associating with a highly experienced company of adventurers. Goodness knows, we're still novices when it comes to exploring the Deeps."

"True enough," said Garum. "Yet, through good luck, we somehow managed to defeat the Black Company and make friends with them. I don't know if you can still consider us novices."

"I'm an experienced server in a tavern and chambermaid for an inn. I've done both jobs for more than a year. But when it comes to the Deeps, or to casting illusions, I've only been at it for a few days."

"And yet, look what you've accomplished," said Garum. "You helped us make our way out of the lowest level of the Deeps on our own and you've mastered Céptianne's wand of illusions. I don't think I've heard of anyone able to make their illusions *solid* before." Garum took Sweetie's hand that wasn't holding a hairbrush and kissed it. "Don't sell yourself short, dear lady."

"Like Prink wanted to sell me an hour or two with his sister's child?"

"The person in the window didn't look like a child," teased Garum. "And the stone that hit your forehead was thrown with both accuracy and force. I doubt a *child* could do that." He moved in front of Sweetie and stood on tiptoe, so he was closer to looking at her eye to eye. "Not that long ago, you were trying to make *me* feel more confident. It's only fair for me to return the favor. Whatever Görthang wants to discuss, we'll sort things out and make the best decisions we can."

Sweetie leaned down and kissed Garum. "Thank you," she said. "That helped convince the hummingbirds in my stomach to sleep for a bit."

"I'm glad," said Garum. He glanced at a picture on a nearby wall that he'd finally determined was magically synchronized to show the face of the clock at the top of the west wing's far tower—another Golden Dome extravagance. "Before we head out, do you think it wise to lock the chest in our room's safe?" he asked Sweetie. "I don't want to carry it with me, and I don't want to risk it being stolen."

"What would you think about me using my illusions to make the chest invisible, *then* locking it in the safe?" asked Sweetie. "If anyone got it open, the safe would look empty."

"I think that's a superlative solution," said Garum. Sweetie removed the chest from her pack, while Garum opened the safe and put the chest inside.

"Step back so I can work, please," said Sweetie.

Garum watched over her shoulder as Sweetie waved her wand. The next time he looked in the safe, it appeared empty. "Nicely done," he said. He adjusted the safe's dial and set its combination to the year his home village of Greenbriar was founded, whispering the digits in Sweetie's ear.

"I'm glad that's taken care of," said Sweetie. "We should leave now. It will take us time to get to the restaurant and we don't want to be late."

Garum nodded and tugged on his tunic to straighten out a few wrinkles.

Sweetie pulled her hair up and tied it back with a green-and-gold ribbon, thoughtfully provided by the staff of the Golden Dome. "I'm ready," she said. "I wonder how many of the others will be there promptly?"

Garum grinned. "Do you think the young men will come early?"

"Xarra and Yarra didn't mention any complaints along those lines," said Sweetie as they left their rooms and walked to the lift. "How do you think this works, anyway?"

"A mastodon turning a wheel in the fourth subbasement?" Garum suggested. He was glad he couldn't see over the wooden wall separating him from a four-story drop to the atrium's floor.

"Could be," said Sweetie. "Though I expect it's a simple enchantment of some sort."

"That's more likely, I expect," said Garum.

"Maybe Vip-vip can explain it to us?" said Sweetie.

"If it's magic, we may get a better explanation from Hrefna," said Garum. "Vip-vip seems more knowledgeable about all things mechanical."

The lift arrived, a literal gilded cage operated by a gray-haired halfling who sat on a seat that folded out from the lift's wall. "Atrium level?" he asked.

"Yes, please," said Sweetie. "We have reservations at the Golden Carp."

"Best dining establishment in Gold Keep Town," said the halfling. "Take a left and a left when you exit, then a right to the west wing. Be sure to try the fried fish."

"Floria gave us the same advice," said Garum.

"She would," said the lift operator. "It's a bit of a joke. Most of the dishes on the menu are fried fish. They bring the fish in fresh every morning by dragonback from the Inland Seas."

"Good to know," said Garum.

"Their fried white tubers aren't anything to rave to your mother about, though," the gray-haired halfling continued.

"Interesting," said Garum. *I wonder what my white tuber crisps recipe would be worth to their chefs?*

Sweetie nodded to the lift operator, then took Garum's hand and led him out into the atrium and along the specified route leading to the restaurant.

A gold-painted model of a fish that might have been a carp, for all Garum knew, hung above the corridor leading to the west wing and helped guide them to their destination. He'd never cleaned or cooked a carp, at least not knowing it by that name, and was more familiar with serving trout, bass, or catfish, so he just assumed the species of the fish model was the namesake of the restaurant.

Flisk, Drain, Prestyn, Arrex, and Crank were waiting by the entrance to the Golden Carp. That establishment was clearly identified by a carp, or at least a fish, painted in gold leaf on a massive sheet of salvaged black glass next to a door that looked more like an entry hatch on a boat than a standard rectangular door. It was an extended oval with a small round window at its top center that reminded Garum of the circular windows at his grandmother's cottage built into the side of a hill back home in Greenbriar near the Great Eastern Confluence.

"Where are the kittens?" asked Garum.

"We left them in the twins' rooms," said Crank. "Jelly is watching them. They love sliding around in the big marble tub."

"Without water in it, of course," said Flisk.

"Sounds like fun," said Garum.

"Have you seen my grandfather?" Sweetie asked them.

"Look behind you," said Arrex.

Sweetie turned and saw Sir Donal and Vip-vip hurrying toward them from the far end of the west wing.

"Sorry, granddaughter," said the old knight. "This little fellow"—he pointed to the vixer—"was so wrapped up in gears, springs, and escapements taking apart the clock in the west wing's tower that we lost track of the time."

"Well, no time like the present to go in for dinner," said Garum. "I expect it's unwise to keep Görthang, Blōgot, Hrefna, and the others waiting."

"Have you seen the twins?" Sweetie asked the young men, Flisk, and Drain.

"They said they were going out, but would be back for dinner," said Prestyn.

"I was out front riding the moving stairs and saw them heading back up the high street," said Crank. "I overheard Xarra tell Yarra they planned to find some of the shirtless men and elves painted on the signs leading into Gold Keep Town."

"What were they planning to use for money?" asked Drain. "From what I've heard, prime beef is expensive."

Prestyn shifted from one foot to the other and several arms of his cloak writhed. "I, uh, may have given each of them a hundred gold pieces from our shared treasury," he told them. "They said they'd, um, make it worth my while, uh, later."

Garum was pleased that Prestyn was no longer stuttering, switching to awkward pauses instead. He wasn't happy about Prestyn's premature disbursement of company funds, however. "That wasn't the brightest thing you've ever done," he said, without showing any hint of anger. All in all, he was more amused than mad.

"Sorry," said Prestyn. "I'll count those as advances against their shares when I figure out our equitable distributions."

"I'm sure you will," said Sweetie. "Now let's go in. It's almost eight and Garum's right about not keeping the Black Company waiting. I'll lead the way."

Garum and the others followed Sweetie inside. He was surprised it didn't smell too fishy or too much like hot oil. *They must have invested in magically powered exhaust fans for the kitchen,* he determined. *I'll bet there are lots of cats congregating around wherever the vents are located.*

The Gold Carp's decor was comparable with the elegance of the Golden Dome. Nets with cork floats hung from the open-beamed ceiling. They were woven from much thicker ropes and had much larger floats than the nets fisher folk used on the freshwater lakes near where Garum grew up. Farther along, a dingy large enough to hold an extended family of halflings or one troll rested on blocks on the floor and appeared to be used for private dinners, with small tables positioned between the thwarts. Wizard globes were hidden inside brass lanterns by booths made of recycled lumber and a massive anchor so large Garum didn't know if even Sir Donal could lift it sat in the far corner of the entryway.

A human wearing a blue uniform with epaulets and lots of gold braid greeted them when they entered. "You must be the *new* Golden Company,"he said. "Right this way. The rest of your party has already been seated." The uniformed man led them all the way to the back of the restaurant and through a door marked *Private Dining.* The room on the other side of the door was spacious and continued the restaurant's nautical theme with ship's pennants, more nets, and harpoons on the walls. Görthang, Hrefna, and the rest of the Black Company were arrayed around three tables set up in a horseshoe pattern, so servers could easily bring platters of food and take away used dishes.

Görthang and Hrefna sat in the center of the table at the top of the horseshoe, with empty chairs to either side of them. Garum held back a smile when he saw that Xarra and Yarra were flanking

Púki at the end of the far table. He kept looking left and right, unsure which direction trouble might be coming from. The twins were talking over him, enjoying his discomfort.

Garum was directed to sit to Görthang's right with Sweetie beside him to *his* right, beside Blōgot. Prestyn sat to Hrefna's left, with Drain next to him. The others filled in to sit in the remaining empty chairs. Servers filled their mugs or goblets. Garum opted for hard cider, while Sweetie picked white wine. When Garum heard Sweetie's decision, he changed his mind and instructed his server that he wanted white wine as well. *A fine establishment like this one must have a good cellar,* he realized. *It will be nice to enjoy a vintage that's old enough to be palatable and young enough not to have turned to vinegar. The wine they offered to officers in the armies I've served in was decidedly second rate. Some wasn't even good enough to cook with.*

Turning to Görthang, Garum started to ask a question. "What did you…" But Görthang held up his palm to stop him.

"Save that for after dinner," said the orc. "Like you saved the conversation *you* wanted to have for *after* that marvelous breakfast you made us."

Garum beamed. He knew the way to a cook's heart was to praise his food.

Sweetie put a hand on his arm and leaned down to whisper in his ear. "Don't drink too much wine," she said. "Görthang wants something, and you'll need your wits about you."

Garum nodded and sat back in his elevated chair to enjoy the meal ahead. It started with a salad of raisins, thinly sliced green and white cabbage with slivers of carrot in a buttermilk, honey, and black pepper dressing. It was accompanied by skewers of sliced, pickled white radishes and parsnips, alternating with sweet preserved cherries. The flavors of the two dishes complemented each other well and Garum was sure they'd do the same for fried fish.

"I hope you don't mind me selecting tonight's menu," said Görthang.

"Not at all," said Garum. "I'm looking forward to your selections if they're anything like what I've tasted so far. My only question is how do you like your fish? I hope it's not nearly raw, like your meat."

"Fish is different," said Görthang. "Biting into a crisp batter is almost like chewing through an animal's fur and skin to get to the tasty flesh inside."

"Thank you," said Garum. "I'll treasure that image."

Sweetie nudged him, which Garum interpreted to be her way of telling him not to start trouble.

Garum was rescued from a potential *faux pas* by the arrival of several large baskets of batter-fried fish, bowls of boiled white tubers with parsley in butter, and shallow metal dishes holding faded green peas. *This is the cuisine at the best restaurant in Gold Keep Town?* thought Garum. *I could make something better than this after I spent my first year in a kitchen.* Then he tasted the fish and changed his mind.

The batter had hints of ale and cider, but the fish it surrounded was thick and white and so flaky and flavorful that it practically melted in his mouth and begged to be replaced with a second piece, immediately.

"Try it with the malt vinegar," said Görthang.

Garum took a second piece of battered fish from the basket in front of him, put it on his plate, and splashed a generous amount of piquant amber vinegar on it from a repurposed wine bottle. This time, the fish went from delicious to ambrosial. The batter soaked up the vinegar and transformed it from good to great, improving with each mouthful. "I see why you wanted to eat first and talk later," Garum told Görthang.

"Now if only these white tubers were as good as the ones…" Görthang began.

Garum held out his palm to stop Görthang this time. "I want to sell the head chef my thin crisps recipe," he told the orc. "Or perhaps I'll let Crank do it. He should be able to get a good price for teaching the chef's staff the technique."

"You're a generous halfling," said Görthang.

Sweetie nudged Garum again, a further warning that Görthang wanted something.

Garum slowly nodded to let Sweetie know he'd received her message. He tried the boiled white tubers and could only manage to swallow a small morsel before deciding the tubers weren't worth eating. The ones Crank had made during the cook-off back at Veridan Green's inn were far better than these. *If they had my crisps recipe, they'd double their number of patrons,* Garum decided. *Now for the peas, I suppose.* He took a small spoonful, chewed slowly, and was intrigued. They didn't taste so much like peas as like tiny spheres of spice—pepper, nutmeg, cinnamon, cloves, ginger, and more he didn't have time or inclination to identify. The spices melded together on his tongue, but released individual bursts of flavor as their outer skins were broken or dissolved.

"The peas are good," said Sweetie. "I like them. The fish, too."

"Not the white tubers?" whispered Garum.

"Crank's were better," Sweetie replied softly, confirming Garum's assessment.

Soon, the baskets of battered fish were empty and Garum noticed the servers weren't replacing them. He looked at Görthang and the orc understood his unspoken question. "The head chef allocates a certain amount of fish per party, being a bit more generous for dining parties with giants, trolls, ogres, sylviants, and humans in their teens, as I understand it," he said. "Otherwise, the Golden Carp would need wheelbarrows to get guests back to their rooms."

"That's quite a compliment to the chefs and kitchen staff," said Garum.

"Indeed it is," said Görthang. "They usually give diners some time to digest before bringing out dessert—your choice of peach, pear, or apricot sorbet, chilled by a cold box—so now would be a good time to have our discussion."

"I'm listening," said Garum.

"You know we enjoyed working together with you to cook at the Rose and Crown," said Görthang.

Garum and Sweetie both nodded, focused entirely on Görthang although half a dozen other conversations were in progress around the table.

"And you know we agreed to a truce between our two companies, at least for the present," Görthang continued.

"Right," said Garum, wondering what Görthang was leading up to.

"Well," said the orc. "It's not good for our bloodthirsty reputation for us to be working so closely with you, a company with the same name as our most bitter enemies."

"And…?" said Garum.

"We've agreed that it would be better all around, instead of giving the appearance of being friends…" Görthang's voice trailed off to a whisper.

"Better all-around if?" said Sweetie.

"If you hired us," said Görthang.

Chapter 5

Wait. What?

"Wait. What?" said Garum.

"Why?" added Sweetie.

"Because then we'll have an easy explanation for why we're associating with you," said Görthang. "For the past five years, the Golden Company has been our nemesis, finding all the best treasure and magical artifacts from the Deeps and beating us, one way or another, when we've fought. The Mages' Guild in North Keep Town has even made a chess set in our likenesses."

"With Hrefna as your queen," said Sweetie.

"Yes," said Görthang.

From Sweetie's right, Blōgot, the orc archer and Görthang's lover, spoke up. "I wasn't particularly happy about that, but there's no denying Hrefna is more powerful than I am."

"You're queen of my heart," said Görthang, giving her a smile that showed off more of his fangs.

"Other names for a queen on a chess board are vizier, chief counselor, and prime minister," said Hrefna. "I prefer using those instead of queen in this context."

Sweetie nodded and Garum shook his head.

"You think that having us *pay* you to accompany us will make things look better?" asked Garum.

"It will, at least as far as the Mages' Guild is concerned," said Görthang. "They liked being able to play the Golden Company and the Black Company off against each other, as the chess pieces in their courtyard demonstrates. It was one of the ways they got Aubericht to reduce his fees for finding items they wanted. If he wanted too much gold, they'd threaten to give the Black Company the assignment."

"Aubericht and the Stone Prince would often up their price when they didn't want to do a job," said Hrefna. "That meant *we* were stuck with the worst missions, like retrieving a nasty-tempered metal armored turtle-like creature from the Deeps below one of the southern keeps."

"The sort that has a sharp beak and a bite strong enough to take your arm off?" asked Garum.

"Exactly," said Görthang. "It was a long trek to get there, and we spent even longer in the Deeps carefully searching for the beast." Görthang started to stand, rising with what seemed to be a growing anger at a past injustice. "We had to put up with so much—"

"Sit back down," said Hrefna, putting a massive arm on Görthang's shoulder to enforce her command. "That was years ago."

"The worst of it was that it was one of Aubericht's not-so-little jokes," said Görthang. "He'd never wanted the job. While we were off hunting a jeweled turtle, he and the original Golden Company were finding an enchanted diamond the size of a turkey's egg on the seventh level under Herb Keep for a senior mage. He and his company got to keep a dozen unenchanted sapphires as big as robin's eggs found with the diamond as their fee."

"They got gems, you got manure," said Garum.

"Right like the meat of a walnut," said Görthang.

"Excuse me?" said Garum.

"In a nutshell," said Hrefna.

"I'm still not sure I understand," said Sweetie. "How would us hiring you improve *your* reputation?"

"That's easy," said Görthang. "We're a *mercenary* company. We'll do jobs for anyone who pays us. No one will fault us for something like that. But they will think it strange for us to associate with any version of the Golden Company, new or old, without a contract, since Aubericht and I are sworn enemies."

"But working for a company you've been competing with for half a decade?" said Sweetie.

"It doesn't *sound* great," said Görthang, "but anyone who bothers to look can see that Garum's not Aubericht and you're not Céptianne. It's a clean slate for both companies, contract-wise.

But if we just associate, without a contract, tongues will wag like happy hounds' tails and potential clients will worry."

"Worry about…" said Garum.

"The Black Company going soft," said Görthang. "Nobody would even consider you beating me in a fight, to say nothing of your company beating mine."

"Ours," said Hrefna.

"Ours, then," said Görthang.

"Even though we did," said Sweetie softly.

"You agreed never to talk about that," said Hrefna.

"And I don't plan to," said Sweetie. "But it's still the truth."

"The truth is what people can be persuaded to believe," said Hrefna.

"The truth is the truth," said Garum.

Görthang, Hrefna, and Sweetie stared at Garum.

"Just kidding," he said, after a pause. Out of sight below the table, his fingers were crossed. There were facts, and there was manipulating those facts to your own advantage, but that didn't negate the facts' truth. *The new Golden Company did beat the Black Company, thanks to Jelly, but I don't need to rub Görthang's nose in that fact,* thought Garum. *Besides, I like Görthang and the rest of his company and want us to keep working together. If paying them is the easiest way to make that happen, we'll pay them.*

"How much do you want?" asked Sweetie, anticipating the question Garum was about to ask.

"We'll work for scale," said Görthang.

"What scale?" asked Sweetie. "Cooks' scale? Silversmiths' scale?"

"Dragons' scale," said Hrefna. "One gold dragon's scale is worth a thousand gold pieces."

"How often?" asked Garum. "Is that per month? Per year?"

"Weekly," said Hrefna. "We'll take gems or gold pieces in lieu of actual dragon scales, of course."

"Of course," said Garum. His pay as a cook and slinger for most of his military assignments was two gold pieces a day, double the wage of an ordinary foot soldier and four times what was paid to cook's assistants. He did some quick calculations. *One thousand gold pieces for seven people over seven days is just over twenty gold pieces per person per day, about what a heavily armored knight was paid to support him or herself, his mounts, his pack animals, and his retainers,* thought Garum. *Given the Black Company's reputation, it wasn't a completely unreasonable number,* he considered. *But I expect there's some room for negotiation.* "Five hundred a week," said Garum.

"Nine hundred," said Görthang.

"Six hundred," Garum replied.

"Eight hundred," said Görthang.

"Seven hundred," said Garum.

"And a forty percent share of any treasure accumulated when we're working together," said Görthang.

"How did you come up with forty percent?" asked Sweetie.

"Eleven of you, seven of us," said Hrefna.

"That's just over thirty-eight percent for you," said Sweetie.

"We like round numbers," said Görthang.

Garum looked at Sweetie. She nodded. "Done," he said. He shook Görthang's hand and was pleased when the orc didn't try any dominance games by squeezing too hard. Garum knew he could never match Görthang's strength, to say nothing of Hrefna's.

"I'm glad that's settled," said Sweetie.

"We'll have Floria arrange to have a formal contract drawn up," said Görthang.

"And we'll read every word of it carefully," said Garum.

"Both of us," said Sweetie. "And probably Drain, too. I expect she has a lot of experience with contracts for sewer work."

"Did I hear my name?" asked Drain from beyond Hrefna.

"Yes," called Sweetie. "I'll tell you about it later."

"Good," said the dwarf. "Kléppri is telling us a story about what happened when dwarves found a gold seam while digging a sewage channel for gnomes, and I want to hear how it ends."

"Carry on," said Sweetie.

"Now that our business relationship is settled," said Garum, "perhaps you can tell me how the Black Company formed. Our tale is simple—we were all at Veridan Green's inn when the original Golden Company was hiring retainers for their most recent trip to the Deeps."

"Do you want to tell it, or should I?" Görthang asked Hrefna.

"You start," said the troll mage. "I'll correct you when you overelaborate."

"As usual, then," said Görthang. He smiled, showing more of both his upper and lower fangs. "I was a warrior in the army of the king of the Starlands…"

"A few hundred miles west of the Keeps," said Hrefna.

"And when I mustered out, Blōgot and I were already involved, so she came east with me to seek our fortunes together."

"Görthang was so romantic," said Blōgot. "He asked me if I wanted to spend all my time shooting arrows at distant enemies across battlefields or would rather shoot shafts at monsters in corridors of the Deeps for treasure. I liked him, so I opted for the monsters."

"I ran into the two of them sitting at a table at the Pewter Mug in North Keep Town," said Hrefna. "The other mages in the guild weren't exactly welcoming. My mother taught me magic, and I think I make most mages nervous. There aren't many troll mages, you know."

"I don't imagine so," said Sweetie.

"We got to be friends over mugs of ale," said Görthang. "Then Kléppri showed up and hired us to find a gnomish relic…"

"A jeweled scepter," said Kléppri from past Drain.

"Right," said Görthang. "Gêrdun was at a nearby table and overheard us talking. Every party of adventurers needs a healer, and he assured us he had the necessary skills even though he'd been thrown out of the college before he'd graduated."

"His healing potions taste terrible," said Hrefna.

"I can help with that," said Arrex. "Gêrdun and I plan to meet after dinner to discuss techniques."

"We're benefiting from working together already," said Görthang. "Now where was I?"

"About to start the quest for a jeweled gnomish scepter," said Hrefna.

Görthang nodded and collected his thoughts. "We ran into Púki when he tried to filch my purse on the way to North Keep from the Pewter Mug. Hrefna caught him and picked him up by his collar and held him off the ground. He convinced her that he could be an asset to our party instead of having her throw him over the wall. We figured we could use someone with a light touch and Púki told us he was good at defusing traps and opening locks, so by then the Black Company was almost fully assembled."

"And Chophorn?" asked Garum.

"He was one of the guards at the top of the stairs to the Deeps," said Hrefna. "It was the last day of his enlistment and he'd been unhappy he'd spent two years *guarding* the surface from the Deeps without ever visiting them. He figured we were tough enough to help him stay alive, so he asked to come along."

"The rest is history," said Görthang.

"Why did you name yourselves the Black Company?" asked Sweetie. "Was your armor black when you first started?"

"That came later," said Görthang. "The Golden Company name was already taken, and we didn't think the Purple Company, or the Green Company had the same cachet."

"He wanted to call us Görthang's Gang, but I wouldn't go for that," said Hrefna.

"But why pick Black?" asked Garum.

"Because of what happened when we recovered the enchanted scepter," said Görthang. "It was in the middle of a small room, on top of a black onyx pillar. The room was completely black, floor, walls, and ceiling, with no wizard globes. Only the glowing jewels in the scepter provided any light."

"I generated a few wizard globes so we could see what we were doing," said Hrefna.

"And I noticed there were small, black, cast-iron pots every few feet around the room's perimeter," said Görthang.

"Those come in later," said Hrefna. "I lifted Púki over to the pillar and he shimmied up and removed the scepter."

"I missed a pressure switch," called Púki from his spot between the twins.

"The cast-iron pots were *smudge* pots," said Hrefna. "When the scepter was removed, they started smoking. It was a thick, black smoke that soon filled the room and made it hard to breathe. The air was so dark we couldn't even see the door."

"How did you get out?" asked Sweetie.

"I tossed a small fireball in the direction I hoped the door was," said Hrefna. "I was wrong, but I managed to make a hole in the wall to a neighboring chamber. Most of the smoke was drawn there and I could see the door. Púki got it open for us, redeeming himself at least a little for his mistake, and we made it back out at North Keep as fast as we could manage."

"When we got to the top of the stairs, the guards started laughing," said Görthang. "Every exposed surface on our bodies and all our clothing, gear, and weapons were covered in a layer of soot."

"The captain of the guards said, 'Looks like the Black Company made it out,'" said Hrefna.

"And we've been the Black Company ever since," said Görthang. "Though I still would have preferred Görthang's Gang."

"You'd be a gang of one if you'd kept that name," teased Hrefna.

"Only kidding," said Görthang.

"Sure you are," said Blōgot.

"When did you buy the house and find Mother?" asked Sweetie.

"Mother found us that afternoon," said Blōgot. "We were trudging back to the Pewter Mug and Cornelius Malton, the proprietor, was standing in the door enjoying the last of the afternoon sun. He took one look at our filthy selves and told us we weren't going inside until we were clean."

"We can laugh about it now," said Görthang, "but I was so angry at Cornelius at the time. I *really* wanted a mug of ale to clean my pipes."

"Not the same way I do," teased Blōgot.

Görthang gave her comment the lack of attention he surely felt it deserved and picked up the rest of the tale. "Mother was standing in the front door of the house across the street from the Pewter Mug. He'd been operating it as a bed and bathhouse, but the staff providing the bed part had left for more lucrative employment elsewhere. The baths were still functioning, however, so Mother invited us in, helped us get clean, and put us up for the night. Kléppri paid him for his trouble, using some of the money we'd earned for recovering the scepter."

"That's quite a beginning," said Garum.

"Yes," said Görthang. "Afterwards, we decided we liked the name, and I had my black enameled armor made."

"When did you buy Mother's house?" asked Sweetie.

"Not long after that," said Hrefna. "After we were paid for rescuing a party of senior mages who hadn't returned from a trip to one of the lower levels. They were stuck in a chamber that negated magic and hadn't thought to bring any other specialists along with them."

"Not even a healer?" asked Arrex.

"Even if they had, healing is a form of magic," said Hrefna. "It wouldn't work, either."

"How did you get them out?" asked Garum.

"That's a tale for another time," said Görthang. "Suffice it to say, they paid us quite well for their rescue."

"As for the house," added Hrefna. "Mother was eager to sell. The place needed a *lot* of work."

"Which you hired him to handle?" asked Garum.

"Yes," said Görthang. "Mother's problem was never his competence as a manager. His issues were due more to a fondness for drink and a tendency to expect free samples from his staff."

"We cured him of both problems," said Hrefna.

"Permanently," said Görthang.

"Poor Mother," said Garum under his breath.

"What's next on tonight's agenda?" asked Sweetie after she shook her head in response to Garum.

"Dessert," said Hrefna.

"Then bed," said Blōgot.

"I don't expect you'll be displeased with either of those," said Görthang with a fang-bearing smile.

"Not at all," said Garum.

"In the morning, we'll go to the bank together," said Görthang. "We expect to be paid in advance."

"Why would I ever have thought otherwise?" asked Garum.

Laughter washed over the table like waves, subtly contributing to the restaurant's nautical decor.

Garum's apricot sorbet was delicious, though not nearly as delicious as the time he spent horizontally with Sweetie *after* dinner.

Chapter 6

Vaulting Ambitions

"Are you sure you have everything memorized?" Garum asked Sweetie as they walked from their rooms to the lift.

"Yes," said Sweetie. "I can recite all the account numbers backwards and forwards *and* know all the pass phrases." She shook her head slowly as she stepped to the corner of the central block where the closest lift was located. "It's not like Aubericht selected particularly difficult phrases."

"Do I want to know?" asked Garum.

"Imagine something along the lines of 'Görthang Sucks' and you won't be far off."

"That's not really one of his pass phrases, is it?" asked Garum.

"No, but I'm glad we'll be in private when we give them," said Sweetie. "You should memorize all the account numbers and pass phrases, too, in case anything happens to me. I can teach them to you while you recover for a second round of lovemaking tonight."

"Wouldn't that be more likely to ensure there isn't a second round?" asked Garum.

"Don't be so sure," said Sweetie. "Some of Aubericht's pass phrases are pretty racy."

"Really?" asked Garum.

"Yes, really," said Sweetie. "It can be something for you to look forward to."

"Any hints?" asked Garum.

"Sweetie has nice…"

"On second thought, I can wait," said Garum. They reached the lift and when it arrived a few seconds later they stepped on. *I'd never even heard of such a thing as a lift before yesterday,* thought Garum. *Now I've entered one like it's the most natural thing in the world.* "Atrium," he told the gray-haired halfling operator.

"Figured that," said the operator. "Where to this time?"

"The Golden Dome Bank," said Sweetie.

"A right and a right, then a left this time," said the operator. "Halfway down the east wing, then take the stairs if you're headed for the vaults. If you just want to talk to a manager, their offices are on the atrium level. Did you make an appointment?"

"I didn't know I needed to," said Sweetie.

"Those bankers are every bit as protective of their time and deposits as the guardians are about protecting us from the Deeps," said the operator.

"I hope they're *more* diligent than that," said Garum. "I've seen the keeps' guards operate."

"Every one of them has their hand out, I know," said the operator. "I just keep operating this contraption and try to stay out of trouble. I had enough of that when I was younger." He smiled at Garum and Sweetie when the lift's gates opened. "That's good advice for you folks, too," he said. "This job may have its ups and downs, but it's a living."

Garum put his hand on Sweetie's arm. "Wait," he said. "I need to do something." He stepped back into the lift, removed a gold piece from his pouch, and handed it to the operator. "Thanks for saying that," he told the gray-haired halfling. "I've been wanting to say it since the first time we got in your lift, but I didn't. I figured you heard that joke dozens of times a day."

"You'd be right about that," said the operator. "Anyone who pulls it on me gets bad directions, so I'm glad you held your tongue." The gray-haired halfling smiled and said, "Thank you for the tip. I have a tip for you, too."

"What's that?" asked Garum.

"If they give you a hard time about not having an appointment, tell them the Lady of the Golden Leaves sent you."

"I appreciate the tip," said Garum. Then, as if he couldn't help himself, he said, "Where are you from, Old-timer?"

"A little village south of the Great Eastern Confluence named Greenbriar," said the gray-haired halfling. "You've probably never heard of it."

"You're right about that," said Garum. "Take good care." He took Sweetie's arm and hurried them both away.

"What was that all about?" asked Sweetie when they'd turned into the east wing of the Golden Dome.

"I think the operator may be one of my great-uncles," he told her. "I'll have to figure out which one tonight."

"Don't put too many things on your list for this evening," said Sweetie. "There are still things I want to try in that tub and on the bed in our suite."

"Understood," said Garum. "But it's going to bother me until I figure it out."

"You can do that on your *own* time," teased Sweetie. "When we go upstairs tonight, it's *our* time."

"I'll do my best," said Garum.

"You always seem to," Sweetie replied. "And your best is quite good, in my opinion."

"As is yours, dear lady," said Garum. He spotted a sign on the wall and stopped abruptly. "Here are the stairs to the vaults," he told Sweetie. "Should we go there directly or speak to one of the managers first?"

"Probably the latter," said Sweetie. "They'll be expecting Aubericht the Magnificent, not Garum the Cook and Sweetie the Server."

"Remember," said Garum. "We're not those people any longer. We're the leaders of the new Golden Company."

"I doubt if it matters," said Sweetie. "Floria has probably told everyone in the place from the dwarves who operate the sewer pumps to the people who clean the guest rooms exactly who we are. Our reputation likely precedes us."

"That's Görthang's doing, I expect," said Garum. "By the way, do you have any idea who's paying for our rooms and who put up the money for dinner last night?"

"You don't think it's the Black Company?" asked Sweetie. "I assumed they were treating us well to get us to hire them."

"That could be," said Garum. "But as their employers, I'm going to be particularly interested in whether or not the contract they try to get us to sign includes a clause about covering *expenses.*"

Sweetie turned to face Garum and raised both eyebrows. "You think they want to stick us with the bill for all this luxury?"

"I wouldn't put it past them," said Garum. "I expect our suite costs more than a hundred gold pieces a night, and that amazing dinner was probably ten or twenty times that."

"Then I guess we'll have to hope that the original Golden Company has a vault full of treasure," said Sweetie. "If not, I've got plenty of experience washing dishes."

"So do I," said Garum. "If it comes to that." *If need be, I can always sell the heartstone to pay our bills,* he thought. *And turn back to North Keep Town to see what the Mages' Guild would give me for the enchanted chest. They, at least, should recognize its value, and its power.*

"Have you heard any rumors about the wealth of the Black Company?" asked Garum. "If they're considered the second most powerful company of adventurers in the Sixteen Keeps, it would be reasonable to expect they've collected their share of treasure."

"I assumed that was why they were willing to let us hire them for a relative pittance," said Sweetie. "I thought it was for the principle of the thing, not because they needed the gold."

"Maybe so," said Garum. "We won't know until we start the process to open the Golden Company's vault."

"This isn't the only bank listed in Aubericht's records," said Sweetie. "There are five more here in Gold Keep Town and six smaller banks noted in keeps spread out along the ring road."

"That many accounts implies a sizable collection of gold and gems," said Garum.

"And perhaps even larger denominations, like dragon scales," said Sweetie. A smile brightened her face.

Garum hoped it was a real one, and not just an attempt on her part to make *him* feel better.

Together, they passed the stairway to the vaults and opened the door to the bank's offices, which were every bit as opulent as their suite upstairs. Dozens of private offices lined the sides of a room large enough to host a banquet for half a thousand people. Free-standing dark wood desks with gold-plated corners and drawer pulls filled the space remaining in the center. Each desk had a wizard globe hanging from the end of a u-shaped metal tube to provide illumination. At a single desk in the front of the room sat a short man with fuzzy sideburns. He was dressed in dark green robes dotted with large circular gold pieces, like Domo. The man rose as Garum and Sweetie approached him.

"How many I help you?" asked the man.

"We want to access our vault," said Sweetie.

"Do you have an appointment?" said the man. "I don't have any vault visits listed on my calendar for today."

"Our visit is rather spur of the moment," said Sweetie.

"We're the *new* Golden Company," said Garum. "We've inherited Aubericht the Magnificent's treasure and everything belonging to the members of the original Golden Company."

"By what right do you claim their treasure?" asked the man.

"By right of survivorship," said Sweetie. "They died in the Deeps, and we inherited their arms, armor, artifacts, and worldly wealth."

"I'm glad to hear that," said the man. "Floria told me you checked in last night. I must say I look forward to working with the two of you in the years ahead instead of Aubericht, the Stone Prince, and their lot. Do you have their vault numbers and pass phrases?"

"We do," said Sweetie.

"Excellent," said the man. "My name is Ledger, by the way. We can go to my office and see to the required paperwork expeditiously. It's this way," he said, indicating an office four doors down on the left. "I'll just get a replacement manager for the front desk, and we can get started." Ledger knocked on an office door near his own and a tall woman wearing the same sort of dark green robes with gold disks moved to the front desk. She had gold-piece earrings that coordinated with her robes.

"I thought it might be harder," whispered Garum as they followed a few steps behind Ledger.

"I think you're right about Floria," said Sweetie. "She's on our side. None of the staff at the Golden Dome seem fond of the Golden Company."

There wasn't time for them to say more before they found themselves sitting on comfortable wooden chairs in Ledger's office across a wide desk from the manager. "First things first," said Ledger. "Let's see to your privacy." He pulled a cord on the wall behind him and a man wearing dark green and gold robes—in a wizard's flowing cut—entered, unfurled a scroll, and read from it in a monotone. The floor, ceiling, and sides of the office sparkled with planes of magical energy and the wizard left as silently as he'd entered.

"What was that?" asked Sweetie.

"A privacy field," said Garum. "The officers used to invoke them when they didn't want their battle plans to be overheard."

"Ours are very much the same," said Ledger, "but operate at a higher level of impermeability than any military privacy spells used for ranks below a general's staff."

"Interesting," said Garum.

"What is the vault number?" asked Ledger as he consulted a thick codex that seemed packed with columns of numbers.

Sweetie told him.

"Oh, yes," said Ledger. "That one."

Sweetie and Garum exchanged glances.

"Don't worry," said Ledger. "It's nothing you've done. Aubericht and his company contrived to steal a dragon's egg from Dragon Keep and stored it in that vault, representing it as an artifact, not an egg. We had quite a time getting the dragon out to the surface and picked up by dragon keepers without burning down half the walls in the complex."

"I'm sorry," said Sweetie.

"You had nothing to do with it and therefore no reason to apologize," said Ledger. "The Golden Company was fined for storing contraband, which covered our out-of-pocket costs, and a few years later, when the dragon matured, it decided to bank with us—our first winged and scaled client."

"All's well that ends well?" said Garum.

"Precisely," said Ledger. He turned to Sweetie. "And the pass phrase for the account?"

Sweetie recited the pass phrase, blushing crimson in the process.

"Very good," said Ledger. "Meeting you, I can see why Aubericht found the phrase memorable."

Sweetie managed a weak smile and Garum took her hand so he could offer some small measure of comfort.

"You have the key, I presume?" said Ledger.

"Right here," said Sweetie. She pulled a key from her sleeve. One end was a square conjoined to a hemisphere, like a miniature version of the central block and dome of the Golden Dome. The key, of course, was gold.

"It's steel," said Ledger, seeing Garum's puzzled expression. "It's only painted gold. A key made of gold wouldn't be strong enough to turn in a lock."

Garum had no idea how Sweetie had obtained the key to the vault but now was not the time to ask her.

There was little actual paperwork. Sweetie and Garum provided their names, which were duly recorded in the codex along with tiny drops of blood from each of them. *Healers' magic,* thought Garum.

"That's that, then," said Ledger, stroking the bottoms of his long sideburns. "I'll escort you to your vault."

They proceeded down three levels into what was surely chambers carved from bedrock and paced east for a hundred feet, passing dozens of identical rectangular steel doors until Ledger stopped in front of one. "This is yours," he said. "Or at least the one you asked to open." He inserted a key he held into the upper of two locks while Sweetie put hers in the second. "Turn on three," he said. They did, with no confusion on Sweetie's part about turning *on* three or *after* three. "I'll stay outside," said Ledger. "Let me know if you need any bags or boxes to transport things."

"Thank you," said Sweetie.

Garum nodded to Ledger, who stepped ten feet down the corridor where he couldn't see into the vault. Garum opened the door, allowed Sweetie to step in, and entered behind her.

When their eyes fully took in the contents of the vault, saying they were surprised would be the understatement of the century. It was empty.

Chapter 7
Hidden Treasure

"What the…" said Garum.

"Shut the door," said Sweetie.

"Are we sure it will open from the inside?" asked Garum.

"It will," said Sweetie. "They don't want clients to lock themselves in."

"That makes sense," said Garum as he closed the door slowly, so it wouldn't clank. "But what *doesn't* make sense is the vault being empty. Where's all the original Golden Company's treasure?"

"I don't know," said Sweetie. "I expected it to be here."

"Could it be hidden behind secret panels?" asked Garum. "Under the floorboards?"

"Don't be silly," said Sweetie. "The floor is made of solid stone, not wood, and so are the walls and ceiling. That's sort of the point of a vault."

"So we're broke?" said Garum after shaking his head. "We'll have to wash dishes for seven years?"

"Maybe not," said Sweetie. "Maybe Céptianne pulled the same trick I did earlier."

"She made the Golden Company's treasure invisible with her illusions?"

"We can hope," said Sweetie. "Put your back to the door, close your eyes, and stay out of my way."

Garum initially followed Sweetie's instructions, then he opened one eye part way. He saw her holding her wand and smiled as she made it swish and flick through the air. Sweetie started to turn around so he closed both eyes so she wouldn't catch him.

"Oooo!" said Sweetie. "You can open your eyes now."

Before he did, Garum said, "The last time I heard you say, 'Oooo!' like that was our second time last night.'" He opened his eyes completely and repeated Sweetie's syllable of rapturous pleasure, perfectly matching her intonation in a slightly lower register. The vault was now filled to the point of being stuffed with treasures.

Bags of gold pieces as big as well-fed Salt Town merchants' bellies were stacked along the back wall. Some were so full their tops had opened, and coins were spilling out. Small soft-leather pouches with drawstrings were on shelves above the bags under signs on the wall above them labeled diamonds, rubies, sapphires, and emeralds. Necklaces, bracelets, and rings with precious gems were displayed on an unfurled bolt of fine black velvet on a shelf on the left-hand wall above piles of expertly crafted weapons and armor the Golden Company must have earned by combat over a decade.

The right-hand wall had bolts of expensive cloth—silks, damasks, brocades, and more Garum didn't recognize. He saw rolled up carpets with hints of their elaborate designs showing and some finished robes and tunics neatly folded to show off the embroidery on their cuffs and necklines. Garum's eyes were particularly drawn to the shelves above the clothes and fabrics where plates, cups, mugs, and goblets made from shiny metals gleamed. He saw a stack of engraved silver serving trays worthy of an emperor's banquet hall and a gorgeous gold goblet more than a foot tall decorated with rubies, emeralds, sapphires, and pearls.

"Looks like we won't need to wash dishes after all," said Sweetie.

"Not unless this is another of your amazing illusions," said Garum.

"It's real," said Sweetie. "What wasn't real was this vault being empty. Céptianne must have come with Aubericht and done the same thing I'd done with the chest in our room's safe."

"Made the contents invisible," said Garum. "No wonder they could get away with hiding a dragon's egg in this vault." He noticed a long, narrow, unlabeled box painted with gold leaf on the shelf beside the gem-encrusted goblet and picked it up.

"It was easy to cancel Céptianne's illusion," said Sweetie. "And it will be easier still to renew the treasure's invisibility with an illusion of my own when we leave."

"Good," said Garum. "Take a look at this," he said after he'd opened the narrow box and showed her what was inside.

"They look like big poplar leaves," said Sweetie. "Only gold."

"I think they're the dragon scales Görthang and Hrefna were talking about," said Garum. "Each one is worth a thousand gold pieces, maybe more."

"So that one box holds over a hundred-thousand gold pieces of value?"

"I haven't counted them, but that seems close to it," said Garum.

"Should we take the box with us?" asked Sweetie.

"I don't think so," said Garum. "It's probably hard for most merchants to make change for a dragon scale. But it would be fun to take a few of them so we can pay Görthang and the Black Company using the method they requested."

"I wouldn't," said Sweetie. "It's rude, like paying your taxes in copper pennies and making the tax collector count them all— not that anyone *I* might know would do such a thing." She put a finger to her nose and smiled.

"Of course not," said Garum, returning Sweetie's smile. "What should we take, then?" he asked.

"A bag of assorted gems, perhaps," said Sweetie. "And a few hundred gold pieces? We can pay the Black Company with gems and use the gold pieces for food, lodging, bribes, and incidental expenses."

"Sounds like a plan," said Garum. "You select the gems, and I'll try to find a smaller bag than those huge ones for the gold pieces."

"There are extra bags of various types and sizes in a niche beside the door," said Sweetie.

"I hadn't noticed them, thanks," said Garum. He collected a small, soft-leather bag for Sweetie and took a much larger canvas bag big enough to hold one of Wuid's melons for himself. While she was selecting gems and he was scooping coins, he noticed she was eyeing the goblet on the right-hand wall.

Sweetie noticed him following her focus on the goblet. "It's beautiful, isn't it," she said.

"Not as beautiful as you are," said Garum.

Sweetie laughed. "You don't have to do that *all* the time," she said. "I do like it but comparing me to a priceless work of exquisite craftsmanship like that goblet is a bit much."

"I'm not saying things to make you more likely to take me to bed tonight, or this afternoon, or whenever we get back to our rooms," said Garum. "I know that's something we both want to do anyway." He moved behind Sweetie and put both his arms around her waist. "I said what I said in all sincerity. That goblet is beautiful, a great work of art and craft—but it can't look at me the way you do, or tease me the way you do, or kiss me the way you do." He put the side of his cheek against her back. "To me, that makes you more beautiful than the goblet."

"Awww..." said Sweetie. She rotated in Garum's arms to face him and embrace him. "I'm still not sure I'm buying what you're selling, but I like it—and I like you. A lot."

"That's a good start," said Garum.

"Should we bring the goblet with us?" asked Sweetie.

"I wouldn't," Garum replied. "It's sure to be heavy and I wouldn't want to risk damaging it in transport."

"You're right," said Sweetie. "I'll just have to make a mental picture of it I can summon up in my mind whenever I need to contemplate its beauty."

"I have a mental picture of a different subject in *my* mind," said Garum.

Sweetie kissed Garum's forehead. "I wonder if anyone has ever made love in one of these vaults?" she asked.

"We could ask Ledger," said Garum.

"Are you *trying* to make me blush?"

"Maybe a little," said Garum. "If we tried, at least we'd have privacy."

"Like we had in Ledger's office after the wizard cast his spell?" asked Sweetie.

"Only if we sent Ledger off on a time-consuming errand first," teased Garum.

After one last hug, they broke their embrace and returned to their tasks.

"I've got enough gems," said Sweetie.

"And I've got enough gold pieces," said Garum. "This bag is about as heavy as I can lift comfortably," he said, patting the bag, which jingled.

"Grandfather can carry the bag when we head to East Keep," said Sweetie. "Its weight will be so many feathers for him. For now, I'll see if I can disguise the sound of those gold pieces rattling together as well as making the bag invisible."

"And I'll ask Ledger if he can sell me a backpack," said Garum. "That would be a much easier way to carry our haul."

"The gems will fit in my belt pouch," said Sweetie.

"Good," said Garum. "Ready to leave?"

"Almost," said Sweetie. "I have to renew the treasure's invisibility."

"Do I have to close my eyes again?"

Sweetie paused for a moment, then said, "Yes."

Garum closed his eyes and sensed the swish-flick of Sweetie's wand. Then he felt warm lips on his, making part of him want to try making love in the vault, despite the lack of a comfortable spot to recline. When their kiss ended, Garum opened his eyes and smiled up at Sweetie.

"You didn't need to close your eyes this time," said Sweetie. "I just wanted to kiss you when your eyes were closed."

"All I know is that I'm glad it was you kissing me instead of Ledger."

"Oh, you!" said Sweetie, gently whapping Garum's chest with the dangling edge of her robe's deep sleeve.

Ledger was waiting a discreet distance down the corridor. He smiled when Garum and Sweetie left the vault, then used his key while Sweetie turned hers to relock the vault and secure it. Ledger opened a cabinet inset into the walls of the corridor and produced a small backpack in response to Garum's request. It made the bag of gold pieces much more comfortable to carry.

As they climbed the stairs, Ledger asked Garum and Sweetie if the service provided by Golden Dome Bank had been satisfactory.

"Other than not having a lift up from the vaults?" asked Garum.

"Oh, I'm sorry," said Ledger. "Of course, there's a lift. We use it for major deliveries and withdrawals. What was I thinking? My apologies for not asking your preference earlier."

"Don't worry about it," said Garum. "We just got back from a trip to the Deeps and there were a lot of stairs to climb to get back to the surface."

"That's perfectly understandable," said Ledger. "I'll be sure to have a question about preferred ways to reach our vaults added to our standard protocols."

"A wise idea," said Sweetie. "How is the rental of our vault arranged, by the way?"

"Aubericht set it up to be automatically renewed every five years," said Ledger. "Payment is taken from an account with the bank that is quite well supplied with funds, so I don't anticipate any issues. You're only in the second year of five, so there's plenty of time to make any necessary changes."

"I don't think we'll need to change anything," said Sweetie. "But I would like to have details about that account you mentioned. Would funds there be accessible at all of the sixteen keeps?"

"Yes," said Ledger. "All but Silver Keep and Ice Keep, of course."

"Of course," said Sweetie.

They stopped back at Ledger's office when they reached the atrium level. Sweetie showed Garum the funds in the original Golden Company's account and both of them raised an eyebrow. Even without the treasures in the vault, they were in no danger of needing to wash dishes.

"Thank you again for all your help," said Sweetie when she rose to leave, with Garum beside her.

"It's our pleasure," said Ledger. "A letter with a few questions about your satisfaction with our services will be delivered to your suite this afternoon. I would greatly appreciate your honest responses."

"Anything other than *superlative* is a black mark, eh?" said Garum.

"I'm glad you understand," said Ledger.

Garum held back a smile. When Garum was chief cook for his unit, some otherwise well-meaning captain tried to circulate similar letters to the troops about the quality of the food he served. Garum hadn't learned about it until later but some of his assistants had collected the letters, steamed them and mashed them, then fried them up and fed them to the captain as an imported delicacy. Garum always thought the best way to judge the quality of a cook's work was by how many soldiers asked for second helpings. He was glad most of his superiors had agreed.

"It's nice to know we don't have to worry about the cost of our stay here," said Sweetie as they headed for the lift to their rooms.

"We have to be careful not to get too used to luxurious living," said Garum. "I think we'll need to find more affordable accommodations in Herb Keep and East Keep."

"Given what we just saw in the vault and the amount in our account with the Golden Dome Bank, do you think that's really necessary?" said Sweetie.

"As we both told the others," said Garum, "it's not really our money."

"That's true," said Sweetie, "but I'm still fine with spending another night in our suite—and that big bed."

"Agreed," said Garum. He rubbed his chin as he remembered something. "We can leave tomorrow morning. At some point, we need to talk to Prestyn about his inventory of the treasure we collected from the original Golden Company when they disappeared," he said. "It's only fair that the others have some gold pieces to spend while they're in Gold Keep Town."

"Like the hundred gold pieces each he gave to Xarra and Yarra?" asked Sweetie.

"Along those lines, yes," said Garum. "After."

"After lunch?" said Sweetie. Then she smiled. "Oh. *After* after."

"That bed is almost as big as the vault, don't you think?" said Garum.

"I like the way your mind works," said Sweetie. "And your body."

"You two look like you have big plans for the rest of the morning," said the gray-haired halfling when the lift doors opened. "Express to the fifth floor, at your service."

"Thanks," said Garum. He tipped the operator two gold pieces this time and enjoyed Sweetie's hand holding his as they walked to their rooms. Something was nagging at his brain, however, distracting him from the fun ahead. *Right,* thought Garum. *I still have to find a buyer for the heartstone, though that's less of an issue now that I know we're already rich—even if it is the original Golden Company's treasure. Maybe I'll hang on to the heartstone for a drizzling day.* That settled, Garum smiled at Sweetie and as the door to their rooms opened, he promised himself to give her his full attention.

Chapter 8

Lunch for Eleven

Before Garum and Sweetie settled in to enjoy their big bed, they rang for someone on Golden Dome's staff and were both surprised when Floria herself knocked on their door.

"This is an unexpected pleasure," said Sweetie.

"My shift just started, so when you rang for assistance, I decided to help you personally," Floria told them. "I've heard excellent reports about the *new* Golden Company from the servers at the Golden Carp and Ledger at the bank, to say nothing of the kind words about you from Squire, the lift operator."

"Squire?" asked Garum. "Is that his title? He never told us his name."

"He hasn't told me, either," said Floria. "From what I've gathered, it's not a title. It's supposedly short for *Squirrel*."

That's nuts, thought Garum.

"I'm glad we haven't disappointed you," said Sweetie.

"Far from it," said Floria. "Now, how can I be of assistance?"

"We'd like you to arrange a late lunch for us and the other members of our party," said Garum. "Somewhere private, if possible."

Floria tilted her head in thought. "There are eleven of you, I believe," she said. "Unless you want Görthang and his associates to join you?"

"No, just the new Golden Company," said Sweetie.

"Come to think of it," said Garum. "It would be great to arrange a dinner with our team *and* the Black Company for tonight, if you could suggest a good place?"

"Other than the Golden Carp?" asked Floria.

"Yes, please," said Sweetie. "If only to try someplace new."

"You could eat at the Golden Calf, another one of the Golden Dome's restaurants," said Floria. "It's under the clock tower at the far end of the west wing. I have it on good authority that your vixer has already mostly repaired the tower's clock, by the way. Thank *you* for that."

"You can thank Vip-vip yourself, next time you see him," said Garum.

"I'll make a point of it," said Floria. "As for lunch, I would suggest using one of the Golden Dome's smaller banquet rooms, the sort that we typically use for business meetings with twenty guests or fewer. Shall we say at one o'clock?"

Sweetie looked and Garum and they both nodded. "Better make it two o'clock," said Sweetie. "No need to rush anything."

Floria looked from Sweetie to Garum and back, then smiled and nodded. "In three hours, then," she said. "That will give the chefs time to arrange a lovely lunch for you."

"Sorry for the short notice," said Garum, thinking about how much he disliked last-minute changes to his own cooking schedule. *Then again, cooks at a high-end place like this must be used to it.*

"One more thing," said Sweetie. "We need to get word about the lunch to everyone on our team, and we're not sure where everyone is," she told Floria.

"The young men are still in the Golden Dome," Floria replied. "The one with the quarterstaff is riding the moving stairs out front for the twenty-seventh time. Your healer is talking about techniques for setting bones with the Golden Dome's resident healer and the mage with the squirmy cloak is in his room scribbling figures on a piece of scrap parchment, according to the person who cleaned for him this morning."

"And the others?" asked Garum.

"Drain is helping our sewage maintenance specialists disassemble a pump and, as you know, your vixer is fixing our clock. If he succeeds, we'll comp his room. It will be worth it to the Golden Dome to have the clock working again."

Good for Vip-vip, thought Garum. *And good for Drain.*

"What about my grandfather?" asked Sweetie.

"He's arm wrestling the Black Company's troll mage in her suite," said Floria. "He's up seven bouts to five, but they're going to twenty-one, so there's plenty of time for the lead to change. Most of the staff is betting on your grandfather, but Hrefna has her supporters."

"I notice you haven't mentioned the twins," said Garum.

"I was getting to them," said Floria. "It's a rather delicate topic."

"Not that Xarra and Yarra are the least bit delicate," said Sweetie.

"As you say," said Floria. "We normally don't follow our guests around on the jaunts through Gold Keep Town, but Major Domo suggested it might be wise to make an exception for the young ladies."

"Thank him for us for that," said Garum.

"Gladly," said Floria. "But there's more."

"Tell us," said Sweetie.

"The twins went to a very high-end establishment, looking for the man who appeared shirtless in the painting they saw on the road from Rose Keep," said Floria. "Domo said he was available, but his rate was over a hundred gold pieces an hour. The young women decided to pool their funds and jointly hire his services."

"So far I don't see a problem," said Sweetie.

"I think I do," said Garum. "Now I understand why you answered our request for assistance personally."

"Ah, yes," said Floria. "The man in question—a celebrity of sorts here in Gold Keep Town—was, shall we say, overwhelmed by the twins. He called for support from three of his colleagues at his own expense and together they managed to 'show the twins a good time.'"

"I must be missing something," said Sweetie. "What went wrong?"

"Nothing," said Floria.

"How much did the establishment offer the twins?" asked Garum.

"A thousand gold pieces a day to sign up with them," said Floria. "Plus twenty-five percent of all fees collected, and they can keep their tips."

"Oh," said Sweetie. "Looks like we're down two fighters, then."

"Not at all," said Floria. "Your twins didn't accept the offer. From what Domo heard third-hand, they said something about not wanting to lose their amateur status when they were still so young. At eighteen, they have plenty of time to change their minds."

"Good for them," said Garum.

"Where are they both now?" asked Sweetie.

"Cheering on your grandfather in Hrefna's suite," said Floria. "We can get word to all of them about the lunch, and the dinner, shortly."

"Please do," said Garum. "And now…"

"I'll take my leave," said Floria. "With your authorization, I'll arrange for a generous tip to be sent to the four professionals who serviced the twins?"

"By all means," said Sweetie. "Make it *very* generous. And Floria—"

"Yes?"

"See that we're not interrupted between now and a quarter to two."

* * * * *

Garum tapped on the side of his wine goblet to get everyone's attention. When all eyes—even the twins'—were on him, he continued. "I know we're all enjoying our time here in Gold Keep Town," said Garum, his glance lingering over the twins as he spoke until Sweetie coughed. "Unfortunately, we're not here for our own pleasure. We have a mission to accomplish and have to get the enchanted chest we found to East Keep so the College of Healers can figure out how and if the members of the original Golden Company can be restored to their normal bodies."

"I don't see why we should bother," said Drain.

"If our roles were switched, I'm sure we'd want Aubericht and the others to try to restore us, right?" said Sweetie.

"I doubt it," said Crank.

"We can show them we're better than that and take our responsibilities as their retainers seriously," said Garum.

"Galingálë did start to show me how to shoot better," said Flisk.

"See," said Garum. "We owe it to the original Golden Company and to ourselves to at least *try* to restore them."

"Why should we, Your Majesty?" asked Sir Donal.

"Because we need to prove we're better than they are, or were, or whatever," said Sweetie. "Aubericht wasn't a nice man and he used to chase me around his rooms when I'd clean for him, but he doesn't deserve to be disintegrated and not restored. At least not without us trying to restore him and the others. Flisk says Galingálë was nice to him, and Barton DeCláre and Alderōn were decent people."

"Wait," said Sir Donal. "Aubericht used to chase you around his rooms? Why didn't you *say* something, granddaughter?"

"Because I needed a job," said Sweetie. "And because I can take care of myself. Aubericht is lucky he never caught me, since I would have nailed the back of his hand to his nightstand with my dagger if he'd touched me."

"You are your mother's daughter," said Sir Donal.

"I know," said Sweetie. "And some of the time, you even remember my mother."

"All of the time," said Sir Donal. "I just don't remember to *say* it some of the time."

"Thank you, grandfather," said Sweetie.

"The Stone Prince took one look at me when I walked into the Green Doors and decided I was unworthy of a second glance," said Drain after gulping several ounces of beer. "That hurt. It always hurts. Dwarves usually cherish their women, since there aren't that many of us, and treat us well. But the Stone Prince looked my way, saw a sewer mason, and pretended I didn't exist. He can stay gone, as far as I'm concerned."

Arrex put a hand on one of Drain's shoulders and Prestyn did the same for the other. The dwarf stared down into her beer mug and seemed to want to hide inside it. She shrugged off the young men's hands and whispered, "Just leave me alone."

Garum wasn't sure what to do. Sweetie was the best thing that had happened to him in years, and he'd thought his fellow adventurers were becoming his friends. Now everything seemed to be unraveling. He wanted to hold Sweetie and rub her back and tell her she was wonderful but knew that wasn't what she needed right now. He wanted to hug Drain and tell her she was a good friend and would be a wise dwarf's first choice as a marriage partner someday but was positive that wouldn't be well-received. Still unsure how to proceed, he was about to stand when Xarra and Yarra beat him to it.

"I know we're young," said Xarra.

"And may seem irresponsible," said Yarra. "But we're not."

"Or not that much, anyway," said Xarra. "We're just sowing our wild oats."

"And having fun while we can," said Yarra.

"In many cases, our response to bad behavior would be to say, 'Screw it,'" said Xarra.

"Or often 'Screw you, and you, and you, and you,'" said Yarra, smiling at Prestyn, Arrex, Crank, and Flisk.

"But we were raised on a farm," said Xarra.

"And farm folk look out for each other," said Yarra.

"If someone's barn burns down, we'll all come together and raise them another one," said Xarra.

"It doesn't matter if the farmer who lost his barn kicks his dog," said Yarra. "We've all had days like that."

"The important thing is that we're a community," said Xarra.

"And we help each other when help is needed," said Yarra.

"I think we need to take the chest to the College of Healers," said Xarra.

"So do I," said Yarra.

The others around the table sat in stunned silence, thinking their own thoughts, when the twins sat down.

"Shall we put it to a vote?" asked Garum.

"No," said Sweetie. "We should show we're better than Aubericht and do the right thing." She looked at every face around the table. No one, not even Drain, was willing to disagree. "Well, then," said Sweetie. "We'll leave for East Keep in the morning."

"GUP?" said Vip-vip, sounding more tentative than any of them had ever heard him before.

"Yes, GUP," said Garum, "if everyone agrees?" He looked around the table and moved his hand in a circular motion, encouraging responses. "All in favor?" he said. This time, everyone nodded, willing to accept Sweetie's peremptory decision. "We can leave in the morning," Garum added, "though I think it might be better to start after lunch. We'll stay overnight in Herb Keep. I've heard it's a great place to replenish my herbs and spices."

"Can we take magecoaches to Herb Keep?" asked Xarra.

"Can we, can we?" added Yarra.

"Tell you what," said Garum. "Let's walk the six miles or so to Herb Keep tomorrow afternoon to work off last night's dinner, our lunch today, and our dinner tonight with the Black Company at the Golden Calf, and we can take magecoaches from Herb Keep to East Keep if we can find any to hire."

"Yay!" shouted the twins.

"We're having dinner with the Black Company tonight?" said Arrex. "That's good. I promised to talk to Gêrdun about making healing potions taste better."

"Yes," said Sweetie. "Dinner is at eight, just like last night. We can all meet at the clock tower at the end of the west wing."

"BONG!" said Vip-vip.

"You got the clock working?" said Garum.

"BONG BONG!" said Vip-vip, which Garum took to be, "Yes."

"Don't get into too much trouble between now and dinner time," said Sweetie to the entire table, with particular attention given to the twins.

"Prestyn," said Garum. "Are there enough gold pieces in your inventory to give everyone here five hundred of them to spend?"

"Not *that* many, but if you count valuable gems, there's plenty," said the young mage.

"Pass out the funds," said Sweetie. "Remember, only four hundred for Xarra and Yarra."

"That should be plenty," said Xarra.

"More than enough, really," added Yarra.

"We had our fun earlier," said Xarra.

"Now we want to buy some nice clothes, and presents for our friends," said Yarra.

"We can have more fun with *these* young men tonight," said Xarra, looking at Prestyn, Arrex, and Crank.

"They can unwrap their presents," said Yarra.

"By which we mean remove our new clothes," said Xarra.

Yarra smiled at Crank. "Be sure to bring Jelly," she said. "We need to thank him for watching the kittens."

"Thank him the best way," said Xarra.

"What fun!" chimed in Yarra.

From the far end of the west wing, the great clock chimed four.

Chapter 9

Conversations in Bed

When they returned to their rooms, Garum did have a chance to hold Sweetie in his arms. It was easier horizontally, since the top of his head only came to her collarbones when they were both standing. Still in tunic and robes, they hugged for several minutes without speaking, just letting the warmth of each other's bodies provide reassurance.

Sweetie had her head on Garum's chest and took deep breaths that thankfully didn't turn to sobs.

Despite the joyful amorous play they'd enjoyed before lunch, and the glow they'd shared from it, the conversations around the table after their meal had been painful.

Garum fought back a desire to sever Aubericht's hamstrings, assuming they managed to restore him, of course, because of the leader of the original Golden Company's behavior. He had to relax his jaw so Sweetie wouldn't sense the tension he held there.

He still saw red when he thought about Aubericht chasing Sweetie around his rooms and attempting to grab her. She was only trying to do her job and clean them, after all. Garum wondered if the young halfling, Veridan Green, who'd been so kind to him when he'd first arrived at the Green Doors had been aware of Aubericht's attempted assaults. From what Sweetie had told him, the original Golden Company were part owners of the Green Doors, which put Veridan in a difficult position, but still. Then he thought about his own feelings of jealousy when he thought Sweetie and Aubericht might have been lovers and heat of a different sort washed over his cheeks.

More shame invaded his brain when he realized how he'd failed as a leader at lunch.

I should have been the one to say what the twins said, thought Garum. *I grew up in a farming community, too. For all that halflings could be narrow-minded, clannish gossips, the families in and around Green-briar could come together to help others in need.* Thinking back, he wondered how much of this was seeing his past through the rose-colored lens of childhood. *No,* Garum considered. *The halflings of his hometown had also helped a party of humans who lost wheels on two of their wagons and a dwarf who'd broken a leg in a rabbit hole by the side of the road going north to Three Rivers. The dwarf had recuperated at a neighbor's home for half a year.*

Garum smiled, remembering how he and several other halfling lads and lasses had listened to stories of the wider world for hours.

"What?" said Sweetie, feeling his muscles move.

"I was just thinking back on the stories I heard from a dwarf recuperating from a broken leg back in Greenbriar," he said. "His tales may have been a big reason I left home when I did." *Along with the threats from my lover's older brothers.*

"Good for you," said Sweetie. She pulled away a bit so she could see Garum better. "I would have done it, you know."

"Done what?" asked Garum.

"Pinned Aubericht's hand to his nightstand with my dagger."

"I never doubted that," said Garum. "You'd be fully in your rights to do so."

"That's why Veridan moved me to a room by the kitchen," said Sweetie. "I originally had a small room on the same floor as Aubericht, the Stone Prince, Céptianne, and Khrusósha, but when I told Veridan I'd heard someone trying the lock several nights in a row, he moved me."

Garum took a moment to think better of the halfling innkeeper, then thought of something else. "Didn't the threat of your grandfather smashing Aubericht's nose dissuade him?"

"Grandfather was a building away in the men's dormitory," said Sweetie. "Besides, I'm sure Aubericht was confident he and his enchanted swords could stop my grandfather, even with his vambraces."

"I would like to see that match-up," said Garum. "Or maybe I wouldn't. I'd hate to see your grandfather injured."

"I'm glad it didn't come to that," said Sweetie. "I was close to having enough money to leave the Green Doors and find somewhere else to live. I decided to see if I could be hired by the Golden Company because if our pay for the expedition would have been large enough, we could leave—and because my grandfather would be there to keep Aubericht in line."

"Oh," said Garum. *And I had no idea. Idiot.*

"And then there was you," said Sweetie. "You didn't push. You left it up to me to make the decision—and I decided to take a chance."

"Thank you," said Garum.

"I'm very glad I did," said Sweetie. She hugged Garum close.

He wasn't sure if she might be crying, but knew tears were forming in the corners of his own eyes. "Where had you hoped to go when you left the Green Doors?" he asked after a long pause.

"I'm not sure," said Sweetie. "Wages are higher at the Sixteen Keeps than elsewhere, and my grandfather was starting to feel at home at the Green Doors. Veridan found jobs for him to do, and he liked that. It was easy for grandfather to move heavy casks and cut firewood."

"People like to feel useful," said Garum.

"I stopped cleaning Aubericht's rooms when he was at the inn," said Sweetie. "Fortunately, the Golden Company was off hunting or adventuring in the Deeps often enough the place didn't have time to become a pigsty."

"Was Aubericht the only one to give you trouble?" asked Garum.

"Besides visitors to the inn trying to pinch me?" asked Sweetie.

"Anyone else in the Golden Company," said Garum.

"The Stone Prince never tried to grab me," Sweetie replied. "Dwarves have different notions about sex from humans and halflings."

"So I've gathered from Drain." *And from talking to dwarves in the axe companies when I was a military cook.*

"He was mostly just disdainful, like it was my privilege to breathe the same air he did," Sweetie continued. "Barton DeClâre was a gentleman, as I'd said, and Alderōn even caught me once when I stumbled carrying a try of ale mugs and didn't try to take any liberties."

"It's good to know at least a few of them weren't horses' asses," said Garum.

"I'm not done yet," said Sweetie. "Galingálë once asked me if I wanted to see her 'special arrows,' but I declined her invitation and left it at that. Céptianne, however, was the worst of the women. She was like a mare in heat all the time and it didn't matter if her partners were men, women, orcs, trolls, or giants."

"Interesting," said Garum, in a tell-me-more tone.

"She made the twins look like celibates," said Sweetie. "It was all I could do to put down my disgust and pick up her wand."

"And I didn't even notice any reluctance," said Garum.

"I did my best to hide it," said Sweetie. "And you had other things to think about."

"We all did, after it happened," said Garum.

"The odd thing is nobody really knows Céptianne's true appearance," said Sweetie. "She could be an obnoxious ogre or a gray-haired halfling man like the lift operator you think is your great-uncle. Given her illusions, there's no way to tell."

"I'm glad she never made a play for me," said Garum.

"She would have, if she hadn't disappeared," said Sweetie. "It would have been only a matter of time."

"I guess I can be happy for small favors, then," said Garum.

"That's what is pulling me apart," said Sweetie. "I tell the others that all the original Golden Company's treasure isn't really ours. That we have to do what we can to bring them back—when what I truly want is for them to *stay* gone and have all their wealth to myself, or for *us* now, and my grandfather." She giggled.

A good sign, thought Garum.

"I'd even be glad to split the treasure with the others," said Sweetie. "There's *so* much of it." She shook her head. "Does not wanting Aubericht and the original Golden Company to come back make me a bad person?"

"It's not what you want, it's how you act," said Garum. "I've served under officers I despised enough I would have gladly poisoned them at the dinner table, but I never actually did it."

"Because you'd be caught and hung?" asked Sweetie. She giggled again.

"What?" said Garum, thinking Sweetie's face looked more sixteen than twenty-four at that moment.

"I was just thinking you were hung already."

Garum laughed. "Thank you for the compliment," he said. "No, I didn't poison anyone because I was afraid of facing the consequences of military justice. I did it because I'm the sort of person who might think such a thing but would never *do* it. Despite my rough life, I'm still a halfling lad from a small farming village on the inside. That wasn't how I was raised. I might steal, but I'd never kill someone who wasn't trying their best to kill *me* first."

"That's why I was only going to pin Auberict's hand to his nightstand," said Sweetie. "It's an injury Barton DeClàre could fix with a single healing potion, but the pain of the blade might make Auberict think twice about trying to grab me again."

"I don't know if that would have had the results you hoped for," said Garum. "I've met enough arrogant warriors in the various armies where I've served that would just take such a thing as a challenge—as if you were playing hard to get."

"I *am* hard to get," said Sweetie. "The second time anyone tried to paw me, my blade would be inserted between their ribs instead of the bones of their hand."

"Thank you for not pulling a dagger on me," said Garum.

"Thank *you* for never giving me a reason to want to," said Sweetie. "When you said you had a firm rule about romance— always let the other person indicate interest first—I knew you were different."

"From?" asked Garum.

"From the drunks who try to pinch me in places where I don't want to be pinched," said Sweetie. "That's why I told you how to find my room."

"To clearly indicate interest?"

"I tried to make it as clear as an axe blow between your eyes," said Sweetie. "Then Alderōn had to come in with his news about that chest."

"The one in our safe?" asked Garum.

"The one no one can *see* in our safe," said Sweetie, grinning.

"Would you have made love to me if I'd come to your room that night?" asked Garum.

"I might have, if you didn't give me a reason not to once you got there," said Sweetie. "Instead, you teased me for hours as we tromped through the Deeps, making me want you even more and keeping me from being too nervous about what might happen to us without the original Golden Company's protection."

"You gave as good as you got, dear lady," said Garum.

"You mean last night, and this morning?"

"I mean when we were in the Deeps, and you know it."

"I *do* know it," said Sweetie. "And I'm so glad we got out alive."

"So am I," said Garum. "And now, here we are, in a featherbed the size of my mother's vegetable garden, with more gold pieces in our not-so-metaphorical pouches than I ever would have dreamed possible as a wee halfling lad."

"Now that you mention it, I do have to," said Sweetie.

"Have to what?" asked Garum.

"Wee," said Sweetie. She disengaged from Garum, slid off the bed, and headed for the garderobe next to the bathing room.

Garum laughed at himself. *I walked into that,* he thought. *Don't lose this woman,* Garum told himself. *She's a bigger gem than the ones on that gold goblet in the vault. We were both feeling down, and our hugs and shared conversations made things better somehow. I'm still conflicted about restoring the Golden Company, but if Sweetie is willing to do it, I can, too.* He heard water running from the bathing room and then Sweetie calling to him.

"Aren't you going to scrub my back?"

"Coming, dear!"

They were still in bed at seven-thirty, having gotten some rest, of a sort. Garum even gave the lift operator a three-gold-piece tip.

Chapter 10
The Golden Calf

"Now *this* is meat cooked just the way I like it," said Görthang.

Garum looked at the slab of steak on Görthang's thick bread trencher and saw it had been barely seared on each side, the same way he would have cooked beef for orcs, trolls, and ogres in his field kitchens back in the army. For himself, he preferred medium rare to meat that could likely still *moo.*

"My fillet is tasty," said Sweetie. She had a cut of steak about the size of her hand on her plate, smothered in butter and mushrooms. Garum could smell the garlic in the butter and had wisely ordered the same thing as Sweetie, since garlic-breath kisses wouldn't matter if they both had it. Sweetie teased him about eating lots of asparagus, which was also on *their* trenchers. Garum wondered if *her* inner thirteen-year-old found something entertaining in that vegetable's phallic appearance. "Even if it does make our pee smell weird," she added.

Garum didn't know if he'd have any energy for more active pursuits in bed that night, but considered that with the proper, or properly improper inspiration he might still rise to the occasion. *Thank goodness thirty-nine for a halfling is comparable to mid-twenties for a human,* he considered, not for the first time.

The Golden Calf had a much different decor from the Golden Carp. Auroch horns far wider than Garum was tall were mounted on the walls. So were the tools of cowherds—ropes, brands, saddles, bridles, and spurs, all in gold or decorated with that metal. A gilded bronze sculpture of a calf at twice life size—nearly as big as Hrefna—filled the spacious lobby where guests waited to be seated. Garum *hoped* it was gilded. A sculpture that big cast from solid gold would be too valuable to leave in a lobby.

"These white tubers are better than the ones in the Golden Carp," said Crank from across the U-shaped tables.

"You can't get much simpler than letting them bake in coals for a few hours," said Garum.

"When I was smaller than Púki," said Görthang, "my father took me to a place near the stockyards at Portage."

"The city at the south end of the longest Inland Sea?" asked Garum. "Where cargoes bound for the Big Muddy used to be carried overland?"

"Before the canal was finished, yes," said Görthang. "There were only three items on its menu: thick steaks, baked white tubers, and salad greens with herbs, oil, and vinegar." Görthang laughed. "For us, the greens were optional."

"I've been to Portage," said Garum.

"You have?" said Sweetie.

"I get around," he teased.

"Yes, you certainly do," Sweetie replied.

"That was when I was younger," said Garum.

"You're not old now," teased Sweetie. She blew Garum a kiss, ate a bite of her fillet, and turned to talk to Blōgot on her right.

Save for what was on the walls, the private room where they were dining was nearly identical to the room where they'd had dinner the previous evening. One big difference was the loud clacking and whirring of the clock mechanism in the tower above them. They'd all been seated precisely on schedule while it was striking eight times.

Görthang tapped Garum's elbow. "When are we going to East Keep, boss?" he asked.

"Don't *do* that," said Garum.

"Touch you?"

"Call me *boss*," said Garum. "If you have to call me anything like that, call me *chief*, as in chief cook. Some cooks in mess tents put on airs and wanted to be called *chef*, but I thought that was pretentious. To my mind, chefs cook fancy food. I just cooked good food and plenty of it."

"I'm sure your troops were pleased you were in the kitchen, chief," said Görthang.

Garum laughed. "Now that I think about it, just call me Garum. It's odd to have someone who's twice my size and has your reputation call me chief."

"Fine, Garum, then," said Görthang. He grinned, showing upper *and* lower fangs. "When are we going to East Keep, Garum?"

"I was thinking we'd walk to Herb Keep in the morning, spend the night, then press on and walk to East Keep the next day," said Garum.

"Walk?" said Hrefna from Görthang's left. "What about traveling by magecoach?"

"Garum said we could take a magecoach from Herb Keep to East Keep," said Xarra.

"I've never ridden in a magecoach, and I want to try it," said Yarra.

"How does it move…" said Xarra.

"…without horses," Yarra completed.

"It's magic," said Hrefna.

"You're no fun," said Xarra.

"We want to know," said Yarra.

"So, the two of you want to study magic as well as swordplay?" asked Hrefna.

"Just enough…" said Xarra.

"…to understand magecoaches," said Yarra.

"Talk to Prestyn," said Hrefna. "He might be willing to instruct novice wizards."

"I'm still a mostly novice wizard myself," Prestyn protested.

"Did you really tell the twins you'd take a magecoach to East Keep from Herb Keep?" asked Görthang.

"Yes, why?" asked Garum.

"Because there are hardly any magecoaches to hire in Herb Keep," said Görthang. "Most travelers pass Herb Keep by on their way to consult the College of Healers."

Xarra waved a fork at Garum. "You were trying to trick us!"

Yarra waved a fork with a morsel of meat on. "Did you know you can't hire magecoaches in Herb Keep?"

"Of course not," said Garum. "I've never ridden in a magecoach myself. I don't think I trust them to stay on the road. Horses, mules, and oxen won't stray off their set path."

"Unless they're hungry and there's green grass beside the road," said Xarra.

"Ask her how she knows," said Yarra.

"That wasn't my fault," said Xarra.

"Was too," said Yarra.

"The best place to hire magecoaches is here at the Golden Dome," said Görthang, stepping on the twins' exchange. "They can get us to East Keep in five or six hours."

"But I want to stop at Herb Keep to replenish my supply of herbs and spices," said Garum. "And I'm more comfortable walking than riding in a magecoach."

"How do you know?" asked Arrex.

Garum looked up at the young healer in surprise. Other than a vague disquiet about magecoaches' motive power, he wasn't sure. "Maybe it's some sort of innate dislike for machines more complicated than a forge bellows, or a wind—I mean, *water* mill," he said. "It's a halfling thing."

"You've taken the lift to our rooms enough times," said Sweetie.

"And you rode up the moving stairs out front," said Crank. "I rode them fifty times."

"We know," said Xarra and Yarra in unison.

"And we still haven't had a chance to spend much time in Gold Keep Town," said Crank. "I've only been here at the Golden Dome."

"Whose fault is that?" asked Xarra.

"We invited you to come with us," said Yarra.

"I have a proposal for you," said Görthang.

"Which is?" asked Garum.

"If you must walk, why don't *you* leave for Herb Keep after breakfast, buy what you need there, and spend the night. We'll enjoy another day here in Gold Keep Town and pick you up in a magecoach, if you decide to rest your legs, or walk to East Keep yourself the next morning."

"What about my safety on the road?" asked Garum.

"Does the leader of the new Golden Company require protection?" asked Hrefna with a smile.

"Yes," said Garum. "I'm just a small halfling cook and slinger."

"Who stood beside me against a Shambling Shocker," said Görthang.

"I like the idea of having another day in Gold Keep Town," said Sweetie. "Though I *don't* like the idea of spending a night in our big bed alone."

"I'd be glad to keep you company," piped up Púki.

"We plan to tie you to a chair in our suite tomorrow night," said Xarra, putting a hand on one of Púki's shoulders.

"And make you watch," said Yarra, putting her hand on Púki's *other* shoulder.

"Works for me," said the shortorc.

The twins each pressed down harder and Púki's body slid on his chair until only his nose, eyes, and forehead were showing.

"I don't feel comfortable continuing to wear Céptianne's robes," Sweetie whispered to Garum. "With an extra day I could buy new ones, have them altered, and pick them up in the morning before we leave two days from now."

"That makes sense," said Garum. "Maybe I can find a few more tunics and braies for myself before I leave. It's not as if they have to fit closely."

"We can shop for clothes *together!*" said the twins in a single voice.

"Why don't you come clothes shopping with me," Sweetie suggested. "Garum's likely to pick the first options the tailor shows him and be done with it."

"That's no fun," said Xarra.

"Trying on clothes and having them fitted is the point," said Yarra.

"More for you than for me," said Garum. He opened his arms wide to take in the members of both the Black and the Gold Companies. "Does anyone *want* to walk to Herb Keep with me?" he asked.

Púki poked his head up higher, looked left, then right, and finally shook his head *no*.

"Sorry, I don't like walking when I don't have to," said Hrefna.

"I could be your bodyguard, Your Majesty," said Sir Donal.

Garum noticed Sweetie's subtle head shake in his peripheral vision. "I couldn't ask that of you, good knight," he said. "Sweetie needs you to help guard her and the twins while they're shopping."

"Service to beauties, before royal duties," said Sir Donal.

Garum turned his head toward Sweetie so her grandfather couldn't see his lips and mouthed, "Really?"

Sweetie kissed her fingertips and touched them to Garum's forehead with a smile. "I don't know where he comes up with things," she whispered.

"Crank?" asked Garum.

"I need new clothes, too, and I want to ride the moving stairs a few more times," Crank replied.

"Drain?"

"Fine," said the dwarf. "Take me away from the soothing sounds of the most exquisite sewage pumps I've ever seen."

"Stay, then," said Garum. "I won't deprive you."

"Prestyn? Arrex? Flisk?"

Garum received three head shakes in return. *Oh, that's right. The twins have evening plans for Prestyn, Arrex, and Crank. Flisk is probably their default kitten wrangler at night since I expect Jelly is invited to their horizontal get together—not that I expect everything happens only horizontally.* He tried to push the images in his head off to one side, especially since he'd be sleeping alone tomorrow night.

A small voice came from the far end of one of the tables. "GUP?" said Vip-vip tentatively.

"You want to walk with me?" said Garum. "That would be great!"

"GUP!" said Vip-vip with more enthusiasm. "GUP! GUP!"

"Not tonight, tomorrow after breakfast and a stop at a tailor's shop," said Garum. "Maybe we can get your healers' robes adjusted while we're there.

Vip-vip smiled and raised his ogre-sized arms over his head, shaking them.

"I think he likes the idea," said Görthang.

"Upon reflection," said Chophorn the sylviant, "and with all due deliberation, I find that I might have business to transact at Herb Keep Town tomorrow as well. If it meets with your approval, I would like to walk with you."

"The more the merrier—and the warier," said Garum. "You're a lot taller than we are and can likely spot trouble much farther off than we could. Vip-vip and I would welcome you as a traveling companion, thank you."

"We leave at dawn?" asked Chophorn.

"Probably more like nine or nine-thirty," said Garum. "Halflings are fond of a hearty breakfast."

"And I'll ask Floria to have the kitchen staff pack a lunch for you to eat on the road," said Sweetie.

"I can do that," said Flisk.

"No, you can't," said Xarra.

"You promised to watch the kittens—tonight *and* tomorrow night," said Yarra.

"Did I?" said Flisk.

"You must have," said Crank, using his hands to add an unspoken *please* to his statement. "Jelly will be tied up."

"No, that's *me*," said Púki. Two strong hands on Púki's shoulders pushed the shortorc's head out of sight.

Garum turned to Görthang. "Any recommendations on where to stay in Herb Keep?" he asked.

"The Bowl and Brew," Görthang replied. "Ask anyone where to find it. You'll like the place, and they have rooms sized for sylviants and halflings."

"I can guide you to there," said Chophorn.

"Great," said Garum.

"I'm glad that's settled," said Görthang. "Now who wants dessert? I hear they make an amazing cream pie topped with whipped and stiffened egg whites."

Garum didn't even have to glance down the table to see Xarra, Yarra, and Púki's eager faces. He knew they were there.

Chapter 11
Chophorn

It was hard to believe, but Garum found himself missing Xarra and Yarra's verbal jousting on the road to Herb Keep. Vip-vip was chattering in his characteristic monosyllables, but the box on his belt seemed to be malfunctioning and failed to translate his speech. *How can a vixer who seems to be able to fix any mechanism not be able to repair his translation box?* Garum wondered. *Perhaps part of the box functions by magic? Vip-vip had never demonstrated any expertise in that area.*

Chophorn, on the other hand, stayed mostly quiet as they walked. The rare times he did speak, he had a tendency to use sixty-four gold piece words instead of simple silver shilling ones. The lack of conversation bothered Garum. He'd enjoyed bantering with Sweetie, especially when it was flirting banter, and reflected on the pleasure he took in talking to his cook's assistants as they worked together to prepare meals.

Garum took no little pride in knowing he could have produced dishes comparable to the ones he'd recently enjoyed at the Golden Carp and Golden Calf. *Except, to be fair, the fried fish.* A few more steps made Garum remember. *Blast! I hadn't tried to sell the Carp's chef my crisps technique.* He shook his head in disgust. *Maybe Crank will do it? It would be good for the young man's ego to make some money from a recipe, even if it was mine.*

They'd gotten an early start since it had only taken half an hour for Garum to select four new tunics and matching braies from a tailor who had come to their rooms instead of Garum having to go to her. It was quite a change for him to buy clothing without worrying about what it cost, though he did avoid the tunics cut from expensive fabrics in favor of more sturdy long-wearing options. He was particularly fond of a pair of braies made of soft indigo-dyed cotton that came with an unusual feature—four pockets of material for storing useful items, one on each hip and one on each side in the back. With a tunic over the braies, the pockets couldn't be seen. *Sweetie will be picking them up for me tomorrow morning,* thought Garum.

Traffic on the road was light. A white magecoach had passed them an hour ago. Its windows were made from salvaged black glass, so Garum couldn't see who was inside. The driver wore the livery of the Mages' Guild, however, so perhaps it was an official visit of some sort. Garum blinked. For an instant, he thought he'd seen a team of six white unicorns pulling the magecoach, but then it passed him, and no sign of the unicorns remained.

Was there an illusionist in the coach? Garum speculated. *Was he, she, or they trying to prank me, or amuse me?* Garum knew wands of illusion were very rare, and mages who could use them well were rarer still. *Now Sweetie is one of their number,* he thought. *Will she have to join the Mages' Guild?* Garum wondered. He knew there *were* mages who operated independently, but the guild at North Keep was powerful and did what it could to encourage magic users of every sort to ally with them.

Were there Cooks' Guilds in larger cities? Garum wondered. *If so, I feel for anyone trying to run one. It would be more difficult than Flisk trying to rein in seven kittens, though Jelly, with his ability to sprout pseudopods when needed, had an advantage.* "Cooks are artists," Garum said, not realizing he'd spoken out loud.

"What?" said Chophorn.

"NU?" said Vip-vip.

"I was thinking about the challenge of organizing a guild of cooks," said Garum. "We're all artists, of a sort, and once we are skilled enough to run our own kitchens, we don't take well to being told what to do."

"In my considered opinion, which is not extensive on culinary topics, since my palate is unsophisticated," said Chophorn. "Especially given that sylviants as a class are more interested in a dish's nutritional value than its gustatory stimulation, but given pecuniary realities, don't cooks have to subsume their own creative urges to the desires of their employers?"

"When you put it that way, yes," said Garum. "A wise cook will prepare dishes their employers like—but wise employers will give their cooks a great deal of latitude, so long as the cooks are able to surprise and delight."

"Delight, more than surprise, I surmise," said Chophorn.

"If an employer has a bland palate, dishes too highly spiced with hot peppers or cumin are indeed unwise," said Garum. "Particularly if bread, rice, milk drinks, or ices aren't available on the menu to reduce the heat."

"Am I to assume this is a hard-won lesson drawn from your own experiences?" asked Chophorn.

"Draw whatever conclusion you want," said Garum with a smile. "I admit nothing."

"Your answer is in the affirmative, then?" said the sylviant.

"Maybe," said Garum, still smiling. "Let's talk about something less incriminating for a bit," Garum suggested.

"Do you have a topic in mind?"

"Where are you from, for a start," said Garum. "I'm from a small farming village south of the Great Eastern Confluence."

"What a remarkable coincidence," said Chophorn. "I'm not."

They both laughed and the box on Vip-vip's belt made a sound like a waterfall of glass shards for a few seconds.

"My roots are farther north," said Chophorn, "in the center of the large peninsula between the Inland Seas."

"You must mean the Mitten," said Garum. "Was it a nice place?"

"It was, until the axe-men arrived," said Chophorn.

"What happened?" said Garum.

"My family and I were living in a lovely little forest there. It was filled with old-growth oaks, maples, beeches, and even a few birches and willows clustered along a narrow stream that ran nearby. I was just a sapling, along with my three brothers and a sister. Our parents tended the forest, pruning back dead branches, removing creepers that would sap the trees' strength, and making sure the squirrels, birds, and chipmunks had plenty of nuts to eat and plant."

Garum looked up at his companion and nodded.

Chophorn continued. "I can still remember the sweet aroma of my mother's acorn-flour bread baking in the sun."

"That sounds like a lovely childhood," said Garum.

"OO-OOO," said Vip-vip, sounding like a deep-voiced owl.

"It was, until the axe-men cut down all the trees in our forest and sent their wood down the stream to be turned into houses and furniture in Portage," said Chophorn. "They didn't select the trees that could be safely culled—they cut them all down, indiscriminately." The sylviant smacked the butt of his axe handle on the road's smooth paving stones. "My mother was in shock. She just stood there, rooted to the spot and horrified, when a thoughtless axe-man chopped her down, thinking she was just another tree. They killed her."

"That's terrible," said Garum.

"It was worse to witness," said Chophorn. "My siblings and I rushed to our mother's side, but she was gone. They held her, but I felt my sap rise, in a way of speaking. I picked up one of the axe-men, shook him until he dropped his axe, then threw him twenty yards. He slid across the ground until the top of his head hit a stump that had recently been one of the trees I had cared for."

"Did you kill him?" asked Garum.

"No," said Chophorn. "But I did pick up his axe and threaten to make stumps of both his legs. He ran back to where the other axe-men were camped and I chased him, swinging his axe and vowing vengeance on all humans."

"Did they leave?" asked Garum.

"No," said Chophorn. "Some of them lured me farther away, shouting insults about sylviants being moss-covered and stupid beyond be-leaf. I proved their point, because I was unwise enough to follow them." He paused, and so did Garum and Vip-vip. Three long breaths later, he said, "They killed my brothers, sister, and father, too, while I was some distance from our home. I found their bodies at twilight. The axe-men had stripped off their bark garments and left their naked bodies in the mud to rot."

"I'm so sorry," said Garum. *If I'd know a simple thing like 'Where are you from?' held so much trauma for Chophorn, he never would have asked the question.* That realization didn't stop Garum from asking another question. He'd been going to say, "Did you kill the axe-men?" but switched to the less accusatory, "What did you do?"

"First, I circled back and pulled down all the axe-men's tents after dark, collecting their axes so they couldn't cut any more trees," said Chophorn. "I chopped all their tent poles to kindling and sent a stampede of forest bison through their encampment for good measure. They decided to leave after that and headed back south along the stream, following the trunks of the trees they'd consigned to their mills."

"Confusion to the enemy," said Garum. "I would have liked to see that."

"Indeed," said Chophorn. "Though it would have been difficult to appreciate the entirety of the axe-men's disarray in the dark."

Garum smiled and Vip-vip made his glass waterfall sound again. "What then?" asked Garum.

"I dug six deep holes, buried my parents and my siblings, and planted trees over their graves," said Chophorn.

"VEE?" said Vip-vip.

"I think he's saying *FIVE*," said Garum. "There were only five members of your family lost. Why six holes?"

"I put the axes in the sixth hole," said Chophorn. "All but three of them. Those I reforged into the axe I now bear."

"That explains it," said Garum.

"Explains what?" asked Chophorn.

"Why a sylviant carries an axe."

It was difficult to read Chophorn's expression, especially given the difference in heights between them, but Garum thought he could sense a note of irony from the way the sylviant raised one bushy eyebrow.

"It's not the traditional weapon of my people," said Chophorn.

Garum nodded. "What did you do afterward?"

"I wandered," said Chophorn, "that is, I just walked around aimlessly for more than a year. Then I learned who'd hired the axe-men and burned his sawmill to the ground."

"Oh," said Garum.

"The next day, I burned his home in Portage to the ground, too."

Garum stared at Chophorn.

"Don't look at me that way," said the sylviant, responding to the accusation in Garum's stare. "No one was home. No one was harmed." Chophorn shook his head, as much as any being with very little neck can. "I may be a member of the bloodthirsty Black Company, but you should know by now that our reputation is for show, not a true representation of our natures."

"I'm coming to realize that," said Garum.

Chophorn stroked a bit of mossy beard below his mouth. "After the fires," he said, "I came south to the Keep Lands and served as a stair guard in North Keep. It seemed a better plan than staying near Portage, all things considered. The leaders of the Mages' Guild and their senior guard officers like my kind. We're strong, imposing, and much less volatile than giants, trolls, and ogres."

"I've served with and cooked for many sylviants," said Garum. "I share the same assessment."

The halfling, the sylviant, and the vixer walked on in silence for a quarter of an hour. Then Chophorn spoke.

"Would you like to look at the cliffs?" asked the sylviant, coming to a stop.

"I'm too short, and so is Vip-vip," said Garum.

"Let me lift you," said Chophorn.

In a single, smooth motion, Chophorn scooped his broad palms under their buttocks and lifted Garum and Vip-vip up to where they could step out onto the top of the wall separating the road from cliffs. The bottom of the depression formed by the Deeps far below was still full of fog that would probably burn off by noon. Here and there, small lakes reflected sunlight and patches of something silver glinted under the fog. A few tiny towers, much smaller than any of the great keeps, emerged in clusters from the upper surface of the Deeps. Garum remembered an officer who'd trained at South Keep Town told him the tiny towers had no doors or other ways to enter them.

I wonder how anyone got down the cliffs to check, thought Garum. *It would take an awful lot of rope to lower anyone down.* Garum mentally smacked himself in the head. *I'm a fool,* he told himself. *They probably flew down on dragonback.* He rubbed his chin. *I've seen dragons close up and cooked for them, too.* Garum enjoyed seeing dragons high overhead during battles, but it wasn't wise to have them land near his mess tents. *Quartermasters have ended up losing a three-week supply of beef on the hoof after an unexpected visit from a single dragon. And they made the soldiers nervous.*

To Garum's right, Vip-vip was also gazing down at the upper surface of the Deeps. Garum couldn't make out exactly what Vip-vip was saying, but it sounded something like CHIP! CHIP! *I don't understand what he means, but that might be a good term for my thin fried white tubers,* Garum considered.

"We'd better keep moving," said Garum. "I need to get to the herb and spice markets while they're still open."

"Let me help," said Chophorn. He strapped his massive axe across his back, scooped up Garum and Vip-vip again, and started striding along the ring road in a clockwise direction, covering more distance in one step than the halfling or the vixer could do in ten.

"You don't mind carrying us?" said Garum.

"Not at all," said Chophorn. "You're not as light as feathers, but you're not heavy, either. Just don't squirm and enjoy the ride."

"I *do* like the higher vantage point," said Garum.

"Welcome to my world," said Chophorn. "I'm so tall, if I'm not careful, birds try to nest in my hair."

"You're kidding?" said Garum.

"Check behind my left ear, if you don't believe me," said Chophorn. Garum looked and didn't see anything.

"Got you," said Chophorn.

"Yes, you did," said Garum, shaking his head and laughing.

"It's nice to know the leader of the new Golden Company is every bit as gullible as the leader of the Black Company."

"Görthang fell for that one?" said Garum.

"Twice," said Chophorn.

Vip-vip wasn't looking around. He was tapping on the small metal box on his belt. "Good luck fixing it," Garum told Vip-vip. "It would be nice to have real conversations with you again."

"My turn to ask you questions," Chophorn told Garum. "What sorts of herbs and spices do you need to get at Herb Keep?"

Garum started counting items off on his fingers. "I'll need eleven secret herbs and spices for my special fried chicken recipe…"

"Those are just a myth," said Chophorn. "Everybody knows about them, but nobody knows what they are."

"A cavalry colonel in one of the bigger campaigns on the Sleeve told me," said Garum. "But he swore me to secrecy."

"I have sincere reservations about the veracity of that statement," said Chophorn, sounding more like he did when he was trying to show off his vocabulary than he had while telling Garum about the loss of his family.

"The proof is in the eating," said Garum. "If I can get what I need, I'll make fried chicken for everyone some night when we're on the road."

"If only I had a discriminating palate and could appreciate it."

"Your loss," said Garum. "I am running low on some basic spices, and do need an assortment of dried herbs, but the real reason I want to visit Herb Keep Town…"

"Is to get long leaf?" asked Chophorn.

"No," said Garum.

"Toothed leaf?" Chophorn offered.

"I don't smoke," said Garum. "Smoking makes it more difficult for me to adjust subtle flavorings. Good cooks try to retain their discriminating palates, not destroy them."

"Your loss," said Chophorn.

"I do get hickory chips for smoking meats and cedar chips for smoking fish," said Garum. "But I try not to inhale."

"Again, that's your loss," said Chophorn.

"I think halflings and sylviants' lungs may work differently," said Garum.

"In that, I'm sure you're correct," said Chophorn. "If you see any cubeb, please buy a pound of it for me."

"A *pound*," said Garum. "I barely use a couple of ounces of cubeb in a year."

"That quantity would be perfect for my needs, however," said Chophorn. "It provides the same mellow feeling for sylviants that seven-lobed toothed leaf does for most other subspecies, with the added benefit of lethe-like forgetting."

"So you can reduce the pain of your family's deaths?" asked Garum.

"So I can reduce the pain of not doing more to make the people who killed them suffer," said Chophorn.

"I'll see what cubeb I can find for you," said Garum.

"Good," said Chophorn.

"GUP!" said Vip-vip, pointing ahead.

Herb Keep and the walls circling Herb Keep Town rose up ahead of them. Both were overgrown with the fast-growing twining plants with large leaves and purple blossoms that Garum knew as goat vines, because it took a large herd of goats munching day and night to keep the vines in check. It reminded Garum of the climbing rose vines on the tower and walls at Rose Keep. Unchecked, goat vines were said to grow so fast you could almost watch them move.

Garum hoped the guardians at Herb Keep and Herb Keep Town budgeted for plenty of goats. He didn't want to consider going to sleep tonight and waking up completely wrapped in vines. He'd rather wake up in Sweetie's arms, but he was here because he wanted to be.

"On, to the herb and spice markets!" said Garum enthusiastically. The prospect of visiting those markets made him as excited as he was on a visit to a confectioner's shop on a family trip to Three Rivers when he was ten.

"I know the way," said Chophorn. "Hang on tight."

"GUP!" Vip-vip repeated.

"I'll buy you an ale at the Bowl and Brew when I'm done," said Garum.

"Just buy my cubeb," said Chophorn. "That will be enough."

Chapter 12
The Market

Garum's excitement was over the Moon and perhaps a few of the planets as well. For a military cook whose spices and herbs were often limited to salt and whatever he could pluck along the line of march, Herb Keep Town's herb and spice market was a banquet of culinary riches. Chophorn had put him down in front of the market's arched and elaborately carved main entrance and had gone off with Vip-vip—and Garum's pack—to reserve rooms at the Bowl and Brew.

The market itself wasn't like other markets Garum had visited, either. It wasn't set up under canvas in a town square and it wasn't held only once or twice a week. *This* market was permanent, a veritable arcade of hundreds of shops around the periphery of a rectangular building with a glass roof to let in sunlight. Much like the central block of the Golden Dome, it had the market building had five levels and low walls around its open court at each level to prevent any merchants or their customers from falling.

The scents wafting around Garum were almost overpowering. They teased his nose and challenged his discernment. He could sense common herbs like basil and oregano, aromatic oils like chamomile and myrtle, and concentrated spices like ground mustard and red pepper powder. On top of those was the savory smell of skewers cooking over charcoal braziers and adding their own smoky aromas.

To Garum's annoyance, most of the stalls at the ground level were for basic ingredients, featuring a wide range of meats, vegetables, grains, flours, and sweeteners. From where he was standing in the entryway, he spotted kiosks for sellers of locally collected honey, conical loaves of white and brown cane sugar from far to the south, tree-sap sugar from the north, and huge round roots bigger than Garum's head arrayed on trays under a sign reading, *Our Sweet Roots*

Beet Sugar in Price and Taste. Garum saw the merchant had a plate of sliced roots beside her for tasting and resolved to make sure he stopped there on his market explorations.

How does anyone find anything in all this? Garum asked himself. *Is there some sort of guide or directory? And more importantly, is there a lift to the fifth level?* He was surprised how quickly his stay at the Golden Dome with its advanced luxuries had accustomed him to its conveniences. *So why wouldn't you ride a magecoach?* part of his brain berated him. Before Garum could start an internal debate on *that* question, however, a halfling woman not much older than he was, wearing a lavender apron embroidered with *Ask Me Anything,* stepped from an opening on the right side of the entryway and greeted him.

"Good morning," said the woman.

Garum was pleased to meet someone his own height and sub-species. He admired the woman, who looked quite attractive in an off-white, knee-length tunic, purple pants, and black pigskin boots much like the ones Garum was wearing. "Good morning," he said in return, after a short pause.

"You look lost," said the woman. "First time to the Herb and Spice market?"

"Yes," said Garum. It seemed like his tongue was unwilling to function properly and a single syllable was all he could manage. Too many years had passed since he'd seen a halfling woman who'd had that effect on him, even if his current preference was for someone taller, and human.

"I could tell," said the halfling woman. "Go ahead, ask me anything."

"Umm, what's your name?" asked Garum.

"Not original, but a start," said the woman. "I'm Marigold—one of the greeters at the market." She saw that the *I'm overwhelmed* look on Garum's face was still there and tried again. "What's *your* name?"

"Garum." He tried counting is teeth with his tongue and was finally able to convince that organ to do his bidding. "Does this place have a lift?" he asked. "I don't like climbing stairs."

Marigold laughed. "That's an excellent question, and one I hear most often from other halflings. There *is* a lift in the back. It's powered by Otis—he's a giant—and members of his family. Unfortunately, it's not open for public use and is only for official members of the market to transport their heavier goods to the shops upper levels."

"I have to walk, then?" asked Garum.

Marigold could see that Garum didn't relish that prospect. "You look so unhappy about climbing stairs you must have just come up from the Deeps."

"How did you know?" asked Garum.

"You did? You really did?" Marigold exclaimed. "Here in the market that's just another way of saying *tired*."

"Climbing seven thousand stairs two days ago still has *me* tired," sighed Garum.

"Seven thousand steps!" said Marigold. "You went all the way to the lowest level? I'm impressed."

Part of Garum wanted to say, "I'm the leader of the *new* Golden Company, you *should* be impressed," but his innate good sense opted for other words. "It wasn't something I'd planned on," he said. "I'm a cook, and was hired by an experienced party of adventurers."

"Well, then, as a cook I can understand why you're here in the market," said Marigold. "Are you looking for anything in particular? My job is helping customers find what they need." She looked Garum over from boots to forehead.

Garum nodded. He was pleased he looked better now in a new tunic and braies than he had when he'd first trudged into the Green Doors and met Sweetie. She'd liked him, unwashed, after days on the road. Marigold seemed to like him in his relative finery. *Focus, Garum,* he told himself. *You've got a good thing going with Sweetie. Don't make your life more complicated.* He shifted from nodding to smiling, then realized Marigold was waiting for an answer and was wise enough not to give an eager male's answer of *I need you.*

"May I be of service?" said Marigold to fill the awkward silence.

To Garum's surprise, she took his hand and pulled him out of the entryway and over to the right and into a tea shop. She directed him to a wooden chair at a table for two and left Garum sitting alone and feeling overwhelmed in multiple dimensions. Soon, Marigold was putting a mug of some sort of tea in front of Garum and taking the seat across from him.

"The market can be a lot to take in," said Marigold after she'd had a few sips of tea and watched Garum do the same. His was very sweet.

"I'm not usually like this," said Garum after another sip.

"Tongue-tied like a halfling lad two feet tall?" asked Marigold.

"Well, yes, but more like feeling I've fallen in a river and can't breathe," Garum replied. "I think everything in the past few days is finally catching up with me."

"I've heard the Deeps can do that to people," said Marigold. "I saw lots of adventurers returning from the Deeps at my parents' inn at North Keep Town. Few were brave enough to risk the lowest level."

"I'm more lucky than brave," said Garum. "You wouldn't be related to Veridan Green, would you? I was at the Green Doors three nights ago."

"Veridan is my younger brother," said Marigold. "I left North Keep Town when he sold a quarter-interest in our family's inn to the Golden Company." She frowned in a way that made Garum think Sweetie wasn't the only woman that Aubericht had tried chasing around a room. "What name does your group of adventurers use, by the way?" she asked.

Garum smiled and shrugged. "The *new* Golden Company," he said.

Marigold's face brightened. "Did something happen to Aubericht and the others?"

Garum found himself opening up to Veridan's sister and gave her a brief account of what had happened.

"Good," said Marigold. "He got what was coming to him."

"Well," said Garum, "my friends and I *are* trying to see if we can restore them."

"That's because you're good people," said Marigold. "I understand you're doing what you need to do. Just don't try *too* hard to bring them back. To my mind, the world would be a better place without most of them in it."

"We're headed to East Keep to see if anyone in the College of Healers has any idea about how to bring them back," said Garum. "I needed to replenish some of my cooking supplies, and I've always wanted to visit Herb Keep Town's market, so I left Gold Keep Town early to stop here."

"Good for you," said Marigold. "This really is a great place for cooks. I'll show you all the best merchants."

"That would be nice, thank you," said Garum.

"By the way," said Marigold. "Do you know Sweetie and her grandfather, Sir Donal Tilter? They came to the Green Doors shortly before I left and are really the reason I could leave in the first place. I wouldn't leave without my brother having someone to help him run the inn and tavern."

"Uh, Sweetie and her grandfather are part of the *new* Golden Company with me," said Garum.

"Isn't she the nicest human," said Marigold. "I did warn her to watch out for…"

"Sweetie and I are very close," blurted Garum. "Very close."

"I see," said Marigold. She stuck out her tongue at Garum. "You must really like *tall* women, then." She held a grumpy face for two beats then shifted to a wide smile. "I'm teasing," said Marigold. "I like Sweetie a lot and I'm glad the two of you are close. It's been hard for her having to look after her grandfather as his mind has slipped more and more into the past, especially with him being so strong and all."

Garum let out the breath he'd been holding and smiled back at Marigold. "It has," he said.

"But with Aubericht gone," said Marigold, "things should be easier for her—and for my brother."

"How are things easier for Veridan in Auberichť's absence?" asked Garum.

"The Golden Company—Auberichť's version—helped my brother out by buying a quarter-interest in the Green Doors," said Marigold. "Aubericht said all their drinks and food and board were now free, so instead of *making* money on their investment, he was losing it."

"Ouch," said Garum. "Let me guess—if Veridan protested, Aubericht would start to slide one of his swords from its scabbard or Khrusósha's cloak would decide to push valuable crockery off the table like a cat confirming objects still fell down."

"It's like you were there to see it happen," said Marigold.

"No, but I have a good imagination," said Garum.

Marigold gave him a long, sensual look, licked her lips, and smiled. "I'm sure you do." Then she shook her head and slapped the back of one of her hands with the fingers of the other. "Stop that!" she told herself in a scolding voice. She shook her head and composed herself. "Sorry," said Marigold, looking back up at Garum and turning both her hands outward to him in some sort of request for supplication or forgiveness. "It's just that there aren't many halfling men in Herb Keep Town and still fewer who are anywhere near the right age to be interesting."

"I understand," said Garum. "And if I wasn't already spurs over crown in love with Sweetie, I'd be glad to court you."

"Now you're just teasing me," said Marigold. "But I deserve it. Let's be good friends and keep it that."

"It would be my pleasure…" Garum began, then restarted. "I'd like that," he said. "Halflings should stick together."

"I agree," said Marigold. She wrapped both her hands around her mug of tea and kept them there.

Garum did the same.

"Do you have any particular herbs and spices you're looking for?" Marigold asked, glad to change the subject.

Garum recited a long list that just happened to include the eleven herbs and spices needed for his colonel's fried chicken recipe, without any of them being grouped close together.

"Those are easy," said Marigold. "And they're mostly at vendors only one level up, so you won't have too many stairs to climb. Ask me for something challenging."

"Does the market have any silphium?" asked Garum, keeping his expression perfectly neutral.

Marigold frowned at him and wagged a finger in front of Garum's nose. "Silphium has been gone since long before the Deeps," she told him. "It's the infamous lost herb of the most ancient ancients."

"Really?" said Garum. "I've seen it and even used it in dishes. It grows wild on the hills above Greenbriar, my home village."

"You're joking," said Marigold.

"I'm not," said Garum. "It's true."

"I don't think I'm going to tell the rest of the market vendors," said Marigold. "They'd probably dig up all the silphium plants by the roots and drive it extinct again."

"I agree," said Garum. "That's why I lied."

"About the silphium existing?" said Marigold.

"About its location," said Garum.

"Wise halfling," said Marigold.

"I can be, sometimes," said Garum. "Other times, not so much."

"That's the human—and halfling—condition," said Marigold.

"Oh, I almost forgot," said Garum. "One of my traveling companions asked for a pound of cubeb. Do you know where I might find some?"

"On the southern islands," said Marigold.

"Now you're teasing me," said Garum.

"Sauce for the hen is sauce for the tom," said Marigold.

"I deserved that," said Garum.

"Your companion must be a sylviant. I've heard what that spice does for them. There are three cubeb sellers on the fourth floor," said Marigold. "Each one is on a different side of the arcade. You'll get a better price if you play them off against each other. I can't do it for you, since the market collective pays me."

"Understood," said Garum. "But you *can* advise me, and I appreciate it. Are you sure there's no way I can ride the merchants' private lift to the fourth floor?"

"No customers allowed," said Marigold. "But there are ogres for hire by the back left stairway who will carry you up as far as you want to go for the right fee. Ask for Tiny—he bathes regularly."

"Got it," said Garum. "You've been *very* helpful."

"Wait a moment," said Marigold. She pulled a square of parchment from her belt pouch. "This is an enchanted map of the market," she told Garum. Marigold tapped several squares representing shops on the second and fourth levels above them. "I've marked the best places to get all the items you mentioned," she said. "When you're done shopping, drop the map in the red box by the exit."

Garum twisted to look over his shoulder and saw what Marigold was referring to. "I'll be glad to," he said.

"Don't forget," said Marigold. "I get a commission on every sale."

"And here I thought you were simply helping me out of the goodness of your heart," said Garum.

"Not to mention the fact that you're at least a little bit handsome, even if you did lie to me about the location of the silphium."

"It was in a good cause," said Garum.

"That's what they all say," teased Marigold. "Tell me, where are you staying in Herb Keep Town?"

"The Bowl and Brew," said Garum.

"Really," said Marigold. "I didn't take you for the sort of person who would stay there."

"Some friends recommended it," said Garum.

"Just try not to inhale," said Marigold.

"Inhale what?"

"Anything," answered Marigold. "The toothed-leaf smoke can get pretty thick in the tavern there."

"I thought the *bowl* part of the place's name referred to a soup bowl," said Garum.

"Think again," said Marigold. "It's a *pipe* bowl."

"Interesting," said Garum. "I'm not fond of smoke, except for cooking meat."

"Neither am I," said Marigold. "If you want to avoid smoke, you could always stay with me. I have a spare room, and the door locks."

"I don't want to tempt either one of us," said Garum. "I'll pick up some bread, sliced meat, cheese, and fruit and eat in my room at the B&B."

"Ah, well," said Marigold. She took the map back from Garum and marked a few more stalls on it, many of them on the ground level. "If I'm not going to have the pleasure of your company, at least I can get a commission on your dinner."

"I like a woman who keeps her priorities straight," said Garum. He looked up at the rows of shops above him before turning his eyes back to regard Marigold. "By the way," he said. "What's on the fifth floor?"

"If you have to ask, you can't afford it," said Marigold.

"No, really, what's up there?"

"Meeting rooms for the merchants' cooperative, dealers in truly exotic herbs and spices used exclusively by mages and healers for their own mysterious purposes, and purveyors of high-priced non-edible perfumes," said Marigold. "It also has a break room. The cooperative put the break room on the fifth level to keep their members in better shape after losing twelve of their associates who were too fond of good food and too adverse to exercise in a single month."

"Thanks for telling me," said Garum. "I think I'll take the stairs myself instead of hiring Tiny."

"That's wise," said Marigold. "It's better for your health—and I was lying about Tiny bathing regularly."

"Good to know," said Garum. Marigold blew him a friendly kiss and he blew her one back before finding a staircase and starting to climb.

Chapter 13
The Magecoach

The tavern part of the Bowl and Brew was every bit as smoke-filled as Marigold had promised. Carrying cloth bags filled with herbs, spices, and assorted more substantial items for his dinner, Garum opened the door to the tavern part and promptly closed it after billows of not-so-fragrant smoke rolled out like a dragon's belch and surrounded him. Holding his breath, Garum stepped back from the now-closed door and walked ten paces to the right to the section where the door to the inn-part of the Bowl and Brew was located.

Since it's both an inn and a tavern, I would have named it the Bed, Bowl, and Brew, thought Garum, *but I'm sure I'm a better cook than an innkeeper or tavern owner.*

Garum was pleased there was a door between the tavern and the counter where he picked up his room key. The innkeeper said he would be glad to deliver a box—holding hundreds of dried cubeb berries—which the merchant he'd purchased them from attested were from one of the larger islands far to the south and of the high-est quality. Cubeb, with a taste between allspice and black pepper, was a spice Garum seldom used, and for the sylviant it was more of a medication than a flavoring, anyway. He hoped it would give Chophorn a few hours of the temporary peaceful oblivion he desired.

With enough food for breakfast in the morning as well as for dinner in his room last night, Garum shouldered his pack, which had been delivered to his room earlier, and made his way down *two* flights of stairs to the inn's front counter, where he tried to pay for all three of their rooms.

"You only owe me for two rooms," said the innkeeper, an older human man with wispy white hair who kept reaching for handfuls of shelled walnuts from a bowl beside him on the counter.

"Why so?" asked Garum.

"That little healer friend of yours got the ceiling fans working in the tavern again," said the innkeeper. "Lately, too many potential customers wouldn't go in there for lunch because they had to stay alert to go back to work afterwards. Then that round-headed young fella with big eyes tightened the belts and oiled the bearings and now the fans are working perfectly. All I have to do to keep them turning is walk on a treadmill behind the bar, and that will likely keep me going another decade until I'll need to go to the College for a healing potion the size of a hogshead."

Garum was doing his best not to smile as he listened. *A free room is a free room.*

The innkeeper took a quick breath and continued. "The fans aren't even squeaking when they turn now, and they always used to. It would set my teeth on edge to hear them *squeak, squeak, squeak* like a mouse the size of a sow or a billy goat. Some days, when I spent too much time in the tavern passing out smokes and brews—ale's my drink of choice, none of this beer with bitter hops, though I wouldn't turn down a good hard cider—I was sure I saw mice that big staring up at me from under the tables. Your fix-it friend has eyes like that, did you know? Big oval mouse eyes, but the ones I saw under the tables had big ears to go with them, and shoes and white gloves and long tails."

"That sounds like a nightmare," said Garum.

"It was, it was," said the innkeeper, "but now my long nightmare is over, and all because of your friend." The man took Garum's payment for his room and Chophorn's and counted out a few silver shillings in change.

Garum handed the silver back to him. "Keep the change," he told the man.

"I will, if you tell your friend his money's not good here," said the innkeeper. "Not that it will cost me much for the offer, since your round-headed friend only ordered water in the tavern."

"He's quite a person," said Garum.

"Even if he is mighty quiet," said the innkeeper.

"Vip-vip speaks with his hands as much as his mouth," said Garum.

"What kind of a name is Vip-vip?" asked the innkeeper. "Not that it's any of my business to be prying, but in my line of work, asking questions is as natural as taking a pull from a mug."

"You're right," said Garum. "It's not any of your business, though thank you for not charging my friend for his room." Garum looked up the stairs and down the hall but didn't see Vip-vip *or* Chophorn. Then he heard the front door open and turned to see Vip-vip stick his head through the opening, the hood of his healers' robes down around his shoulders.

"GUP?" asked Vip-vip.

"Where's Chophorn?" asked Garum.

Vip-vip pointed out to the street.

Garum nodded, turned, and followed out.

Chophorn picked Garum and Vip-vip up again and began striding toward the gate that led to the ring road.

"Take us by the Herb and Spice Market first, please," said Garum. "I need to say goodbye to someone."

"I'll be glad to," said Chophorn. "Thank you for the cubeb. It helped last night."

Garum nodded. *I wonder what it must be like to forget the pain of bad decisions for a few hours, just by eating dried berries?* He smiled. *Who am I kidding? One full human-sized mug of ale or hard cider and I'm asleep.*

Chophorn's long legs ate up distance, even with him generously carrying Garum and Vip-vip's packs, so they were at the market in minutes. It was almost ten in the morning by the clock in the market's tower. Garum hadn't even noticed the clock tower yesterday. He'd been too excited to notice anything except the entryway in his eagerness to go inside. From what he could tell now, *this* clock didn't need help from Vip-vip to function. When Garum glanced down from the clock tower to the carved wooden arch marking the entrance to the market, he was surprised to see Marigold, in her lavender apron and purple pants, standing outside.

"I thought you might stop by," said Marigold.

Chophorn put Garum down.

"It seemed like the right thing to do," said Garum.

"So does this," said Marigold. She crossed the distance between them, wrapped her arms around Garum, and gave him a hug that was only a few ounces of pressure more than what one friend might give another. Garum returned the hug, staying on the safe side of that line. Marigold seemed too nice a person to give her any false hopes.

Their hug was still in progress when a gilded magecoach with an image of the Golden Dome outlined in brighter gold on a black door pulled up beside them. "Herb Keep's Herb and Spice Market, as requested," the driver, a woman with almost as many freckles as the twins but with skin as dark as Aubericht's, called down to the passengers inside.

"You've earned your bonus," Garum heard Sweetie's voice reply. He took two steps back from Marigold and rushed to the door of the magecoach to open it and help Sweetie step out. She looked stunning in a white dress and Garum simply stared at her for a few seconds, still amazed to see her so soon.

"I see you've met Marigold," Sweetie teased him. "Did he behave himself, Goldilocks and the Three Bares?"

"Yes, blast it, Dulce de Lecher," said Marigold. "I even invited him to spend the night at my place and he turned me down for a room at the Bowl and Brew instead."

Sweetie hugged Garum using a level of intimate pressure that not only crossed the line of mere friendship but leapt over it into *we're going to make love at the first available opportunity* territory. After embracing long enough for both of them to want to shift from *first available opportunity* to *as soon as possible,* Garum reduced the strength of his hug, allowed a few inches of space to intrude between him and Sweetie, and looked up at her.

"Did you two set all this up to *test* me?" he asked both women.

"No," said Sweetie.

"We didn't," said Marigold. "Really. But we've been friends for over a year."

"You told me you didn't leave the Green Doors until Sweetie showed up with her grandfather and they could help Veridan," said Garum. "I expect I should have known you were friends, but I didn't expect you to have pet names for each other."

"Those weren't pet names," said Sweetie.

"They were names we gave each other out of frustration due to lack of petting, and kissing, and fu…" began Marigold.

"…fun of other types," finished Sweetie. She grinned at Garum to get his attention then waggled her eyebrows.

"We didn't plan this," said Marigold.

"But when it turned out you were set on going to the herb and spice market on your own…" said Sweetie.

"She knew me well enough to guess what might happen," said Marigold. "So congratulations. Even though there wasn't really a test, you passed anyway."

Garum took Sweetie's hands in his and moved a few feet back so he could look at her eyes instead of her chest more easily. "You didn't trust me?" he said.

Sweetie shifted her gaze to Marigold. "No, my love," said Sweetie. "I didn't trust *her*."

"Because she knows me so well," said Marigold, who made a small curtsy and winked at both Garum *and* Sweetie.

Garum dropped Sweetie's hands. "So," he said, "you took a fast magecoach early this morning hoping to catch me kissing Marigold in front of the market?"

"Or in bed with her at her apartments, or in your room at the Bowl and Brew," said Sweetie. "I told the driver our next stop was Marigold's, if we didn't find you here."

"You think I would sleep with Veridan's older sister so soon after I found *you*?" asked Garum.

"Did I think you *would*?" said Sweetie. "No." She tilted her head in a way that made Garum want to kiss her. "Did I wonder if you *might*? I certainly did, and I was quite pleased to see Marigold hadn't talked you into doing more than hugging. She can be very convincing."

Marigold and Garum exchanged glances, doing their best to look guilty—of something, at least.

"Wait," said Sweetie. "Did you two actually spend the night together? Was the hug I saw more than it seemed?"

"Will you tell her, or should I?" Garum asked Marigold.

"You, probably," said Marigold. "She'd take it better from you."

"As you wish," said Garum. "Last night, while I was pining for you in my bed upstairs at the Bowl and Brew, Marigold climbed up the vines outside my window, slipped inside, and joined me for a night of carnal pleasure."

Marigold couldn't keep a smile from her face.

Sweetie smiled for a few seconds before her smile transformed into a laugh. "Nice try," said Sweetie. "You had me until you talked about Marigold climbing vines."

"That was wrong?" asked Garum.

"Yes," said Sweetie. "Marigold isn't fond of heights, and she hates getting dirty. That's why she sold her half-interest in the Green Doors to her brother. She wanted to buy into the merchants' cooperative and used her share in the inn and tavern as her stake. Veridan had to sell twenty-five percent of the Green Doors to the original Golden Company to come up with the full amount of her lump-sum payout."

"Wait," Garum said to Marigold. "You told me you left the Green Doors only after Aubericht and company bought in."

"Correct," said Marigold. "Because that's when my younger brother could afford to pay me. You made your own assumptions about why I left."

"So Aubericht wasn't chasing you around his rooms while you were cleaning them?" asked Garum.

"Upstairs?" said Marigold. "Cleaning his rooms? That's not me." She shook her head. "No, Aubericht was chasing me around the bar on a slow night when my brother talked me into serving mugs of ale—before Sweetie and her grandfather arrived."

Garum shook his head and rubbed his chin. "If you've bought a share in the merchants' cooperative at the market..." he began.

"Several shares, now," said Marigold. "I'm on the cooperative's executive committee."

"If that's the case," said Garum, trying again, "why are you working as an *Ask Me Anything* guide at the front entrance?"

"Because it's the best way for me to stay in touch with the needs of our customers and figure out ways we can do better," said Marigold. "It's also because I hate climbing stairs. I have an office behind the tea shop on the ground floor where we talked yesterday."

"I'm confused," said Garum.

"Then my mission here is done," said Marigold. "You have an accurate understanding of the situation."

"But..." said Garum.

Marigold gave him a quick hug that stayed firmly on the friendship side of the line. "Have fun in East Keep Town," she told Sweetie. "Be careful," Marigold added. "We've been hearing reports about trouble on the arc of ring road you'll be traveling. Stay alert."

"We will," said Sweetie, who waved goodbye to Marigold and tugged at Garum.

"I don't want to ride in that thing," Garum protested.

"Get in," Sweetie told Garum as she opened the near door of the magecoach and pushed him toward the steps to climb into it. "We have to get moving."

"But I hate magecoaches," said Garum.

"Would you do it for me if I asked nicely?" asked Sweetie.

"Yes, but I'd probably resent you for making me," said Garum.

"What if we have the interior of the coach to ourselves?" asked Sweetie. "I could make it worth your while."

Garum took a deep break, looked at Sweetie, looked at the magecoach, and looked back at Sweetie. "It doesn't have horses," he told her.

"Is that all you're worried about?" said Sweetie. "I can go one better than horses." She pulled her want from her sleeve, concentrated, waved it back and forth, and suddenly a matched team of snow-white unicorns were harnessed to the magecoach.

"How did you..." Garum began, trying to determine whether or not Sweetie had been in the white magecoach he'd seen on the ring road yesterday morning, pulled by similar unicorns.

"It's an illusion, silly," she said, without giving Garum time to react. She pushed him into the interior of the magecoach with a rod of solid illusion.

Garum flopped onto the floor of the coach then clambered up on the forward-facing seat. "What about Chophorn and Vip-vip," he asked Sweetie.

"I'll carry the vixer," said Chophorn. "I think I'm starting to understand some of his speech, and I wouldn't fit inside that coach, anyway. I stand guard on the back of one when I travel with the Black Company. I can walk almost as fast as your magecoach when I really stretch my legs."

"See you in East Keep Town," said Sweetie. "I plan to book us rooms at The Hands of the King."

"Excellent choice," said Chophorn. Soon the sylviant and vixer were far behind them as their magecoach reached the ring road and their driver poured on more speed.

Garum heard the bell-like tones of the unicorns' hooves hitting the cobbles but could no longer see them from inside the coach. He held Sweetie's hands like they were a rope, and he was drowning.

"Would you like me to try to distract you?" asked Sweetie.

"You can try, but I'm not sure it will work," Garum replied.

"Trying is fun," said Sweetie.

She kissed him and a few minutes later Garum was oblivious to everything in his surroundings except Sweetie's soft lips on his.

Traveling by magecoach isn't so bad, thought Garum half an hour later. *In fact, I could even learn to like it.*

Chapter 14

The Highwaymen

It must have rained overnight, for the surface of the ring road shimmered in the morning sun as Garum and Sweetie's magecoach traveled the miles between Herb Keep and East Keep, the home of the College of Healers.

Garum, now completely relaxed, held Sweetie's hand as he looked out the coach's windows at the scenery. *The road is not quite a ribbon of moonlight,* he thought, *but it is romantic to be alone with Sweetie, hurtling along at three times the speed of an oxcart.* He chuckled at where his mind had taken him. *Not much moonlight during the day, fool,* he told himself.

There were low hills, moors, really, visible out the left window away from the cliffs and the Deeps. They were covered in purple heather, which for some reason made Garum think of Marigold's lavender apron and purple pants, despite having just made love to Sweetie a few minutes ago. *What's going on in my brain?* he asked himself. *Why am I thinking of another woman when I have such a wonderful one right beside me?*

"A shilling for your thoughts," said Sweetie.

"They're not worth more than a copper ha'penny," Garum replied.

"They are to me," said Sweetie with a smile. "Were you thinking about her, or about me?"

"Uh, both," said Garum. "The purple flowers on the moors reminded me of Marigold's pants and my mind just went there."

"I bet you'd like to get into them," said Sweetie.

"Into what?" said Garum. "The flowers on the moors?"

"Marigold's purple pants, of course."

"I'm not responsible for where *that* part of my brain wants to take me," said Garum, looking down at his braies. "Only for my actions."

"You can't get into my pants today," Sweetie told him with a smile.

"And why is that?" asked Garum, thinking that was closing the barn door after an entire stable full of horses had already left.

"Because I'm not wearing any, as you well know," Sweetie announced. She raised her long skirts, revealing her shapely legs before smoothing the fabric back down. "Not to mention the fact that, clothing details aside, you just did."

"Was that you?" teased Garum.

"No," said a voice that sounded like Marigold's.

Garum blinked, because now it was Marigold in the magecoach with him, not Sweetie.

"Oh Marigold, Marigold, how I've wanted you!" said Garum.

"Blast," said Sweetie, reverting to her usual appearance. "I can't even have fun with illusions with you anymore."

"I was interested in your sweet self before you got your wand," said Garum. "Anything more would be gilding the lily, and that's far from necessary. Goodness knows, the decorators at the Golden Dome have shown me the folly of gilding everything in sight."

"Would you like me to gild my eyelids?" asked Sweetie. "Or my nipples?"

"No, thank you," said Garum. "Your eyelids and nipples are perfect just the way they are."

"You say the nicest things," said Sweetie.

"You inspire me," said Garum.

"Let's stop now," said Sweetie. "I expect we could keep exchanging endearments for as long as Xarra and Yarra could keep an argument going, but I'm going to need a few hours before I'll be ready for more of *your* wand."

Garum reached over and squeezed Sweetie's arm. "If you can't tell, I'm really enjoying being with you."

"I'm enjoying being with you as well," said Sweetie. "Especially when we aren't at the lowest level of the Deeps, afraid for our lives."

"I liked being with you even then," said Garum.

"You certainly gave *me* more reasons to want to get out with all your talk about featherbeds."

"It's probably time to change the subject," said Garum. "I think my wand will need a few hours before it can wave again, too, so talking about featherbeds isn't productive." He stretched and when his arm came back down it slid around Sweetie's waist instead of on her shoulders, because she was enough taller than he was for the angles not to work. "Were you able to pick up my new tunics and braies from the tailor's?" he asked.

"Yes," said Sweetie. "And three new dresses for me—this is one of them." She smoothed the fabric down along her legs again. "I also got more practical clothing of the sort I'd want to wear if we decide to return to the Deeps or if the original Golden Company is restored and I have to go back to serving ale and cleaning guests' rooms."

"I don't think you'll ever need to go back to *that,*" said Garum, thinking of the heartstone in his belt pouch.

"I might if Céptianne comes back and reclaims her wand of illusions," said Sweetie. "A woman has to be able to support herself, somehow."

"Did you find any nice fabrics to be turned into illusionists' robes for *you?*" asked Garum. "I always thought that Céptianne's were too gaudy You deserve something more tasteful and less like a quilt made by a collection of random children who'd never seen a bright color they didn't like."

"I like bright colors," said Sweetie. "I even like lots of them, in combination."

"Like a rainbow," said Garum.

"Exactly," said Sweetie. "But it's much easier for me to project patterns of illusions on a neutral background and it could be handy to change the apparent colors of my robes with just a tiny bit of my magic."

"That makes sense," said Garum. "Is your choice of white for *this* dress based on the same thinking?"

"It is," said Sweetie. She slid her hand into the sleeve where she kept her wand and changed the color of her dress to the same shade of purple as Marigold's pants.

"Don't be mean," said Garum.

"Maybe I'm just trying to restore your interest and mine a bit faster."

Garum shook his head, then smiled. "Are there limits to how you can change your own appearance using your illusions?" he asked. "For example, when you changed to look like Marigold earlier, you stayed the same size. You didn't look like a halfling."

"If I'm disguising my appearance, instead of projecting an illusion from whole cloth, I am limited by the dimensions of my own form," said Sweetie. "But I can create an illusion—even a solid illusion—of someone Marigold's size, or your size, if I wanted. I think I could make myself disappear at the same time, so it would look like Marigold replaced me."

"Could you do the same with someone bigger, like Hrefna?" asked Garum.

"Probably," said Sweetie. "I don't think I want to try that here in the coach, though. To make it believable, I'd have to give the projection weight, and the shift in how the magecoach's load was distributed might confuse our driver."

"That's sensible," said Garum. "You can experiment in our room tonight."

"If we don't end up making other plans," said Sweetie.

"Which would also be nice," said Garum. An important thought came to him, and he rubbed his chin. "Did you bring *it* with you?" he asked.

"The box?" said Sweetie. "Of course I brought it. It's under our seat."

"Good," said Garum. "It needs to stay close to at least one of us."

"Promise me you won't go off on your own again," said Sweetie. "I didn't sleep well while you were in Herb Keep Town."

"Neither did I," said Garum, "but that's a promise I can't really make. I don't know what might happen in the future and there might be a very good reason why we need to separate—temporarily."

"You're right, but I won't like it," said Sweetie.

"Do you have another attractive friend ahead of us in East Keep to tempt me?" asked Garum.

"No," said Sweetie. "And I told you Marigold and I didn't *plan* what happened." Sweetie kissed Garum's cheek. "Not to forget you *did* prove you care about me and didn't succumb to Marigold's charms."

"You've said that. Several times," said Garum. "It still feels like a lack of trust."

"I'm sorry," said Sweetie. "I didn't mean it to seem that I didn't trust you."

"Thank you," said Garum. Now it was his turn for his lips to kiss Sweetie's cheek.

Before he could lean up and do so, they heard a loud *thump* from the front of the magecoach, followed by a *thud*. After a few moments, the sound of blades being drawn from scabbards came from outside. A beat later, a deep and ominous voice penetrated into the coach's interior.

"Be it known that you have the privilege of being robbed by Capt'n Hugh the Highwayman. Prepare to be boarded."

Sweetie shot up and started toward the door just as Garum got to his own feet and tried to do the same. The two of them collided and fell to the floor of the coach, face to face, with Sweetie sprawled on top of Garum. They heard a heavy boot crash against the coach's door, and it flew in, its lock shattered. Garum was in no position to stop the thin edge of the door from slamming into the top of Sweetie's head.

Sweetie moaned and became a dead weight pressing down on Garum. He hoped she was just unconscious. Drops of blood from her bleeding scalp landed on Garum's neck and face. He heard something cylindrical—*Sweetie's wand?*—roll under the backward-facing seat opposite them. Garum was on his back, his limbs tangled up with Sweetie's. His hands were trapped, and he couldn't reach his dagger-sword or sling, not that there was any space to use a missile weapon. It took all his willpower and battlefield experience not to panic.

"What have we here?" said the deep voice of the man Garum assumed was Capt'n Hugh—a seaman, not a soldier, if his *prepare to be boarded* command wasn't misdirection.

Garum's nose was wedged in Sweetie's cleavage, which would have been pleasurable, under other circumstances. He couldn't see the man who went with the deep voice but was ready to take action as soon as that was feasible.

"Aren't you a lovely lass," said Capt'n Hugh, "Even with blood in your pretty hair."

Garum pulled air into his lungs, a difficult feat with Sweetie pressing down on his ribs. He sensed Capt'n Hugh's hands at Sweetie's shoulders.

"Let's see if you're as pretty from the front as you are from the back," said the Capt'n as he rolled Sweetie over.

Prepared to act, Garum pulled his leather bag of lead and stone sling ammunition from his belt in one quick move. He tilted his own head back to get a sense of where Capt'n Hugh's head must be and swung the weighty leather bag with as much force as he could manage from his position on the floor. It didn't catch the highwayman on his forehead, but it did strike his cheek just under the man's right eye. Garum heard a crack and Sweetie's right arm and that side of her torso fell back on him.

Capt'n Hugh shouted louder than a Stinking Screamer from the Deeps and let out a stream of imprecations that Garum would have gladly written down for future reference if he hadn't been too busy trying to stay alive. Hugh had dark hair past his shoulders, wore a broad black hat with a raven's feather in the band, and sported a black felt coat over a frilly, once-white shirt. A cutlass was in his right hand. Capt'n Hugh was standing in the door of the magecoach now, filling that space with his bulk. He kicked out at Garum, using his working left eye for somewhat less than fully successful target identification. The first two kicks from the heavy boots the Capt'n wore missed Garum, though one did connect with Sweetie, making it even more difficult for Garum to stay in a soldier's calm as he fought back.

Garum had gotten to his knees and faced Capt'n Hugh as the third kick came forward. He bit into his leather bag and held it between his teeth while he caught his attacker's swinging boot in both hands and twisted. The highwayman landed on his back with the upper half of his body lying outside the coach door. Garum opened his mouth, caught his leather bag as it fell, lifted it over his head with both hands, and brought it down as hard as he could on the juncture where the legs of the Capt'n's navy blue canvas pants came together.

The highwayman just grunted this time. He didn't shout or scream, but he pulled his knees up to his chest and the momentum of that motion sent his entire body out of the coach's interior and after a backwards somersault, Garum assumed he was—at the very least—moaning on the smooth surface of the ring road. Working his way to the side of the magecoach's splintered door, he took a quick glimpse around outside.

He was right about Capt'n Hugh's location, but there were two more highwaymen, another man and an orc woman, holding drawn swords on either side of their leader, trying to determine whether they should be tending to Capt'n Hugh's injuries or immediately charging into the magecoach. Off to the right, he saw the coach driver face down on the road. He couldn't risk looking at her long enough to tell if she was breathing. Sweetie *was* breathing, he confirmed, though blood was pooling around her head. *Scalp wounds are like that,* he told himself, hoping she wasn't seriously hurt.

They're going to run inside, Garum decided after taking two seconds to think. *There's not much they can do for Capt'n Hugh and the orc woman, at least, looks like she has some sense of initiative. Thank goodness the door's too narrow for them both to enter at once.*

Garum moved to the far side of the magecoach and crawled up on the front-facing seat with his back against the coach wall. *Looks like there might be just enough room to use my sling after all,* he thought. Garum put four lead bullets, his most effective and lethal missiles, in his left hand and took his sling from his belt. Fitting one bullet in his sling, he slowly rotated his weapon and waited. As expected, the man was the first one through the door. *That orc woman is smart,* Garum noted. *I need to change tactics.*

When the man's sword and body entered the coach, Garum aimed a crippling shot at the man's front shin, not a lethal shot at his head. His bullet flew true, and Garum heard the man's shinbone crack like a stroke of lightning in the narrow confines of the coach. The man fell forward on top of his sword, clutching his lower leg.

Garum realized his miscalculation in seconds. The man, with his sword still reflexively gripped in his hand, was less than a foot away from Sweetie. A second lead bullet smashed the man's temple in, and he lay quiet.

"If you come out quietly, I won't kill you," came a voice that Garum determined must belong to the orc woman.

"If you *do* kill me, the Black Company, especially Blōgot, will use you for target practice," shouted Garum.

"Who's Blōgot?" asked the orc woman.

"You must be new to the Keep Lands," said Garum.

"We thought we'd try our hand south of the Inland Seas where the pickings are richer," said the orc woman. "I don't know any Blōgot, and I've never heard of any Black Company. Let me get a torch and a bundle of straw to toss in your coach, and I'll see how you get on without breathing."

If I can just keep her talking, I can be sure of her location, thought Garum. *Just a few words more.* He put another bullet in his sling and started slowly twirling it. "If he's Capt'n Hugh, are you his first mate?" asked Garum.

"I'm the admiral," said the orc woman. "At least that's what I tell Hugh when he tries to order me around."

The orc woman is standing to my right, outside the magecoach door. It's hanging loose, half off its hinges, or I'd never be able to make this shot. Garum jumped across the gap to the backward facing seat and sent his bullet racing against the edge of the open door, right where the wide lock mechanism gave him a better target for a ricochet shot. The lead bullet hit the place where the lock, now hanging off the swinging door, would have engaged. It bounced outside at an angle, and Garum heard a cry of pain.

He rushed to the open door with another bullet already in his sling and didn't even bother releasing it. He hit the orc woman over the head with the stone in his sling and she slumped down to join Capt'n Hugh. Pulling out another bullet, a stone one this time, and used the same technique to ensure Capt'n Hugh would join his *admiral* in unconsciousness.

Now I can see to Sweetie! thought Garum after confirming there had been only three attackers. Her eyes were closed, but her breathing was steady. Ripping strips of fabric from the hem of her dress, he bound her head wound and mopped up the blood on the floor, pulling one of the pillows off the backward facing seat to put under her head. He felt for her pulse, too. It was steady.

Time to check on the driver, Garum realized. He stepped down from the magecoach and found the driver starting to get up on her own. "How are you feeling?" he asked.

"Like the wind was knocked out of me, and I might have a few broken ribs," the driver replied.

Garum helped her stand and adjusted a wide leather belt she wore to help bind her ribs. He saw that the highwaymen had rolled a log under the front wheels of the magecoach and must have followed that up by shoving the driver off her seat on top of the magecoach with a tree branch. Both the log and the branch were on the ground.

"Thank you," said the driver. "I thought I was a dead woman."

"I'm glad you're not," said Garum. "Can you still drive?" he asked. "Sweetie is hurt, and we need to get her—and you—to healers as fast as possible."

"I don't think I have a choice," said the driver. "Help me climb up."

Garum wished he had Sir Donal's vambraces to give him strength, but somehow, between the two of them, the driver resumed her spot atop the front of the magecoach.

"Get in," she told Garum. "I won't hold the horses."

"I just wish there *were* horses," said Garum, but not loud enough for the driver to hear. He stood on a seat and tapped the roof with the hilt of his sword-dagger.

The driver got his message, and they were off.

Chapter 15

Lark of the Morning

"Where can I find a healer?" Garum heard the driver say after he felt the magecoach slow, then stop.

"Throw a stone or toss a cat and you'll likely hit one," said a gruff, but not unfriendly man's voice that Garum assumed belonged to a gate guard. "This is East Keep Town, and healers are everywhere."

"Then point me at a place where I can get a couple of healing potions," said the driver. "We were just attacked by highwaymen on the ring road from Herb Keep. I have broken ribs, and a woman in the coach is badly injured."

"Keep going on the high street and stop at any shop showing a white sign with a red stripe down its center," said the guard. "My cousin runs the third one on the left, and I'll vouch for his skills and potions."

"Thank you," said the driver. She didn't waste time getting the magecoach moving again.

Garum was glad he hadn't needed to speak. He'd been shaky following the struggle—the usual letdown after fighting for his life—and hadn't been good for much except sitting next to Sweetie on the floor and holding her hand.

A few dozen heartbeats later, the magecoach stopped, and Garum heard the driver dismount. She stuck her head in through the partly open door, which was still hanging loosely on one hinge. Garum saw her wince as she moved.

"I'm going into the shop to get help," said the driver. "I'll be back as fast as I can."

Garum couldn't do more than nod. He heard the driver's footsteps as she walked away, then knuckles knocking on what sounded like a wooden door. The knocking repeated once more, then again. A window shutter opened somewhere close by and Garum heard an older woman's voice.

"He won't answer," said the older woman. "I've never seen his face before noon, if then. Too fond of certain of his own concoctions, he is, and always out too late carousing with his cousin in the gate guards."

"His cousin sent me here, more's the pity," said the driver. "I need a healer immediately. So does an injured passenger in my coach. Where can I get healing potions—quickly?"

Garum nodded his agreement, not that his nod could be seen outside the magecoach. Before the woman could answer the driver, footsteps approached. Someone on the high street was walking toward the coach.

"Is there anything I can do to help?" Garum heard someone say. She was young, female, and human, from what Garum could tell based on her voice.

"Thank goodness," said the driver. "You're a healer. Can you help my passenger? She's hurt."

"I'm just a novice healer," said the young woman. "But in my last year. I did earn top marks for my healing potions and have several with me, however. Is your passenger still in the coach?"

"Yes," said the driver. "The door's open—it can't close, for that matter. Please see to her, and then to me. I think I broke a few ribs falling off the coach when we were attacked."

"Attacked?" said the older woman from the window.

Garum was pleased the novice healer didn't bother to ask about the attack and focused on the needs of her prospective patient, Sweetie. He saw a young woman in white healer's robes with three thin red vertical stripes down their center instead of one broad stripe. *That signifies someone in their last year of training,* he remembered. *Several of the healers he'd met in various military units had the same three stripes and were getting extra experience before returning to the college to finish their programs.*

The novice healer nodded to Garum and sat beside him and Sweetie on the floor of the coach, seemingly oblivious to the drops of blood Garum hadn't managed to wipe up she was getting on her robes. She watched Sweetie's chest rise and fall, held her wrist to check her pulse, and bent even further to put her ear over

Sweetie's left breast and listen to her heart. Then the healer lifted Sweetie's eyelids to check the size of her pupils.

Garum looked at the young healer, waiting for her to speak.

"She'll be fine," said the healer. "At least she will be after she drinks one of my potions and gets some rest."

"Wonderful," said Garum. He somehow felt even more tired yet exhilarated at her news. "How can I help?"

"Sit her up," said the healer. "I'm Lark, by the way."

"Garum," said Garum. "Shouldn't I call you Arrex?"

"Not until I've formally graduated," Lark replied. "Support her back, please. We need to get her into a position where she can swallow a healing potion and most of it will go down."

"Gladly," said Garum. He moved to sit cross-legged behind Sweetie and lifted her upper torso. "Do you need me to open her jaw?" he asked.

"I can do that," said Lark in a calm, reassuring tone. "Just hold her up. You're doing great."

"How is the driver?" asked Garum.

"Feeling better soon, I expect," said Lark. "I gave her a potion vial before I came in. She could swallow it on her own. Her ribs should heal in a few hours, and I don't think she had any major internal injuries."

"Good," said Garum.

Lark pulled Sweetie's jaw down, tilted her head back, and poured the contents of a blue ceramic vial marked with three narrow red stripes around it into Sweetie's mouth. Sweetie swallowed reflexively, then shuddered and sighed.

"That should do it," said Lark. "Now she just needs rest." The healer examined Sweetie's head wound, removed Garum's makeshift bandages, and replaced them with clean ones from a pouch on her belt. "You did a nice job," Lark told him. "Too bad you're too old to enroll in the college."

"I learned as a military cook," said Garum. "I've bandaged a lot of soldiers over the years. There were only so many healing potions to go around."

"I'll probably do a stint with one of the armies north and east of here," said Lark. "There's no better way to get experience than to serve with an army—unless it's going down into the Deeps."

"I just came back from the lowest level of the Deeps at North Keep," said Garum.

"I don't know about doing that myself," said Lark. "Being that far underground isn't for me and I've heard there are *so many* stairs to climb down and up."

"You're right about the stairs," said Garum. "My calves still ache."

Lark reached for a green vial on her belt and handed it to Garum. "Drink this," she said. "It will help your calves and your shock."

Garum drank and promptly felt better, physically, than he had in months—discounting times spent in bed with Sweetie. "Thank you," he said.

"Glad to help," said Lark. "It's my own formula, with some of the same components as healing potion, but it's much faster and easier to brew up."

It was easy to give Lark a smile. "I wish it had been available when I was bandaging soldiers."

"Maybe someday it will be," Lark replied. "Just don't mention it if anyone asks," she said. "I'm only supposed to administer healing potions in emergencies, which your friend and the driver certainly were. I'm not authorized to hand out anything else except willow bark tea without a more senior healer's approval."

"What other potion?" said Garum, referring to his planned answer to any inquiries.

Lark smiled then. "You said you went into the Deeps at North Keep?" she said. "One of my friends from the college, a year ahead of me just went to North Keep Town a week ago. His name is Jenner. Perhaps you met him?"

"I don't recognize the name. What does he look like?"

A fairly generic description from Lark followed. Young, brown hair, green eyes. One robed healer looked much like another.

"Sorry," said Garum.

"He wanted to find Barton DeCláre, part of the Golden Company, and learn from him," said Lark.

"Then I *do* know your friend," said Garum, "but not as Jenner. He told us to call him Arrex, the standard name for new healers. From what I've seen he's a fine, resourceful young man—now part of the *new* Golden Company. I expect him to be arriving in East Keep Town by magecoach this afternoon."

"How delightful!" said Lark. "The *new* Golden Company? It sounds like he'll have a lot of tales to tell."

"Indeed he will," said Garum. "We plan to stay at an inn called The Hands of the King. Do you know it?"

"Know it?" said Lark. "Everyone in East Keep Town knows it—it's the best place here. All the senior mages from North Keep Town and top military people from South Keep Town stay there, along with nobles and wealthy merchants. You must have a lot of gold."

"I have enough for my needs," said Garum. "If you can get free, you're welcome to stop by the common room at the inn and see your friend. I'll tell him you helped us."

"Wonderful!" said Lark, her face lighting up like a wizard globe. Then the light went suddenly out. "But I didn't ask about the most important thing you told me," she said. "My instructors always tell us to ask our patients about the details of their lives. You said you were *attacked?* On the *ring road?* There's never been trouble on the ring road. "

"There was this morning," said Garum. "Our magecoach was stopped by highwaymen, former sailors from the Inland Seas. Three of them, two men and an orc woman."

"And the three of *you* fought them off alone?" said Lark. Garum thought her eyes looked almost as big as Vip-vip's.

"Just me," said Garum, shrugging his shoulders to minimize his accomplishment. "The driver fell off her seat and was face down on the road when they attacked. My friend and I were on the floor. She was hit in the head when the leader of the highwaymen kicked the coach door in."

Lark looked over at the door dangling from one hinge.

Garum could tell she was about to ask him why he and Sweetie had been on the floor, but she put a hand to her mouth and wisely decided not to, hiding her mouth in the process.

"Was anyone else hurt?" Lark asked.

"Two of the highwaymen were incapacitated," said Garum. "I had to kill the third. He still held his sword after I broke his shinbone and was too close to Sweetie."

"Goodness!" said Lark. "I'd always taken halflings to be peaceful folk, and here you've done all that just this morning."

"Most halflings *are* peaceful," said Garum. "Not many of us have spent more than a decade in various armies. I served as a slinger as well as a cook." He shook his head. "I'm peaceful myself, when someone or something isn't trying to kill me."

"That's nice to know," said Lark. "I suppose I should tell the guards about what happened and let the college know so they can send a red-striped magecoach out to pick up the highwaymen you injured—and the one you killed."

"If they're still there," said Garum. "If they're smart, they'd be running back to the Inland Seas as soon as they were able."

"You're probably right," said Lark. "But I should notify the guard and college anyway. It's unsanitary to leave dead bodies lying around on the road. I had to take an entire semester's course on public health last year and learned to tell time of death from the presence of flies and maggots on corpses and everything."

"Sounds fascinating," said Garum, who'd seen far too much death on battlefields.

Just then, he heard someone shouting his name. It was Chophorn. A moment later, the sylviant was leaning down to peer inside the coach. Vip-vip was by the steps into the coach, looking up.

"There you are!" said Chophorn. "We wondered if you were responsible for the three injured sailors we found on the ring road."

"Three *injured?*" asked Garum. "I thought I killed one of them with a lead bullet to his head."

"The man's head must have been harder than you thought," said Chophorn. "Vip-vip carried one of them, and I carried the other two here into East Keep Town. We put them down outside this shop where the gate guard sent us. Do you know where we can find a healer? No one seems to be opening the door to the shop."

"OWTCH-Y!" said Vip-vip.

"I'm a healer," said Lark. "But this little round-headed dwarf or halfling or something is wearing senior healer's robes. Couldn't he help?"

"It's a long story," said Garum. "But no."

"I'll stay and heal the highwaymen," said Lark.

"Good," said the coach driver, who'd poked her own head into the coach after Chophorn stepped back to let Lark exit. "I'm feeling a lot better. Do you still want to go to The Hands of the King?"

"Yes, please," said Garum.

"Yes, please," echoed Sweetie, whose eyes fluttered open as Garum spoke.

"We'll follow you there," said Chophorn.

"GUP!" said Vip-vip.

"I'll see you in the common room at the Hands tonight," said Lark. "It was nice to meet you, even if under these less than pleasant circumstances."

"Nice to meet you, too," said Garum. "And I'm glad I didn't kill anyone."

"So far today, at least," said Sweetie. "But *I* might want to. Where's my wand?"

Chapter 16
The Hands of the King

The rest of Garum's compatriots arrived at The Hands of the King by mid-afternoon. The establishment's exterior was made from a light-blue brick Garum had never seen before, with all the window molding painted a darker blue that made a quite attractive contrast. It was soothing, which was exactly what Garum needed after his far-too-exciting morning. *That's what I get for letting Sweetie talk me into riding in a magecoach,* he thought.

The interior—at least the public rooms—matched the exterior, with more light blue on the walls and dark blue woodwork. Even the lighting inside was soft and soothing. Robins-egg blue paper lanterns around wizard globes reduced the room's glare and encouraged rest and relaxation, supported by their subtle serenity.

He had left word with the woman registering guests to let the other members of their extended party know Sweetie was resting. Garum was confident Chophorn would tell the new arrivals every detail he knew about the attack, even if his long-winded style of speaking would make the recounting last for more than an hour.

They'd all agreed to meet in the common room before going to dinner at seven. When Sweetie was napping, he'd gone back to the front desk person he'd spoken to earlier and learned Görthang had reserved one of the smaller private dining rooms off the common room for their dinner.

"It's decorated in black and gold," said the woman. "You'll like it."

Garum did like the symbolism of the room's decor, including the colors of both companies, but he decided it made more sense to go back to his room now and nap next to Sweetie. She was curled up on top of the bed's quilt, clutching her wand and moving her arms and legs in her sleep like she was trapped in a bad dream. Garum spooned against her back and held her until her restless motions stopped, her hands opened, and her wand fell on the quilt. Soon, Garum was also sleeping as deeply as he would have if he'd swallowed the same potion Arrex had given Sir Donal in the Deeps.

A few hours later, Sweetie rolled over to face Garum and snuggled into his neck. Garum woke slowly and took a deep breath, inhaling Sweetie's warm scent that reminded Garum of roses. *Must be the soap she used to wash her hair back at the Rose and Crown,* his half-awake brain decided. Another part of his brain said the Golden Dome might have rose-scented soap as well, but he couldn't remember. His soap had smelled like mint.

"What time is dinner?" asked Sweetie.

"Seven," said Garum. "We'll meet in the common room and then move to a private meeting room."

"Good," said Sweetie. "By the way, thank you for saving my life."

"You're welcome," said Garum. "I was kind of saving my own life, too."

"That doesn't negate my appreciation," said Sweetie. "In fact, I'm as glad you saved yourself as I am you saved me."

"I just reacted," said Garum. "When I'm in a situation where people want to kill me, my training takes over."

"I thought slingers killed from a distance," said Sweetie.

"Most of the time, we do," said Garum. "But one of my unit commanders—who was quite fond of my cooking, by the way—told me that sometimes enemies get close enough to stick a sword or a knife in you, and it's best to know how to prevent that from happening."

"What *did* happen after our coach was stopped?" asked Sweetie. "I remember we tripped over each other and fell, then the door to the magecoach hit my head, and the next thing I know I'm starting to wake up, feeling a lot better than I had any right to feel."

"Lark gave you a healing potion," said Garum.

"Who's Lark?" asked Sweetie.

"A novice healer in her last year at the college," said Garum. "I think she's friends with Arrex, or wants to be, at least. I told her to meet us in the common room and should probably invite her to join us for dinner."

"If she helped save my life, I definitely want to meet her and thank her."

"I think you would have lived through your concussion," said Garum. "But you wouldn't have survived being skewered by Capt'n Hugh's cutlass."

"I remember someone shouting, and the name *Capt'n Hugh*," said Sweetie. "Was he the leader of the highwaymen?"

"Seems like it," said Garum. "The town guards are holding them for trial. Seems they may have robbed several merchants bringing wagons full of spices to the market in Herb Keep Town earlier in the week."

"I have a hazy memory of Marigold telling us to be careful on the road," said Sweetie.

"You must be starting to recover," said Garum. "Let's both get a nice cold shower to clear our heads and get dressed for dinner."

"A cold shower?" Sweetie protested. "You can have one of *those* by yourself. I want a nice warm bath."

"Would someone to wash your back in that bath be appreciated?"

"I don't know," said Sweetie. "I might be able to get that sort of service at the Golden Dome, but I'm not sure about here."

"Unless we told the staff it was for therapeutic purposes," said Garum.

"I think you're all the therapy I need right now," said Sweetie. "Let's get wet."

* * * * *

When Garum and Sweetie entered the common room, they were surprised to be greeted by applause and huzzahs from their friends *and* from other guests at The Hands of the King. Word of Garum's actions had spread, and a collection of locals—merchants, students at the college of healers, and town officials—had also gathered to await their arrival. Many wanted to see the valiant halfling warrior who had fought off an orc and two humans, or ten orcs and fifteen humans and a giant, or an entire company of highwaymen led by a former ship's captain who had once been a nobleman in the

Langstrand near the Sleeve. There seemed to be no limit to what the gossips of East Keep Town could inflate Garum's accomplishments to include.

Hrefna, Görthang, Blōgot, and Gêrdun, the Black Company's ogre healer, now disguised as a wealthy ogre mine owner from Iron Keep, formed a protective wall around Garum and Sweetie with their bodies. Sweetie used her illusions to create duplicates of herself and Garum and sent them out of the common room and toward the stables out back. Most of the crowd followed the decoys, giving Garum and his friends a chance to find their private dining room.

Garum saw Lark talking to Arrex and moved to stand beside her as they shuffled out of the common room. "You're welcome to join us for dinner," Garum told the novice healer.

"Thanks," said Lark. "Arrex already invited me. I hope there's space for one more at the table."

"If not, we'll make room," said Sweetie. "I understand you saved me from a giant-sized headache and several weeks of recuperation."

"My professors at the college say my healing potions are outstanding," said Lark. "I guess I have a gift for making them."

"I'd have to agree," said Sweetie. "My head wound has disappeared, and you can't even see a bruise where the highwayman kicked me."

"I'm so glad," said Lark. "How about the potion's taste?" she asked. "I'm always trying to improve my work."

"I could give you a better answer if I was conscious when I drank it," said Sweetie. "Maybe next time."

"I hoped there's *not* a next time," said Garum. "And that's the last time anyone is getting *me* in a magecoach."

"We'll see," said Sweetie.

A large finger tapped Sweetie on the shoulder. "I hope you're feeling better," said Gêrdun. "What do you think of the disguise Blōgot made for me?" He pointed to a dark wig that resembled an abandoned bird's nest and a velvet hat with a silver broach pinned to its turned-up brim. "Don't I look prosperous?"

"You do," said Sweetie. "And it's probably easier to make you look like a wealthy ogre than to use my illusions to make you look like an orc."

Blōgot smiled at Sweetie.

"I like it better this way, too," said Gêrdun.

"So does Görthang," said Blōgot.

"What now?" said Görthang, hearing his name.

"Nothing you need to worry about," said Blōgot.

Görthang nodded and continued trying to get more details about Garum's fight with the highwaymen out of Chophorn.

Garum walked faster, tugging Sweetie's hand to get them both into the private dining room before the crowd realized they were chasing illusions. Only when everyone was inside and the door had closed did Garum release a sigh. "Have a seat, everyone," he said. Garum waved to Lark, still next to Arrex. "This is Lark, a healer in her last year at the college. She's good friends with Arrex and gave Sweetie a healing potion in time to spare her a lengthy recovery from a blow to the head," said Garum. "Lark, these are the members of the Black Company, and *these* are the new Golden Company."

"Hi Lark!" came a chorus of voices.

"I'm hoping she can advise us on the best people at the college to talk to about *you know what.*"

"No, what?" said Púki.

Xarra and Yarra squelched him and received a round of applause. Lark joined in, but Garum could see she was just doing so to be polite.

Members of both companies, plus Lark, found seats around a round table, or rather a ring-shaped one with the center missing and a few degrees of arc open for convenient access by servers. Garum liked the configuration of seats. It was easier to see everyone and didn't suggest any high and low table stratification.

Unlike the formality of the fancy dining establishments connected to the Golden Dome, the Hands of the King's kitchen served their meals family style, with bowls and platters delivered every ninety or one hundred-and-twenty degrees. Prestyn conveniently sat on one side of the gap so his cloak could pass dishes across.

Garum was surprised when a pair of servers placed a roasted turkey nearly as big as he was in front of him. It made more sense when a third server handed him a broad-bladed kitchen knife, a sharpening steel, and a long-handled fork. "Looks like I'm carving," said Garum. "Who wants white, and who wants dark?"

Sweetie, seated beside Garum, started to giggle when it seemed like the majority of the members of the new Golden Company asked for white meat while most of the Black Company opted for dark meat. Lark requested some of both. He piled meat on the platter, took a slice of white for himself, and sent it around the table. "I should have known you'd prefer breast meat," said Sweetie.

"I'm also fond of legs and thighs," Garum answered, glad Sweetie's flirting, playful banter had returned. This prompted another round of giggles. *I'm more used to smiles and sultry looks than giggles from Sweetie,* thought Garum. *She may still need more time for a full recovery.*

Instead of stuffing, Garum found the turkey's cavity was filled with a plump duck. He saw that its head had been removed and laughed.

"What's so funny?" asked Görthang.

"There's no head on the duck," said Garum, pointing to the waterfowl he'd extracted from inside the turkey.

"I don't understand," said Görthang.

"Without its head, I don't get the bill!" said Garum.

Groans circled the table and Hrefna offered to pass Görthang her club-wand so he could tenderize Garum for sharing his joke. Görthang declined her club-wand and opted for a slice of duck breast dripping with savory juices instead. Soon the duck was carved, and a second platter of meat followed the first on its circular sojourn.

Instead of laughing this time, Garum shook his head when he realized the duck was stuffed with a small chicken. He'd heard about such things at royal feasts but had never tried making a turkey-duck-chicken when he cooked for soldiers. *I don't think they would have appreciated the extra work needed to get to their favorite fowl,* thought Garum. Instead of carving the chicken into slices, he simply disjointed the bird into several pieces and put them all on a third platter.

Sweetie tugged on Garum's sleeve and pointed at what had been inside the chicken's cavity—a golden egg that reminded Garum of the hard-boiled eggs wrapped in sausage, rolled in breadcrumbs, and fried that they'd eaten in the Deeps. This egg wasn't hard boiled, however. It was gold-plated and had a thin line around its circumference.

"I think you're meant to open it," said Sweetie. "Pull it apart and see what's inside."

"Could you open it?" asked Garum. "My hands are greasy."

"I can help with that," said Sweetie. She took Garum's hands in hers, one at a time, brought his fingers to her lips, and sucked off the grease while wiggling her nose. Garum nearly fell off his raised chair and the others around the table began to clap in a shared rhythm, encouraging Sweetie's efforts. Garum felt his face get as red as the bog-berry sauce for the turkey.

When Sweetie had finished, Garum held up the golden egg to display it and pulled the halves apart with a flourish. A small piece of light blue paper fell out and landed on Garum's plate, which so far had only included one slice of turkey.

"What does it say?" asked Hrefna.

"Let's find out," said Garum. He picked up the paper and read it to himself.

"Tell the rest of us," said Görthang.

Sweetie removed the slip of paper from Garum's now thoroughly cleaned fingers and read the note out loud so everyone at the table could hear. "We need to talk. Please join me in my office tomorrow morning at nine." Sweetie paused. "It's signed, 'The Provost.'"

"Oooo!" said Lark. "You must be *really* important if the Provost of the College of Healers herself wants to talk to you."

"I wonder how she knew we wanted to meet with senior healers," said Garum.

"She could just want to thank you for dealing with the highway-men," said Arrex.

"The Provost usually lets the town council deal with issues regarding service to the keep and the town," said Lark. "I don't think I've *ever* heard of her meeting with someone who's not on the town council, a top healer, a powerful mage, a high-ranking military leader, or a tenured scholar at the university."

"And maybe one of the bankers from Gold Keep who manages the college's funds," added Arrex. "I've *never* heard of the Provost meeting with a halfling, to say nothing of the unorthodox way you were invited."

"It hasn't been the *strangest* way I've been invited to a meeting," said Garum.

"Do tell," said Sweetie.

"Later," said Garum. "It's a very long story and I'm still trying to live it down."

"Fine," said Sweetie. "How do we know the note in the egg is legitimate?"

"You could send a messenger over to ask at her office," Drain suggested. "I could do it. Healers, even healer-administrators, don't intimidate me."

Garum turned the two halves of the gold egg in his fingers. Something was written at the bottom of the big end. Holding it close to his eyes, he saw four words written in tiny letters: *Official Business. Eat Me.* Garum considered the words. *I'm either being insulted or instructed, possibly both.* Hoping to halt future discussion about the note, Garum decided to take the advice written inside the shell—and bit into it.

The gilded eggshell tasted far better than Garum expected. In fact, it reminded him of the brown logs that came out of the wall in the rooms Vip-vip had shown them in the Deeps. As Garum chewed, the taste of the shell grew sweeter and richer, like crepes made with almond milk, fresh raspberries, and whipped cream. A smile of contentment formed on his face and his eyes unfocused like he'd been sitting at a bar filled with too much toothed-leaf smoke for hours. Garum's head started to loll, and his chin was tracing back and forth along his collarbones as his neck muscles lost any power to support his skull.

"What's happening to you?" asked Sweetie.

"Oooommm," said Garum as more of a controlled exhale than a word.

Lark was out of her seat and standing beside Garum before any of the others could react. She picked up the other half of the gilded egg, broke off a piece of it, and slid it into Garum's mouth. Then she pushed his chin up and down and massaged his neck, so he'd swallow what he'd just masticated.

A few seconds later, Garum's eyes snapped back into focus. He shook his head from side to side and looked like he was ready to fight another trio of highwaymen, plus Görthang and Hrefna before dessert.

"The message really *must* be from the Provost," announced Lark. "She's the best at the college with potions that affect the mind. I think she must have coated the edible eggshell confections with two of them."

"What made you think the other half of the egg held the antidote to whatever I ate first?" asked Garum, who now seemed to be fully himself again.

"It's her style," said Lark. "She believes in combining chastisement with praise. All the students at the college think it's a way for her to seem forceful, without being hated."

"I think *I'm* starting to hate her," said Garum. "I don't like being manipulated."

"In that case, you're *definitely* not going to like the Provost," said Lark.

"I'll say," added Arrex.

"Nine o'clock tomorrow morning," said Garum. "At her office. Who can tell me how to get there?"

"I can," said Arrex.

"So can I," said Lark. "But it might be better if you do it," she told Arrex. "I still have to graduate."

Garum turned left to Görthang and right Sweetie. "Who should come with me—and Arrex?"

"I think it might be better if only Sweetie goes with you," said Görthang. "She appears less threatening."

"While being more dangerous," added Hrefna.

"We'll meet you in the common room at eight-thirty," said Garum.

"Sounds like a plan," said Sweetie. She stood up, took Garum's hand, and waved to Hrefna. "Time to get my heroic halfling here and my dainty, unthreatening, but dangerous self, to bed. Goodnight, all!"

Chapter 17

The Provost

Arrex guided Garum and Sweetie to the building for senior college administrators only a few blocks from The Hands of the King but would leave them at the entrance.

"Here we are," said Arrex, "Her office is on the top floor."

"It would have to be," grumbled Garum.

"As a student," Arrex continued, "I would have been quaking in my sandals at even the slight possibility of meeting the Provost or even crossing her shadow on the street. She could expel any of us on a whim, and her reaction to Gêrdun's assault and property damage was legendary." Arrex looked up and down the otherwise empty street like a small dog wondering if a bigger dog was waiting to jump out and steal his bone. "They said the Provost threw a marble mortar *through* the wall of her office and had aim good enough to toss the matching pestle into the hole after it from a dozen feet away."

"Sounds like quite a formidable woman," said Garum.

"That she is," said Arrex.

"Don't worry," said Sweetie. "So am I."

Of that I have no doubt, thought Garum. *Then again, it might have been a thin wall.*

Garum turned to Arrex. "Given what you say about the Provost, I'm confused. I thought you told us the healers are more interested in helping people than in wealth or power?"

"I was talking about senior healers like my preceptors at the College," said Arrex. "Not the Provost." He shook his head. "Some of my instructors worked one or two days in ten treating the afflictions of poor people without the funds to pay for healing potions," Arrex continued. "The Provost isn't like that."

"Thanks for the warning," said Sweetie.

The building before them was made of high-quality limestone blocks with a slight blue tinge. Two pillars of marble in a deeper blue and circled by carved serpents flanked the front entrance. A lintel of the same blue marble as the pillars bore the incised words *Healing the World*. Garum was pleased there were only four steps up from the street to the building's door.

"You can go," Garum told Arrex as he noticed the young man's uneasiness. "Buy Lark breakfast or something. I think she's sweet on you."

"Lark?" said Arrex. "You think she *likes* me?"

Garum didn't immediately say what he was thinking. *You'd have to be a fool not to be able to see that she liked Arrex.*

"Trust me," said Garum, deciding Arrex *did* need to hear it. "She likes you."

"Well, then…" said Arrex. He waved goodbye and strode off deeper into the campus of the college.

"I expect spending time with the twins has given Arrex more confidence with women," said Sweetie.

"That remains to be seen," said Garum. "He seemed comfortable with Lark when he only thought of her as a friend, but it's still possible for him to put his foot in his mouth up to the ankle with her if he's not careful."

"I have confidence in Arrex *and* Lark," said Sweetie.

"Let's hope we can have similar levels of confidence in our own ability to handle the Provost," said Garum.

"I'm more concerned about handling three more flights of stairs," said Sweetie.

"If need be, I'll carry you," said Garum.

"Sure you will," said Sweetie. She took Garum's hand, and they entered the building together.

A plump man in sky-blue robes standing at a lectern inside the door looked up from the book he was reading and addressed Garum and Sweetie. "You're here for your nine o'clock?" asked the man. Garum heard sounds, but didn't truly *hear* the man's question. He was too busy taking in the long flight of stairs leading to the next level above them.

"We are," said Sweetie, covering for Garum's distraction.

"Fourth floor," said the man, pointing up the staircase.

"Do you have a lift?" asked Garum when his attention returned.

"For administrators' use only," said the man.

"We're using it," said Sweetie. "Take us there. Now."

The man looked at Sweetie, then at Garum, then back to Sweetie.

"I nearly killed three highwaymen yesterday morning," said Garum. "You don't want to make me angry."

"That was *you?*" said the man.

"It was," said Sweetie.

"Right this way," said the man.

This lift was smaller than the ones in the Golden Dome and it ran without an operator. The man in sky-blue robes simply pushed a lever on the wall labeled *4* to the up position and hastily backed out. The lift's doors closed, and it started to rise.

"What made you think he'd jump when you barked?" asked Sweetie.

"My instincts told me the Provost would surround herself with such individuals," said Garum. "I saw the same thing in the army. People like her only want subordinate toadies, not anyone with initiative."

"So, when you said *jump,* you knew his response would be *how high?*" said Sweetie.

"I'd hoped his answer to *how high?* would be the fourth floor, by lift, not my sore legs."

"My sore legs and I appreciate that," said Sweetie. "Though my legs aren't really that sore after taking Lark's healing potion."

"Neither are mine," said Garum. "She gave me a different sort of potion to treat my shock after the fight and it filled me with energy."

"Bring all that energy to our meeting with the Provost," said Sweetie. "Should we mention *you-know-what?*"

"Not until after we find out what the Provost wants to discuss," said Garum. "She may have a quite different topic in mind— maybe even hiring the Golden Company."

"Are we open to taking on assignments?" asked Sweetie.

"Not really," said Garum. "But it would depend on the details."

Sweetie nodded.

The lift reached the fourth floor and its gate opened as if by one of Sweetie's invisible solid illusions.

A woman half again Garum's three-foot-six-inches and about his age stood outside the lift waiting for them. Her dark black hair had bright blue highlights and her robes were white healers' robes, marked with the single wide red stripe of a graduate of the college.

Not the Provost, Garum decided. *Her chief lieutenant, most likely.*

"You're right on time," said the woman. "The Provost appreciates punctuality."

"And we appreciate riding the lift up to her office," said Garum. "Without that courtesy, we would have been late." *Giving the Provost the advantage when we met.*

"Climbing stairs keeps the heart healthy," said the woman.

"Does the Provost climb the stairs?" asked Sweetie.

The woman didn't answer but guided them through a nearby door into an outer office. She tapped on a second door.

"Bring them in," called a voice in a deep alto register that reminded Garum of Hrefna. It had power, carried a slight hint of menace, and suggested someone with the vocal control of a professional singer, public speaker, or politician. *Perhaps she's all three,* thought Garum.

The woman with bright blue highlights opened the door to the Provost's office and gestured for Sweetie and Garum to enter. She did not follow and closed the heavy wooden door behind them. It sounded like one of the solid metal doors in the Deeps closing, but with a *thunk* rather than a *clank.*

The Provost did not look anything like what Garum had expected. His mind had pictured a woman carved from the same stone as one of the generals of an army he'd served in years ago—hardened body, lined face, steel hard determination in her bearing. The woman who crossed the office to greet them was human, in her late thirties or early forties, with short blonde hair the color of straw and blue eyes that sparkled with enough merriment and mischief they reminded Garum of Púki. She was a few inches taller than Sweetie, but shorter than the twins, with a much smaller count of freckles. She reminded Garum of a taller version of several halfling women back in Greenbriar who ran businesses selling cheese, baked goods, or vegetables. Those women had been quite capable. *Don't underestimate this woman,* Garum reminded himself. *I expect too many people have underestimated her and regretted it over the years.*

"Welcome to the College," said the Provost. Sweetie took the woman's offered hand and Garum shook it. Her palm was soft, but he felt thick calluses from holding a quill for too many hours. She invited them to take comfortable seats on the side of her office closest to the windows and fifteen feet from the desk where the Provost had been sitting before their arrival. "Sorry for the unconventional invitation, but I had to meet you," she said.

"Why?" Garum blurted. *Watch yourself, fool. Keep your guard up. You're probably being manipulated. First praise, then a verbal blade when you're not expecting it.*

"You're the halfling of the hour," said the Provost in response. "One against three highwaymen," she said. "I had to see for myself who such a hero might be."

"No hero, just someone defending myself, and my friend," said Garum.

"He's *my* hero," said Sweetie. "But he was before the highwaymen."

"I can see that the two of you are close," said the Provost. "I was glad Lark happened by to assist you. She's one of our most talented students. And I understand that Jenner is working with you?"

"We call him Arrex," said Garum.

"Which is perfectly proper practice," said the Provost.

"He's been an exemplary part of the *new* Golden Company," added Sweetie.

"Yes," said the Provost. "You're the *new* Golden Company. I'd heard word of Aubericht's disappearance from my sources at Rose Keep. The Golden Company's name will be a challenge to live up to, but I can't say I'll lament Aubericht's demise, even if he was pretty to look at, with all those muscles. I once used him as a model for an anatomy lesson."

A private one, Garum speculated. *For all of Aubericht's impressive reputation, it sounds like few people liked him, though they weren't averse to using him for their own ends.*

"You knew Aubericht?" asked Sweetie.

"The College had cause to hire him and his company for various projects from time to time," said the Provost. "Sadly, the Stone Prince was every bit as arrogant as Aubericht, and as for Céptianne, the less said about *her* the better. Barton sent me updates about the company's activities every month. He's the one I'll miss the most."

Barton DeCláreClare was spying on the Golden Company for the Provost? thought Garum. *Interesting.*

"Well," said Sweetie.

Garum sensed she was about to bring up the chest and spoke over her. "Well," he said, repeating Sweetie. "Is having a chance to see me face to face the only reason you extended your invitation? I hope the fact that I'm not as tall as a giant with muscles on top of muscles, like Aubericht, hasn't proved too great a disappointment."

The Provost laughed and it seemed so genuine that Garum had to remind himself it might be more manipulation.

"The reports *said* you were a halfling," noted the Provost. "I wasn't expecting a giant or an Aubericht."

"Garum is Garum," said Sweetie. "He's one of a kind." Her body language added *and he's mine.*

The Provost understood Sweetie's subtext. "Of course," she said. "Now that I've met him... now that I've met you both, that's obvious. What I also wanted to discuss is whether or not the *new* Golden Company might be interested in a little project I have in mind—to recover something from the Deeps below East Keep."

"Thank you for not wasting our time with more blandishments and getting to the point," said Garum.

"Oh, they weren't blandishments," said the Provost. "I really did want to meet you, and I have to say that so far, I haven't been disappointed."

"You're not the person we were expecting," said Garum.

"I have to play the ogre to keep the students and the instructors at the College in line," said the Provost. "I'm sure you've realized that and know it's easier to reveal the soft glove inside *after* showing the steel gauntlet."

Sweetie nodded. "Tell us about this recovery project," she said.

"Getting right to the point, I see," said the Provost. "I like that."

"And I'd like details," said Sweetie.

"Fine," said the Provost. "Are you familiar with transformation potions?"

"Not really," said Sweetie. "Mages are always threatening to turn people into frogs. Are they something like that?"

"In a way," said the Provost. "But mages' spells are typically temporary. Transformation potions can be permanent, and they usually require rare and exotic components."

"So, you want us to get you ingredients for a recipe?" asked Garum.

"I'd forgotten. You're a cook," said the Provost. "That's an apt analogy. I need you to locate and retrieve a Golden Chalice."

The Golden Company's vault had a jeweled golden chalice, Garum remembered. *Perhaps it has properties particular to mixing up transformation portions?* He sensed his brow wrinkle involuntarily. *But she'd said the Golden Chalice was an ingredient, not a mixing vessel…*

"What sort of chalice or goblet would we be looking for?" asked Sweetie. "And where?"

"This chalice isn't a goblet, though it is cup-shaped when it's mature," said the Provost. "It's a type of mushroom, shimmering gold in color, with a stalk about a foot long and a broad cap that turns up to form a cup holding a pint or two."

"Oh," said Sweetie.

Garum nearly matched Sweetie's expression but kept his face neutral. "And where do we have to go to find it?"

"How deep into the Deeps?" asked Sweetie.

The Provost tilted her head. "A few up from the lowest level, but it's said to be on a dark level. No wizard globes. Strong light harms mushrooms. From what I've learned, the special fungus garden where the Golden Chalice can be found is no more than half a mile from the stairway leading down from East Keep."

"Why aren't you sending any of your own people to get it?" asked Sweetie.

"Because transformation potions, once prepared, are quite powerful," said the Provost. "I'm afraid one of my rivals might keep the Golden Chalice and use it to supplant me."

The perpetual challenge of leadership, thought Garum. *You always have to watch out for someone who wants your job.*

"And?" asked Garum, sensing there was more.

"And it's well guarded, but I don't know by what."

"So, we're pawns to sacrifice," said Garum. "You're hoping some of us get back to give you more information."

"I'm *hoping* some of you get back *with* at least one mature Golden Chalice," said the Provost.

"What do *we* get out of it?" asked Sweetie.

"You get my help restoring Auberight and the rest of the original Golden Company," said the Provost.

"How did you…" Sweetie began.

"No," said Garum. "That's not the question. We know she has sources in Herb Keep Town and Gold Keep Town. Any of the servers at our meals could have sold that information."

"I guess you're right," said Sweetie.

"The chest that took the original Golden Company is a magical artifact known as the Grand Acquisitor," said the Provost. "It has a long history and is rumored to draw on its magic to acquire anyone who opens it." She turned up her hands and shrugged. "The chest was placed at the lowest level of the Deeps below North Keep for a reason—to prevent it from acquiring anyone else. Auberight and his associates didn't have the good sense to leave it alone."

"And you think the Golden Chalice mushroom will bring the original Golden Company back?" said Garum.

"I think Auberight and the rest are inside the chest, shrunk down to the size of ants," said the Provost. "Mushrooms like the Golden Chalice have a long history of supporting size changes. We have a saying at the senior levels of the college about capsules made from chalice mushrooms."

Sweetie looked at the Provost as if waiting for more.

"Oh, of course, the saying. One pill makes you larger, and one pill makes you small," said the Provost.

"But a pill didn't make them smaller, the Grand Acquisitor did," said Sweetie.

"The other pill, or rather, a potion with the right ingredients, should restore the Golden Company to their original heights."

"An Aubericht the size of an ant would explain the tiny screams," said Garum.

"You *have* the chest?" asked the Provost.

"We do," said Sweetie. "But I don't understand. It doesn't sound like Aubericht and the others were on your list of favorite people. Why do *you* want to restore them?"

"I mostly want to restore *Aubericht*," said the Provost. "I want him back so I can tell him face-to-face what I really think of him."

The Deeps have no dangers like a woman scorned, thought Garum. He knew he didn't have all the details about Aubericht and the Provost and he wasn't sure he wanted them. *There are some things I can't support, however.*

"Well?" asked the Provost. "Will you take the assignment?"

"No torture?" said Garum.

"Maybe just a little," said the Provost.

"That's fine, then," said Sweetie.

It is? thought Garum. *Add Sweetie to the twins on the list of people I don't want angry at me, though I expect she's already on it.*

"When do you want us to start?" asked Sweetie.

"This afternoon, if possible," said the Provost. "The Golden Chalice is only mature for a brief period, and by my calculations, that window starts today." She extended her hands to touch Garum and Sweetie's forearms and said, "By the way, feel free to call me Galena."

"Why?" asked Garum reflexively. He mentally kicked himself. *You're an idiot.*

"Because it's my name," said the Provost.

Chapter 18

Quest Preparations

It's impressive how quickly an expedition can be ready to enter the Deeps if the most powerful person in both Keep and Town wants to make it happen, thought Garum. Görthang, Hrefna, and the rest of the Black Company were glad to be part of the quest and get on the good side of the Provost in the process. Garum's own team, to his surprise, were glad to return to the Deeps, especially with Görthang's much more experienced team for company.

Sweetie and Garum didn't go into details about their mission, explaining only that they had to find something the Provost needed for a potion to restore Aubericht and the rest of the Golden Company, but none of the members of either team seemed to mind. *If I didn't know better, I'd think they trusted my leadership,* Garum considered. Then he reconsidered. *Maybe they trusted Sweetie, not him.*

At Galena's insistence, Lark would be coming with them. "You may need plenty of healers, and Gêrdun never did formally graduate," the Provost had told Garum and Sweetie. Garum was fine with that. Lark's potions were remarkable. Then he considered the extent of the Provost's knowledge—of Galena's—revealed by her statement.

She knew about the chest. She knows about Gêrdun. What doesn't she know about? Garum asked himself. He shrugged. *Lark will probably be reporting back to her, too. Maybe Arrex as well.* Garum rubbed his chin, glad for the ten-thousandth time halfling men didn't have to shave. *I wonder if Arrex told Galena about the chest? Did loyalty to the College of Healers override loyalty to your comrades in facing danger? It might,* thought Garum. *None of them really knew each other before they interviewed for support roles with the original Golden Company.*

"You're in charge of our food and drink," Sweetie told Garum as they stood off in a far corner of the private meeting room at

The Hands of the King where they'd had dinner the previous evening. The others were making their own preparations for their descent along the opposite wall, giving Sweetie and Garum space for confidential conversations.

He didn't hear her, however, since he was too busy following a maze of twisted passageways in his brain, like wondering if Prestyn might be a spy for the Mages' Guild. Was he telling everything that went on to his parents, who then informed the guild heads—or maybe one or both of Prestyn's parents were *on* whatever body set policy for the mages. And Drain and Flisk could be reporting back to dwarvish and elvish authorities, respectively. Crank could be planted by someone at the Scholars' University in West Keep Town. Even the twins might be spying, though Garum couldn't figure who would be foolish enough to employ them—unless their bickering was only meant to put him off guard.

Garum's convoluted collection of mental somersaults and switchbacks were abruptly disrupted when Sweetie grabbed Garum at his waist, lifted him up, and gave him a series of passionate kisses that redirected his thinking in one of the nicest ways possible. When Sweetie broke the kiss and put Garum back on his feet, they were both smiling.

"Sorry, my dear," said Garum. "I'd gotten lost down a maze of badger burrows." He stood on tiptoe and kissed the end of her nose. "I was imagining *everyone* was a spy for the Provost."

"You're probably not wrong," said Sweetie. "She seems to have ears everywhere."

"Kiss me again," said Garum.

Sweetie did.

Garum took a deep breath. "The problem with that kind of thinking is there's no end to it," he said. "It's like thinking too hard about crossing the room. First you go halfway, then half the remaining distance, then half again and if you think about it too much, you'll never get there."

"Yes, you will," said Sweetie. "At some point you're close enough to touch the opposite wall, so you've made it."

"Correct as always," said Garum. "You're good for me."

"I know," said Sweetie. "And you're good for me. But I'd told you you're in charge of our food and drink, which wasn't really an order, or a request, but more a recognition of your superior qualifications for that part of our preparations and an expectation that you'll handle the details of what we'll eat and imbibe."

"I will," said Garum. "Just give me a handful of minutes. I'll give Galena's people a list of what I'll need."

"I hope it doesn't take us long to find what we're looking for," said Sweetie.

"From what Galena said, it can't," said Garum. "If it does, the object of our quest will be past its prime."

"And I know cooks prefer the freshest of ingredients," said Sweetie.

"Depends on the dish," said Garum. "Some ingredients—certain cheeses, wines, and cured meats—improve with age."

"Certain men—and halflings—do as well," teased Sweetie.

"You don't mind being robbed from your cradle?" asked Garum, teasing back.

"Not if there's a possibility the two of us might be needing a cradle for a joint project of our own someday…"

"That might be nice," Garum replied. "Someday." *I'm not feeling a need to leave town,* Garum realized. *That's what I usually do when a woman starts talking about having children together. Either I'm getting ready to settle down or I'm truly in love with Sweetie, or more likely, both.*

Lark stuck her head into the private dining room, saw Sweetie and Garum, and approached them holding a dark-blue leather scroll case as long as the distance from Lark's elbow to her fingertips and as big around as her slender wrist. "This is for you," she said, holding the case out to them. "The Provost told me to give it to you. She said it will help you find the object we're seeking, whatever that is."

"Thank you," said Sweetie.

"Thank *you* for letting me join you," said Lark.

Garum noticed that she looked lumpy, like she'd gained thirty pounds since he'd seen her a few hours ago. "Are you carrying a lot of healing potions?" he asked.

"Does it show?" Lark asked. She patted her torso and Garum heard ceramic vials clink. "That's a silly question," Lark went on. "Of *course*, it shows. I brought all my healing potions because the Provost said I should be ready for anything."

"Did she also ask you to report back to her on everything we do?" asked Garum.

"How did you know?" asked Lark.

Garum could have said, *I didn't, until now,* but he gave a response that was more considerate of Lark's feelings. "The Provost told me that was her plan," he said. "She must have a lot of confidence in you."

"I think she doesn't want one of the other senior healers to go with you," said Lark. "No sense in giving some would-be future Provost a chance to get what she wants first."

I'm going to have to revise my thinking about Lark, thought Garum. *She's more attuned to political realities than I expected in someone her age.* "That could be a factor as well," Garum replied.

Lark left them to talk to Arrex, her novice's white robes with three vertical red stripes billowing as she clinked with every step.

"She's going to need to belt those robes and cinch them tight," Garum told Sweetie. "Anyone or anything in the Deeps that wants to attack us will be able to hear her vials from hundreds of yards away."

"Maybe so," said Sweetie. "I'll talk to her about carrying fewer potions and padding the ones that remain."

"Good," said Garum. "I have to start writing up my detailed kitchen order."

"Before you start," said Sweetie, "I want to say I'm glad we're not on a suicide mission."

"What makes you sure we're not?" asked Garum.

"If we *were,* Galena would be sending several of her rivals along with us, hoping the Deeps will do what she can't, all without making her look bad. Instead, she's sending Lark."

"This expedition seems like a lot of work just to bring back an old lover who jilted her, or whatever it is that has Galena so angry with Aubericht," said Garum.

"Oh, my dear halfling hero," said Sweetie, patting his arm. "Galena doesn't plan to bring back Aubericht and the Golden Company using the Golden Chalice. She just told us that so we'd fetch the fungus for her."

Garum nodded. "I figured that much out myself," he said softly. "Her story leaked water like a colander."

"Speaking of colanders," said Sweetie, "do you know how to make long, thin noodles with wolf-peach sauce and grated cheese?"

"Of course, though you haven't tried my flat noodles with bacon, cheese, and cream sauce," said Garum. "It's much better—but why are you changing the subject? Either you don't *know* the game Galena is playing and are trying to make me think you do, or you *do* know her game and don't want to tell me. Which is it?"

"Maybe I'm just having a craving for wolf-peaches turned into sauce," said Sweetie. "Sweet, ripe, wolf-peaches exploding with flavor, with a pinch of oregano and another of basil, and plenty of sautéed garlic."

Garum wiped off a line of saliva that had formed on his lips. "If you're having odd cravings, there may be a third option, but I've been diligent about wearing my charm against conception whenever we've..." said Garum. His hand reached under the neck of his tunic. "Ah, it's still there. What are you trying to do other than make me hungry, make me want to cook, and make me think I've lost my charm?"

"Sorry," said Sweetie. "You're always charming to me." She held up a hand. "I was only trying to get my own thoughts in order before explaining." She ran her tongue over her lower lip and frowned. "Do you remember about who Lark told us were the only people the Provost ever meets with?"

"The corresponding senior people at North Keep, South Keep, and West Keep," said Garum.

"Right," said Sweetie. "The most powerful people in the Keep Lands."

"What if the transformation potion using the Golden Chalice would give her the power to control the others?" asked Garum. "Healers' skills work on minds as well as bodies."

"That has a certain level of plausibility," said Sweetie, "but there's not much we can do about it now."

"Except to stay vigilant," said Garum.

"Except that," said Sweetie. "Now let's look at what's in the scroll case."

"Galena wasn't very precise in identifying the location of the chalice," said Garum. "Maybe there's a map with an X where we'll find it."

Sweetie pulled off the case's cap and slid out a roll of parchment.

Garum looked around, but none of the others were paying attention to them, except Görthang, who looked over at Garum and waved before returning to sharpening his twin blades. Xarra and Yarra, seated next to the leader of the Black Company, were following Görthang's example and sharpening Aubericht's swords.

Sweetie unrolled the parchment on the floor, holding one end down with the scroll case and the other end with her hand. A corner curled up and Garum used his palm to smooth it down. They were both pleased to see it *was* a map and seemed to be one of the Deeps below East Keep. On the left side was a stylized staircase drawn in black ink, with a red arrow marking two levels up from the bottom. Small red letters reading *Start Search Here* were above the arrow.

"That seems straightforward enough," said Garum. "There are three pie wedges showing the arc of the Deeps clockwise between East Keep and Yew Keep."

"I'm guessing the middle one is the level with the arrow," said Sweetie. "The other two wedges must be for the level above and the level below."

"Galena has marked off areas of interest on all three areas," Garum pointed out.

"And labeled them One, Two, Three," said Sweetie.

"One is on the middle level," said Garum. "And two is one level down."

"So, three is one level up," said Sweetie, pointing with a finger from the hand that wasn't holding down the map."

"Should we do them in numerical order, do you think?" asked Garum.

"I wouldn't," came a deep voice above him. Garum looked over his shoulder to see Görthang standing above him. "You'll want to descend through the levels one at a time, instead of backtracking. You two should know that climbing *up* stairs is a lot harder than climbing down them."

"What do you suggest?" asked Sweetie.

"I'd take them in Three-One-Two order," said Görthang. "We can practice our tactics on Three, and if we're lucky enough to find what the Healer Boss wants there, we're done. Otherwise, we can keep going down until we find it, refining our tactics as we go." He chuckled, sounding like bits of iron rolling around in a barrel. "There's also the matter of the only *entrance* to the Deeps from East Keep that's anywhere near these areas is at the level labeled Three. That's where we'll *have* to enter, since nobody has ever managed to blast a hole in the side of the Deeps."

"I guess we'll go in at that level, then," said Sweetie. "Unless we want to use a higher entrance and walk down stairs *inside* the Deeps instead of outside."

"No thank you," said Görthang.

"It's supposed to be dark where we're looking," said Garum, just remembering what Galena had said. "No wizard globes and we can't use bright lights."

"Orcs, half-orcs, trolls, ogres, gnomes, and dwarves have better vision in low light," said Görthang. "We'll be your eyes."

"I'll see if Prestyn has any scrolls for red lights," said Garum. "They shouldn't bother what we seek."

"I'm already a step ahead of you," said Görthang. "I asked the Healer Boss's minions to get you folks with weak eyes headbands fitted with small red-light lamps. They won't be much, but you should be able to see well enough to avoid stepping off ledges or into deep pits."

"Good thinking," said Sweetie.

"One other thing," said Görthang. "The Bird Girl…"

"Lark," said Garum.

"Whatever her name is—she's too noisy. I asked her to give everyone in the combined parties a vial of healing potion. Sometimes there's not enough time for a healer to get to someone who's injured, and having a potion on hand can be a literal life saver."

"Another excellent idea," said Sweetie.

"Want to look over the map with us in more detail?" asked Garum.

"Don't mind if I do," said Görthang. "Tell me, what is it we have to find again…"

Garum and Sweetie told him.

Görthang slapped his knee. The steel on his gauntlet made a heavy clunk against his leg armor. "A mushroom," he whispered. "Aubericht and the original Golden Company used to have a gem-encrusted golden goblet. It was pretty. I wonder what happened to it?"

Garum and Sweetie chose not to enlighten him.

Chapter 19
Back to the Deeps

They didn't have to pay to enter East Keep, or even offer bribes to the guards at the stop of the stairs. Görthang tried to hand their commander a small bag of gold pieces, but she declined to accept it, saying, "Provost's orders," as she shrugged and mouthed a silent *Thanks, anyway.*

East Keep's stairs into the Deeps were different from the ones at North Keep and Rose Keep. Instead of spiral stairs in the center of a circular tube, the stairs below the home of the College of Healers were built around all four sides of a square shaft as they descended, with small landings at every corner.

"There must have been a lot of up and down movement when these were built," Görthang told Garum. "The landings make it easier for ascending and descending parties to pass each other."

Garum would have been happier if there'd been a portion of the stairway with half-height treads, but figured that with his luck, that section would be beside the drop into the central shaft instead of tight up against the outer wall. He shuddered to think of falling over the edge, only stopping when his body hit the floor at the lowest level. Like everyone, he'd heard the joke about an orc falling off and asked how he was doing midway. "So far, so good," was the punchline. Garum kept his right shoulder close to the wall as he took each high step down.

Sweetie had seen the fear on Garum's face when he'd gazed over the inner edge of the stairway, so she insisted he should take the wall. The two of them side by side were narrow enough that she was more than a yard away from the sheer drop.

Garum watched his feet—the human-sized treads were a challenge—and not for the first time wondered why there wasn't a railing to prevent accidents along the side of the stairs by the central shaft. *Because when you're defending against monsters of the*

Deeps coming up *the stairs, you* want *to be able to push them off,* Garum realized after a few moments to think. This trip into the Deeps was different. Then, he'd been a simple cook following Aubericht's orders. Now, he was the reputed leader of two adventuring companies.

Görthang and Blōgot were in the lead as they trudged their way down. Garum and Sweetie came next, not taking up much room, followed by Hrefna, who was wide enough she didn't have a companion beside her. Kléppri and Drain, maintaining an uneasy silence, were behind the troll mage, and Xarra and Yarra, with Púki between them, formed the next rank.

Lark, Arrex, Gêrdun, and Vip-vip formed a knot of white-robed 'healers' on two steps behind the twins and the shortorc. Gêrdun had returned to wearing his healers' robes—with a zig-zag red stripe of his own devising—after Garum had told him the Provost was well aware of his identity and had no interest in causing trouble for him.

Prestyn came next, then Flisk and Crank, with Jelly riding on top of Crank's backpack. Chophorn and Sir Donal were their rear guard. Chophorn had decent night vision—not quite as good as the orcs, but good enough to potentially see enemies sneaking up behind them.

I'm glad we left the kittens with three of Lark's roommates, thought Garum. *They had a four-legged kitten and were glad to temporarily look after the seven six-legged felines placed in the Golden Company's keeping. I don't want to be responsible for herding a chaos of cats as well as the members of the Black and Golden companies.* Garum chuckled to himself. *I know the proper collective noun is 'clowder,' but 'chaos' seems so much more appropriate.*

Garum wore a headband with a small red-light lamp positioned so the lamp was centered on his forehead. The lamps were provided by the Provost, or rather, by her minions—of which there were multitudes. To Garum's eye, the luminous ball inside the tiny lamp looked like a typical wizard globe, save for its size and the fact that it gave off a soft reddish light instead of a bright white glow. The lamp had a shutter he could close to cut off the red light, but for now, having it open gave Garum some assurance he could make his way on otherwise dark levels.

He looked over at Sweetie and saw she'd managed to make the headband she wore hold back her long hair. Garum wondered if their lamps would clink together if he tried to kiss her. *Probably not, given our height differences and the applicable angles,* thought Garum. He saw Blōgot and Görthang together ahead and expected Blōgot to be counting levels while Görthang stayed alert for anything that attacked them.

Any monsters from the Deeps would have to get past the guards on the landings first, thought Garum. *We're probably safe from attack while we're still on the stairs. I hope.* He looked over at Sweetie and saw she was biting her lower lip.

"Something worrying you?" he asked her softly.

"You mean something more than our general circumstances?"

"Yes," said Garum. "I can worry enough about those for both of us."

"I'm sure you can," said Sweetie. "I'm worried about my illusions."

"I have no illusions about how wonderful you are," said Garum.

"No, those are your *delusions,*" teased Sweetie. "I don't know how effective my illusions will be in low light. They depend on our foes being able to *see* them, and these red lights may make them useless."

Garum reached over and squeezed her hand.

"I don't *like* feeling useless," said Sweetie.

"Even without your illusions, you're anything but that," said Garum.

"I've been practicing as we've walked," said Sweetie. "I send tight reeds of *very* bright light down the central shaft and across to the wall on the other side. I'm thinking I can use them to blind our opponents, without damaging the Golden Chalice with light like a standard wizard's globe."

"That makes sense," said Garum. "As for that, I'm not sure how useful I'll be in any sort of battle. Halflings like homes cut into hills, but we keep them well-lit and like lamps over our shoulders even when reading by the side of a fire."

"I'm the same way," said Sweetie. "Sometimes I'd read by the big hearth at the Green Doors, but I had a follow-me wizard globe the size of an apple that hovered over me to help me read. A visiting wizard I'd been serving for more than a week made it for me. She said I spent so much of my time looking after my grandfather, I deserved something nice for myself."

"I think I like that wizard," said Garum. "And I feel the same way. Are you still interested in us buying an inn of our own, someday?"

"I'd greet the guests and you'd do the cooking?" said Sweetie.

"That seems like an intelligent division of responsibilities," said Garum.

"Is that a business proposal or something more?"

"Let's wait until we survive this trip to answer that question," said Garum.

"Good enough," said Sweetie.

Garum was looking when he saw a smile like a standard wizard's globe flash across Sweetie's face.

"What should we call it?" she said.

"Our inn?" said Garum.

"Of course, our inn," said Sweetie. "The Cook's Delight," she suggested.

"You want it to be named after you?" asked Garum with a smile.

"Maybe not," Sweetie replied.

"Dulce de Lechery," teased Garum.

"That's a better name for a different sort of establishment," said Sweetie. "But we could license the name to someone and sell them candy and pastries."

"I like the way you think," said Garum.

"Short Order," Sweetie suggested. "No, that's better for a restaurant than an inn with a tavern and food, even if both of us are far from tall."

"We'll have to keep thinking about it," said Garum. "It's not something we'll need immediately."

"But we will, someday," said Sweetie.

"I hope," said Garum. *Interesting,* he thought. *I really mean that. Opening an inn with Sweetie would be nice.*

"The halfway-point guard station is coming up in a few flights," said Görthang.

"Or rather, will be coming *down* a few flights," Blōgot clarified.

"You have the pass the Provost gave us, don't you?" asked Sweetie.

"I'm carrying it," said Blōgot. "Görthang tends to leave important papers like that in the wrong pouch and blames me for not having them."

"Hey," said Görthang. "I can be organized when I need to be."

"How often is that?" asked Blōgot.

"Not that often, because you organize things *for* me," Görthang replied. "And I *do* appreciate it."

"Just don't take it for granted," said Blōgot.

"I won't—and I don't," said Görthang.

Blōgot shook her head and handed Görthang the pass. He held it up for the stair guards to see the Provost's seal and signature giving them free passage on the stairs without any need for payment—and by implication, without paying any of the usual and customary bribes. Despite the official pass, Görthang took a leather jacketed bottle from his belt and handed it to the guard captain.

"It's Gold Keep Reserve applejack," said Görthang as the captain took the offered container. "Don't drink too much at one time—it packs a punch."

"Thanks," said the captain of the guards on the landing. "It means more because we know you didn't have to give us anything. The Provost's pass was very explicit. It says we're supposed to help you *any way we can,* but I'm sure we'll do our part to distribute this token of your appreciation in the very near future."

"One swallow at a time, eh?" said Görthang. "When you see him, tell the guard captain at the top of the stairs that I'll have a similar bottle for him, later. I couldn't hand it to him with the Provost's people looking on."

"It's a pleasure dealing with someone who understands the ways of the world," said the halfway-point captain. "Good hunting, whatever you're seeking."

"We'll need it," said Görthang.

The combined Black and Gold Companies passed the halfway-point landing without incident and continued their descent. Garum overheard Drain asking Kléppri about encounters with monsters from the Deeps on the stairways.

"In all your expeditions," said Drain, "did you *ever* have to fight *in* the stairways leading up to the keeps?"

"Just twice," said Kléppri. "And the first time didn't really count. We were running from slug-trolls close to the bottom of Iron Keep and thought we'd closed the doors to the Deep behind us, but one of the slugs stuck a pseudopod through the door before it sealed and we had a major fight on our hands at the base of the stairs," said Kléppri. "None of them started climbing, so I can't really say they were *on* the stairs."

"I know what a slug is, and I know what a troll is," said Drain. "But what's a slug-troll? I don't think I've seen one anywhere in the sewers. Do they look like trolls?

"No," said Kléppri. "They look like *really* big gray-black slugs, with upper bodies as big as Hrefna."

"But much uglier," Hrefna added.

"Well..." said Púki until a look from Hrefna shut him up.

"They also have two massive arms, long, tapering tails, and leave trails of stinking slime everywhere," said Kléppri.

"Sounds unpleasant," said Drain. "How do you fight them?"

"With difficulty," said Hrefna. She flicked her club-wand left and right with enough force to decapitate a bison.

"With axes and fire," said Kléppri. "Their slime trails and the oils oozing out of the pores on their warty skins are both highly flammable," said the gnome. "Once you light one up with a torch, they're so distracted you can easily chop them up into segments. I used a slug-troll segment as a camp stove years ago. It was great for boiling water for tea.

"You mentioned a second time you fought monsters on the stairs?" Drain reminded Kléppri.

"Oh, yes, the whirlybirds," said Kléppri. "They fly, if you didn't know. Flying monsters have a natural advantage when it comes to heading up to the surface."

Garum was going to turn around and ask if Drain hadn't said, "What's a whirlybird?" a second later.

"They're odd creatures," said Kléppri. "You know about the tiny birds that sound like bumblebees, don't you?"

"Yes, we dwarves call them *hummers*," said Drain.

"Almost everyone calls them hummers," chimed in Hrefna.

"Whirlybirds are like hummers in that their wings beat very fast," said Kléppri. "Instead of beating up and down, their wings spin in a circle, like a child's top. They can move great distances vertically and horizontally in an eye blink."

"They sound cute," said Drain.

"They would be, if they weren't as big as mosquitoes scaled for giants and didn't have sharp stingers the size of poignards," said Kléppri. "Their wings are like knife blades, too. When they fly, they make an ominous whirling sound like a swarm of approaching locusts. A dozen of them got out into the foot of the outer stairwell below Gem Keep, they stopped attacking us and spun up toward the surface."

"Did the stair guards stop them?" asked Drain.

"A few of them," said Kléppri.

"I killed five," Blōgot announced from the front rank. "Five arrows. Five kills."

"That was nice shooting," Görthang told her.

"What happened to the rest of them?" Drain demanded.

"The weighted nets at the top were released," said Kléppri. "They trapped the whirlybirds and dragged them down to the bottom on top of us. We were stuck in the netting, too."

"With sharp-winged angry spinning creatures sporting dagger-like tails," said Hrefna. "There were only four of them by then, thank goodness."

"How did you deal with *them?*" asked Drain.

"Görthang and Chophorn cut us out of the nets," said Kléppri. "Then I skewered one with my extensible spear."

"I crushed two more with my club-wand," said Hrefna.

"And I sliced the last one into quarters with my swords," added Görthang. He smiled and flexed his arm muscles.

"That's impressive," said Drain. "I'm glad nothing is in the stair shaft now."

"We don't usually have that sort of problem on the way *down*," said Kléppri.

"Only on our way *up*," said Blōgot. "Thanks for the story, by the way. It made the descent go faster. There are only eight more flights until we're at our entry point three levels up from the bottom."

"How does it work when the lowest entrance isn't on the lowest level of the Deeps, like it is at North Keep?" asked Garum.

"I've never been down this far under East Keep," said Görthang, "but I expect the shaft just ends."

"Looks like reality has matched your expectations, then," said Blōgot. "We're here—and the doors to the Deeps are much the same as the ones we've seen at the lowest levels elsewhere."

"Check your equipment, everyone," said Garum. "Especially your red-light lamps. Sweetie and I will pass out honey cakes so we can all have a little extra energy. Once that's done, we'll enter. The dark section isn't right on the outer edge, it starts several hundred feet in, so we won't be without light immediately."

Sweetie whispered to Garum as he gave her a stack of honey cakes to distribute. "I like being in the dark with you," she said. "Once the lights are out, we can see what develops."

"Save that thought for *after* we retrieve the Golden Chalice," Garum whispered back.

"I will," said Sweetie softly. "And for the record, *this* isn't the part of our project for the Provost I'm most worried about."

Chapter 20
Puddles in the Dark

"Watch your step," said Görthang as he took a few paces into the Deeps. "The floor is damp and may be slippery." He was in a large, oval chamber with the curved corridor that circled the Deeps stretching out to the left and right and a wide, tunnel-like opening directly ahead leading toward the inner sections of the underground complex. Puddles were present in low spots where moisture had pooled. Some of them appeared to have been there long enough for moss to start growing in them.

"Mushrooms like high humidity," Garum whispered to Sweetie as they entered and waited for the rest of their combined companies to pass through the heavy double doors, made from the same gray metal as most of the Deeps.

"I know," said Sweetie. "I've picked enough over the years. They also like to grow in manure, and I don't smell any of that—yet."

"They also tend to be found on dead tree trunks and other decomposing matter," added Garum. "Those don't smell—or at least they don't smell as strongly. From what Galena said, I got the feeling that the Golden Chalice mushrooms were being farmed and tended, not just growing wild."

"Or as wild as anything grows in the Deeps," said Sweetie.

"Other than the hungry *wild* monsters who want to eat us, you mean," said Görthang.

"Galena—the Provost—didn't give us any details about monsters that might be on this level," said Garum.

"Powerful people like her never do," said Görthang. "They sit in Keeps and send us to do the hacking, slashing, bleeding, and dying."

"Let's resolve not to die on this expedition," Blōgot told Görthang.

"I'm with you on that," Görthang replied. "But we don't always have a choice in the matter." He looked around the faces in the chamber and curled his lips to show more of his fangs. "We're a stronger party now than usual, Arrow-Through-My-Heart. We should be able to defeat anything that wants to kill us."

Garum was glad that Blōgot didn't counter Görthang's assertion of their larger size and strength with the fact that more individuals in their party meant more potential candidates for death. If they ran into something really powerful, like a giant Drake of the Deeps, more than one of them would be in trouble. The Drakes could shoot fireballs from their bills and their webbed feet would have great traction on damp floors. From what Garum had heard and read, the creatures were very rare, so their odds encountering one today would be low.

"Pay attention to your peripheral vision, people, said Hrefna. "There could be Argus-spheres at these levels, and you don't want to look at one straight on."

"What happens if I do?" asked Crank.

"Every muscle in your body locks up and you freeze in place like a statue," said Hrefna. "The effect lasts for hours, and we'd have to carry you with us, since you'd be easy prey for any beast or monster that happened along in the meantime."

"Don't look at the ball of eyes," said Crank. "Got it."

"That's not the worst of it," said Hrefna. "Some of an Argus-sphere's eyes can make you so scared you collapse in into a weeping heap on the floor."

"Or both could happen at the same time if you look at both types of eyes," said Kléppri.

"Remember when I wasn't paying attention and saw two of their eyes?" said Görthang. "Once I was afraid—then I was petrified, but with dear Blōgot here by my side, somehow I survived."

"Only because I carried you up seven thousand steps," grumbled Hrefna.

"You *are* the strongest one in the party," said Blōgot.

"I'm strong, too," said Sir Donal. "I can carry anyone who gets stoned."

"Turned to stone metaphorically, grandfather," said Sweetie.

"I knew that," said Sir Donal.

Xarra and Yarra planted themselves directly in front of Garum and Sweetie. Their swords were unsheathed and their blades formed an X between them.

"Are you going to tell us what we're looking for now?" said Xarra.

"Or do you plan to keep playing games with us?" added Yarra. "I'm not a child."

"Neither am I," said Xarra.

"And we don't appreciate being kept in the dark about our mission," they said simultaneously.

"We were just about to tell everyone," said Garum.

"The Provost—the person *paying* for this expedition—told us not to say anything about why we're here until we entered the Deeps," said Sweetie. "She didn't want her rivals in the College of Healers to know what we're doing."

"What *are* we doing?" asked Kléppri.

"Searching for a Golden Chalice," said Garum.

"Aubericht and the Golden Company had a gem-encrusted one of those," said Kléppri. "Any idea what happened to it, Görthang?"

The orc shrugged. "Who knows? They could have sold it, melted it down, or stuck in a vault somewhere."

"It was more a goblet than a chalice, anyway," said Blōgot.

"What's the difference?" asked Crank.

"A chalice is made from thicker glass and has a more rounded bottom than a goblet," said Prestyn.

"But this one is supposed to be gold," said Crank. "It's not made of glass."

"Healers use chalices in their graduation ceremonies," said Arrex. "They drink a special potion made from…"

"Jenner!" said Lark. "That's a secret of the college. The Provost wouldn't like it if…"

"Stuff the Provost," said Arrex. "Who cares if graduates drink distilled white tuber-mash infused with raspberries?"

"Is *that* what you were drinking?" Lark protested. "You didn't let me taste any."

"Because it's only for graduates," said Arrex. "It didn't taste that good, anyway. You didn't miss anything."

"It also made you and the others act like—" Lark began.

"I think we all know what students' celebrations can be like," said Garum. He tried to get the conversation, and their mission, back on track. "The Golden Chalice isn't metal *or* glass. The Provost told us it was a special kind of mushroom, just starting to bloom now. It's cap inverts and it *looks* like a chalice."

"And it's apparently about the same size as a chalice you drink from, too," said Sweetie.

"Oh," said Xarra. "Why didn't you just say so…"

"…in the first place," said Yarra.

"She told us why," said Xarra. "The Provost told her to keep quiet about it."

"Never mind, then," said Yarra.

"Where *is* it?" asked Flisk. "On this level?"

"It might be," said Garum. "We've been told there are three possible locations to check. One on this level and others on the two levels below us."

"The fact it's a mushroom explains why you night-blind people need red-light lamps," said Drain. "Fungi can be sensitive to light."

"That's our understanding," added Sweetie. "We have black canvas bags that block bright light to put them in after we pick them."

"What's the Provost going to use the Golden Chalice *for*?" asked Prestyn.

"Some sort of potion, I think," said Garum. "We're not sure."

"I remember my parents talking about a magic mushroom with powerful effects on the brain," said Prestyn. "I'll try to remember what they said. Something silly, if I remember correctly."

"Psilocybin," muttered Arrex.

"We'd appreciate it," said Sweetie, responding to Prestyn. "We're not sure we *want* to give the Provost such a potent ingredient…"

"…but," Garum completed, "she said she needs it to help restore Aubericht and the original Golden Company."

"The Provost says lots of things to get what she wants," said Lark. "That doesn't mean they're true."

"Well, why don't you and Arrex and Gêrdun think about why the Provost might want it and share your best theories with us in an hour or so when we get to the first dark zone," said Sweetie. "We can determine how wise it might be to give the Golden Chalice to her afterwards."

"Right," said Lark.

"I have some familiarity with the properties of exotic mushrooms— as poisons," said Hrefna. "Potion crafting is one of the magical arts common to both healers *and* mages. There are some practitioners in both fields who believe the *mites* responsible for mages' magic and the *clerks* who handle healing are actually the same tiny animalcules, with the difference being only one of nomenclature."

"Dwarves' *masons* are definitely *not* the same," said Drain. "They don't require scrolls *or* potions *or* wands to be summoned," she elaborated. "They respond to any dwarf who knows the proper ways to attract them."

"Such as?" asked Hrefna.

"If you've seen dwarves work magic, you'd know without me telling you," said Drain.

"Simply a matter of laying hands on metal and stone, then?" asked Hrefna.

"That, and mental attitude," said Drain. "It takes a dwarf to not only call, but out-stubborn the little *masons*."

"So that explains it," said Flisk. "Dwarves' stubbornness is legendary."

"Keep that up and I'll ask the *masons* to anchor your feet to the metal floor," said Drain.

"My apologies, good dwarf," said Flisk. "Elves are sensitive to the flow of *xylem* and *phloem* in all living things, but here in the Deeps, we're at a disadvantage. I expect you dwarves are neither more nor less stubborn than you need to be to coax your *masons* into action."

"True enough," said Drain.

Garum noticed her frown for Flisk had changed to a smile and was glad to see it. Teasing was one thing, actual animosity between subspecies of humans, be they elf and dwarf, or orc and troll, wouldn't be good for their combined parties.

"Lead the way," said Sweetie after a wave in Görthang's direction.

The big orc walked straight ahead along the wide corridor leading deeper into the Deeps with the rest of them forming up behind. This passage, at least, had wizard globes lighting their way, though their illumination reflected off puddles that seemed randomly distributed.

"Be careful," said Blōgot. "We don't know how deep those puddles are."

"Or what might lurk in them," said Kléppri.

Garum had his doubts that the puddles were anything more than half an inch deep. The metal of the floor seemed solid to him, and he hadn't seen any holes in it on his previous trip to the Deeps. *But you've only been down here once,* he reminded himself. *The Black Company has been on hundreds of expeditions below.*

After they'd walked for a quarter of an hour, Sweetie whispered to Garum. "I think we'll be turning soon, if my memory of the map is accurate."

Before Garum could reply, Görthang held up his hand and the company halted. They had reached a spot where a medium-sized corridor crossed their own. "We go left," he told the others. This passageway was *not* lined with wizard globes and Garum could see the light from the main corridor only penetrated the darkness for a few dozen paces.

"Red-light lamps on," said Garum as he adjusted his to be centered on his forehead. He blinked several times to get used to the way the lamp altered his vision. Colors faced away, but Garum expected he could still see shapes in the dark with something resembling sharpness if there was anything in the corridor to see.

"At least Argus-spheres aren't likely to be nearby," said Görthang.

"They like light bright enough for their potential victims to see them," Blōgot clarified.

There were *more* puddles in the narrower corridor, with fewer opportunities to avoid them. Garum was glad he wore pigskin boots and smiled to himself, remembering the carefree barefoot days of his childhood when the soles of his feet were tough enough not to mind sharp stones. *I wasn't all that fond of stepping in cow pats and goose droppings, though,* he considered. *Not all of my childhood was idyllic.* His right foot inadvertently stepped in one of the puddles—they were hard to see in the red light—and Garum was glad his guess about the water being only a fraction of an inch deep was correct.

"Garum," said Sweetie.

"Yes, dear lady?" Garum answered.

"Where is the water in the puddles coming from?"

Garum shrugged, then realized his gesture might not be easily noticed in low light. "I don't know," he said. "I haven't noticed any dripping down from the ceiling."

Sweetie generated a thin rod of solid illusion and dipped it into a puddle a few steps ahead, then brought the tip of the rod back to her face. She sniffed it and rubbed her small sample between two solid-illusion 'fingers.'

Garum turned and was pleased he could see well enough to tell Sweetie's brows were furrowed. "What?" he asked.

"I don't think it's water," she said.

"Is it ale?" asked Garum, knowing full well it wasn't. He was more than familiar with the smell of ale.

"No," said Sweetie. "I think it's slime—or mucus."

"What could leave so many puddles of slime that large?" asked Garum. He didn't have to wait long for an answer. Tentacles the size of the arms on Prestyn's cloak shot out from the darkness ahead and wrapped around Görthang and Blōgot before the two orcs could react. Then the tentacles began to retract, pulling them both out of range of Garum's red-light lamp.

Kléppri extended his enchanted spear, hoping to snag one of the tentacles with its hooked point, but was unsuccessful. Vip-vip pulled out his red and blue wands and was about to send heat energy from the red one down the corridor when Sweetie stopped him.

"No," she told the vixer. "You might hurt our friends!"

"SHELZ!" shouted Vip-vip, waving his wands in the direction where Görthang and Blōgot had disappeared.

Garum felt powerless, knowing his sling and dagger would be useless against any creature big enough to have tentacles thicker than one of his legs. He was nearly knocked off his feet by Drain, who had drawn the Stone Prince's hammer-axe and was charging past him with Chophorn by her side.

"It's chopping time!" Drain shouted as she ran.

"Hoooom!" said Chophorn as the sylviant kept pace with the dwarf and matched her fury.

The two of them were soon out of sight down the dark corridor and Garum began to hear what sounded like axe blades crunching on stone, followed by screams of pain that Garum didn't think were coming from Drain or Chophorn. Sir Donal and the twins started to go after the axe-wielders, but Sweetie held her arms out to stop them.

"My strength can help!" said Sir Donal.

"We'll chop those tentacles…" Xarra began.

"…into tiny pieces," Yarra finished.

"Wait a moment, grandfather," said Sweetie. "Let's see if Drain and Chophorn *need* assistance, first."

"But they'll get all the glory," said Xarra.

"And it sounds like *gory* glory," said Yarra.

"I expect there will be plenty of battle fame for everyone before the day is through," said Sweetie.

After a few more crunching axe blows echoed up the corridor, they heard Drain call out. "We could use some help here!"

"I'll send the twins and Sir Donal," Sweetie shouted back.

"No!" came Drain's voice. "Send healers, not swords."

Lark, Arrex, and Gêrdun trotted ahead into the dark with the rest of their combined parties following behind. Hrefna generated a large red-light wizards' globe to provide better illumination once they all arrived at the scene of the crunching carnage.

Garum saw Görthang and Blōgot were on the floor of the corridor, still wrapped in tentacles, though those tentacles were no longer attached to anything and oozed a dark ichor from their cut ends. Beyond the orcs were fragments of what looked to Garum like snail shells studded with spear points.

"Squid-snails," said Hrefna. "I should have suspected them, from the puddles of slime." She tapped the end of her club wand on the floor beside a puddle to illustrate her point.

"I've never heard of them," said Garum.

"Then you've lived a shell-tered life," said the troll mage. "This is what, your second time in the Deeps?"

"Correct," said Garum.

"Squid-snails are *very* strong," said Kléppri.

"But not very fast—or smart," said Hrefna.

"Axes are particularly effective against them," said Kléppri. "Spears, not so much."

"Neither are clubs," said Hrefna. "I remember pounding their tentacles flat and they just swelled back up whenever I stopped pounding."

The three healers were kneeling beside Blōgot and Görthang. Gêrdun had managed to unwrap the tentacles around both orcs and the two human healers were pouring healing potions down the orcs' throats.

"They're not injured," said Gêrdun, "but the tentacles' slime has mild paralytic properties…"

"…nothing like the gaze of an Argus-sphere," added Hrefna.

"And we need to give Blōgot and Görthang something to counteract the slime's effects," said Gêrdun.

"They should be fine in five minutes," said Arrex.

"If not sooner," said Lark.

Garum noticed Arrex had his arm across Lark's back as she checked Görthang's pupils and respiration.

"What hit me?" asked Görthang as he suddenly sat up, knocking Lark over onto Arrex and landing them both with their buttocks on the corridor's floor—luckily *not* in a puddle of slime.

"You're getting slow," said Kléppri. "It was a snail."

"A squid-snail," said Hrefna. "They're not the same."

Görthang noticed Blōgot's eyes fluttering as she was still on her back beside him. "Maybe I can wake her with a kiss?" he said.

"Try it and you'll need another healing potion for a lacerated kidney," said Blōgot. "Now is definitely *not* the time." She smiled at Görthang, grabbed his shoulder, and used his body to lever herself up to a sitting position as well. "Squid-snails?" she said, looking at the large collection of broken shell fragments.

"Just two of them," said Sweetie.

"It's unfortunate arrows don't work on those creatures," Blōgot noted. "Shafts bounce off their shells or just stick in their flesh without doing any real damage."

Görthang laughed and hugged Blōgot. He looked up at Hrefna. "Did Chophorn axe them both?"

"He got one," said the troll wizard.

"And I got the other," Drain announced. She nudged the shell debris with the hammer side of her hammer-axe until she found the tightly wound curve at center of the shell's spiral. "I think I'll keep this as a trophy. If I plate it with gold or silver, it would make a nice necklace."

"You're welcome to the one from mine, too," said Chophorn. "You could make matching earrings."

"Thank you, but one is fine," said Drain. "I can wear a necklace charm under my tunic, but don't want to wear earrings on both ears and advertise my gender. Too many male dwarves act odd around females."

"Then let me trim and re-glue your beard when we're out of the Deeps," said Sweetie. "It's looking ragged."

"That would be appreciated," said Drain.

Once Görthang and Blōgot were on their feet and seemed themselves, Garum said, "The Golden Chalice won't find itself. Let's get moving."

They reformed their order of march and set off. Garum didn't think Lark saw him notice her collecting a few ounces of squid-snail slime in two empty healing-potion bottles. *I'm with you,* he thought. *A mildly paralytic liquid might come in handy.*

They continued on—more confidently—into the dark Deeps.

Chapter 21
Images on the Wall

Garum had remembered enough about the map the Provost provided to have a general sense of where to find the first possible location for the Golden Chalice. It was a large, rectangular chamber farther along the corridor they were following, and had been marked with thin lines looking like tiers or the stepped fields farmers sometimes used to make a hilly area easier to plow. He wondered what monster or other terrifying denizen of the Deeps would attack them next, but no attack came before they opened the door to the specified location.

Sweetie and Garum stepped into the chamber shortly after Görthang and Blōgot. *I'm a halfling,* thought Garum with a smile. *Everything I do is short.* The room was dark, but Garum's red-light lamp cast enough of a glow he could see the thin lines on the map marked six levels of comfortable seats, rather than six tiers for planting crops. He ran his hand over the cushions of the nearest seat. It was soft and touching it felt like petting a kitten. The wall opposite the seats was tall and looked either gray or white, though it was hard to tell with the limited illumination available.

"No mushrooms here," said Görthang, stating the obvious. "Shall we take a short break before heading down a level to the next marked location?"

"Sounds good," said Garum. "These seats look comfortable, and we can afford ten minutes to rest."

"Should I unpack some snacks?" asked Sweetie.

"I'll take a quart of hard cider," said Púki.

"You'll take whatever you're offered," said Xarra.

"And *like* it," said Yarra.

The twins guided Púki to a chair and found seats for themselves on either side of him.

"Beauty and the Beasts," said Púki.

"Shall we?" Xarra asked her sister as she pulled one of the black mushroom collection bags from her pack.

"Indeed," Yarra replied as she helped Xarra fit the bag over Púki's head and tug the drawstring snug.

"Mmnmph-ph!" said Púki.

"Be sure not to suffocate him," said Sweetie.

Garum found a seat in the middle of the front row for himself after giving Sweetie half the shortbread squares and passing out his own half. Sweetie joined Garum in the seat beside him and allowed her body to sink into its soft cushions.

"This is *comfortable*," she said.

"I'll need to be sure I don't nod off," said Garum. "We shouldn't stay here long."

Following Garum and Sweetie's example, the others in their combined parties found seats of their own and nibbled on shortbread in the dark. Then fuzzy moving images began flickering across the wall opposite the seats.

"Are you doing that?" asked Garum.

"My wand is still in my sleeve," said Sweetie. "What do you think it *is?*"

"I don't know," said Garum. "Let's watch a bit longer."

Music from unseen stringed instruments swelled. A dozen trumpets blared a stirring fanfare as the moving images sharpened into a night sky filled with tens of thousands of twinkling stars. The stars began to dance. They swirled into spiral whirlpools and shrank down to a spinning disk that suddenly exploded outward across the wall, revealing the head of a huge red dragon. Before any of them could react, the dragon opened its jaws, roared like a mile-high waterfall, and exhaled a blast of white-hot flame directly at them. Garum and the others crouched back into their comfortable seats, expecting to be roasted alive, but they felt no heat or fire. A low tone, almost at the edge of his hearing, filled Garum with an unshakable sense of impending doom.

Sweetie gripped Garum's forearm. "What *is* that?" she asked, voicing the question they all shared.

"Perhaps it's a Scare Room," said Garum, whose knuckles were white from the tight hold he had on the arm of his chair opposite Sweetie. "Young halfling lads and lasses would put on masks and costumes after the harvest season and lead their younger brothers and sisters between high rows of hay bales in barns, jumping out to frighten them," Garum suggested.

"If it's trying to scare us, it's succeeding," said Sweetie.

"Nothing scares *me*," said Görthang with what Garum took to be feigned bravado.

"If you're not scared, why are you holding my hand so tightly?" said Blōgot, her own voice quivering.

"To reassure you," said Görthang.

Sweetie let out a small laugh, then covered her mouth with the hand that wasn't clutching Garum.

For Garum's part, he wanted to crawl under his chair, where he hoped the dragon wouldn't be able to flambé him. He reluctantly watched the wall opposite and saw the dragon disappear in an eye blink, only to be replaced with new images of silvery metallic pie wedges covered with sparkling lights, gleaming against a backdrop of more stars.

The pie wedges were moving from left to right on the wall and thin red ropes extended from three wedges in the back toward a single wedge that was more of a long, narrow, loaf-shape, Garum realized on closer examination. The loaf was throwing red ropes at the pie wedges now, and the music from unseen instruments grew louder. Each time a red rope extended, Garum heard a sound like a live shock-eel pulled from a pond and dropped in a scalding hot cast-iron skillet.

"Did you bring any pie?" Sir Donal called to Garum from several chairs to the left. "This is making me hungry."

"Eat your shortbread, grandfather," said Sweetie.

"I did," said Sir Donal. "And I'm still hungry."

"No pie, sorry," said Garum.

"GORP!" said Vip-vip, from near Sir Donal. Garum kept one eye on the wall ahead, which had now changed to showing images of particularly ugly and shaggy horned cattle crossing a plain of ground rock particles that seemed far drier and more desolate than the sands along the edge of the great Eastern Ocean. With half his attention, Garum saw Vip-vip pull a small white bag from his belt pouch and put it on the floor in front of his chair. The vixer pulled out his red rod, manipulated it in some fashion, and shot a beam of heat at the white bag. Seconds later, the bag expanded to four times its original size, popping like small, wet pebbles in a hot campfire.

The dark chamber with the chairs was soon suffused with a wonderful smell. *It's like roasting ears of corn in the coals,* Garum realized. Vip-vip opened the bag, took a few irregular shapes the size of soldiers' dice from inside, and passed it to Garum. He took a handful, tasted them, licked his lips, and passed the bag to Sweetie. "It's good," he told her. "But it needs salt."

Sweetie took a handful herself. "And melted butter," she suggested.

"Agreed," said Garum. "But it's pretty tasty without either." He turned to the vixer and whispered, "Thank you, Vip-vip."

"GORP!" Vip-vip repeated.

The bag was passed along the seats until everyone had enjoyed a taste, then passed back to Vip-vip, almost empty. The images on the wall had changed from yellow sand to blue-white ice, like the surface of the Inland Seas in winter. Men and women were scurrying about in an ice cave loading barrels, boxes, and crates on wagons that crawled, rather than rolled around the cave on wheels. Some of the wagons were shaped like moths or birds as well.

At least these images aren't making me hungry, thought Garum. *Though I would have loved to have all their equipment for moving heavy things around when I had to manage supplies of food for an army.*

Vip-vip clapped using all three pairs of his hands when a collection of vixers appeared on the wall. They were gathered around what Garum thought looked like an octopus mounted on a cooking tripod, if the tripod was big enough to support a giant's cauldron. "CAP!" said Vip-vip. "CAP! CAP!"

Garum looked down the row of seats and saw more than half of both companies had their eyes closed. He stood up, moved in front of the wall, and shouted, "Time to go! The Golden Chalice won't find itself." Most of the members of the combined parties opened their eyes, grumbled, and started to move, then one of the vixers on the wall stepped down and put an ogre-sized hand on Garum's shoulder. Garum pushed back against the vixer's torso, but his hand didn't meet any resistance.

Is the vixer real? Garum asked himself. *Or is it somewhat like Sweetie's solid illusions? Only solid when and where she wants it to be.* The vixer 'image' spoke to Garum. He turned up his palms in what he hoped was a universal gesture of *I have no idea what you're talking about.* Vip-vip moved to stand beside Garum and he 'talked' with the vixer who'd stepped off the wall for several minutes.

Sweetie, meanwhile, was trying to get the others up and moving. It was a task on par with herding felines ranging in size from tigers to house cats. Still, she managed to get the rest of the party into some sort of order and heading toward the exit.

Garum was edging away from Vip-vip and the other vixer himself, easing his way toward the door and closing the distance between himself and Sweetie. He moved faster when a tall warrior in odd-looking black armor resembling Görthang's enameled plates appeared on the wall. Garum heard labored breathing of the sort he'd only heard from people who'd been working around clouds of dust in the mines for too many years.

The vixer talking to Vip-vip moved back onto the wall and disappeared off to the right, out of site. The tall warrior stepped down off the wall and moved toward them, but their party was already gone. Garum closed the door behind him and ran to catch up to the others.

"What *was* that?" asked Görthang.

"I have no idea," said Garum.

"I do," said Hrefna. "I think those were illusions generated by the Deeps— perhaps to help train illusionists like Sweetie in improving their skills or practicing combat." The troll mage looked at Sweetie. "Did you feel any vibrations from your wand?"

"I… I might have," Sweetie replied. "But I was too frightened at first to pay much attention."

"Perhaps you can return to that room someday and see if your illusions can interact with the illusions on the wall," said Hrefna. "You should bring the vixer with you. He seems to have an innate understanding of how the wall operates."

"I have a better idea," said Sweetie. "We could continue our quest, find the Golden Chalice, and never come anywhere *near* that room again. That black knight was unnerving."

"I'm with her," said Görthang, waving at Sweetie. "Let's get the mushroom as fast as we can and head back up the stairs without wasting time."

Garum and Sweetie left Görthang and moved several paces away to assume their usual spot in their line of march behind Hrefna.

"The Provost would be pleased if we found the Golden Chalice quickly and simply handed it to her with no questions asked," whispered Garum to Sweetie.

"Yes," said Sweetie softly, "but will we like what happens when she gets it?"

"In for a copper, in for a hundred gold pieces," said Garum quietly. "We'll just have to see. It seems like the only way we're going to be able to restore the original Golden Company."

"I don't know if I want to give back Céptianne's wand," said Sweetie. "It feels like part of me, now."

"We can sail that sea when we get to its shore," said Garum.

"*We can sail that sea* is easy for you to say," said Sweetie. "You didn't take any of the original Golden Company's artifacts. I doubt if the twins will want to give back Aubericht's shield, swords, and armor, and my guess is Drain will be reluctant to part with the Stone Prince's enchanted hammer-axe and gear."

"Nothing says we *have* to give back the Golden Company's artifacts," said Garum. "Maybe they'll be happy just to be rescued from the chest?"

"Would you be?" asked Sweetie.

"Probably not," Garum replied.

"I wonder…" said Sweetie.

"Wonder what?" asked Garum.

"Whether the Black Company would stand with us against the original Golden Company, or with Aubericht?" said Sweetie. "We're getting along quite well now, but I get the sense Görthang really wants another chance to fight Aubericht one on one, as individuals, and as the Black Company against the original Golden Company."

"But Görthang and his people are working for us," said Garum.

"Yes," said Sweetie. "But I really think we're going to want to look at the fine print of our mutual contract when we get back to the surface."

"I thought it was going to be sent to us at East Keep Town from Gold Keep Town so we could review it thoroughly before we signed it?" said Garum. "We both need to go over it with nit-combs."

"Umm," said Sweetie. "I was in a hurry to see you at East Keep Town, so I signed the contract when Görthang gave it to me without checking the details." Sweetie put her hands on her cheeks. "That wasn't smart, was it?"

"No," said Garum. "Not even a little bit."

"But we'll get through it?"

"We will," said Garum. "Somehow."

Chapter 22

Sweetie's Revelations

The red-light lamp on his forehead didn't illuminate the floor in front of Garum unless he looked down, so he focused his eyes on Hrefna's feet ahead of him. The troll mage wore big black boots with turned down tops that Garum probably could have fit his entire body inside, so they were a large target for his attention. Sweetie's news about her signing the contract without a thorough review by *both* of them had his mind spinning like the wheels of an overloaded wagon careening downhill.

How could she do that? Garum's mind screamed. He took a breath. *Face it,* he told himself. *You're more dismayed by Sweetie turning out to be less than perfect than you are about the contract.* Garum knew he was in love with Sweetie. *I've let the rose-colored haze of my emotions blind me to the reality that nobody is perfect.* He snorted. *I know I'm certainly not, and Sweetie still tolerates me. No, it's more than that. She has affection for me.* He shook his head. *Stop trying to minimize it, fool. You're in love with each other.*

"Can you forgive me?" asked Sweetie, sounding like a small child who'd stolen a honey cake meant for dinner.

"I said we'll get through it, somehow," Garum replied in a forced whisper. "But you should have known better than to sign a contract without examining its terms in detail."

"I know," said Sweetie. "But I *really* wanted to get to East Keep Town early and surprise you and I had clothing to pick up from the tailor's and…"

"It was still unwise," said Garum.

"You're right," said Sweetie. "I'm *so* sorry." She lowered her eyes to watch Hrefna's boots and walked beside Garum without saying more until they'd returned to the wide main corridor leading back to the exit to East Keep.

Garum heard Sweetie talking to herself as they walked but couldn't make out what she was saying. He thought he heard the word *fool,* but wasn't sure if she was referring to herself, or to him. After another minute, she spoke.

"Did you ever wonder how I ended up working at the Green Doors?"

"I assumed you needed somewhere to live and work where you could stay with your grandfather," said Garum.

"I *did* have a place like that," said Sweetie. "We lived on the tip of the Sleeve, just across the river from the thumb of the Mitten."

Garum knew the Mitten was a large peninsula thrusting northward between two of the Inland Seas. "And?" he said.

"And I lived with my parents there," said Sweetie. "They had an inn and I learned the business from them. It was near the ferry taking people and wagons across the river, so we had a steady trade. That was when grandfather was still a knight and counselor for various nobles on the Sleeve—before his mind began to wander."

"I didn't know that," said Garum.

"Because I hadn't told you," said Sweetie. "They were crossing the river to look into buying land for an inn on the Mitten side…"

Garum heard Sweetie's voice change as pain infused her words like adding vinegar to cake batter.

"I saw it happen," said Sweetie. "It was still in sight of the shore in deep water a long bow shot from the dock. There was a heavy wagon on the ferry, and I watched the pair of oxen yoked to the wagon pull it to one side—maybe because a dog barked. I'll never know." Sweetie sniffed and Garum touched her hand, then squeezed it.

"Did it…?" he began.

"Yes," said Sweetie. "The ferry capsized, and my parents couldn't swim. I lost them both."

"I'm sorry," said Garum.

"Sir Donal rode west from Castle Garter once he'd heard," Sweetie continued. "That's when I saw how far his own mind was gone. He insisted I was still a child of five and had to return to the castle with him. Sanchez, a retainer of the count of the Garter who came with him, told me my grandfather was released from the count's service after he'd destroyed three out of four sails on the count's most profitable wheat-grinding windmill."

"That obsession of Sir Donal's goes back a few years, then?" asked Garum.

"It's a particularly strong delusion," said Sweetie. "He thinks they're four-armed giants."

Garum held Sweetie's hand now and took long strides as they walked together.

"I tried running my parents' inn on my own," said Sweetie. "But I couldn't make enough at it to pay my town taxes. The mayor of Mittenferry offered to cover my taxes in return for a share of the inn."

I can see where this is headed, thought Garum.

"And I signed the contract he gave me without reading all the clauses."

Of course she did, thought Garum.

"Which is why I *should* have known better," said Sweetie.

Yes, she should have.

"How long did it take before he owned the inn and sent you and your grandfather off?" asked Garum.

"Only a few months," said Sweetie. "We made our way to the Keep Lands, North Keep Town, and the Green Doors on foot."

"That's more than fifty leagues," said Garum.

"And my legs felt every step of the trip," said Sweetie. "We had very little money and I had to learn new skills to keep us fed." She wiggled her fingers in Garum's grip.

Sweetie must mean she learned how to pick pockets, Garum realized.

"That's why I *should* have known better than to sign the contract with the Black Company."

Garum squeezed Sweetie's hand again and shook his head, even though he expected she couldn't see it. "It wasn't smart," he said. "But it would take hours—no, days—to list all the foolish things I've done in *my* life."

"You're not angry at me?"

"Of course I am," said Garum. He paused for a moment to inventory his thoughts and emotions, then continued. "But I also love you."

"You do?" said Sweetie. "Still?"

"People who love each other can still be angry with each other," said Garum.

"My parents were like that," said Sweetie. "They'd have an argument and then, a few hours later, they'd tell me to go outside and play or send me off on an errand for a while. But I knew why. My parents could be noisy."

"You take after them that way," teased Garum.

"You're not much of the strong, *silent* type yourself," Sweetie teased back. She squeezed Garum's hand this time.

"Be that as it may," said Garum. "I thought about it and realized that I do love you—*all* of you, wise and foolish, tender and hard, clever and…"

"…not so clever," said Sweetie. "I was hoping you wouldn't ask about the contract but know that was just compounding my foolishness. I love you, too—*all* of you—and want you to know you've got credit with me for doing foolish things of your own. I'll keep a tally for us."

"That's not a good approach," said Garum. "Partners shouldn't keep score with each other. We should support each other and help each other when we stumble, not count the piles of stones representing each other's shortcomings."

"How did you get so wise?" asked Sweetie.

"To the extent that I may be wise," said Garum, "it's from somehow surviving my own dumb mistakes, and I've had more years to make them than you have."

"So there's hope for me to improve?" asked Sweetie. "At least on contracts and business matters?"

"That probably depends on the fine print of the agreement with Görthang," said Garum. He rubbed his chin. "Come to think of it, if I'm the leader of the *new* Golden Company, could you even rightfully sign on behalf of the company?" Garum laughed, softly. "Of course you could," he conceded. "Everyone can see that you and I lead the company together."

Sweetie laughed too, at the same low volume. "When we get back to The Hands of the King, I'm going to be *so* nice to you in bed." She touched her cheek. "Oh, is that appropriate? Is it keeping score, in a way? You forgive me and I treat you like a king—Your Majesty?"

"I think we can call that a loving couple's basic reciprocity," said Garum. He hoped Sweetie could hear the smile on his face even if she couldn't see it in the dim red light of the lamps on their foreheads.

"Re-ci-proc-ity," said Sweetie, breaking the word down into its parts on her lips. "I think I'll like using that as a new euphemism for lovemaking. Want to indulge in *reciprocity* with me, my dear halfling?"

"Yes," said Garum. "And you've succeeded."

"At what?" asked Sweetie.

"At making me not mad at you," Garum answered.

"Too bad any makeup *reciprocity* will have to wait until we're out of the Deeps," said Sweetie.

Any response Garum was formulating was halted by Görthang calling to them from the front of their line of march. "We're back at the entry chamber to this level," he said. "Any idea how to get down to the next location, given that the stairs from East Keep don't go any deeper?"

"You have more experience in the Deeps than I do," said Garum. "What do you suggest?"

"Sometimes we find internal stairways," said Hrefna. "They're often near the exits leading up to the Keeps."

"Do we just start trying doors, then?" asked Prestyn. "My parents talked about moving stairways in the Deeps."

"Moving, as in switching locations—or moving as in the stairs themselves going up and down, like the ones at the Golden Dome?" asked Crank. Jelly, on top of Crank's pack, extended two tentacles and waggled the end of one up and the other down.

"ELLY!" said Vip-vip. He waved them along the curving corridor to their right until they reached a section of the inner wall marked with a double-headed arrow pointing toward the ceiling and the floor. The vixer pushed on the lower arrow and stood back as it started to flash yellow, then green. Two panels of the corridor next to the arrows slid apart, revealing a room big enough to hold a fully loaded hay wagon. Vip-vip entered the room and the others followed. Seconds later, the panels closed and Garum felt himself sinking.

"Wait," he said. "This must be a lift!"

The sound of a bell came from an unseen musician somewhere over their heads. *Bing!* The panels in front of them separated and Vip-vip led their combined parties out into a dark, gently curving corridor much like the one they'd just left.

"I wonder what level we're on?" asked Blōgot.

"With our luck, we'll be on the bottom, instead of one up from there," said Görthang.

"Only one way to tell," said Sweetie. "Start counting doors and see which level on the Provost's map best corresponds to our location."

"Good," said Garum. "If we're on the next-to-the-bottom level, there should be a door on the left about two hundred paces along the corridor leading deeper into the Deeps."

There wasn't. But there *was* a door on the right, four hundred paces farther.

"Looks like we've reached rock bottom," said Garum, after confirming the door configuration matched the map of the lowest level.

"It's not *rock* bottom," said Drain, smacking haft of the Stone Prince's hammer-axe between her feet. "The floor is still metal."

Garum decided not to belabor the point and assert his statement wasn't meant to be taken literally. They had a location where the Golden Chalice might be found to check on *this* level. Best to get on with it.

Görthang opened the door to the right and led them all inside.

Beside him, Garum heard Sweetie reciting some sort of rhyme under her breath. He smiled when he was able to make out what she was saying. It was, *"Re-ci-PROC-ity, re-ci-PROC-ity…"* repeated over and over.

Suddenly, Garum was less worried about what the Provost might use the Golden Chalice for, and more interested in simply getting safely back to The Hands of the King with Sweetie. *A halfling has to have his priorities.*

Chapter 23

Simulation

Görthang followed the Provost's map to the second possible location for the Golden Chalice Galena had specified. The floor was still damp, so everyone stayed wary about more squid-snails with their spiky shells and powerful tentacles. Drain and Chophorn held their weapons at the ready, prepared to shatter spiral shells or sever rope-like limbs as necessary.

Adventuring parties, like kingdoms' armies, are always best prepared to fight their last battles, mused Garum. *I'm less worried about more squid-snails than I am about whatever* new *menace will decide to attack us.*

The door to the designated chamber was marked with a glyph that looked like five identical circles close together, arranged horizontally. Vip-vip saw it and said, "BZZZT! BZZZT!"

The vixer's word reminded Garum of the shock-eels-on-skillets sound that accompanied the red lines joining the pie wedges and the loaf of bread in the room two levels up where they'd all nearly fallen asleep. *Maybe it's another rest and relaxation room with food logs,* thought Garum, but those were marked by five circles of decreasing size, arranged vertically. He did have some meat pies wrapped in heavy dough caskets, as such crusts were called, as part of the rations he'd ordered from the Provost's kitchens. *Perhaps we'll have a chance to enjoy them in the near future?* Garum considered. *No,* he reflected. *Better to save them for dinner if we're still in the Deeps by that time.*

"Ready, everyone?" asked Görthang. His excellent eyesight in low light noted confirming nods from the rest of the combined companies and a waving tentacle from Jelly, so he opened the door and led them inside, into a brightly lit room with a ceiling twice as high as the corridor's usual ten feet.

Garum nearly stepped back *out* of the chamber when he saw the creature perched atop what looked like a giant metal toadstool twice

Garum's height on the far wall. The creature seemed to be made of spherical segments, each the size of a fat dwarf's belly, that came in multiple colors and patterns. Each one had a pair of large, dark, oval eyes, and two insect-like legs that oddly twitched in a way that reminded Garum of a sleeping dog having a bad dream. The six upper segments of the creature were stacked vertically on the 'toadstool' with several dozen more coiled snakelike around and beside it. Dozens more spilled over the edge and trailed down to the chamber's floor.

The circular mouth of the creature's uppermost segment was sucking on a cigar the size of Garum's forearm and from the smell, Garum supposed only the outer wrapping was long leaf, since the characteristic skunky smell of burning toothed leaf permeated the chamber. To Garum's surprise, the creature removed the cigar from its mouth and spoke in a deep voice so low it made the hairs on Garum's toes stand up.

"You're here," it said. "I've been expecting you." The voice had a curious metallic quality, like the sounds emitted by the box on Vip-vip's belt.

"A giant centipede," said Xarra.

"A *sentient* centipede," said Yarra.

"More like a *bead*-ipede," said Drain. "The individual segments look like beads and the creature itself resembles some sort of colorful necklace."

"Could it be a caterpillar instead of a centipede?" asked Flisk.

"Probably not," said Blōgot. "Caterpillars are soft and this creature's segments appear hard, shiny, and chitinous."

"I am what I am," said the creature. "And as for *what* I am, I—or rather we—are *hoojahs*. We're here to test you."

"Test us?" said Sweetie. "Test us *how*?"

"And why?" asked Garum.

"I *like* tests," said Prestyn. "Especially ones with numbers."

"Save it for the classroom," whispered Crank, perhaps not as softly as he'd intended. "We don't know what it intends to test us *on*."

"We intend to test your readiness," said the *bead*-ipede.

"Readiness for combat," said the hoojah's first segment, a red one. It separated itself from the other components of its bead-like body, stood on one leg, and waved its cigar with the other. The next segment, an orange sphere, took the cigar from the first segment, inhaled deeply, and puffed out a perfect ring of smoke the same color as it was.

"You could also call it readiness to defend yourselves," said the orange sphere.

The red segment pressed a foot-hand into a spot on the surface of the metal toadstool and nineteen crimson rods, each of which appeared to be a foot long and an inch in diameter emerged from the edge of the toadstool facing the combined Black and Golden Companies. The orange segment nodded to the red segment, who pressed the same spot again, causing the rods to shoot out from the toadstool, sprout wings, and flutter-glide over to every party member like so many migrating butterflies drunk on nectar.

"Catch!" said the orange segment when Garum and the others grasped their rods as their wings retracted.

Vip-vip smiled, waved one of his human-sized arms, and shouted, "BZZZT! BZZZT!" He pointed one end of his rod at the red sphere and squeezed it. A thread of scarlet light sped out from the rod and painted a small circle on the chitinous exterior of the red bead-ipede segment, accompanied by the same shock-eels in a cast-iron pan sound they'd heard in the room two levels up. Something that sounded like a bell chimed from the ceiling above the toadstool.

The red sphere rolled to the edge of the metal toadstool, clutched both its leg-arms to the spot where Vip-vip's beam had struck it, and said, "You *got* me," with the same dramatic tone of voice Garum might have used as a child playing knights and squires with another young halfling after he'd been touched by his playmate's stick 'sword.' The red sphere then rolled off the metal toadstool and bounced twice on the floor in front of the combined companies before coming to rest and emitting a convincing death rattle, accompanied by a broad wink from its eye facing them. A rod like the ones they'd been given skittered from the red sphere toward Garum and his comrades.

Jelly extended a pseudopod and collected the red sphere's rod, so he'd have one as well.

"That was a free shot, to serve as an example," said the orange sphere. "If we shoot all of you in a quarter hour, you fail your test." It put the cigar in its capacious mouth again and blew out three concentric orange rings, each inside the previous ones, forming a sort of target. "If you shoot all of us first, you pass."

"What happens when the light from a rod hits one of you—or one of us?" asked Sweetie.

"A bell will chime, and you'll be temporarily immobilized," said the orange sphere. It detached itself from the segment behind it and like a ripple crossing a pond all the other *beads* detached and held rods at the ready.

"Wait!" said Sweetie. "There must be a hundred of you and there are only nineteen of us."

"Twenty," Crank corrected.

"Twenty of us, then," said Sweetie. "How is that fair?"

"We never said it would be a fair test," said the orange hoojah. "It's a test of your readiness to survive in the face of poor odds. Be glad there are only a hundred of us at present." It took one last puff on the cigar and put it down on the upper surface of the metal toadstool. "Now prepare to defend yourselves! We start in…"

The yellow sphere behind the orange sphere said, "One."

The green sphere, next in line, promptly said, "Two."

And the blue sphere, directly behind the green sphere, completed the count with, "Three!"

Garum shot the blue sphere before it could close its mouth. It grimaced and rolled off the top of the toadstool to join its red spherical counterpart on the floor. Ready to tuck himself into a ball and roll himself to be more difficult to hit, Garum glanced left and right, only to see that everyone in the combined Black and Golden Companies had disappeared, replaced by *hoojah*-like spheres in an assortment of primary and pastel colors. *It must be one of Sweetie's illusions,* he thought, *but I can't tell her how brilliant she is because speaking might give away my position and get me shot.*

The blue sphere's rod slid away from its body and disappeared. *More of Sweetie's doing?* mused Garum. *Probably Sweetie and Jelly combined.* He kept his head down but did see all the *hoojah* beads disconnect from their *necklace* and scatter around the chamber on their jointed leg-arms. Several of them were struck by red threads of energy, accompanied by the same distinctive sound, and fell over, unmoving. A few added theatrical 'death scenes' like the red sphere.

The top of the metal toadstool would provide a great vantage point for shooting hoojahs, Garum realized. He crawled his way to the central column supporting the toadstool and saw there was a double arrow symbol pointing up and down near its base. *A lift?* He pushed the up arrow and a door large enough for a hoojah or halfling opened. Garum entered and three heartbeats later he was on the upper surface of the toadstool. He threw himself on his belly and moved to the front edge, finding what he and his fellow slingers used to call a *target-rich environment.*

Scores of multicolored hoojahs, their thin leg-arms churning, were running around the chamber in apparent confusion, scuttling about like fat barnyard fowls chased by foxes. They weren't sure where to direct their rods to hit members of the Black or Golden Companies, who were disguised into invisibility by Sweetie's illusions. Garum saw red threads of energy shoot out from empty air, striking spheres and rendering them immobile. Bells chimed from overhead. The hoojahs sent red beams to converge where the shots had come from, but so far, it hadn't seemed like they'd hit any of Garum's friends. At least bells hadn't tolled for any of them.

Caroming off walls crisscrossing the floor with their spinning bodies trying to locate the members of the Black and Gold Companies, Garum kept his head down, allowing only his eyes and forehead to show. He extended the tip of his wand out far enough to shoot and hit ten hoojahs in half that many seconds before a close blast from a hoojah caroming off a nearby wall caused him to retreat. When he stuck his head up again, the last hoojahs had been hit and all five score of them were arrayed across the floor in a seemingly random pattern, like peas inadvertently dropped from a counter by a careless junior cook.

The other members of the combined parties transformed back into themselves as Sweetie dropped her illusions disguising their appearance. Crank and Jelly tapped their rods together in lieu of hitting palm with pseudopod.

Garum then saw the hoojahs reassemble into their original *bead*-ipede form. One of the arms of Prestyn's cloak pulled him off the top of the metal toadstool just before the composite creature could reinstall its red *head*—still somehow holding the cigar it had reclaimed from another segment—and smiled. The expression on its reflective chitinous face seemed pleased.

"Nicely done," said the first segment. "You're competent and work well together. We approve."

I'm so glad, thought Garum, though he refrained from commenting.

"We should get medals," said Púki. "And a reward."

"We'll give you a reward," said Xarra with a tone of teasing menace.

"And see you get what you deserve," added Yarra.

"No medals," said the first segment. "But please, keep your rods as tokens of your accomplishment. They will be key to providing security in your new roles."

"New rolls?" said Garum, remembering he hadn't done any real baking in weeks.

"I think it means roles as in jobs or responsibilities," said Sweetie.

"Unless we've just successfully auditioned for parts in a play," said Hrefna.

"Somehow, I don't think that's it," said Blōgot.

"We'd best be getting on with our business, then," said Görthang.

I should have said that, thought Garum.

"Remember," said the first segment, waving its cigar toward the exit. "Respect everyone, but trust no one until they've earned your trust."

"Always," said Hrefna. The troll mage kept watch on the segments of the *bead*-ipede as if to reinforce the redhead's message.

Garum slid his rod into his belt and saw the others, except for Jelly, do likewise. Feeling more optimistic about their mission after passing this unexpected test, he stepped to the door and led the Golden and Black Companies out into the corridor.

"Only one more place to look," said Sweetie.

"We hope," said Garum.

Chapter 24
Third Time's the Charm

Once they were all out of the room with the *bead*-ipedes and had made their way to a lighted stretch of corridor, Garum called a halt and checked on how everyone was doing. "Were any of you zapped by beams from the segments' rods?" he asked.

"I was," said Púki, managing to insert a tone of innuendo into two short words. "It made me a little stiff." He leered at the twins and waggled his eyebrows.

"Little being the key description, I assume," said Xarra.

"Probably *very* little," said Yarra.

"Why don't you confirm that you're in error for yourselves?" teased Púki.

"Enough!" said Sweetie. "Get a healing potion from Gêrdun if you need one," she told the short orc.

"I'd rather drink vinegar," said Púki.

"That can be arranged," said Gêrdun. He took a step toward Púki, but Lark intervened, inserting herself into the space between Gêrdun and Púki.

"You can have one of my healing potions, if you'd prefer," said the young healer-in-training.

"I'd rather have *you*," said Púki, redirecting his leer.

"You can have one of my arrows up your..." began Blōgot.

Both twins jumped in. "Can we help?"

"Settle down," said Görthang. He glared at the twins, who pretended to be suitably chastised, then he winked.

Xarra and Yarra took up stations on either side of Púki, crowding his personal space.

"Enough foolishness," said Garum. "Save it for the surface. We still have to find the Golden Chalice."

"There's only one more place to look, according to the Provost's map," said Drain. "It's one level up, if I remember correctly."

192

"True," said Sweetie, "but I don't know how to get up one level. Maybe Vip-vip can make the lift take us there?"

Garum saw Crank and Jelly waving their wands at the far end of their line of march. It seemed like they were practicing combat moves, and Garum was pleased to see the young cook and his pet—*or is it vice versa? Garum wondered*—taking combat skills seriously.

"We could take the stairs," suggested Prestyn.

"What stairs?" asked Garum.

Prestyn used several extensions from his Cloak of Arms to point down the corridor. "Those stairs," he said.

Garum saw a stairwell, well illuminated by wizard lamps, had appeared next to Crank. "How did we miss that earlier?" he mused aloud.

"We didn't have keys then," said Crank, holding the rod he'd been given by the *bead*-ipede earlier and twisting his wrist to swish it from side to side. Behind him, Jelly was mimicking Crank's motion with *his* rod held in a coil of tentacle.

Suppressing a laugh, Garum nodded. "That could be it," he said. "There's no help for it. We'll have to climb."

"It's only one flight," said Sweetie.

"We hope," said Garum.

"We'll still have to figure out where we are on the map once we go up a level," said Sweetie. "This staircase isn't marked—or at least I don't think it is."

"Once we're on the next-to-the-bottom level, we can look for correspondences to what's on the Provost's map," said Görthang.

"And we'd better hurry up about it," said Hrefna. "From what the Proctor said, the Golden Chalice has a short lifespan."

"We'd best get about it, then," said Garum.

"The journey of a thousand miles begins with the first step," said Prestyn, quoting an old proverb.

"Just so long as we're not talking about a thousand steps *up*," said Garum.

"If it's more than two flights, I'll carry you," said Hrefna. She mimed grabbing Garum by the ankles and tossing him over her shoulder.

"Let's hope that won't be necessary," said Garum. "I'd rather walk than be treated like a sack of white tubers."

"I'd be gentle," said Hrefna.

"That's my department," said Sweetie.

Reluctantly, Garum started up the stairs with the rest of the combined companies trailing along behind. To Garum's relief, there *were* only two flights of stairs. The door at the top of the second flight opened of its own accord, revealing a well-lit corridor stretching out to the left and right. Ahead of them was a blank wall, except for a broad white arrow pointing to the right. On top of the arrow was an outlined picture of a wizard's lamp with a slash through it.

"I guess we go right," said Garum.

"Since that's the dark direction?" said Drain.

"Right," said Garum.

"You already said that," teased Drain.

"We'll have to keep walking and see if the pattern of side passages corresponds to anything on the Provost's map," said Sweetie.

"Form up our defensive line of march," said Garum, "and stay alert. There must be a reason the Provost didn't fetch a Golden Chalice herself."

"Because she valued her *own* skin a lot more than she values ours," said Görthang.

I think that goes without saying, thought Garum.

Görthang and Kléppri took the lead. Hrefna, ready to throw spells, and Blōgot, ready to shoot arrows, were directly behind them. Garum and Sweetie came next, with Sweetie holding the Provost's map and looking for corridor correspondences. Sir Donal and Drain guarded their rear, with Flisk and Prestyn as archer and mage in front of them. The rest of the party filled out their line of march with the twins flanking Púki, Vip-vip beside Chophorn, and the healers in the center. Crank and Jelly shifted their positions forward and backward, as if unsure about where they wanted to be.

Crank doesn't really know where he fits, Garum considered. *Perhaps he can find out where he belongs in time.*

They passed two doors on the right, one on the left, and another on the right as the combined parties continued along the slightly curved corridor.

"There should be a passageway coming up on the left leading into a dark area," said Sweetie. "At least there should be if the map is accurate, and I've correctly identified our location."

"I wonder how many people died collecting the information needed for this map?" asked Hrefna.

"Why do you suppose any of them died?" Blōgot replied.

"Because the Provost would have sent *them* to get the Golden Chalice instead of us," said Hrefna.

"If any of them had lived," said Blōgot.

"I think she didn't want any potential competitors for power getting the Chalice," said Lark from a few ranks back. "I'm too junior to be a threat, and the rest of you don't share the Provost's goals."

"Ultimate rule of the Keeplands?" asked Garum.

"I think the Provost is more subtle than that," answered Lark. "Why rule directly when you can influence the minds of the rulers."

"You're talking about the Senior Mage of the Mages' Guild," said Prestyn.

"And the Marshall of the Martial Academy," said Xarra and Yarra in unison.

"Martial Marshall," said Púki in a sing-song voice.

"Quiet, you," said Xarra and Yarra.

"Plus the Dean of the Scholars' University," added Crank.

"And maybe a few bankers from Gold Keep," chimed in Kléppri.

"Do we *want* Galena to have that kind of power?" asked Garum.

"That *is* the question, isn't it," said Sweetie. "And what about her promise to help restore Aubericht and the others?"

"I wouldn't hold my breath about that one," said Lark. "The Provost is known for her self-interest, not her altruism."

"Unless she has a *use* for the original Golden Company," said Garum.

"I think we're proving equally useful in the meantime," said Sweetie. "If we can bring back a Golden Chalice."

"The corridor ahead is dark," said Garum. "Turn on your red-light lamps if you need them."

That task accomplished; the combined parties pressed on.

"There should be a corridor coming up leading left," Sweetie called to Görthang.

"I see it," replied the orc. "How far to the chamber with the Chalice once we turn?"

"Two hundred paces or so, if I've got the scale of the map right," said Sweetie as they reached the corridor and took it to the left.

"There's someone or some*thing* down there already," said Kléppri.

Gnomes can see even better in the dark than orcs, Garum remembered.

"What is it?" asked Sweetie.

"I'm not sure," Kléppri replied. "It's a little fuzzy."

When they got closer, even Garum could see that Kléppri was right about it being fuzzy. The being standing in the corridor outside the door where the Golden Chalice should be found, according to the Provost's map, was a giant squirrel. It was gray and taller than Garum, with a frizzy tail and a strip of extra-long fur stretching from between its extra-long tufted ears to the base of its bushy appendage. That unusual fur stuck out in all directions as if the squirrel had recently been struck by a bolt of lightning. Garum couldn't be sure in the dim light, but he thought the fur between its ears was a different color from the gray of the squirrel's body—maybe red or brown or even blue.

The combined parties approached to within a spear's length.

"Go away!" said the squirrel. "None shall pass. I am the Guardian of the Fungi, and I'm rabid. One bite and you'll die an agonizing death from lockjaw."

"I think he's trying to scare us," said Lark. "I don't see any evidence he has rabies."

"Well, I might. Sometimes squirrels are asymptomatic," said the belligerent creature.

Lark pulled a ring of thick copper wire from her belt, held it up, and looked at the squirrel through it. "Nope," she said. "No rabies."

Garum had seen battlefield healers using similar copper rings in the past, but he didn't realize Lark had one.

"I still have big teeth and claws," said the squirrel.

Görthang smiled, revealing his own large incisors. He pulled one of his swords from its scabbard, waggled it at the squirrel, then resheathed it.

The squirrel flipped its tail in a gesture Garum interpreted as *I get your point, big guy. And I'm not interested in getting the point of your sword anywhere near my body.*

"What are *you* doing here?" asked the squirrel in a deep voice after regaining its equilibrium. It chittered after its words in some sort of squirrel-ish affectation, or as a show of bravado.

"Looking for mushrooms," said Görthang. "One special mushroom in particular."

"You can't have a Golden Chalice," said the squirrel. "They're mine. I've been waiting for them all year."

"We were sent to get one," said Görthang.

"By the boss healer?" asked the squirrel. "She always wants a Chalice, but I make sure to eat them before she can get them."

"I didn't know squirrels *ate* mushrooms," said Crank, who had moved up close to the front of the line of march with Jelly.

"Squirrels eat everything," said the squirrel. "Is that thing on your shoulder edible?"

Jelly adjusted his body into a ball shape then separated into two hemispheres, showing a huge maw lined with sharp teeth.

"Never mind," said the squirrel. "I guess he's wondering the same thing about me."

"Jelly isn't for eating," said Crank. "Who and *what* are you," he asked the squirrel, "if you don't mind the question?"

"If you can't tell *what* I am, you're dumber than a fungus," said the squirrel, "but as for *who* I am, the name's Chátter, short for Chátterjee. Who might you crowd be?"

Since it no longer seemed like Chátter was likely to fight them, Garum introduced the members of the party with all due politeness, explaining his own role last.

"You're a cook?" asked Chátter.

"I am," said Garum.

"And a good one, too," added Crank.

Garum nodded to Crank, pleased that the young man was over his rivalry.

"Can you cook mushrooms?" asked Chátter.

"In dozens of different ways," said Garum.

"How about sautéed with pine nuts in a cream sauce?" asked Chátter.

"Of course," said Garum. "Though I don't have any pine nuts with me."

"That's no problem," said Chátter. "I have nuts to spare."

Xarra and Yarra giggled while Sweetie rolled her eyes.

"How about this," said Chátter. "If there's one ripe Golden Chalice, it's mine. But you can have the others if you'll cook up some smaller mushrooms for *me*."

"Done," said Garum. "What are the odds of more than one being ripe?"

"You can never tell," said Chátter. "Some years it's just one, some years as many as five."

"Let's hope it's not one," said Garum.

"Agreed," said Chátter. "I wouldn't want to fight you for it."

"Because you'd lose," whispered Drain.

Sweetie turned back to the dwarf and made a shushing motion with her finger.

"If there's only one," said Garum. "We'll give you some delicious honey cakes."

"Honey cakes?" said Chátter. "Golden Chalice mushrooms are good, but if there's only one, there's always next year."

"Excellent," said Garum. "I assume they're on the other side of that door?" He pointed to the outline of the portal Chátter was guarding.

"Correct," said the giant squirrel. "Do you have black bags?"

"We do," said Garum. He motioned to Xarra and Yarra, who handed him two bags each. Chátter bowed to Garum and wiggled the tips of his tufted ears.

"You're going in alone?" asked Sweetie.

"I'm going in with Chátter," said Garum. "We have an understanding. If I don't come out and he does, he won't get honey cakes or sautéed mushrooms."

"You're in good paws," said Chátter. He opened the door, and Garum entered with the squirrel right behind him.

I'm glad Chátter didn't go first, thought Garum. *I'd have a face full of tail.* Garum smiled, thinking of times with Sweetie where that description would also apply.

The door to the chamber shut behind them and in the dim illumination of the red wizard lamp strapped to his forehead, Garum could make out a long table filled with rich soil. The air around him was humid and filled with the musty scent of dried dung and fungi. Lots of small mushrooms dotted the surface of the table like small heraldic charges strewn across a shield. Four tall stalks a foot high and several inches in diameter were evenly spaced along the length of the table. They had broad caps that had begun to invert and each one was lit by a deep yellow aura that seemed to come from inside their flesh.

"Wonderful!" said Chátter. "It's a good year!"

"Is one enough for you?" asked Garum.

"I suppose," said Chátter. "If you will cook me up some of the small mushrooms and add in a honey cake."

"Gladly," said Garum. "Is there a special way to collect a Golden Chalice?"

"Cut them off near the base with a sharp knife, or front teeth," said Chátter. "Leave the tendrils in the soil to grow back next year. The caps will finish turning up into chalice form over the next few hours, even after they're cut."

The squirrel collected a few dozen of the smaller mushrooms in a mesh bag that Garum hadn't noticed before, because it was made from twine the same gray color as Chátter's fur.

"Good to know," said Garum. He set to work with his knife and three of the four black bags, carefully placing one Golden Chalice in each bag.

Chátter cut his Golden Chalice off with his teeth and held it delicately in his front paws.

"Do you want a black bag for yours?" asked Garum.

"No," said Chátter. "I'll eat it here." The giant squirrel started nibbling on the mushroom from the base up. By the time the last of the cap was consumed, he'd begun to glow with a soft golden light of his own. "Delicious," announced Chátter. "Worth waiting a year for."

As Garum watched, Chátter grew several inches until he was taller than Garum and his tucked-in tail added another two feet above that. "Let me guess," said Garum. "Before you started eating Golden Chalice mushrooms, you were a typically sized squirrel?"

"What's typical?" asked Chátter. "I'm the height that I am—and right now I feel full of energy, enough to take those three Golden Chalices away from you and eat them, too."

"I wouldn't advise that," said Garum. He held the black bags tightly in his left hand and pointed the tip of his knife at Chátter with his right. "I killed three highwaymen—two orcs and a human—on the way to East Keep Town, and I have no qualms about separating your tail from your torso if you give me cause." *I didn't actually* kill *them,* thought Garum, *but the squirrel doesn't need to know that.*

The tops of Chátter's tufted ears twitched and his tail swayed from side to side before snapping back into position directly behind him. "Sorry about that," he said, eying Garum's knife. "Eating a Golden Chalice always makes me think I'm invincible. Tell me about these honey cakes."

Garum had to shake his head at Chátter's rapid change in attitude. "I'll do better than that," Garum told Chátter. "I'll give you a honey cake as soon as we get back out in the corridor."

"Thank you," said Chátter. "There's something about the smell of the fungi nursery that makes my fur stand on end."

How can he tell? thought Garum. *His fur always looks like it's standing on end.*

"Come on," said Chátter, moving to the door. "We don't want to be here when the Guardian comes back."

"I thought *you* were the guardian of the chamber," said Garum.

"Oh, no. I'm just an opportunistic thief trying to steal a Chalice. The real Guardian is truly terrifying."

"If you say so," said Garum as he followed Chátter out into the corridor. "I've got three Golden Chalices," he told the other members of his party. "Please give Chátter a honey cake."

Sweetie handed the long-tailed rodent one of the sweet confections and Chátter bit into it, then smiled.

"Delicious," he said. "Could use nuts, though."

"I sometimes put slivered almonds in my honey cakes," said Garum. "But we were given these by the Provost's bakers. I'm not sure what they include."

"Maybe some acorn flour would improve the flavor," said Chátter.

"I'll mention that when we get back to East Keep Town," said Garum.

"Can we leave now?" asked Hrefna. "Those mushrooms are supposed to have short lifespans."

"I don't see why not," said Garum, though he wasn't looking forward to climbing back up all those stairs.

With little warning, the walls and floor began to vibrate, as if being struck by the massive clapper of a gigantic bell. Garum watched his friends glance left and right, wondering what the vibrations signified. He didn't have to wait long for an answer.

"That's the Guardian," said Chátter. "Time to go." He scampered off down the corridor at high speed, leaving tiny bits of honey cake behind him like a trail of breadcrumbs.

"Form up," said Garum.

"And move out," added Görthang. "Whatever that Guardian is, we want nothing to do with it!"

"I'll second that," said Drain.

They sped back to the stairway Crank's key had unlocked and descended.

Chapter 25
The Guardian

Garum looked over his shoulder as they hurried down the stairs. The walls and the stairs themselves were vibrating with greater intensity and the thudding, kettledrum-like booming behind them was growing nearer. A shadow of a massive creature with four tree-sized limbs appeared on the wall beside the topmost stairs.

"Run!" said Drain from her position in the rearguard.

"We're moving as fast as we can," called back Blōgot. "These stairs are steep!"

They're twice as steep for me, thought Garum. *Nobody thought of halfling's legs when they built them.*

A bellow akin to the roar of an ancient dragon with a tooth-ache filled the stairwell and now the thud of heavy feet echoed only yards behind the combined companies.

"What *is* it?" cried Sweetie.

"I can't see anything," replied Drain.

"Neither can I, granddaughter," said Sir Donal. "But fear not—I'll smite it and defeat it even if it's the size of house."

"If it's that big, they should be able to see it," said Sweetie, half to herself and half to Garum. "I'll fall back and see if it's cast some sort of illusion."

"Please don't," said Garum. "We shouldn't stop moving until we've made it to the bottom of the stairs and closed the door behind us."

"You're probably right," said Sweetie. She shouted back along the line. "Be careful, grandfather! Let us know if you *do* see any threat!"

They heard no cry of alarm from Sir Donal and reached a broad landing at the base of the stairway without any of them tumbling over each other in their haste. Görthang, assisted by Blōgot, tried to wrestle open the door blocking their exit to the lowest level of the Deeps, but that portal was locked.

"We're trapped!" shouted Púki.

"Quiet, you," said Xarra, whose words were reinforced by her sister's finger-wagging an inch in front of the short orc's nose.

The hair on Garum's arms stood up when the bellow of an old dragon in need of a tooth extraction repeated at an even higher volume. It seemed to come from somewhere *inside* the party.

"Where *is* it?" asked Sweetie.

Four ponderous footfalls akin to a giant smith striking a granite mountain with a marble hammer echoed around the landing like peals of thunder.

Garum shook his head in an unsuccessful attempt to stop his ears from ringing and spotted a small gray creature the size of a mouse near his feet. He stepped back and considered the beast in earnest.

Its proportions were all wrong for a mouse. Its legs were more like the great battle unicorns who grew their own armor he'd seen depicted in block prints or the huge snake-nosed pachyderms carrying castles on their backs he'd come across in old bestiaries. Legs as big as tree trunks didn't make sense on something the size of a mouse.

The entity beside Garum's feet was built like a centaur, with a pair of arms as strong as legs hanging off shoulders that made blacksmiths' arms look like pieces of string. Topping its relatively wide shoulders was a saucer-shaped head resembling a ball of dough compressed before baking into flatbread. The creature took a step toward Garum, and the thunder echoed again. The sound was definitely coming from the odd-looking new arrival on the floor below him.

Wait a second, thought Garum. *The creature isn't gray—it's bright pink. It's wearing a gray tabard.* Garum squinted and squatted. *The tabard is some sort of herringbone pattern that keeps shimmering in and out of focus.* Garum rubbed his eyes, stood back up, and pointed toward the floor. "We have company," he said.

"And *you* have my Golden Chalice mushroom," came a voice that was a hundred times too loud to be reverberating out from something its size.

"You're the Guardian?" said Sweetie.

"I am," boomed the creature. "My name is Thumpthudder Maxsenex, but you can call me Thud. Return the Golden Chalice, and I won't trample you all into a flat paste spread across the metal of this landing."

"That's quite a boast for someone so small," said Kléppri, who—as a gnome—had issues regarding his own size.

"I may be small, but I'm mighty," said Thud. "I won't smite you—yet, but I'm more massive than I seem. See if any of you can lift me."

Sweetie quickly designated the three strongest members of their combined parties: Hrefna, Görthang, and her grandfather, to make the attempt. The troll mage leaned over and cupped both hands around Thud, then straightened her back, or tried to, but Thud remained as firmly on the floor of the landing as if he'd been carved from its substance.

"I don't understand," said Hrefna. "I can't sense any enchantment, but I can't lift him."

"You'll never lift me," said Thud. "I contain multitudes—and have no need for magic."

"Let me try," said Görthang. He removed one of his scabbarded swords from his back and tried to use it as a lever to lift Thud, using a thick, triple-baked travel biscuit with the consistency of solid stone as a fulcrum.

Garum refused to make such biscuits, since in his experience they were more likely to break teeth than break fasts.

Görthang pushed down on his sword, using the extra leverage to magnify his strength, but he had to stop when he could tell his blade was coming dangerously close to snapping. "What *are* you, Thud?" he asked.

Are you dense? thought Garum about the orc and his question. Görthang was smart—smart enough to use a lever—but was missing the point. Thud *was* dense, so dense he couldn't be any sort of normal being.

"I came here from a far distant land tens of centuries ago," said Thud. "The only thing preserving my long life is an elixir I prepare using the macerated flesh of the Golden Chalice. Without it, my life will end."

"We can spare him one, can't we?" Sweetie asked Garum.

"I don't see why not," said Garum. "I also don't want to risk being turned into a flat paste on floor, and I have a feeling Thud isn't exaggerating his capabilities in that regard. We haven't even been able to lift him, after all."

"Let *me* try," said Sir Donal. "I never got the chance."

"If Thud doesn't mind," said Sweetie. "Would you be willing to give my grandfather a chance to lift you?" she asked the small, but immensely heavy individual. "He has enchanted vambraces that greatly increase his strength."

"Give it your best, Sir Donal," said Thud. "I've never had someone with strength-enhancing magic try to lift me."

Sir Donal squatted in front of Thud, nodded to him to confirm it was acceptable to make the attempt, and gently slid his hands around the left and right sides of Thud's body. "One, two, *three,*" said the old knight.

At first, nothing happened. Then Sir Donal's vambraces began to glow, radiating golden light that filled the landing. Thud was more surprised than anyone when he felt himself rising, held carefully in Sir Donal's hands, and presented to Sweetie. "My strength is as the strength of ten thousand, because my heart is pure," he said.

"He's only strong because of those vambraces," Hrefna muttered softly to Görthang.

"Maybe so, my friend, but he *could* lift him," Görthang replied.

"There must be something in the enchantment that negates Thud's weight," whispered the troll mage.

"How... *how* did you *do* that?" Thud asked Sir Donal. "No one here has *ever* been able to lift me before. Only people from my far-off home have ever managed it before."

"It's like he's defying gravity," said Prestyn.

"Would you like me to put you down?" Sir Donal asked Thud.

"I think that would be wise," said Thud. "I don't know what would happen if I fell from a great height."

"You're only three or four feet off the ground," said Púki.

"Quiet, you," said Yarra this time. The sisters were about to toss Púki into the air, but Thud called out to stop them.

"I'll do it," he said. "Despite Sir Donal's unprecedented feat of strength, I need to demonstrate my own prowess to show you why you have to surrender your Golden Chalice to me."

Sir Donal put Thud back on the floor and the small, pink, centaur-like being thumped his way over to the twins and the short orc. While everyone watched, Thud used one of his arms to grab Púki by the heel of his boot and lift him six inches off the floor. With what seemed like negligible effort, the small being tossed Púki into the air, spinning him four times before his buttocks smacked against the ceiling. The short orc fell, only to be intercepted by the twins on his way down.

"Nice," said Xarra to Thud.

"Better than we've managed," said Yarra. "Best we've done is *three* spins."

"Thank you for the compliment," said Thud, "but back to important matters. Will you give me the Golden Chalice voluntarily, or will I have to beat it out of you?"

Garum considered saying, "You and what army," but after seeing just how strong Thud was, he kept silent.

Sweetie answered instead. "We'd be glad to give you *the* Golden Chalice," she said, making it seem like they had only one, not three. Sweetie put a black bag holding one of the special mushrooms on the floor by Thud and he set off back up the stairs, making the vicinity shake with his every step.

"Thank you," said Thud over his broad shoulder as he climbed. "And guard the other two Chalices with your lives. Don't allow them to be used for evil ends."

"So much for your attempt at deception, making Thud think we only had *one* Golden Chalice," Garum whispered to Sweetie.

"It was worth a try," said Sweetie. She raised her voice and called after the Guardian. "Any advice on how to open the door?" she asked.

"You need a key," said Thud, turning his saucer-shaped head over his other shoulder this time.

"I'm on it," said Crank. He removed the rod he'd been given in the room filled with *bead*-ipede segments from his belt and touched it to the door in front of him, causing it to slide open noiselessly, revealing what seemed to Garum like endless flights of stairs leading up. "A piece of pie," said Crank.

"Don't *say* that," Drain told Crank. "You're making me hungry."

"And it's cake, not pie," said Arrex.

"He can say pie if he wants to," chimed in Lark. "I know we're healers, but we can still be creative, not prescriptionists."

"I think you mean *proscriptionists*," said Arrex.

"I meant what I said, and you're missing my point," said Lark.

"I like pie *and* cake," said Crank, "but I can stick to the more common idiom if it will make you happy."

"Next time I have access to a kitchen, I'll make plenty of cakes and pies for all of us," said Garum.

"Savory or sweet?" asked Xarra.

"The pies, not the cakes," added Yarra.

"Both," said Garum. "And I knew you meant the pies. Can we please go through the door now? I shouldn't have to remind you that Golden Chalices have a finite lifespan. We don't want to have gone through all this trouble only to have the Provost tell us the relevant fungi are past their prime."

"Assuming we actually decide to give her a Golden Chalice," said Hrefna.

"Why wouldn't we, if we've already gotten this far?" asked Kléppri, the gnomish warrior.

"Because we don't trust her," said Gêrdun. "At least *I* don't. She expelled me from the Healer's College."

"The way I heard it," said Lark, "you were thrown out for smashing your potion instructor's head through a slate board *and* the wall behind it."

"Maybe so, but she deserved it," said Gêrdun.

Lark shook her head, then turned away.

"There are worse places to get a concussion and broken skull bones than inside the College of Healers," said Arrex.

"The fact that the instructor was fine the next day after drinking two healing potions does not mitigate the poor judgment of Gêrdun's actions," said Lark. "The Provost was right to expel you."

"She just doesn't like ogres," said Gêrdun. "And *this* ogre doesn't like her, either."

"Can we *please* get on our way to the surface?" asked Garum. "You all know I hate climbing stairs even more than most of you do, but we can discuss what to do with the Chalices at a much higher landing."

"Fine," said Görthang. "Form up, everybody—and lift those knees."

"Whatever," said Púki in a tone of voice that made him sound like a petulant youth.

"Oh no you don't," said Xarra.

"We can see right through you," said Yarra.

"You're trying to tick us off enough," said Xarra.

"That we'll carry you," said Yarra.

"It was worth a try," said Púki.

"Why don't we drag him, instead?" asked Xarra.

"By his legs," said Yarra.

"So his head will bounce on every step," said Xarra.

"Works for me," said her sister.

"I can walk," said Púki.

Cheered by the twins' byplay, Garum squeezed Sweetie's hand and began to climb.

Chapter 26

Steps to a Decision

Garum had tried counting steps to distract himself from the big decisions ahead, but lost track when he'd made it over a thousand because Sweetie had gotten a bit ahead of him and it was more interesting to watch her than to count. "Let's talk while we climb," he said to the others. "We need to figure out what to do…"

"Regarding the Provost," said Sweetie.

"And the original Golden Company," added Görthang.

"Aren't they interconnected?" asked Hrefna. "The Provost *did* say she'd help restore Aubericht and the others."

"I don't know how much I'd trust her about that," said Lark. "She told me I had to do everything I could to get you to bring her the Golden Chalice without delay, but I have my own reservations about giving it to her."

"Because?" asked Arrex.

"Because Galena is only interested in what's good for Galena and she'd lie without a second thought if it would get her what she wants," Lark replied. "And because I don't think what's good for Galena is what would be good for the Keep Lands."

Garum envied the effortless way Lark seemed to gracefully glide up the stairs with minimal effort. *I wonder if she's part elf,* he thought. "It's good to know you're not her spy," he told the young healer.

"But she thinks I am," said Lark. "She's making my graduation from the College contingent on my obedience, but my ultimate loyalty is to the profession of Healing, not to the Provost."

"We can be expelled students together," Gêrdun told Lark. "If the Provost kicks you out because you wouldn't spy for her, you can start your own college, and I can be your first student."

"You *are* good enough to teach classes, not just take them," Arrex told Lark. He put his arm around her shoulder as they ascended and he smiled at her, receiving a smile in return.

Garum lifted his knees and took the next four steps two at a time to catch up with Sweetie and squeeze her forearm. They exchanged smiles as well and Garum felt a small portion of the boundless energy of youth Lark exhibited flow into his tired calves. "How bad do you think it could be?" he asked Lark.

"If Galena got the Golden Chalice?" said Lark. She shook her head. "Pretty bad, actually. I told you I think she could use it to craft a potion that would allow her to influence other leaders of the Keep Lands. She could end up as a *de facto* dictator, ruling from the shadows."

"That sounds like a very good reason *not* to give her a Golden Chalice," said Blōgot.

"What are our alternatives?" asked Görthang.

"Could *you* make the same kind of potion the Provost was going to brew up and use it to control *her*?" asked Gêrdun.

"I probably could," said Lark, "if I had my copy of *Principia Potio Nostrumque* I'm sure I could make one."

"I have a *PPN*," said Gêrdun. "I *liberated* it on my way out of the College."

"I can go one better," said Arrex. "I have *your* copy. You loaned it to me last semester and I'm so sorry, but I forgot to return it. I've got it in my backpack."

"*You* had it?" said Lark. "I wondered where it had gotten to. I had to borrow a copy from the College library."

Arrex kept his eyes on his feet as he climbed. "I said I was sorry."

"You probably kept it to have a reason to see Lark again," said Xarra.

"Because you're sweet on her," said Yarra.

"Thanks a lot," said Arrex. "You two are like the younger sisters I never had—and never wanted."

"Insults," said Xarra.

"He gives us insults," added Yarra.

"It's not like this is news to Lark," said Xarra.

"Look how red her face is," said Yarra.

"Look how red Arrex's face is," said Xarra.

In near perfect unison, Arrex and Lark asserted something clearly untrue, especially to anyone with functioning eyes and the proper vantage point. "My face is *not* red!"

They'd just reached a broad landing about halfway up to the surface by Garum's estimation. He called a halt to rest his legs and give Lark and Arrex a few minutes to recover from the others' teasing. He was surprised to see the two young healers ascend a few steps and sit side by side with their heads together, talking softly, while the others arrayed themselves around the inside walls of the landing, leaning back. Some even closed their eyes for a quick nap.

After less than half a dozen minutes, Lark and Arrex stood and addressed the rest of the combined companies while holding hands.

"Lark thinks she *can* replicate the potion Galena had planned to brew up," said Arrex. "She'll need some standard cooking equipment…"

"…I can provide what you need in that department," said Garum, mentally inventorying the contents of his pack.

"I was counting on that," said Lark. "It won't take me long—just an hour or so, especially if Garum helps me with the chopping and dicing."

"I'll be helping, too," said Arrex.

"Let me know what I can do to assist," said Gêrdun.

"I'm expecting *you* to handle the pulverizing," said Lark.

"Something I'm good at," said Gêrdun.

"I'm sure," said Lark. "I'll use one Golden Chalice to make the influence potion."

"And the other for the growth potion needed to restore Aubericht and the others inside the chest," said Arrex. "That will take another hour."

"Are you sure you can do what's necessary to make them?" asked Hrefna.

"Lark is the best student with potions in three generations," said Arrex. "The professors even ask her for advice. She can do this."

"I'll try my best, anyway," said Lark. "The Provost had asked me about making an influence potion, so I know what she'd planned to brew up."

"What about the growth potion?" asked Görthang. "I'm not all that fond of Aubericht, but I *do* want to cross swords with him again. There wasn't a clear victor the last time our blades met."

"That one's actually easier than the influence potion," Lark replied. "The Golden Chalice's natural tendencies are to increase and enhance. Increasing height is much more straightforward than increasing suggestibility."

"Like Chátter growing into a giant squirrel," said Flisk.

"Let *me* have some of the growth potion, then," said Púki. "I'm tired of being short."

"You're enough of a pain already," said Xarra.

"There's no sense in making you a bigger one," said Yarra.

"Every male in the Keep Lands wants a bigger one," Púki asserted.

Garum nodded to the twins and they crowded around Púki, convincing him to pipe down, at least temporarily. For himself, Garum was at peace with his own size *and* his male equipment. *Sweetie hasn't had any complaints, at least,* he thought. He remembered old stories about halfling heroes drinking beverages prepared by sylviants and growing taller than dwarves—tall enough even to ride horses—but wrote those off as literal *tall* tales told by ancient gaffers drinking ale around an inn's crackling fireplace after the harvest was in.

"Sounds like a plan," said Sweetie.

"There *is* a problem, though," said Lark. "A challenge, really. Or two challenges to be accurate."

"What are they?" asked Sweetie.

"First, how do we get Galena to *drink* the influence potion—and second, who drinks the influencer's version of the potion?"

"Influencer's version?" asked Garum.

"The one who is doing the influencing," said Lark. "It has one extra ingredient. The primary version isn't so much an influence potion as a susceptibility to influence potion."

"We'll need to get the Provost to drink the susceptibility version?" said Sweetie.

"Yes," said Lark. "But who do we trust to drink the influencer's version?"

Garum was surprised when everyone's eyes turned to him. "Not me," he said. "I don't want that kind of power."

"And that's exactly why *you* should have it," said Hrefna. "I wouldn't trust myself with it—and I certainly wouldn't trust Görthang with it."

"Agreed," Görthang replied. "I wouldn't trust me with it, either."

"What about Sweetie?" Garum suggested. He turned to Sweetie and saw she was pointing at him with the index fingers of both hands and vigorously shaking her head rejecting Garum's suggestion.

"No way," she said. "I'd trust you with drinking the influencer potion much more than I'd trust myself. There are too many people I'd like to *influence* to jump off cliffs."

"Present company excepted, I hope?" said Garum.

"Of course," said Sweetie, giving Garum a smile and a small curtsy.

Garum looked at the individuals assembled around the landing and those standing a few steps up the next flight of stairs leading to the surface. One by one, they nodded as his eyes held theirs. "You're sure about this?" he said.

"We're sure," said Hrefna. "Just remember one thing…"

"With great power comes great responsibility?" asked Garum.

"No," said Görthang. "Just don't fuck it up."

"Understood," said Garum. "Now, what cooking gear are you going to need—and will any of these potions cause my pots permanent damage?"

* * * * *

The potion-making process proved much simpler than Garum had expected. Lark directed him and her other assistants with the same skill Garum brought to organizing a kitchen to cook a five-course banquet for forty senior military officers. They only had to make the equivalent of three dishes, rather than twenty, though the recipe for each dish—or rather, each potion, took at least two dozen steps. Lark had most of the necessary ingredients in her pack, but asked Garum for honey, salt, and a few spices, such as sage, thyme, and mint leaves.

"I only have dried mint leaves," Garum told Lark. "I hope they will still be effective."

"Mint leaves aren't essential to the formulation," said Lark. "The mint—and the honey—are to make it taste better."

Garum noticed Gêrdun paying close attention to his conversation with Lark and hoped that meant the taste of the ogre's own healing potions might soon improve.

Hrefna filled three small metal bowls with flames using her magic and Garum put one of his nesting pots on a lightweight tripod supporting a pot above each bowl. After completing his chopping and dicing duties, Garum watched Lark work her healers' magic.

"What else goes into these potions?" asked Garum, "beyond macerated Golden Chalice mushrooms, of course?"

"The smaller the number of people who know that, the better," said Lark. "The growth potion for Aubericht and his team includes seeds—the exact type doesn't matter—but they're there to encourage the *clarks* to help whoever drinks the potion grow, like seeds grow after they're planted."

"What are clarks again?" asked Garum.

"They're like mages' mites and dwarves' masons," Lark replied. "Tiny animacules that do the actual work of healing. When I craft potions, I try to attract clarks and let them know what I want them to do."

"It's much the same for mages," offered Hrefna. "We are guiding the mites that work magic with our wills."

"What about illusion magic?" asked Sweetie. "Does my wand use mites?"

"I expect so," Hrefna replied, "though I've heard the tiny creatures associated with illusions are called *lulus* instead of mites. They're reputed to be the tricksters of the magical zoo and delight in fooling people."

"No wonder you're so good at using them," said Garum.

"You'd better be teasing me," said Sweetie.

"I am," said Garum. He put his arm around Sweetie's waist and gave her a gentle squeeze. A giant cat's head appeared in front of Garum's face, and a raspy feline tongue extended and gave

Garum's cheeks a bath. He wiped his cheeks with the hand that wasn't on Sweetie's far hip and marveled. "My face is *wet*. How did you manage that?"

"I think I remember someone saying I was good with illusions," said Sweetie.

"Excuse me," Lark interrupted, "but before the two of you need to find a room, could I have some help getting these potions into bottles, please? I can pour from the pots, but it would be better if someone held the bottles steady, so we don't lose even a drop."

"I can do that," said Garum.

"So can I," said Sweetie.

"Allow me," said Prestyn. He stepped closer to Lark and her bubbling pots, giving his Cloak of Arms an opportunity to grab a dozen tiny potion bottles at a time and hold them steady as Lark poured from the first, second, and third pots.

The bottles were only the size of Garum's index finger and Lark's smallest pot only held enough bright red liquid to fill one of them. "That's the influencer potion?" Garum asked as Prestyn's cloak smoothly found a cork stopper beside Lark and expertly inserted it into the open mouth the bottle. Lark nodded, remaining focused on her work.

The middle-sized pot contained a deep blue liquid, enough to fill six small bottles. "Those are for the people you'll need to influence," said Lark. "Starting with Galena." She began filling bottles offered by Prestyn's cloak. "You'll want to drink the red potion first, to help encourage Galena to drink a blue one."

"And after she drinks a blue one?" asked Garum.

"She'll pretty much do whatever you command," replied Lark.

"Don't get any ideas," said Sweetie.

"You mean like giving *you* a blue potion?"

"Why waste one?" teased Sweetie. "Most of the time I'll do what you want, if you ask nicely."

"And vice-versa," said Garum with a smile. "Who are the other five blue potions for?" he asked Lark.

"I'm not sure," said Lark. "We can guess how the Provost planned to use them, on the Senior Mage of the Mages' Guild, the Marshall of the Martial Academy, the Dean of the Scholars' University, and probably the current head of the Bankers' Syndicate at Gold Keep, but since you don't plan to rule the Keep Lands from behind a curtain, I guess we'll just have to wait and see."

"Maybe you can use one the next time a monster of the Deeps wants to eat us?" suggested Prestyn as his cloak put corks in the six new bottles.

"Excuse me, good monster," said Arrex, who'd been close at hand observing Lark. "Before you eat us, could you please drink this blue potion? Thanks ever so much!"

Lark laughed, and so did Prestyn, Garum, Sweetie, and even Gêrdun.

"Too bad it isn't a contact potion," said Garum. "We could spray it on a monster."

"Wait," said Lark. "It *is,* sort of. It's much more effective if you drink it but would still have some effect if you got even a little on your bare skin."

"Good to know," said Garum.

Lark and Prestyn started filling bottles from the largest pot. The liquid was a bright green this time.

"Green for growth?" asked Garum.

"Correct," said Lark, keeping her focus on pouring. This time, a dozen bottles were filled and corked.

"There are only seven members of the original Golden Company," said Sweetie.

"So we'll have five extras," said Lark. "Are you sure you don't want to be a foot taller, Garum? It would only take a drop or two."

"No thank you," said Garum. "I'm happy with my current height. As halflings go, I'm even on the tall side."

"I'm tempted," said Sweetie. "I've always wanted to be taller—but after all these years, I'm used to being short, so I'll skip a drop of green potion."

"I'll drink a whole bottle," said Púki, who'd been following the conversation from ten feet away. "It would be nice to be a tall orc instead of a short orc."

"If you drank an entire bottle, you'd be twenty feet tall," said Lark. "You wouldn't like being a freak."

"I don't know about that," said Púki. "Especially if my equipment was proportionately larger. What would happen if I put a drop of green potion down there?"

"Then your lovers wouldn't need a magnifying crystal to find it," said Xarra.

Yarra slapped her sister's back and the two started whispering and giggling. Garum thought he overheard a reference to hummingbird's eggs. Púki closed his mouth and retreated out of reach of the twins.

Sweetie had used her wand of illusions to generate a soft light and was inspecting all nineteen bottles. Lark was about to transfer the bottles to a bandoleer covered in loops specifically designed to *hold* potion bottles when Sweetie stopped her with a question. "The potions are clear," she said. "What happened to the bits of Gold Chalice?"

"They dissolved," said Lark. "With help from the clarks. You can't sense them, but I can. There were huge clouds of clarks around each pot and now they're swarming like midges in a marsh around each potion bottle."

"Really?" said Sweetie. "I sometimes feel like there's a fog around me when I project illusions. Do you think that might be the *lulus?*"

"Probably," said Lark. "But I can only speak for healers' magic."

"I can sense them," said Hrefna. "Your wand of illusion draws mites, or lulus, or whatever you want to call them. Some mages think all the tiny creatures are the same and we just give them different names when they're used by different kinds of practitioners, by I really don't see the point of making such distinctions, so long as magic works, enchanted objects remain enchanted, and healing potions heal."

"At the University there are charts with the different sorts of mites and how they relate," said Crank. "At least I'm told that's the case."

More confirmation that Crank was originally from the Scholars' University, thought Garum. He helped wash and put away the pots used for potion making.

Hrefna extinguished the flames in the small bowls before collecting them and stowing them in her pack. "Time to go?" asked the troll mage.

"I expect so," so Garum. "Everyone's had a good rest, at least." *His own calves no longer felt like they were burning as hot as the flames Hrefna had generated to cook potions.*

"We'll have a problem when we get to the top," said Sweetie. "We won't have a Golden Chalice to give to Galena so she'll see us and Garum can influence her."

"Didn't I tell you?" said Lark. "We *do* have a Golden Chalice. It turned out I only needed one to make the potions."

"Good to know," said Garum. *That should make things easier,* he thought. *At least I hope so.*

Chapter 27
Under the Influencer

An armed squad of six of the Provost's proctors met the combined Golden and Black Companies five levels below the surface. They carried short swords, small round buckler-style shields the size of dinner plates, and truncheons that looked like they could easily club into submission any student with the temerity to object to one of the Provost's edicts. The squad leader stood her ground as Görthang, in the vanguard, reached the landing where she and her fellow proctors stood.

"It's about time you got here," the squad leader announced. "Hurry it up, the Provost is waiting for you."

"And a good day to you and yours, as well," said Görthang. "Next time your boss needs something retrieved from the lowest levels of the Deeps, you should volunteer for the role."

"That's not our job," said the squad leader.

Garum could see that she was relatively young, not much more than Sweetie's one score and four, so he understood why she was adopting a hard attitude toward Görthang. It was too easy for the orc warrior, with his fierce appearance, to intimidate others. He smiled when Görthang responded to the squad leader.

"Then get out of the way so we can get to the surface and give Galena what she wants."

"You'll give it to us and be on your way," said the squad leader. She managed to keep her face looking stern until the twins, and Púki, began to giggle.

"Take a look at the size of our party compared to yours," said Hrefna, lowering the pitch of her voice to add more menace. "We're the Black Company—and the Golden Company. Both of our companies have fearsome reputations. Those reputations wouldn't be improved by tossing the six of you into the stairwell and having you fall to your deaths, so I suggest you either turn around and head to the surface as fast as you can manage or prepare for battle."

The other squad members looked at their leader then turned and trotted up the next flight of stairs. "We will announce your arrival to our superiors," said the squad leader.

"You have chosen wisely," said Hrefna.

The squad leader turned on her boot heel and sped up the stairs to rejoin the other proctors. Sweetie waved goodbye to the leader's departing back.

"You could have offered to arm wrestle her for the right to go up the stairs first," Hrefna told Sweetie.

"Only after I borrowed my grandfather's enchanted vambraces," Sweetie replied.

"You could have used your illusions to make your grandfather look like you," offered Garum.

"Where's the fun in that?" asked Sweetie.

"It *might* have been a good opportunity to drink the influencer potion and see if your enhanced persuasive powers could convince them to simply let us pass, without any need for intimidation," said Lark.

"That brings up a good point," said Garum. "When should I drink the potion? Does it need time to take full effect?"

"It should start working in minutes," said Lark. "Five at the most."

"And how long will it remain effective?" asked Garum.

"I thought you understood," said Lark.

"Understood what?" said Garum.

"The influencer potion's effect is permanent—or at least quite long-lasting."

Garum's eyes went wide like a fawn caught in the light of a wizards' lamp. His jaw dropped. Then his eyes shifted left and right, like a fox casing a hen house. He rubbed his palms together and a sound like *heh heh heh* came from deep in his throat. "Permanent?" said Garum. The sounds he was making shifted into maniacal cackles.

"Are you well, my friend?" asked Drain.

"Permanent persuasive *power!*" said Garum. "And it will be mine. All *mine!*"

"Nice try," said Sweetie. "But it won't work. I see what you're doing."

"It was worth a shot," said Garum, who had abandoned his attempt to project megalomania as fast as he could put a lid on a stew pot.

"Once we've dealt with the Provost, I can research techniques for countering the effects of the influencer potion," said Lark. "I would appreciate a favor from you first, however."

"Name it," said Garum.

"I'd like you to influence the Provost to let me graduate early," said Lark.

"If anyone deserves that, you do," said Arrex, nodding to Lark. "The Provost should have given you graduate's robes a year ago, but she wanted to keep you around to make potions for her."

"I wasn't unhappy to keep taking classes and labs," said Lark. "And I simply *loved* caring for patients. Dealing with all the self-serving projects Galena assigned me has been my challenge, however."

"It's time for you to graduate," said Arrex. "You can join us as we explore the Keep Lands."

"Join *you*, you mean," said Lark with a smile. She took Arrex's hand. "That sounds like a lot of fun, actually."

"I'm glad you think so," said Arrex as he hugged Lark.

"Less talking and more stair climbing," said Görthang as he started up toward the next level. "We don't want that squad leader wondering where we got to."

"I'd be glad to exert my influence with the Provost on your behalf," said Garum. "After we get to the surface."

"You might as well drink the influencer potion now, then," said Sweetie. "It could make it easier when we talk to the squad leader again."

"Or her commanding officer," added Görthang.

"Onward and upward," said Garum. Lark handed him the small bottle filled with red liquid as they climbed. He was tempted to drop it and let it smash on the stone stairs but pulled the cork and downed it in one gulp instead. Garum immediately felt energized, as if he'd had a bottle of Lark's healing potion instead of this disturbing influencer potion. His calves stopped hurting and he could feel a spring in his step that hadn't been there since the first three levels he'd climbed on the way up.

"How are you doing?" asked Lark.

"I'm doing great!" said Garum. Just saying the words made him feel even better. *I must be influencing myself,* he considered. "Should I be feeling this good?" he asked the young healer.

"I don't know," said Lark. "This is the first time I've ever made *any* of these potions."

"Now she tells me," said Garum to the universe and no one in particular.

"It does make sense that your mind's ability to influence your body should increase," said Lark.

"I'll give it a try," said Garum. "You're not tired at all," he said, noting that everyone who could hear him up and down the stairs seemed to move with lighter steps. Soon, the stairs ended and the squad of proctors, plus a contingent of door guards, blocked their way. "Let us pass," said Garum. "Escort us to the Provost's office."

The door guards opened the door to the surface and the squad of proctors formed up to lead the way across the campus of the College of Healers. "Follow us, please," said the squad leader. "The Provost instructed us to take you straight to her chambers."

Garum nodded to Lark and Sweetie then followed the squad with the rest of the combined companies behind him.

* * * * *

Lark moved beside Garum on his left as they walked and handed him the black bag holding the last Golden Chalice they'd harvested. She also pressed one of the small bottles filled with blue liquid into his palm and watched as he slid it into his belt pouch.

Garum spoke so that only Lark, and Sweetie, on his right, could hear him. "You know the Provost best," he told the young healer. "Should I go in alone or take a few others with me?"

"Galena likes to feel in control," said Lark. "I think she'd be more comfortable one-on-one. I'd hand her the bag with the Golden Chalice, then get her to share a toast with you to celebrate a task well done and slip the blue potion in her wineglass."

"What if she has others with her?" asked Sweetie.

"Then Garum should invite the same number to join *him*," said Lark. "I doubt Galena will have any of her staff with her, though. She doesn't trust many people."

"And we don't trust *her*," said Garum.

"That's wise," said Lark as Sweetie nodded her agreement.

They reached the College's administration building and left most of their party on the ground floor while Garum, Sweetie, Lark, and Görthang, representing the Black Company and providing a potential intimidation factor, rode up the lift to the fourth floor. Their little group was met by the same dark-haired woman with a blue streak in her hair and senior healer's tabard who'd occupied the Provost's outer office on their previous visit. The woman, indicating Garum with a wave of her hand, said, "You can go right in."

"Thank you," said Garum. "Be sure we're not interrupted." The door to the Provost's office was partway open and he could see Galena was alone, standing a few feet inside. He entered and heard the woman with a blue streak pull the door shut behind her. Garum thought he heard a lock click as she did so. He took in more details of his surroundings this time. Galena had a large couch and three comfortable armchairs along the far wall in addition to her huge desk.

"I see you were successful," said the Provost as she indicated the black bag Garum held.

"We were," said Garum. He tried using his most persuasive tone of voice to say, "And I think we should share a toast to celebrate."

"Give me the bag," said Galena.

Garum extended the black canvas sack to her and allowed her to remove it from his loose grip. He spotted what he'd hoped to see on a table behind the Provost's desk. "You've got glasses and a decanter of what I hope is good wine," he said. "Share a toast with me."

"No toast," said Galena as she crossed to behind her massive desk and gracefully lowered herself into a high, well-padded chair. "And *sit down*," she added.

To his surprise, Garum hoisted himself up and sat in one of the two uncomfortable-looking human-sized wooden chairs opposite the Provost's desk. He shook his head. *Didn't the influencer potion work?* he wondered. *I knew I should have tested it more.* "You really should share a toast with me," he tried again.

"And *you* should give me the doses of influencer potion Lark made," said Galena. "Hers are probably better than what I could have crafted, anyway."

"What makes you think Lark did any such thing?" asked Garum, afraid he knew the answer.

"The way you're trying to use a persuasive *command* voice to influence me," said Galena. "That means you must have taken an influencer potion yourself. You didn't know I'd already taken an influencer potion three years ago. That was the last time my proctors successfully harvested a Golden Chalice. Unfortunately, it was too old by the time they brought it to me, and I could only get one dose from it, so I used it to improve my own ability to influence others."

"That explains a few things," said Garum.

"Like how I was able to solidify my control of the College of Healers at such a young age?" said Galena.

"And why you're so insecure about it."

"I'm *not* insecure. If anything, I have to take care to avoid over-confidence."

"Is that the reason you haven't let Lark graduate?" said Garum. "You're so confident you have to hold back excellent students so you can continue to exploit them."

"I'm not exploiting Lark," said Galena. "I'm using her skills effectively for the greater good."

"The greater good?" said Garum. "Don't make me laugh. You really mean for your own benefit. Lark is better than you in *so* many ways. She has more talent at making potions than you ever will—and more, she truly cares about others."

"I care about others," Galena responded. "When they do as they're told."

"Were *you* ever good at doing what *you* were told?" asked Garum.

"Yes, more's the pity," said Galena. "I was a good little student, the teachers' lapdog, always ready to wash pots, chop herbs, and distill tinctures for the faculty. I never stood up for myself and found myself doing what everyone *else* wanted, never what *I* wanted. When I tried to stand up for myself I was bullied and belittled by fellow students and faculty members who told me I was worthless and only good for serving *them*."

"I'm sorry," said Garum.

"I'm not," said Galena. "You don't need to know the details, but after I realized what they were doing—or more to the point— what I was doing to myself, I stopped being a length of carpet."

"And having others walk all over you?" asked Garum.

"Indeed," said Galena. "I promised myself I wouldn't be good at doing what I was *told* but would be the one doing the telling, instead. I researched various influence potions and used them to help me rise at the College. The potion made from the Golden Chalice is the most powerful and most effective. It's how I've gotten to where I am as Provost. I *never* want to be in a position of being told what to do again."

"So you mistreat others because you were mistreated?" said Garum. "That doesn't sound like responsible leadership. If one of my assistant cooks was being bullied, I'd put the bullies on garbage detail and would make it clear they'd be keeping that assignment until they changed their ways and apologized."

"Running the College of Healers isn't the same as cooking dinner," said Galena.

"Leading is leading," replied Garum. "I expect a lot of your students and faculty would rather have one of my meals than have you as Provost—at least without the power of your influence potion."

"I doubt that," said Galena.

"But how would you ever know?" asked Garum. "As soon as I found out the influencer potion was permanent, I asked Lark to find a way of reversing its effects. My friends thought I should be the one to drink it because they knew I didn't *want* that sort of

persuasive power. You, on the other hand, sought it for yourself."
He slid off his chair, stood up, and prepared to leave.

"Wait," said Galena. "What makes you think a dose of influencer
potion is permanent?"

"Lark seemed to think so."

"Lark is misinformed," said Galena. "The potion's effect is long-
lasting, but it does wear off over time. I could feel my control over the
faculty and proctors waning. That's why I sent you into the Deeps."

Garum stood up, stared at Galena and shook his head. "I'm
glad to know the potion *isn't* permanent—and now you've *got*
a Golden Chalice mushroom. We've done what you asked and
delivered it to you. We won't even hold you to your promise to
restore Aubericht and the others. We'll just be on our way, and
you can get on with building walls around yourself until you feel
safe—not that you ever will."

"Sit down," said Galena. "You're not going anywhere."

Garum remained standing. "Remember, influencers can't
command other influencers. I did what you said earlier out of
politeness and because I wasn't prepared to resist. Now I am."

"You *will* give me the potions Lark brewed," Galena insisted.
"I'm realistic enough to know they'll be better than mine. The
clarks seem to love her—why, I don't know."

"I will *not*," said Garum. "And the fact that you can't see why
Lark is a natural healer is confirmation that you're not one. You're
perverting the College into a place for preserving and expanding
your own power rather than serving its proper mission to heal
the world."

"Big talk from a small man," said Galena. "I can have twenty
proctors here in five minutes to *make* you give me Lark's potions."

"And I can have eighteen seasoned adventurers from the Black
and Golden Companies here just as fast," said Garum. "You'd
need a hundred proctors to stand a chance of taking us in a fight."

"I have twice that number of proctors at my command," said Galena.

"And how many of her fellow students would come to Lark's
aid if she called?" asked Garum. "Probably thousands."

"I could influence them to stay in their rooms," said Galena.

"And *I* could influence them to defend her," said Garum.

"Not if you're in a jail cell."

"You'd have to gag me so I don't order my jailers to release me."

"That wouldn't be a problem."

"Tell you what," said Garum. "I can give you one of Lark's potions as a token of good faith, then discuss matters with the rest of my party and see how they feel."

"I'll take the potion, but it's a weak leader who can't make a decision on his own."

"Alternatively, it's a strong leader who gets advice from his people and builds consensus before acting." Garum removed the bottle filled with blue potion from his belt pouch and hopped back up on the seat of the visitors' chair, so he was able to face Galena eye to eye across her desktop. With the dexterity of a skilled halfling slinger, he thumbed the cork from the bottle and tossed its contents into Galena's face, staining her forehead, nose, cheeks, lips, chin, and neck a deep blue.

"You little dastard!" shouted Galena.

"It's no big deal," said Garum, not raising his voice. "Nothing to worry about in the slightest."

"You're right," said Galena. She watched Garum, as still as a dog resting beside a fire, and made no move to even wipe her face.

The woman with the blue streak in her hair called to Galena from the outer office. "Is everything alright?" she asked.

"Tell her everything is fine," said Garum softly.

"Everything is fine, Perga," said Galen. "I'll let you know if I need you."

"Very good," said Garum, pleased that the influence potion *did* work well even when applied externally, not internally. Lark was right about that, as she was about most things relating to her area of expertise.

Garum sat down and held Galena's eyes with his own. "Now," he said, "tell me what you've done and plan to do to gain control of the Keep Lands."

"With pleasure," said Galena. She wiped a line of blue liquid from her cheek with her finger and licked it clean. "It started several years ago when…"

Garum took paper and quill from Galena's desk and began to write.

Chapter 28
Yew Called

After he'd filled a page with the Provost's words, Garum told Galena to request Sweetie, Lark, and Görthang join them. He needed more of his friends to hear what Galena was saying and his hand was cramping from writing for much longer than it took to scribble out a list of comestibles for a supplier. Half an hour later, after the others had entered and found seats of their own, Galena returned to recounting how she'd arranged the previous expedition to get a Golden Chalice.

Lark tapped Garum on the shoulder and whispered in his ear. "We need to craft potions from the Golden Chalice in the bag right away," she told him. "It will soon be too old and we might have uses for more potions."

"Good idea," said Garum. "I'll have Galena order the rest of our combined company to her office and you can make the potions here while we keep listening to her plans."

"Thanks," said Lark. "After watching Galena, I may even have some ideas on how to make a potion that counteracts the influencer potion, in case you decide you want to take it later."

"Make two bottles," said Garum. "We should give one to Galena first."

"That makes sense," said Lark.

Sweetie had taken over Garum's work as a scribe. She was still taking notes about Galena's plans, which had gotten up to two years ago, when the others arrived. Crank helped set out the same pots and Hrefna lit fires to warm them as she'd done earlier. Three hours later, Galena's recitation had finished and Lark had more bottles filled. Two were yellow this time.

"What now?" asked Sweetie as Galena looked at Garum, awaiting further orders.

"Now I tell Galena to move to her couch, drink the yellow potion, and try to get a good night's sleep," said Garum.

"What will *we* be doing in the meantime?" asked Görthang.

"Making our way to Yew Keep Town as fast as possible," said Garum.

"The fastest way would be by magecoach," noted Sweetie.

"Let me rephrase," said Garum. "Making our way to Yew Keep Town as fast as possible with*out* using magecoaches."

"I'll see about hiring ponies and horses," said Görthang.

"Excellent," said Garum. "Make it so."

"Your wish is my command," said Görthang, making a grin that showed off his impressive canines.

Blast it, thought Garum. *It's going to take some time for me to get used to my new persuasive powers. I hope the yellow potion works as Lark expects on Galena. We'll have to wait for word from one of Lark's friends to reach us with details on Galena's reaction. I'll be glad when I can take it.*

* * * * *

Garum was decidedly *not* pleased when Görthang reported there weren't any ponies or horses available for hire. Most healers, he'd discovered, traveled in a sort of magecoach called a RedX that was painted white with a wide red stripe along both sides and in the center of the top and back, forming a red cross on white in the center of its rear doors. The RedXes had long, enclosed decks behind a passenger compartment big enough for six humans, designed for moving injured individuals. Görthang had hired three former RedXes, repainted in black, to transport their combined companies. They moved using the same magic that powered magecoaches, and Garum wasn't ready to climb aboard one.

"I'm *not* getting in a coach without horses again," he protested. "I was attacked, Sweetie was injured, and our driver fell from her seat and needed a healing potion the last time I rode in one."

Sweetie and Görthang wanted to tell Garum he was acting like the back end of the animals magecoaches and RedXes didn't require, but his influencer potion's power wouldn't allow them to force him aboard. Lark, however, had her professional manner to fall back on.

"Have a sip of this, Garum," she said holding out a stoppered vial. "It's good for general anxiety and will relax you."

"That *does* sound useful," said Garum, who was wise enough to recognize when he was being unreasonable. *I'm not going to walk to Yew Keep Town, after all,* he told himself. "What is it?"

"Tincture of chamomile and willow bark," said Lark, "I mix it with honey and take it myself when the Provost wants me to make her special and sometimes questionable potions."

"Sounds like just what the healer ordered," said Garum, who'd used those ingredients himself for a similar effect.

Garum popped the cork on the vial and tasted its contents. He sensed a hint of poppy oil as well and wondered what Lark wasn't telling him. *I'm not going to use my influence to have her tell me the complete formulation,* thought Garum. *That would be like me revealing one of my own secret recipes.* Garum tilted his head back and drank the contents of the far-from-vile vial. *Not bad,* he considered. Then, after the ingredients began to work on him, his opinion changed. *This is really good. I'm feeling great. If I had wings I could fly to Yew Keep Town.*

Sweetie and Lark were whispering and Garum could overhear them, but their actual words seemed unimportant.

"Do you think it's working?" Sweetie asked.

"Oh, yes," said Lark. "Look at his eyes. He's flying."

"Don't want to fly over Yew Keep Town," said Garum after a yawn. "Archers would think I'm a bird and shoot at me."

"Yes, that's true," said Lark. "You can lie down and rest and you'll be safely in Yew Keep Town in no time."

Sweetie nodded to Lark and took Garum's hand, encouraging him to step up into the back of a RedX coach and rest on one of the couches there.

"Couches on coaches," said Garum. "At least this isn't a magecoach."

No more than twenty breaths after he was horizontal, Garum was asleep. Sweetie sat on a bench beside Garum as the repainted RedX rolled.

* * * * *

Garum yawned and opened his eyes to see Sweetie smiling down at him. They were alone in the back of one of the repurposed RedXes.

"Did you have a nice nap?" she asked.

"You mean, 'Did Lark's potion knock me out?'" said Garum. "The answer, obviously, is *yes.*"

"I'm glad you're not angry at her," said Sweetie.

"Her potion was just what I needed," said Garum. "I've been stressed ever since I took that influencer potion, afraid I'd inadvertently tell one of my friends to go jump in a lake and they'd drown."

"Xarra and Yarra are good swimmers," said Sweetie. "They swam in the pond on their farm and would be glad to rescue anyone who jumped in a lake and couldn't swim."

"Nice to know," said Garum. "Now I need to test my influencer powers. Kiss me."

Sweetie's hands squeezed into fists. "Not until you say *please.*"

Good, thought Garum. *She* can *resist my influence when she wants to.* "Please," he said.

Sweetie kissed him, which did a lot more to help Garum wake up.

"Would you have kissed me even if I hadn't influenced you?" he asked.

"I'd planned to," said Sweetie. "Somehow, it was easier to delay following your instructions than not follow them."

"Duly noted," said Garum. "These influencer powers have limits, thank goodness."

"Not that I'd mind being under the influencer," teased Sweetie. "Or on top of or side by side with or…"

"I recognize the landscape you're painting," said Garum. "Save that thought."

"I will," said Sweetie, "and I'm glad you went with landscape instead of still life. I don't plan to keep still."

"I don't either," said Garum. "By the way, where are we?"

"Outside Fletchers' Inn," replied Sweetie.

"In Yew Keep Town?"

"How did you guess?"

"Fletchers make arrows," said Garum. "An inn with that name is most likely to be in the keep famed for its bows, arrows, and archers."

"Blōgot recommended Fletchers," said Sweetie. "She said there's another inn to consider, but it gets a rowdy crowd."

"Let me guess," said Garum. "Quarrels?"

"That's right," said Sweetie.

Garum levered himself up on his elbows then shifted to a sitting position. Sweetie stayed beside him with her arm around his shoulders. They kissed again without any hint of influence from Garum's new abilities. "Have we heard anything from back in East Keep?" asked Garum after he recovered from the delights of shared osculations.

"No," said Sweetie. "And I don't expect to hear anything until tomorrow morning at the earliest. It will take that long for Lark to get word from her sources."

"Is it wise for us to stop only one keep away from East Keep?" said Garum. "Should we push on to Horse Keep and put more distance between us and Galena?"

"We need to rest," said Sweetie. "Not all of us have been sleeping."

"Can't we sleep on the way?" said Garum.

"Blōgot wants more arrows," said Sweetie, "and so does Flisk. We're staying overnight in Yew Keep Town."

"I guess I could pick up more stones for my sling as well."

"In the morning," said Sweetie. "For now, you're taking the first watch, since you slept on the way here."

"Will you be waiting for me to come to bed when I've finished standing watch?"

"I'll be asleep," said Sweetie. "Though with the right incentive, I won't throw you out of bed if you wake me up."

"I'll have to contemplate suitable incentives while on guard duty," said Garum.

"I'm sure you'll come *up* with something," said Sweetie, patting his lap.

"You're making it *hard* to focus on standing watch," teased Garum.

"I don't know if I'll be awake enough to do anything standing," said Sweetie, teasing back.

Garum was spared from replying by a loud triple knock on the coach's door.

"Is he up yet?" called Drain. "Blōgot's got rooms for us, and the innkeeper says our dinner is ready."

"He's up," said Garum. "And he's hungry. Lead the way."

"As you wish," said Drain.

I'm really going to need to be careful with my phrasing, thought Garum. He opened the coach's door, hopped down to the street, and assisted Sweetie with her descent.

Drained waved toward the entrance to the inn, which was marked by a double door underneath a pair of arrows as big as Chophorn was tall and as wide around as Garum's thighs. The points of the huge arrows rested on granite blocks on either side of the doors and the fletched ends almost met to form a triangle above the lintel.

Garum wondered what sort of bird had feathers large enough to fletch the oversized arrows and decided it would be wise to be wary and watch the skies when walking the streets of Yew Keep Town. He'd seen great eagles try to carry off puppies and didn't want to risk a similar fate.

Garum noticed the inn itself was three stories and stretched out for a considerable distance to the left and right of the entrance. It had something of a shaggy look, being covered in what he took to be cedar shakes that reminded him of certain types of boiled leather armor. *No, the armor looks more like pinecones, these are just shingles covering the walls as well as the roof,* he realized. *My brain must still be foggy from the poppy juice in Lark's potion.*

Sweetie tugged Garum through the door that Drain was holding open for them. The delicious smell of roasting goose came from inside, reminding Garum that he was hungry. *Goose feathers and cedar shafts are the raw materials of the fletchers' art,* thought Garum. *It only makes sense to find them here together.*

"Blōgot says the stuffing is particularly tasty here," Sweetie told Garum. "And they have marvelous ways of preparing asparagus."

"There's only one good way to prepare asparagus," said Drain. "Steamed, with butter."

"I can't disagree," said Garum.

"I *love* asparagus, but don't like the way it makes my pee smell," said Sweetie.

"Bogberry juice can help with that," said Garum.

"Good to know," said Sweetie.

They ate in a private room off the inn's common room. The walls of the private room were covered in assorted types of bows, from the small, recurved bows favored by horse archers to the tall longbows able to send dozens of clothyard shafts in a dark rain against opposing armies. A few crossbows were interspersed among the other bows, but Garum guessed they'd be featured more prominently at Quarrels.

Dinner was roast goose, asparagus, mashed white tubers with parsnips, mushrooms, and large yellow onions cut horizontally and baked until they were tender. Garum thought the onion slices looked like what archers shot at and resolved to serve them next time he cooked a special feast for archers himself. The food was plentiful and Garum took care not to eat too much so he'd be able to stay alert while on watch later that evening. He wrapped a handful of small cakes in a napkin for later. One of the servers told him they were made with a flour from the southern islands and appropriately named *arrowroot* biscuits. Perhaps he'd find a way to use that flour in his cooking in the future.

In addition to the usual knives, forks, and spoons, each place was set with narrow, polished slivers of cedar, like arrow shafts that tapered down to points. Garum watched Blōgot and Flisk use theirs like tongs to pick up morsels and convey them elegantly to their mouths. Even Jelly extended pseudopods to try them, though it was somewhat disconcerting to watch asparagus spears appear to float inside Jelly's transparent protoplasm.

"Any idea where I could buy some good bullets for my sling?" Garum asked Blōgot halfway through their meal.

"Yes," said the orc. "There's a big emporium in town specializing in all things related to archery and missile weapons."

"I've heard of it," said Flisk. "It's got an apt name and a clever sign in a red and white concentric rings pattern."

"Right," said Blōgot. "Its full name is long and complicated, but everyone in Yew Keep Town just calls it Target."

"That hits the mark," said Garum. "I'll look for lead and clay slingers' bullets in the morning while you get more shafts."

"I'll give you a shaft tonight, my dear," said Görthang, showing his fangs.

"If it pleases me," Blōgot responded, exposing her own fangs as well. "And if you learn how to ask nicely."

"When am I not nice?" said Görthang.

After that, laughter circulated around the table like platters of tasty sweets being passed.

Soon, dinner was over and Blōgot got one of the innkeeper's assistants to escort them to their rooms—all of which were on the same wing of the inn's third floor. "The better to defend ourselves, if necessary," said Blōgot.

"I'll take first watch in the hall as soon as I see Sweetie settled in for the night," said Garum.

"Better leave the door open so we're not tempted to keep you from your guard duties," teased Sweetie.

Garum gave Sweetie a hug and several kisses, then moved a chair from their room out into the hall. Lark's relaxation potion ensured he was well-rested, so he wasn't worried about falling asleep in the chair. Two hours passed without any threats appearing and soon Crank and Jelly took Garum's place in the hall while Garum climbed into a comfortable featherbed with goose-down pillows and snuggled with Sweetie. He still had energy and teased Sweetie about her quiver, but she didn't push him out of bed. Sometime later, they were both sleeping the sleep of the happily sated.

Loud knocking, like a giant banging a massive mattock on the door to their room, woke them both up faster than if they'd been drenched with ice water.

"I tried to stop her," shouted Crank through the door.

"Let me *in!*" came a voice that sounded familiar. "We have to talk!"

Sweetie found her wand of illusions and had it at the ready as Garum stepped warily to the door, threw the bolt, and opened it.

Galena, the Provost of the College of Healers, stood in front of him looking like she'd just run all the way from East Keep Town pursued by a mob carrying torches and pitchforks. The panic in her eyes was palpable. "Please!" said the Provost. "You've *got* to help me. You're my only hope!"

Garum turned his head enough to catch Sweetie's eye. She nodded. "Come in," he told the Provost. Galena did.

Chapter 29
Horse of a Different Color

"Thank you, thank you, *thank you!*" said Galena as she held Garum's hand with the strength that might be expected from a drowning woman clutching a rope tossed from shore. "They've all turned against me, and I've barely escaped with my life."

"The students are after you?" asked Sweetie.

"No, not the students," the Provost responded. "The proctors—and the faculty! They want to beat me with truncheons and pointing sticks!"

"What did you do to provoke them?" asked Garum.

"Better to say, 'What did *you* do?'" answered Galena. "When you gave me the potion that negated my ability to influence them, all their pent-up resentments against me and my policies boiled up to the surface and exploded."

"I can understand unhappy proctors," said Sweetie. "Every one of them likely resented you using them as your secret police. What I don't understand is what made the *faculty* members so angry?"

Crank, who'd been standing by the door, stepped in and provided his guess at an answer. "The faculty must be furious at every perceived slight stored up since you first took an influencer potion and began to boss them around," he suggested. "In academic circles, the smaller the pond, the larger the conflict," Crank added. "Other members of the faculty must have been quite jealous of you holding a position of authority at a young age without *paying your dues,* as some of them must have seen things."

"You're right about that," said Galena. "Academic ponds can be minuscule in area, more the size of chamber pots than ponds at all."

"And smelling as sweet," said Crank.

This is still more evidence of Crank's connection to the Scholars' University, Garum mused. *I'll have to get back to that later, though. For now, I'd better stick to interrogating Galena.* "You had the faculty dancing to your tune for half a decade, Galena. What made them shift from unthinking obedience to wanting your head on a pike so quickly?"

"It's part of the influencer's enchantment," said Galena. "Faculty members, and the proctors' senior officers, are very strong-willed and used to getting their own way."

"Petty tyrants," said Crank.

"Exactly," said Galena. "Each and every one of them. Suppressing their natural inclinations by influencing them to do what *I* wanted was like erecting a dam in front of the rivers of their wills. Over time, more and more water accumulated behind their dams."

"Which is why you were so anxious to get a new dose of influencer's potion quickly," observed Sweetie.

"When you had me drink the yellow potion to negate the influencer enchantment," said Galena, "it was less than an hour before I was nearly washed away. I had to leave East Keep Town with just the clothes on my back."

"How did you escape?" asked Garum.

"On my horse," said Galena. "Zura is *very* fast and was bred for speed by the best breeders in Horse Keep Town. She's three times faster than any magecoach."

"Sounds like quite a horse," said Garum. "Where is she now?"

"In the stable here at Fletchers'," said Galena.

"I didn't even know this place *had* a stable," said Garum.

"Of course it has a stable," said Sweetie. "A large inn like this one would certainly have a stable. Trust me, I know. I was in the inn business."

"Right," said Garum. *And I'd rather be back* in *this inn's featherbed with Sweetie.*

"What do you want from *us*?" asked Sweetie.

"Protection," said Galena.

That makes at least some sense, thought Garum. *We're a very strong combined party of adventurers.* "For how long?" he asked.

"Until we get to South Keep Town," said Galena. "The Marshall of the Martial Academy owes me and should be able to defend me, assuming the Healers' College faculty and proctors are angry enough to follow me that far. The important thing is staying ahead of the mob."

"Does that mean the streets of Yew Keep Town will soon be filled with angry Healers' College faculty and proctors carrying torches and pitchforks?" asked Garum.

"Along with barrels of tar and sacks of feathers?" added Crank.

"Not exactly," said Galena.

"What, then?" asked Garum, not realizing he was using the power of the influencer potion.

"They're not carrying torches because they have wizard lamps," said Galena.

"Also, because it's not even dark yet," said Crank.

"And they don't have pitchforks," Galena continued.

"Pitchforks are more of an agricultural implement," said Sweetie. "They're not something you'd expect faculty members to have at hand."

"I *told* you," said Galena. "They have pointing sticks. They want to *beat* me with them!"

"What are pointing sticks?" asked Garum.

"They're like extra-long wands," said Crank.

"You must have seen them," said Sweetie. "Teachers use them to point at lessons written on slate boards."

"And they're flexible, with a lot of snap to them," said Galena. "I don't want any of them snapped across my back or buttocks."

"Now I know what you mean," said Garum. "My halfling school instructors just used hickory switches for pointing *and* punishment."

"What about the tar and feathers?" asked Crank. His eyes were wide at the prospect of excitement and Jelly, who'd been sitting in his usual position on Crank's shoulder, extended a pair of pseudopods and began to clap.

"They may be bringing tar," said Galena, "but they don't need to bring feathers. Everyone knows Yew Keep has so many goose feathers they bring in a lot of coin selling pillows and mattresses stuffed with them."

Garum saw Crank's eyes grow wide at the prospect of actually *seeing* someone tarred and feathered. *The boy's still young,* Garum mused. *He hasn't had a chance to realize that some things are better to imagine than to truly see or do.* Garum grinned on the inside. *The same can be said for several shared acts of intimacy.* Garum's attention was jerked back into the here and now as Sweetie changed the subject and focused on the crux of Galena's situation.

"Why should we protect you?" she asked. "What's in it for us?"

"Money," said Galena. "I can pay you handsomely for your services after I sell Zura back to her breeders in Horse Keep Town."

"She must be quite a horse," said Garum. "We're not cheap."

Sweetie winked at Garum, and he saw her mouth the words, *Speak for yourself.*

Now Garum let his grin show on the outside.

"Zura *is* quite a horse," said Galena. "You'll understand why when you see her."

"I expect we will," said Garum.

"I can pay you in more than coin," said Galena. "As the Provost of the College of Healers, I know everyone who is anyone in all sixteen keeps. They all owe me favors, or know *I* know things about them they don't want spread around."

"So you can help compensate us for our protection by blackmailing people into helping us?" said Garum.

"I wouldn't put it that way, but yes," said Galena.

Sweetie tilted her head and Garum could see from her expression that she thought Galena might have something worthwhile, if a touch unsavory, to offer them. Laughter showing at the corner of her eyes also made it quite clear she understood that Galena had triggered Garum's protective instincts.

"We'll get you safely to South Keep Town," said Garum, "but after that, you're on your own."

"Thank you, thank you, *thank you,*" said Galena, inadvertently repeating what she'd said when she'd first entered. She went to her knees in front of Garum, so she was the same effective height as he was and hugged him so hard he felt the air pressed out of his lungs.

"Hey there," said Sweetie. "No one hugs Garum like that except me."

"Sorry," said Galena as she broke the embrace, stood up, and stepped back. "I was just so relieved."

"I'll take a hug, if you're offering," said Crank from the doorway. Jelly, on his shoulder, extended two pseudopods and waved them like a pair of arms to welcome Galena closer.

Garum sensed Galena had temporarily dropped her mask of control when she'd hugged *him* but had resumed that mask when she'd realized hugging Crank and Jelly wouldn't provide the same sort of catharsis.

Galena shook her head and held up her hands. "Sorry, no," she said. "One hug is more than enough."

Garum heard Sweetie mutter under her breath. "I'll say."

"I'm not really a hugger," said Galena.

She seemed like enough of one when she hugged me, thought Garum. Then he remembered the rumors about Galena's amorous appetites and took solace in knowing he was far from the Provost's usual type.

Crank yawned.

"It's late," said Sweetie, realizing it would soon be time for Kléppri to replace Crank on watch.

"Good point," said Garum. He turned to Galena. "Let's get you to bed," he said.

"What?" said Sweetie as she glanced at the bed she and Garum had both recently occupied.

"Not *here*," said Garum. "Have her sleep in Hrefna's chamber. A powerful troll mage should be able to protect her slumbers."

"I'm not going to knock on Hrefna's door and wake her up," said Crank. Jelly was shifting the top third of his pyramidal form left and right in shared negation.

"And you're not taking Galena to Hrefna's room on your own," said Sweetie. "We'll both go."

Kléppri chose that moment to appear in the doorway beside Crank. "What's going on?" asked the gnome. "And what's *she* doing here?"

"It's a long story," said Sweetie. "We'll fill you in at breakfast."

"Now we have to wake Hrefna, so she can guard Galena," said Garum.

"Good luck with that," said Kléppri.

* * * * *

Breakfast was quite good and featured slices of day-old bread dipped in a beaten mix of goose eggs, fresh cream, and spices, then grilled in clarified butter.

"This is delicious," said Yarra as she drizzled honey over a generous helping of the dish.

"Umm-hmm…" added Xarra in affirmation.

I think I can taste allspice, thought Garum. *I'll have to add some the next time I make fried soaked bread. Usually, I just serve it with berries, but that way I can prepare it when berries are out of season.*

Sweetie was eating cooked oat porridge along with her bread. Between mouthfuls, she paused to smile at Garum, lifting Garum's mood each time.

Hrefna was eating a sausage the size of Garum's forearm, delicately carving it into bite-sized pieces with an eating dagger large enough for Garum to use as a sword. Beside the troll mage, Galena was eating fried bread with an exuberance Garum could only ascribe to relief at her successful escape on horseback from an angry mob.

So far, no one at Fletchers' seemed to have recognized the Provost.

For all that Galena was into acquiring and expanding her power, she hadn't been one for self-aggrandizement, Garum considered. *Her face isn't well known. It's not like she had statues of herself erected all over East Keep Town or coins minted with her visage.*

"You there," said Galena, using her fork, to point at a server delivering a heaping platter of bacon to the table where the members of the Black and Golden Companies were seated. "More honey. Now."

If her face isn't likely to be recognized, her supercilious manner may well identify her, thought Garum. He used the command voice he adopted with junior cooks in military kitchens and influenced Galena to literally change her tone. "Be nice," he told her.

"My apologies," Galena told the server. "If you have a chance, we'd appreciate more honey. Please tell the cook everything is excellent."

The server's gaze shifted from Galena to Garum and back again. He nodded and retreated into the kitchen.

"If you could be so kind," said Görthang to Prestyn. "Would you please pass the bacon in this direction."

"It would be my pleasure," said Prestyn, lofting the requested platter toward Görthang with two limbs from his cloak of arms.

"Ever so obliging of you," said Görthang. "Thank you, young mage."

"You're quite welcome, esteemed orc," said Prestyn.

Garum wondered if his command to Galena had influenced others at the table. Then he heard Púki speaking to the twins and was sure of it.

"Might I borrow the raspberry jam bowl for a few moments, lovely ladies?" asked Púki.

"I think he means it," said Yarra.

"That he wants the jam?" asked Xarra.

"No, that we're lovely ladies," responded Yarra.

Xarra smiled and passed the jam bowl to Púki. "Our pleasure," she said.

Garum could see Púki consider a response that would have been more ribald than polite but was amazed to see the short orc squelch himself and simply say, "You're most kind."

Sweetie tilted her head and gave Garum a look that spoke volumes.

"As you were," said Garum in his influencer command voice.

Sweetie's eyes flicked to Galena.

"Except for you," Garum told the Provost.

"As you wish," Galena replied.

I can't wait to take the antidote to the influencer potion, mused Garum.

* * * * *

Blōgot, Flisk, and Garum went to the huge retail emporium with the concentric-circles logo while the others packed up. Flisk found a new quiver and two dozen arrows to fill it. His supply had been running low. Blōgot bought two bowstrings and a selection of arrows with unusual tips, one of which—a green shaft—seemed to be an overstuffed glove.

"What's that for?" Garum asked.

"In case I want to knock an opponent unconscious, not kill them."

"Interesting," said Garum, "but doesn't the glove affect the arrow's range and stability?"

"It's only good for ten yards," said Blōgot.

"Why is it green?" asked Garum.

"Tradition," said Blōgot. "It's from a picture book."

Garum made a mental note to find a copy of the book and went off in search of bullets for his sling. The place had an impressive selection of bullets made from the traditional lead and clay, along with more exotic materials, such as black obsidian, white quartz, and blued razor-edged steel, complete with a special metal-mesh sling to throw them. Garum got six new lead bullets and six made from clay, glad to replace ammunition he'd used fighting monsters in the Deeps. On a whim, he added a pair of bullets made from thick glass, one holding a red liquid, the other a blue liquid. They were each the size of potion vials and the salesperson told Garum the red one would turn into a wall of flame when it broke while the blue one created a wall of ice.

"Don't use them both at the same time," said the salesperson as she took Garum's payment. "The fire will melt the ice and all you'll be left with is a wet floor."

"Duly noted," said Garum. He found Flisk and Blōgot and the three of them rapidly returned to Fletchers' Inn with their purchases.

The black-painted RedX self-powered carriages were waiting out front and most of the members of the combined companies were already aboard them. Their packs and gear were stored on the roofs and various members of their parties took responsibility for such driving as was necessary. Chophorn stood on a platform just below the axle at the back of the rear carriage and Sweetie stood outside the steps of the lead carriage waiting for Garum.

"Oh no," said Garum. "I'm not getting back in a magecoach, no matter what you call them, even *with* one of Lark's potions. I'll just *walk* to Horse Keep Town."

Sweetie was about to speak, but the sound of horseshoes on cobblestones stopped her before she could. Her mouth *did* open in surprise, however.

Garum turned to face the approaching equine and saw that it was a magnificent mare with a sky-blue coat and a dark-blue mane the color of deep water. Galena was riding the mare and smiling down at Garum and Sweetie.

"This is Zura," said Galena. "She's a horse of a different color."

"Quite," said Sweetie. "She's beautiful!"

"I agree," said Galena. "If Garum is afraid of magecoaches, he can ride with me." She reached down and shocked Garum speechless by hoisting him up by the collar of his tunic and twisting him around to sit in front of her.

"But," said Sweetie, her mouth suddenly resembling the entrance to a cavern.

"Don't worry," said Galena. "I'll take *very* good care of him. See you in Horse Keep Town." The look the former Provost gave Sweetie prompted Sweetie to worry quite a bit.

With a tap of her heels on Zura's flanks, Galena and Garum were off at a pace so fast the RedX magecoaches couldn't possibly match it.

Chapter 30
A Long Story

It was several hundred yards before Garum's mind fully took in what had just happened. He certainly didn't like magecoaches but had even less experience riding on full-sized horses. Small ponies and halfling-scale donkeys were another matter—he'd ridden them from time to time to get from one field kitchen to another while serving as a head cook for military expeditions—but falling off a pony or a half-ass, as the taller soldiers called them, was much less likely to break his neck.

I'm very fond of my neck, thought Garum. *I'd like to keep mine unbroken.*

Adding to Garum's discomfort, Galena's arms were on either side of him as she held the reins. Her arms were brushing his own as Zura trotted through the gates of Yew Keep Town and sped down the ring road toward Horse Keep Town. More disconcerting still, Galena's breasts were pressed close enough against his back that Garum could feel the points of her nipples through the fabric of her tunic.

No, thought Garum, reconsidering. *Those are more likely the hilts of daggers sheathed in her bodice for easy access.* Garum shook his head, mentally inventorying all the weapons hidden out of sight in his own garments and footwear. *It's only prudent to have multiple weapons kept easily accessible.*

There was traffic on this segment of the road, but not enough to slow their progress. A few prosperous-looking travelers were mounted, but Zura was moving faster than the other horses and passed them easily. Galena directed Zura around slow-moving oxcarts loaded with bundles of arrows heading south, staying out of the path of similar carts filled with finished tools from Forge Keep Town going north.

"We should be in Horse Keep Town in less than two hours," said Galena after a double handful of minutes. "You can find us lodging while I see what I can get from the horse traders for Zura."

"Find *us* lodging?" asked Garum. "I didn't know you considered our protection arrangement something that would last long enough for you to think in terms of *us*?"

"Only until we get to South Keep Town," said Galena. "Marshall Dylán at the Martial Academy there will protect me from the College of Healers' faculty and proctors—at least he'd better if he wants me to stay silent about certain information regarding his misuse of funds to procure military supplies."

Garum laughed.

"What?" asked Galena.

"You've just described an excellent reason for the leader of the Martial Academy to wish you *dead,* not protected," said Garum. "And it's not like misusing procurement funds is at all remarkable, at least in the armies where I've served. I had to budget ten to fifteen percent for graft on every contract I had with suppliers for everything from flour to fodder."

"No, you're missing something," said Galena. "It's more complicated than that."

"Explain it to me, then," said Garum. He felt Galena stiffen and realized he'd used his influencer voice. She had no choice except to comply.

"Very well," said Galena. "It's a long story."

"We have nearly two hours on our way to Horse Keep Town. Get on with it."

"Over a thousand years ago…" began Galena.

"It's *that* long a story?"

"Yes," said Galena. "But perhaps I need to provide more context. Have you ever been to one of the ancient cities?"

"Of course," said Garum. "I was a member of several teams searching for usable metal and glass when I was younger."

"Did you ever wonder where those cities came from?"

"They're the works of the ancients, of course," said Garum. He carefully moved his left hand from the pommel of Zura's saddle and used it to stroke his chin, gripping even tighter with his right. After a moment's thought, he said, "That's not really an answer, is it?"

"Give the halfling a basket of mushrooms," said Galena.

Garum couldn't see her face, but he sensed the former Provost was being both patronizing and amused. "The existence of the ruined cities means there must have been an ancient civilization—quite an advanced one, at that—long ago. Are you saying the cities are more than a thousand years old?"

"I am," said Galena. "And do you have any guesses as to *why* that civilization fell?"

"I suppose to the extent that I thought of it at all, I just assumed wars, or plagues, or lack of water brought it to an end," said Garum. "Are you saying you *know* why it fell?"

"I am," said Galena. "The senior people here in the Keep Lands all know."

"Go ahead and tell me, then," said Garum. "Start at the beginning. Over a thousand years ago…"

"Before the coming of the Keeps," said Galena.

"Wait! What?" said Garum. "You mean they haven't *always* been here?"

"We will run out of time on the road if you keep interrupting," said Galena. "Zura is *not* a slow horse."

"Fine," said Garum. "Go on."

Galena cleared her throat and organized her thoughts, giving Garum a few seconds to observe their surroundings.

Zura followed a well-worn equine path along the verge to the right between the ring road and the wall beside the cliffs. Just as it had been on his previous travels between keeps, the surface of the ring road itself was constructed of well-maintained cobblestones smoothed flat by dwarven magic. The nearby scenery was different, however. Garum saw rows of neatly planted and tended trees to his left, away from the stone wall on the right separating the ring road from the steep cliffs that surrounded the Deeps. Garum realized that one of the advantages of traveling on horseback was that he could now see over the wall, which matched his own height at three-and-a-half feet and hid what was beyond it from his sight when he was on foot. Now, Garum could dimly see the far cliffs from his position atop Zura.

He looked back left and examined the trees more closely. As he expected, or realized he *should* have expected, there were dozens of rows of tall, straight, red-barked cedars—for arrows—alternating with rows of bushy, green, shrub-like yew trees—for bow making.

A few rows of thorny hedgeapple trees appeared next. They looked like particularly gnarled sorts of apple trees and bore large green fruits. The wrinkled skins of hedgeapples had always reminded Garum of brains. He knew some archers preferred bows made from yew, while others insisted theirs be made from the well-seasoned wood of the hedgeapple. From what he'd heard, it was all a matter of the wood's grain and how well it could provide both compression and tension. Only bowstaves that could bend and be strung without breaking after shaping would serve.

Just thinking about the complexity of bow crafting makes me glad I'm a slinger, not an archer, Garum mused. *All I need is some cord and a bit of leather.*

Zura sped on, and Garum saw—and heard—that the spaces between the rows of trees were occupied by flocks of stout geese, each one nearly as fat as a turkey and likely every bit as surly. They were honking as they ate the grass growing close to the road and between the trees, reminding Garum of the times such sounds had heralded roast goose for dinner. Garum had to focus when he realized Galena was finally resuming her story. Her voice, at least, was mellifluous and didn't remind him of geese honking.

"The Keeps came from the sky," said Galena after she pressed her arms against Garum's to be sure he was paying attention. "They struck the ground like a large stone hitting soft earth and dug their way five hundred feet down…"

"Leaving the cliffs to our right?" said Garum.

"Very good," said Galena. "Your powers of comprehension are truly…"

"While *your* sarcasm isn't appreciated or necessary," Garum interrupted. "It's enough of a challenge to grasp the notion of something as big as the Keeps falling out of the sky."

"You *have* seen falling stars, haven't you?"

"Every child has," said Garum. "I even knew an officer who claimed his sword was forged from one."

"So you'll acknowledge that metal can descend from the sky?" said Galena. "That's what the Keeps did, over a thousand years ago. It's just a difference in scale."

Garum shook his head, trying to take in the implications of Galena's tale. *How can I know that she's not trying to trick me,* he considered. "Do you believe what you're saying is true?" he asked, using his influencer tone.

"I do," said Galena. "But that's just the start. The Deeps weren't the only thing to fall."

"Oh?" said Garum. He thought for two dozen of Zura's hoof-beats. "Oh!" he said as understanding worked its way through his skull. "The civilization that built the ancient cities also fell?"

"According to the archives at the Scholars' University, that civilization fell shortly after the Deeps arrived."

"Brought down by the force of the impact?" asked Garum. He glanced to his right in the direction of the unseen cliffs hidden behind the wall.

"No," said Galena. "Brought down by what escaped from the Deeps."

"The great monsters that made it out before the sixteen Keeps were built to guard the exits?" asked Garum.

"Those didn't try to escape for a century," said Galena. "It was something much smaller, something more familiar to the Healers' College, that brought down the ancients."

"You mean a disease?" said Garum. "That was one of my initial suppositions. It must have killed tens of thousands."

"It was more like tens or even hundreds of millions," said Galena. "But the ancients weren't just killed."

I wish Sweetie were here, thought Garum. *She'd help me get the story out of Galena faster, I'm sure. It feels like Galena is trying*

to torment me by dribbling out details by the quarter teaspoon.
"What, then?" asked Garum.

"Did you ever see sculptures or statues amid the ruins?"

"A few times," Garum admitted.

"Did you see any representations of elves or orcs or trolls or dwarves in stone or metal?"

Once again, Garum gripped the pommel of Zura's saddle with his right hand and stroked his chin with his left. "I wasn't really thinking about it, but now that I reflect on it, all I saw were standard human men and women—and horses."

"Yes, the ancients were fond of equestrian statues," said Galena. "As were the pigeons."

"Is there a point in this digression?" asked Garum.

"There is," said Galena. "Not all the ancients were killed. Some were transformed."

Garum tilted his head then realized Galena wouldn't be able to see his quizzical expression. "Into what?" he asked.

"Into all the diverse peoples of *our* world: giants, sylviants, gnomes, short orcs, and *halflings,* to name a few."

"You mean we're *all* variations on standard humans?" asked Garum.

"How else can there be half-elven or viable offspring from matings between giants and trolls?" asked Galena.

Garum, for once, was glad to be on horseback. Had he been on foot, he would have stopped in his tracks. It wasn't something he'd thought about. Somehow, he just *knew* that everyone was the same under the skin but hadn't given due consideration to the implications of that innate knowledge. In the future, he hoped to have children with Sweetie, after all, even though he was a halfling and she was human—not that humans and halflings were all that different except in size.

"It's starting to sink in?" said Galena. "Is your mind filling with images of gnomes mating with sylviants?"

"Yes, it's sinking in," said Garum, "but no, that particular combination is not occupying space in my head."

"You're more focused on human-halfling matings, then?" teased Galena.

"I'm trying to figure out how something that escaped from the Deeps could transform ancient humans into the diverse peoples of modern times," said Garum.

"It's not like there are that many differences between a troll and a human," said Galena. "Humans themselves vary in size and strength. There are hundreds of breeds of dogs—why not dozens of subtypes of people?"

"Perhaps," said Garum. "What about teeth? Orcs and trolls have long canines."

"From what the Healers' College has been able to determine, the transforming animacules that escaped from the Deeps recruited *clarks* to change teeth, ear shape, skin thickness, and more. For the survivors, it all happened quickly."

"But how do the clarks make the changes?"

"Are you aware of how healers can help people who feel out of step with their physical bodies? Men in women's bodies, women in men's bodies, and sometimes people who feel like both men and women, or neither?"

"I'd heard about it," said Garum, remembering a confidential conversation late at night around the embers of a campfire with one of his senior assistants. The man had told Garum about his own experiences with healers to help effect just such a change.

"Almost all healers can cajole the clarks into changing surface appearances," said Galena. "Flattening a chest or shrinking a phallus are straightforward. The animacules from the Deeps worked differently, however. They changed the hidden plans inside people's bodies, so their children resembled their transformed parents."

"As it is across the animal and vegetable kingdoms," said Garum. "Plant a cabbage, get a cabbage."

"Yes," said Galena. "Can you reason through what came next?"

Garum allowed the rhythm of Zura's hoofbeats to carry his thoughts along. *What would it mean if three of my cousins were permanently transformed into orcs and two more into sylviants?*

To say nothing of the people who died from the clarks' actions and from the chaos that must have followed such radical changes to a formerly all-standard human society? "You said tens, maybe hundreds of millions of ancients died?" he asked.

"From Scholars' counts of skeletons in the old cities, it seems so," Galena replied.

"I do remember a lot of bones on my salvage expeditions," said Garum.

"And that's after centuries of farmers harvesting those bones to fertilize their fields," said Galena. "Whatever held the ancients' civilization together couldn't cope with such losses. Everything fell apart and the varied subtypes of people sought out their own kind for comfort before trying to build anew."

Garum felt like his skull was filled with just-brewed beer beginning to energetically ferment. The pressure built to the point where Garum shook his head, then realized that was not the wisest course of action as the pressure turned into pain behind his eyes and in his sinuses. He wished he had one of Lark's healing potions in his pouch. Garum let out a sigh and realized Galena's long tale still hadn't answered his initial question about why the Marshall of the Martial Academy would protect Galena.

"It's a lot to take in," Galena said to fill the silence. "Very few people know what I've told you."

"Which seems wise," said Garum. "So, what is the *real* reason the Keeps were built, since the transforming animacules had already escaped the Deeps?"

"The traditional story is true enough," said Galena. "The Keeps *were* built to protect the people—of all subtypes—on the surface from various monsters escaping from the Deeps. But the monsters didn't appear immediately. It took them a century."

"And by then, a new society had formed on the literal bones of the old?"

"Correct," said Galena. "The clarks and mites and other tiny creatures had also spread across the world, giving healers and mages and illusionists powers to take on the monsters. Soldiers got enchanted weapons to help *them* fight, as well."

"Let me guess," said Garum. "Dwarves used their *masons* to build the stairways leading down to the doors of the Deeps?"

"Dwarves and gnomes," said Galena. "Healing potions restored the strength of the soldiers who pushed the monsters back inside those doors—or killed such monsters outright."

"All the monsters?"

"All but the dragons," said Galena.

"Dragons aren't transformed humans?"

"The clarks *do* have limits."

Garum was reassured to hear that detail. He'd known a few dragons who'd served with him in various armies over the years, and they'd always seemed quite different from any subtype of *people*. They were intelligent, of course. *Very* intelligent. But their minds were truly alien, as anyone could sense if they looked into a dragon's faceted crystalline eyes. It made sense that they came from the stars. *At least dragons could appreciate good cooking,* thought Garum. *My spicy roast goat, in particular.*

"You understand just how complex things are now?" asked Galena.

"I can appreciate what you've shared," said Garum. He turned his head left, then right, as if trying to consider all the aspects of Galena's tale. "Once more," he said, using his influencer tone. "Do *you* believe what you've told me is true?"

"I do," said Galena. "There are scholars at the University who can show you archives preserved from the first century after the Deeps arrival to confirm every detail."

Convenient that the University is seven Keeps away, Garum considered. *Still, I did use my influence-potion tone when I asked the question. And then there are the dragons—and the Deeps themselves. Why are the Deeps crafted from metal, not stone?* Garum realized Galena had distracted him from providing the real reason why she expected the head of the Martial Academy to protect her. "The information you hold over the Marshall doesn't have anything to do with his misuse of military procurement funds, does it?"

"No," said Galena, responding to Garum's question without elaboration.

"What *do* you hold over the Marshall?" asked Garum. "Some sort of healers' college program to create super soldiers?"

Galena laughed, and Garum realized how foolish his question was. With giants, trolls, ogres, oversized orcs, and even sylviants, there wasn't much more the college could do to create larger or stronger soldiers. Marshall Dylán himself was a powerful orc, reputed to be built much like Görthang. He already had companies of well-trained trolls and giants to use against any escaping monsters.

"That stone didn't strike anywhere near the target," said Galena.

Choosing his words with care, and focusing his influencer tone, Garum said, "Tell me why you think the Marshall will protect you."

"Because of the vials I carry close to my heart."

Garum thought back to when he'd first leaned back against Galena atop Zura. *It could have been vials I felt, not dagger hilts.* "What's *in* those vials?"

"Clarks," said Galena.

Garum closed his jaw and counted to five. "What is it those clarks do?"

"I sent Aubericht and the original Golden Company into the ancient city northwest of here, at the southern end of the long Inland Sea," said Galena. "They found an urn filled with animacules released shortly after the Deeps' arrival."

"The ones that killed tens of millions?" asked Garum.

"The same," said Galena. "The ancients had tried to isolate the animacules so they could be studied, but they all died—or were transformed—before they could do more. The urn didn't just hold the animacules. It also had a collection of clarks trained to multiply and follow the animacules' program on people's bodies. I have two vials filled with clarks extracted from that urn."

"So—you're carrying an incredibly dangerous infection?" Garum struggled to keep from looking over his shoulder at where he assumed the frightening vials must be. He leaned forward to avoid even inadvertently coming into contact with the vials.

"An incredibly dangerous infection that Marshall Dylán wants."

"Why?" asked Garum. "If anything should be sealed away forever or destroyed, it should be that urn—and those vials!"

"Marshall Dylán believes in the superiority of the larger, more powerful subtypes: orcs, trolls, giants, ogres—even sylviants and dwarves. He resents the fact that there are as many humans from the original standard type as all the various other subtypes combined."

"And his solution is to release the same clarks that killed so many a thousand years ago?"

"He believes the clarks will transform still more of the original type humans into one of the subtypes, and thus improve the species overall," said Galena. "Dylán is something of an orc chauvinist. He wants more orcs in the world and doesn't want to wait for the time-consuming usual process of creating them."

"More like something of a madman," said Garum. *Where's the fun in creating new orcs from standard humans instead of through lovemaking?* Garum mused. Inside his head, he could hear a parent explaining to an inquisitive child: *When a mommy orc loves a daddy orc very much.* He didn't smile, however. On the other hand, he *did* notice the scenery to his left had changed, transitioning from rows of trees to rolling hills covered in dark green grass. Small herds of horses with more traditional coat patterns were grazing on the hillsides.

"He's willing to both pay me and protect me," said Galena. "And he's not a madman. He just has a different vision for the world."

An insane, destructive vision, thought Garum. "Once you give those vials to Marshall Dylán, what makes you think you won't die when he releases the transforming clarks?"

"I must not have told you," said Galena. "Any potion derived from a Golden Chalice mushroom is proof against the transforming clarks. That means I'm safe, and so are you."

Garum sat stiffly in the saddle. Sweetie, her grandfather, Prestyn, Crank, and the twins were all standard humans who could be transformed or killed if the clarks were released, to say nothing of all the other standard humans of the Keep Lands and the wider world beyond. Galena and Marshall Dylán were both monsters—one for passing the clarks along and the other for planning to use them. Garum saw a small copse of trees to his left, breaking up the line of rolling hills controlled by Horse Keep. He made up his mind.

"Guide Zura over into those trees," said Garum, using his influencer tone.

Galena did so.

* * * * *

Garum greeted Sweetie with a hug when she stepped down from her RedX just inside the paddock-style wooden gates of Horse Keep Town.

"It's so good to see you," she said.

Over Sweetie's shoulder, Garum could see the massive stone construction of Horse Keep atop a hill on the edge of the cliffs. It was less a tower than a cube and reminded him of a great barn. *That's appropriate enough for Horse Keep, I suppose.*

"How was your horseback ride?" asked Sweetie.

"Fine," said Garum.

"Where's Galena?"

"She's left us," said Garum.

"Just as well," said Sweetie. "I had a bad feeling about her."

"So did I," said Garum. "So did I."

Chapter 31

A Giant-sized Lunch

"Are we staying the night at Horse Keep Town?" asked Sweetie.

"No," said Garum. "Let's press on to Forge Keep Town. We can get an early start the next morning, since I need to deal with a certain matter in South Keep Town."

"I didn't know you knew anyone there," said Sweetie.

"I don't," said Garum. "It's a long story."

"Which can wait," said Sweetie. "It's been hours since breakfast, and we're all hungry. Let's find an inn and get a nice lunch."

"I was thinking we could simply buy some bread and meat and cheese and make a quick meal," said Garum.

"Good idea," said Sweetie. "Stopping at an inn could take a while. We'll want to get some fruit, too."

Görthang stuck his head out of the window of the lead RedX. "And some beer," he added.

"Of course," said Garum. He extended his arm and helped Sweetie back into the RedX.

She turned around and extended a hand to help Garum board as well, figuring—correctly—that a few minutes in a magecoach wouldn't be a problem. "We can travel a few blocks looking for bakeries, butcher shops, cheese shops…"

"And pubs," said Görthang. "For that matter, there *is* a great place for lunch just a bit further along this street that has excellent sandwiches you can order at a counter, plus a courtyard out back with tables to eat in the sunshine. Stopping there will likely take less time."

"Fine," said Garum. "I should have known you'd be familiar with the best places to eat and drink in the Keep Lands. What's this place called?"

"Murphrey's Pubic House."

"Don't you mean *Public* House?" asked Sweetie.

"Pubic House is what's on the sign," said Görthang. "Given Murphrey, it's hard to tell if it's that way because he's a terrible speller or has an even more terrible sense of humor."

"I'll keep an eye out for hairs in my food and beer either way," said Garum. "You're sure this place is good?"

"Best in Horse Keep Town," Görthang asserted.

"Horse meat isn't on the menu, is it?" asked Sweetie.

"Anyone in Horse Keep Town would rather eat stray travelers than one of their beloved horses," said Görthang.

"That's not reassuring," said Sweetie.

Görthang leaned his head out one of the windows on the RedX. "There it is," he said, indicating another block down the street. "I see Murphrey's sign."

Garum waited until the RedX stopped and stepped out. Everyone from both the Black and Golden Companies left their magic-powered conveyances except for Chophorn, who'd been riding on a platform below the luggage storage area at the back of his RedX that was designed for sylviants. He didn't fit well inside a RedX and lowered himself to the ground after the vehicle had stopped.

The street was bare dirt, not cobbled, and a small cloud of dust was in the air, stirred up by the wheels of the RedXs. *Dirt is easier on horses' hooves than cobblestones,* thought Garum. *I expect all the streets in Horse Keep Town are unpaved.*

The facade of Murphrey's reminded Garum of an oversized livery stable with a flat front and a tall, wide pair of swinging doors. An even larger barn-style door, suitable for trolls, ogres, and other larger customers was on the right side of the structure and a broad porch, supported by a dozen fifteen-foot tree trunks, shaded the street side of the establishment. When Garum saw Murphrey's sign, he started to laugh. "It does say *Pubic* House!"

"I told you," said Görthang.

"But you *didn't* tell me Murphrey was also a pawnbroker," said Garum. The sign had a painted representation of a long loaf of bread along with two gold balls, strategically located to emphasize the resemblance between what was painted there and quite generous male 'equipment.'

"You're *sure* this place is good?" asked Sweetie.

"Looks good to *me!*" piped up Púki. "The painter obviously copied from the time I posed for a naked self-portrait."

"Only if the sign painter used an enlarging glass," said Xarra.

"And a great deal of artistic license," said Yarra.

"You could always inspect *my* equipment to check and see how little license was necessary," said Púki. He stopped talking when he realized he'd set himself up for an obvious response from the twins.

Xarra and Yarra didn't speak, however. Xarra held her thumb and index finger an inch apart while Yarra nodded.

Sweetie turned to Görthang. "I thought pawnbrokers used *three* balls as their symbol," she said.

"They do," Görthang replied. "When people point that out to Murphrey, he tells them that he's only a part-time pawnbroker."

"I'm looking forward to meeting the proprietor of this establishment," said Garum. He glanced down the street at the row of five RedXs pulled up along the raised wooden sidewalk that ran in front of Murphrey's and several other establishments. "Who's going to guard our transportation while we're inside?"

Just then, a young woman stepped out from the swinging doors and waved. She was only a bit taller than Sweetie and had tightly braided brown hair hanging down in pigtails.

Something is off about her appearance, thought Garum. *She looks young, but she has enough muscles to juggle our five RedXs.* He turned to Sweetie and gave her a quizzical look.

"She's a giant's child," Sweetie whispered. "Be polite."

Garum smiled and nodded. "I'm Garum, and we're the Black and Golden Companies," he told the giant child, sweeping his arms to take in everyone in their combined parties. "We've heard good things about the food here and wondered if you might have any recommendations for someone who can watch our RedXs?"

"I do," said the giant child. "*Me.*" She smiled back at Garum and the others. "I'm Lilybet, the baby of the family. My daddy is busy handling the lunch rush, but he heard your coaches arrive and sent me out to guard them."

"Is your daddy Murphrey?" asked Garum.

"Uh huh," said the giant child. "Daddy is the pro-pri-e-tor. He's inside making sandwiches and filling mugs."

"Pleased to meet you, Lilybet," said Garum, giving her a small bow. He was glad to see the other members of the Golden Company doing the same, while the Black Company opted for, "Nice to see you again."

"You're in luck," said Lilybet. "We haven't run out of bread yet—and we still have that spiced flathorn meat you like, Master Görthang. Daddy has a supplier who brings it in from north of the Inland Seas."

"That's good to hear, Lilybet," said Görthang, "but I'm no master. Just call me Görthang."

"Daddy said you're a master adventurer," said Lilybet. "Maybe you can take me with you on adventures when I'm bigger?"

"That's up to your father until you're of age," said Görthang.

"My mother would have let me go with you," said Lilybet.

"Your mother, if she was still with us," said Blōgot, "would have told you to wait, as you know your father will, if you're unwise enough to ask him."

"Oh, I'd *never* ask him for anything during the lunch rush," said Lilybet. "But it would be nice to know if you'd consider taking me along someday."

"Thank you for watching our RedXs," said Sweetie. She nodded to Lilybet and stepped up onto the front porch of Murphrey's. "And now, to eat. I'm *hungry*."

Garum and the others followed Sweetie inside the Pubic House, enticed by the delicious smell of fresh-baked bread.

* * * * *

The interior was much as Garum expected, adjusting for the fact that the place was run by a family of giants. There were three solid-looking men twice Garum's height sweeping the floor and cleaning off tables. They had that same sense of youth as Lilybet, along with a similar shade of brown hair, so Garum assumed they were her older brothers. None of them had grown into the stature of a full giant as yet. The person behind a long bar across the room was a different matter, however. At over nine-feet, he was the tallest giant Garum had ever seen.

That must be Murphrey, Garum realized. *I now understand why he can call his place anything he wants without worrying about criticism.* Murphrey wasn't just tall. He was huge, with a body built like a pair of massive barrels stacked one atop the other and arms big and strong enough to carry a fully-armored warhorse under each one. The mature giant's head was shaped like the great round stones tossed by catapults and used to batter fortifications. It was bald, except for a fringe of hair the same shade as his children's. The features of Murphrey's face were craggy, like battlements, though his eyes sparkled and shone with the light of a keen intelligence, as if they were a pair of polished bronze domes topping the towers of a wealthy keep.

Not someone I'd like to meet as a foe on a battlefield, thought Garum. The giant's impressive appearance was enhanced by his rumbling *basso* voice that was so deep it made Hrefna sound like a soprano. Garum refocused from a vibration he could feel inside his bones to realize Murphrey was calling out, "What'll ya have? What'll ya have?"

"A spiced flathorn sandwich with white, spreadable cheese and pickled peppers, if you please," said Görthang.

"An excellent choice," said Murphrey. "And given that it's yourself who's asking, I don't have to guess whether you'll be wanting a half or a whole loaf."

"You know me well," said Görthang. "It's a nice enough day. We'll be eating out at the courtyard, not inside."

"An excellent plan, that," said Murphrey. The giant waved the knife in his right hand from side to side to illustrate that there weren't any available tables with enough room to hold the Golden and Black Companies. A dozen and a half tables for two, four, six, and eight were already occupied by a mixed assortment of human sub-types at various stages of transferring sandwiches stuffed with meats, cheeses, and more from their hands to their mouths.

Murphrey's hands were broad enough to extend from one end to the other of the long loaves he used for feeding his customers. The giant was already cutting one such loaf in half lengthwise, spreading it with a soft, white cheese seasoned with herbs, and layering on slices of a dark meat Garum assumed must be flathorn— the great deer of the north with massive flat antlers who were as much bigger than the white-tailed deer of Garum's homeland as trolls were bigger than halflings. Garum recognized the pickled yellow peppers added to Görthang's sandwich next as the type that was so powerfully hot Garum could toss a single slice to a twenty-gallon kettle of stew and have heat come through in every spoonful.

With a fellow cook's professional interest, Garum examined the bar and surrounding counters where Murphrey was constructing his creations. A knife block held several blades, including a serrated one for bisecting loaves and multiple traditional blades optimized for slicing meats and cheeses. Broad, flat blades were also present for spreading soft cheeses and condiments on the bread as Murphrey assembled the sandwiches with practiced precision.

The giant had already presented Görthang with his order on a thin oval-shaped wooden plate and was assembling Blōgot's—peppercorn venison with cheddar and beer barm—as Garum realized the options for sandwich fillings were listed on chalkboards above and behind the giant's shoulders.

While Murphrey was filling orders for the members of the Black Company, who had the advantage of having dined here before, Garum shifted to get a view of the left-hand board, which had been partially blocked by Murphrey's literally gigantic body. There were dozens of options, featuring several choices of breads, including rye, millet, buckwheat, and oat loaves, in addition to fine white manchet bread and whole wheat. He tugged on Sweetie's sleeve. "Garlic? Onions?"

"I will, if you will," said Sweetie.

Garlic and onions go better if both of us opt to have them, thought Garum. *Sharing garlic-infused kisses can be delightful, whereas one-sided allium-breath is not only impolite but unpleasant.* That important matter dealt with, Garum gave the chalkboards further study while others placed their orders.

Hrefna ordered two full sandwiches made from roast beef with double meat and added layers of horseradish-infused soft cheese as thick as her thumb, which made them as thick as Garum's first three fingers.

Púki looked up at Hrefna and said, "I'll have what she's having."

Murphrey laughed when he saw the twins roll their eyes. It was a laugh that came from deep in his belly, reminding Garum of the sound of the ceremonial military drums made of hides stretched over huge brass cauldrons. The giant lifted a long loaf with one hand then used a finger on his free hand to encourage the twins to tell him where to cut. Xarra used her index finger and thumb to measure a scant inch. Murphrey nodded, and Yarra covered Púki's mouth to stifle his protests. Garum was pleased to see the giant prepare half a sandwich with a single serving of roast beef for the short orc and more pleased to see Púki take the half-sandwich without additional complaints.

I wouldn't want to antagonize Murphrey, either, Garum considered. He smiled when he heard Drain's order of a roast pork, ham, and bacon sandwich on bread spread with lard. *That's real commitment to a theme,* thought Garum, *though I would have gone with mustard, myself.*

Lark asked for sliced chicken breast with farmer's cheese and crushed bogberries, prompting Arrex to do the same. The twins placed identical orders for sausage links with cooked, fermented cabbage and caraway seeds. Garum expected them to use the links to tease Púki suggestively and reminded himself not to smile when they did.

Sweetie requested white-meat turkey with pale rounds of *provola* cheese, chopped lettuce, sliced wolf peaches, onions, and minced garlic, all topped with a mixture of red-wine vinegar, olive oil, and oregano. *That sounds perfect,* Garum realized. "The same for me," he told Murphrey.

The giant made one sandwich to those specifications and flourished a cleaver to cut it in half with a theatrical flair, presenting one half to

Sweetie and the other to Garum. "If you're still hungry when you finish those, come back, and I'll make you another to share," he told them.

Garum and Sweetie smiled, thanked Murphrey, took mugs of cider from a tray held by one of Murphrey's sons, and proceeded after many of the others to the courtyard outside. *Prestyn holds enough of our funds to pay,* thought Garum. *I'm sure he's also wise enough to tip well, including something for Lilybet.*

Sweetie led Garum to a low table for two. It was obviously a square board on top of half an overturned barrel and seemed designed for the comfort of Murphrey's shorter patrons. Garum's feet still dangled when he hopped up on his chair, but Sweetie's didn't when she sat in hers. Still, he was glad he didn't have to ask Hrefna to lift him up so he could sit on a chair built for giants.

"So," said Sweetie, after they'd both had sips of cider. "Tell me more about your ride."

"It was fine," said Garum, not meeting her eyes and uncomfortably aware of the two vials full of transforming clarks in his belt pouch next to two similar containers holding oil and vinegar for salads.

Sweetie leaned close to Garum with her lips close to his ear. "You said that already."

"Uh huh," said Garum.

"Did you kill her?" asked Sweetie.

"Kill who?"

"You *know* who," whispered Sweetie. "You said she left us. Was it for a shallow grave?"

"No," Garum whispered back. "It was worse than that."

"You buried her *alive?*"

"Of course not," said Garum. "I used my influencer voice and commanded her to forget her life as the Provost."

"That doesn't sound too bad," said Sweetie.

"Then I told her to make her way back toward Yew Keep and find a job tending geese."

"You *fiend!*" said Sweetie.

Garum saw Sweetie's face light up as she grinned. "It seemed fitting," he said.

"What about her horse?" Sweetie asked after savoring Garum's actions for a few seconds.

"I led Zura here and sold her before you got here," said Garum. "This *is* Horse Keep Town, after all, and there were plenty of buyers to bargain with."

"Did you arrange to send the proceeds back to Galena?" asked Sweetie.

"No," said Garum. "I'd given her some funds based on what I expected her horse was worth before I sent her back and replaced them with what I received from the sale."

"That's more than I would have done," said Sweetie. "Did I ever tell you about the man who bought an expensive horse for a copper piece?"

"Is that the one where the husband leaves his wife and tells her to sell his horse and send him the money?"

"You've heard it, then," said Sweetie. She took a bite of her sandwich then licked her lips in a way that made Garum want to kiss her.

"Not only that, I've told it," said Garum. He tasted his own sandwich and found himself in agreement with Görthang. Murphrey's was *the* place for a great lunch.

"How long do you think your command to forget her life as the Provost will last?" asked Sweetie.

"Long enough for us to be several keeps away," said Garum. "I hope."

"Her absence means one less thing to worry about," said Sweetie.

"Not exactly," said Garum. "Galena told me the strangest story on the way here, and I *really* need to get Lark's advice about something."

Sweetie waved in the direction of the table where Lark, Arrex, and Gêrdun were chatting and enjoying their lunch.

"We need more privacy for our conversation," said Garum. "Maybe the three of us can share a RedX on the way to Forge Keep Town?"

"If you're willing to ride in a RedX without taking a sleeping potion first, this *must* be serious."

"Very," said Garum.

"If that's the case, Görthang should probably join us," said Sweetie.

Garum sighed. "Agreed."

"I'll arrange it," said Sweetie. "And I'll tell the others that riding on a horse with Galena made you reconsider your irrational fear of magecoaches."

"You're so kind," said Garum. *You're also more right than you know. A magecoach is highly preferred to riding on a horse with someone willing to sacrifice millions.* He'd prefer to walk, but given what he carried, he didn't think the risk was worth it. Garum smiled when he overheard Flisk tell Crank that he thought deep-fried thinly sliced and salted white tubers would go particularly well with Murphrey's sandwiches.

Chapter 32
Vial Dilemma

Garum slipped Lilybet a coin for watching their conveyances while Sweetie organized who was traveling in which RedX. She contrived to have herself, Garum, Görthang, and Lark alone in the lead vehicle.

"What do you need *my* advice about?" asked Lark as she sat across from Garum and Sweetie. All their bodies were swaying as they picked up speed leaving Horse Keep Town.

Görthang, sitting beside Lark and taking up two-thirds of the space on the seat, said, "I'm sure he'll tell us and given that you're here, I expect it has to do with the ousted former Provost."

"Obviously," said Sweetie.

"Has he told you?" asked Görthang.

"Not yet," replied Sweetie. "I'm as curious as you are."

Garum's booted feet dangled over the edge of the forward-facing bench. He'd seen the space beneath the bench was used for storage and swung his heels back to tap what he thought was an over-stuffed duffel. After pausing to take a few deep breaths and collect his thoughts, Garum began to talk, sharing a condensed version of everything Galena had told him. When he finished, he announced, "I'm not sure I believe her, but I am convinced *she* believes what she told me."

"It's nonsense," said Görthang. "Something the size of the Deeps can't fall out of the sky."

"And if it did," said Sweetie, "it would leave a much bigger hole."

"What about the metal walls, floors, and ceilings?" asked Garum.

"Wouldn't it make more sense that the ancients built the Deeps in place after excavating the cliffs?" said Görthang. "I assume you've been on scavenging expeditions. You've seen how far down the foundations of their fallen towers were dug—and they used metal everywhere."

"Well, you *can* see steel rods poking up out of concrete, at least," said Garum. Sweetie gave him a lecherous glance that he interpreted as being fond of *his* steel rod, but Garum tried to not let it distract him. "The point is, I have two vials full of something and Galena says they're a transforming plague." He looked at Lark. "Does that make sense?" he asked. "And if so, what do we do with them?"

"I'd heard about the Great Transformation from a few members of the faculty," said Lark. "So it does make some sort of sense. If you read between the lines in several of the texts on assisting patients with gender dysphoria, you can piece together a story about much more extensive changes to humanity. But I had no idea any of the clarks adapted by the animacules responsible were still in existence."

"Apparently, they are," said Garum. "Now, what are we going to do with them?" He shifted his gaze to each of the others in turn. "Galena says they could kill millions."

"Or transform them," said Görthang.

"More likely, both," added Sweetie. "At least according to what you told us."

"Much as I'd like to study them," said Lark, "I think the wiser course would be to destroy the vials as soon as possible."

"What will it take to destroy them safely?" asked Sweetie.

"Intense heat would be best," said Lark.

"Don't tell me I need to find a volcano to toss them into," said Garum.

"Let's hope not," said Görthang. "It's over nine hundred leagues to the closest one on an island to the east of the Southern Sea, at least according to the maps I've seen."

"Forges for steel and furnaces for glass are hotter than volcanoes, I've heard," said Sweetie.

"And there are both at our next stop, Forge Keep Town," said Garum.

"A stove hot enough to melt lead would work if the vials held the animacules responsible for the plague," said Lark. "But after the clarks have transcribed the animacules' instructions, *they* are much more difficult to dispose of."

"What do you suggest, then?" asked Sweetie.

"We *could* return to East Keep Town," said Lark. "The College of Healers has very powerful incinerators to safely disintegrate dangerous clarks."

"I don't think returning to the College would be wise," said Görthang.

All four of them nodded.

"We're in agreement on that," said Görthang. "What are our other options?"

"How much heat do you need to disintegrate clarks?" asked Sweetie. "Maybe there are specialized furnaces at Forge Keep Town that would do the job?"

"The woman who ran the incinerator told me it was more than twice as hot as a furnace to melt steel," said Lark. "She said it was hot enough to melt *wolfram*."

"And that's really hot," said Görthang. "They use shields made of wolfram to protect soldiers from dragons' flames."

"There's our answer," said Sweetie. "Dragon Keep Town is only four keeps away. We could find a dragon to destroy the vials for us."

"I have *no* interest in traveling a quarter of the way around the Deeps with these vials in my possession," said Garum. "And I'm especially adverse to taking them any closer to Marshall Dylán in South Keep Town than I have to."

"Maybe Drain knows if they have any furnaces hot enough to melt wolfram at Forge Keep Town?" Sweetie suggested.

"Because she's a dwarf?" said Görthang. "Did you ever consider that someone who's *not* a dwarf but has been completely around the Deeps more than a dozen times might have that knowledge?"

"Who is he talking about?" asked Lark.

"Himself," said Garum.

"Oh, sorry," said Lark. "*Are* there any wolfram-hot furnaces in Forge Keep Town?"

"One, I think," said Görthang. He smiled at Lark, showing his prominent canines. "There's a smith named Fess who works with wolfram. I know where he has his forge."

"Great," said Garum. "If he lets me toss the vials in his furnace, we won't have to worry about the Marshall trying to take them from me when we get to South Keep Town."

"Remind me," said Görthang, "why are we going to South Keep Town?"

"To deliver Galena to the Marsh…" Garum began. "Oh. Right."

"Also, to put some distance between ourselves and the mob of irate proctors and faculty from the College of Healers," added Sweetie.

"And that," Garum agreed.

"Do we have any proof for the existence of such a mob?" asked Lark. "I lived in a dormitory at the College for years and the only mobs I ever saw there were when the refectory was serving flavored ices."

"Galena *told* us a mob was chasing her," said Garum.

"And is the Provost someone known for her honesty?" asked Sweetie.

Görthang snorted. "Hardly," he said. "But if anything could whip a crowd into a frenzy, the prospect of giving Galena some of her own back is probably high on the list."

"She was hardly the most popular person at the College," said Lark. "My instructors often grumbled about her when we were in small tutorials—though not in larger gatherings."

"Too afraid Galena would have them flogged if they spoke out publicly?" asked Sweetie.

"More likely too afraid she'd cut off funding for their research," said Lark.

"A fate far worse than flogging," said Garum.

"Some of the faculty would probably *enjoy* being flogged," said Görthang.

"They *do*," said Lark. "Especially with ready access to healing potions afterwards. There's a club for it and…"

"We don't need details," said Sweetie. "The point is, we don't know if there's any compelling reason to go to South Keep Town."

"But there are *two* important reasons to go to Forge Keep Town," said Garum. He gently tapped his pouch where the pair of vials were stored. "Let's deal with them first and determine further steps afterwards."

"Sounds good," said Görthang. "And there's an excellent inn near Fess's forge in Forge Keep Town."

The RedX bounced over a dislodged cobblestone and Garum fell against Sweetie, righting himself by gripping a leather strap next to the coach door beside him and swinging his legs vigorously to help him sit up straight again. His boot heels smacked the duffel under the bench where he sat with quite a bit of force. Garum was surprised to hear a suppressed "Ooof!" come from below him.

Before Garum could react, one of Görthang's massive arms shot out to a spot between and below Garum's legs and *pulled.*

"Let me go!" a high-pitched voice protested.

Garum saw the voice came from the throat of a young human male not much taller than he was. Görthang's grip on the boy's collar was strong enough to keep the soles of his captive's boots a few inches off the floor of the RedX. The captive was kicking energetically to the point where Garum had to shift his legs to prevent himself from being struck and potentially injured.

"I just wanted to go on an adventure!" Görthang's captive wailed.

Looking closely at the orc's prisoner, Garum saw he resembled Lilybet enough to be one of her brothers. *Not a standard human then,* Garum realized. *A young giant.*

"What's your name?" Görthang demanded.

Garum almost said his *own* name before catching himself and hearing the juvenile giant reply with "Nif."

"How long have you been under that bench?" asked Görthang.

Lark shook her head. "I think the answer to that is obvious," she said. "He's been there since before we climbed back in."

"But Lilybet was guarding our carriages," said Sweetie.

"And Lilybet is what—five, maybe six years old?" said Garum. "It would be literal child's play for one of her brothers to distract her."

"Lilybet's *not* my sister!" said Nif. "And she's just turned seven."

"Whatever," said Sweetie. "The issue now isn't *who* he's related to, but *what* we're going to do with him."

And how much of what we'd been discussing he heard, thought Garum. *We have to assume he heard everything.*

Nif shifted in Görthang's grip and pointed an index finger at Garum. "I was asleep and didn't hear *anything!*" he said.

Too conveniently, thought Garum.

"At least not until he *kicked* me!" Nif continued.

"You're welcome to go on an adventure," said Sweetie. "Just not with us." She waved to Görthang, indicating he should put Nif down, but the big orc didn't do so.

"Should I stop the RedX and toss him out?" Görthang asked, waving Nif back and forth like a small banner. "We haven't passed the gates of Horse Keep Town yet, so he won't have far to walk home."

"You should simply allow him to leave the vehicle without any tossing," Sweetie asserted.

"Where's the fun in that?" said Görthang.

"The fun is in *not* having Murphrey the Giant mad at us," said Garum. "We have enough troubles already."

"He said he wasn't Lilybet's brother," Lark reminded them.

"I *said* Lilybet wasn't my sister," Nif protested.

"Isn't that the same thing?" asked Lark. "Or is this one of those logic problems the savants like to pose to their students?"

"A difference that makes no difference *is* no difference," said Sweetie.

Nif tried punching Görthang's arm and Sweetie repeated her gesture until the big orc returned Nif to his feet. The boy, now a bit less irate, turned to Garum. "What do you have in your pouch, Mister…"

"Garum," said Garum.

"You keep fish sauce in your pouch?" asked Nif.

Garum was about to respond when Görthang beat him to it. "None of your business, little man. Don't give me an excuse to throw you out instead of allowing you to climb out on your own."

"Sorry," said Nif, in a voice that sounded less than one percent apologetic. He shook his head and rubbed his neck, then glared at Görthang. "If you want a hot forge, you should take me with you. I know everybody who's anybody in Forge Keep Town."

"I thought you were asleep and didn't hear our conversation," said Lark.

"That was before tall, dark, and fang-y there started threatening me," said Nif. "I really *want* to go on an adventure and really *don't* want to be thrown out into the street. I heard you need a hot forge. Fess has one, but I know someone who's got one even hotter. Are you going to make a sword from wolfram? I've heard they're brittle."

"So are your bones," said Görthang.

"Actually, I'm young enough my bones *aren't* brittle," said Nif.

"Care to test that assumption?" asked Görthang.

"No," said Nif. "I just want to be helpful enough for you to take me with you."

"Why?" asked Sweetie.

"I'm sick of slicing sandwich fixings," said Nif.

But Lilybet's not your sister, thought Garum.

"How old are you?" asked Sweetie.

"Old enough to go on adventures," said Nif.

"Which makes you...?"

"Older than Lilybet."

"Are you ten?" asked Lark.

"Yes," said Nif.

Sweetie nudged Garum with an elbow then raised an eyebrow once he faced her.

Ah, Garum realized. *She wants me to use my influencer command voice on him.*

Before Garum could speak, Nif went with a different approach. "Maybe you *should* stop the carriage and let me out," he said. "Adventures are overrated."

"Agreed," said Görthang. The big orc opened the door to the RedX magecoach and growled, "Be gone, Nif!"

Despite the fact that the coach was still in motion, Nif said, "See you around, losers," and jumped out.

Garum watched Nif's leap and saw him land in the back of a loaded hay wagon, probably delivering fodder to one of the many stables in Horse Keep Town. *What are the odds of a hay wagon coming by, just when Nif needed one,* Garum considered. *Probably pretty high, given all the equines within a mile of the town's walls.*

Sweetie repeated her raised eyebrow, but signifying a different meaning this time.

"He's fine," said Garum, explaining Nif's soft landing.

"Good," said Sweetie.

"I don't trust him," said Görthang. "There's something *off* about that lad."

"I agree," said Sweetie. "As an illusionist, I'm growing more skilled at recognizing illusions."

"You think he wasn't what he seemed?" asked Lark. "He looked like a young giant—one of Murphrey's children."

"I expect that's what we were *meant* to think," said Sweetie.

"If he's using some sort of disguise, that might explain how he was able to get past Lilybet and hide under the bench," said Garum.

"Check your belongings," said Görthang, making a grimace that showed off his orc-ish canines. "Make sure Nif didn't steal anything. For all that he looked like an innocent youngling, my instincts tell me he has more in common with Púki than with Crank."

"You think he's a thief, then?" asked Sweetie.

"Of information, at least, if not property," replied Görthang.

"We certainly gave him enough of that," said Garum. "He knows we have something valuable that must be destroyed by the heat of an intense furnace." He opened his belt pouch and sighed when he saw the two vials were still there. "At least I still have the items in question."

"Perhaps we should set a faster pace toward Forge Keep Town and find Fess's forge before dinnertime," said Sweetie.

"I know I'll be more comfortable once those vials have been incinerated," said Lark.

"I'm concerned Nif might get word to Marshall Dylán somehow," added Görthang.

"How?" asked Sweetie. "We're setting a quick pace and Nif's just a lad."

"You told us yourself he may well be more than that," said Garum.

"And Horse Keep Town is known for swift steeds," said Lark.

Garum nodded his agreement and resolved to listen closely for the sound of rapid hoofbeats overtaking them. His resolution proved to be for naught, however. Soon, his eyes closed, his head leaned on Sweetie's shoulder, and he was well on his way to dreamland. *I shouldn't have had such a big lunch* was his last conscious thought for several hours.

Chapter 33
Finding Fess's Forge

The sun was still above the western horizon when their RedX magecoaches reached the gates of Forge Keep Town. Sweetie had nudged Garum awake a mile back and as he'd become less muzzy-headed, he'd noticed the land stretching off to the left of the ring road was no longer covered in thick green grass. Instead, piles of rocks—ores, rather—in varied shades of red, orange, brown, and black, occupied the ground like so many untidy anthills. Ahead, the impressive steel gates of the town stood open, framing the gleaming metal of Forge Keep's tall tower rising up from the cliffs.

Görthang stuck his head out of their magecoach's window and hailed a gate guard who waved them all through and into the town. Unlike the earthy smells of manure and horses from Horse Keep Town, Garum wrinkled his nose at the smokes and stinks of hundreds of fires for smelting and working metals. Sharp, rhythmic banging assaulted his ears.

"It sounds like bells," said Lark.

Indeed it does, thought Garum. *Those are smith's hammers.* He remembered field kitchens next to the smithies set up to repair damaged weapons and armor many years ago when he first started out as a military cook. The noise made it harder to hear the chief cook's instructions and the acrid odors from heating and quenching steel made it more difficult to adjust levels of spicing—though that was usually just a question of how much salt to add. *When I ran my own kitchens, I set them up far from the smiths,* he reminded himself.

"Now what?" Sweetie asked Görthang. "Do we drive straight to Fess's forge?"

"No," Görthang answered. "There's nowhere to park all our magecoaches there. We should check into an inn and 'stable' the horseless carriages, then find Fess on foot."

"What if he closes in the meantime?" asked Garum. "I don't want to be responsible for these vials any longer than necessary."

"We made good time getting here," said Görthang. "A quarter of an hour to stop at an inn shouldn't make any difference."

"More like half an hour, minimum," observed Lark.

The others nodded, acknowledging the accuracy of Lark's statement.

"When we get to the inn, I'll see to our rooms and the magecoaches," said Görthang. "You can take any of the others you want to accompany you, and I'll arrange for our dinner as well and join you as fast as I can."

"But you're the one who knows where Fess's forge is located," said Garum.

"Blōgot also knows how to find the place," said Görthang. "She can lead you—and you may want to bring Hrefna or Gêrdun along for magic, muscle, and intimidation, if necessary."

"Sounds good," said Sweetie. "How far is this inn?" she asked. "I assume you have a particular one in mind?"

"Of course," said Görthang. He leaned out the window and pointed. "I know all the best inns around the Keep Lands. There it is now."

Garum stood on the bench seat, crowding Sweetie and following the line of Görthang's arm. He saw a squat, wide, two-story structure painted a soft green. *No, that's not paint. The place is sheathed in copper that's been there long enough to develop a lovely patina.*

"There's a frog on its sign," said Sweetie.

Indeed there was, Garum noticed. The sign, hanging from a bright brass pole sticking out from above the inn's front door, was a well-made, embossed depiction of a bullfrog on a lily pad, enameled in a darker green than the color of the building. Small copper circles, like so many freckles, were unpainted and unoxidized. Garum mentally slapped himself when he realized what the name of the inn had to be.

"Welcome to Rivets," said Görthang.

The combined parties' magecoaches pulled up in front of the inn and Görthang sorted out who was going where.

Garum invited Drain to join the group heading for Fess's forge—assuming the dwarf would have a professional interest in such things. *Even sewer masons might find a wolfram forge fascinating,* Garum thought.

After being cooped up in a RedX for hours, Blōgot was more than willing to lead Garum to the forge. It was decided that Hrefna could provide both might *and* magic for their small party, especially given that Sweetie had her wand of illusion and Drain carried the Stone Prince's hammer-axe.

Púki's voice caught Garum's attention before they could set out, however. "Who was the kid jumping out of your magecoach back in Horse Keep Town?" the short orc asked.

"He said his name was Nif," said Lark.

"More like half his name, or his job description," said Púki. "I think I recognized him. He's a gonif—a thief—with excellent disguise skills."

"Takes one…" said Xarra.

"…to know one," Yarra completed.

"What was he doing in your coach?" asked Púki. "No, wait, I can *guess* what he was doing. Count your fingers and toes to make sure he didn't steal any of them."

Sweetie held out her hands and wiggled her fingers. "They all seem to be here," she said.

Garum looked closely at Sweetie's hands and smiled. She'd used her illusions to generate an extra finger on each one. He held up his own and found he could also count to twelve without taking off his boots. Púki was oblivious to Sweetie's visual joke, but Garum wasn't and promised to show Sweetie just how much he appreciated her bit of humor later in their bedchamber.

Púki snorted. "He must have been trying to get *something*," he said.

"We think he might have been hoping to steal valuable information," said Sweetie.

"And he may well have done so," said Lark.

"Let's get moving so Nif can't *act* on that information," said Garum.

"Good advice," said Blōgot. "Follow me. It's not far."

Hrefna, Sweetie, Garum, Drain, and Lark gathered 'round the orc archer and walked farther into Forge Keep Town, turning right and left in a seemingly random pattern as Blōgot led them through a maze of twisting alleyways. Garum was glad Lark was along, since she could likely confirm whether the furnace's heat completely disintegrated the vials and their contents.

They proceeded along narrow streets and saw several forges, but the smiths pounding away at anvils beside them were working iron or softer metals, not wolfram. The streets were busy, with peddlers selling pretzels and drinks, smiths carrying their finished products to customers, and the occasional town guard in a jangling mail shirt covered with a black and gold tabard.

After a few minutes and more turns, Hrefna adopted the voice of a small child and asked Blōgot, "Are we there yet? Are we there yet?"

Blōgot shook her head. "Soon," she told the troll wizard. "I may have missed an alley or two."

"You mean we're lost?" asked Sweetie.

"No," said Blōgot. "Fess's forge is within a couple of blocks of here, I'm sure."

"What's the real reason you're guiding us, not Görthang?" Garum asked as they continued following Blōgot.

"Görthang isn't Fess's favorite person," said Blōgot. "It goes back to the disposition of a flaméleon's armor Görthang was commissioned to recover on an expedition twenty levels down in the Deeps below Forge Keep."

"What was special about the armor?" asked Drain.

"Was it made of wolfram?" chimed in Lark.

"It was," said Blōgot. "It needed to be to withstand the heat of the flaméleon's body."

"What's a flaméleon?" asked Sweetie. "Does it change the color of its flames to match its surroundings or something?"

"Flameleon's are very large and powerful fire creatures who carry whips tipped with sharp wolfram blades," said Hrefna. "They don't change color to match their surroundings, but the flames that radiate from their bodies do move from yellow to red to blue-white when they get angry."

"And they're often angry," said Blōgot.

"Beyond needing to be heat resistant, what was *special* about the armor?" asked Drain, returning to the matter of *her* concern. "And why did its disposition displease Fess?"

"Fess wanted a definitive answer to a longstanding question about flaméleons," said Blōgot. "And for that, he needed its cuirass."

"Ah," said Garum. He nodded, touched the tips of his thumbs together, extended his fingers, and moved both hands to imitate a butterfly in flight.

"Exactly," said Hrefna. "Fess wanted the armor's backplate to answer, once and for all, if flaméleon's had wings."

"One of my instructors at the Healer's College who specialized in treating burns had a painting of a flaméleon in her office," said Lark. "From what I remember, it looked like it had wings."

"That's a copy of a famous painting hanging in the Great Hall of the Martial Academy," said Blōgot. "Many think the wings are simply suggested by the shapes of the clouds in the background. Fess wanted the backplate to see if it had holes cut out for wings."

"So what happened?" asked Sweetie. "Did Görthang refuse to give Fess the backplate?"

Blōgot laughed. "We never managed to defeat the flaméleon," she told them.

"The fight ended in a draw," added Hrefna. "I wrapped the flaméleon's whip around my club-wand and wound it up so it stopped flailing around, but it was so strong…"

"…and gave off so much heat," said Blōgot, "that Görthang called a truce, and we gave up."

"You *reasoned* with a flaméleon?" said Garum.

"It was more like a mutual decision to take a break from fighting," said Blōgot. "We were all parched, and even the flaméleon was starting to tire. Görthang offered it something it couldn't refuse in return for some relevant information."

"What did he offer?" asked Sweetie.

"A small bottle containing concentrated tincture of Dragons' Fire peppers," said Hrefna.

"That's stronger than nitric acid!" said Garum.

"We call it *aqua fortis* at the college," said Lark.

"I *stored* the tincture in an *aqua fortis* container," said Hrefna.

"Then what happened?" asked Drain.

"The the exchange was made. The flaméleon got the tincture and we got the information," said Blōgot.

"*WHAT* information?" shouted Drain, Garum, and Sweetie, their voices echoing off the nearby walls.

"Now I understand," said Lark. She laughed and did a quick pirouette. "You asked the flaméleon to turn around."

Hrefna and Blōgot smiled.

"Exactly," said the troll mage.

"You hit the mark," said the orc archer.

"And?" said Garum.

Drain and Sweetie each raised an eyebrow, though it was harder to tell on Drain, since she was wearing the Stone Prince's helm.

"And what?" said Hrefna.

"And *did* it have wings?" asked Garum.

Hrefna and Blōgot smiled again.

"What?" Sweetie protested. "Tell us!"

"We can't," said Blōgot.

"The flaméleon swore us to secrecy," said Hrefna.

"And Görthang, too," said Sweetie.

"Görthang especially," said Blōgot. "He was the one who'd handled the negotiations with Fess."

"So he sent *you* to see if the wolfram smith could be persuaded to do us a favor..." said Garum.

"...after Görthang reneged on his part of their earlier bargain," said Sweetie.

"No wonder he didn't want to lead us to Fess's forge himself," said Garum.

Blōgot sighed as they reached a T-intersection and she looked left and right, trying to decide which way to turn. "Fess has never met me, but under the circumstances, perhaps it would be better if you talked to him on your own."

"Your influencer potion is still working," said Sweetie. "That should help."

"Right," said Garum. "I'll just *tell* Fess to crank up his forge to its highest heat for an unspecified reason."

"That would probably work," said Lark. "Things like that worked for the Provost, after all."

"Very well," said Garum. "You know I'm not comfortable using my influencer abilities, but I'll do it." He patted his belt pouch. "The sooner these vials are destroyed, the happier I'll be."

"If we can just find Fess's forge," said Sweetie.

"Wait a second," said Drain. "Isn't a fess a horizontal bar across the middle of a heraldic shield?"

"Yes," said Sweetie. "And a pale is a vertical bar."

"There's a white sign hanging outside a building at the end of the alley to the left that has a black horizontal bar painted on it between a wolf's head at the top and a ram's head at the bottom," said Drain.

"That's it!" said Blōgot. "The sign all but announces Fess's Wolf Ram forge."

They all began to move down the alleyway at a trot until they came to a halt like hitting an invisible wall five yards away from the forge. A slender man not much taller than Garum stood by a squad of a dozen soldiers in the mottled green livery of South Keep's Martial Academy. They were armed with halberds and backed by a pair of orcish wizards, also in livery, with wands at the ready. A similar contingent was approaching from the other end of the alley.

"We meet again," said the slender man.

"Nif," said Garum. "You've aged."

"Not really," said the thief. He slid his open hand over his face from his forehead to his chin and suddenly took on the appearance of the young giant he'd assumed when he'd hidden under the seat in the magecoach. Sliding his hand back up returned his face to its current, more mature appearance. "It's a simple enough thing after taking the right potion," Nif asserted.

"What do you want from me?" said Garum, sadly sure he knew the answer.

Nif gestured toward Garum's belt pouch as the squad beside Nif began to move.

Blōgot reached for her bow while Sweetie drew her wand of illusions and Hrefna started to flourish her club-wand. Before they could take action, one of the soldiers had stepped behind Lark and put the edge of her short sword along Lark's throat.

Nif spoke in a tone that was not quite a sneer. "As I said," he announced to Garum. "You have something I—or more precisely, my employer—wants. Hand it over and nobody will get hurt."

Unless the clarks in the vials are released, thought Garum. He considered the effectiveness of Lark's healing potions and weighed that against how much good they'd do the young healer if her throat was cut, and she couldn't drink one. Garum's shoulders slumped. He nodded to Nif and slowly reached for his belt pouch.

Chapter 34
Sounds of Silence

"You don't want to do this," said Garum, remembering the power of the influencer potion and using the same tone he'd use to stop a junior cook who was about to toss a wet chicken leg into a pot of boiling oil.

Nif looked over at Lark then back at Garum. "Hand it over," he said, pointing to Garum's pouch.

"Release the healer," said Garum, changing the focus of his command to the soldier holding Lark instead of Nif. He opened his belt pouch and palmed something he took from inside it.

The soldier began to comply, but Nif shouted, "I'm the one giving the orders around here! As you were."

Why wasn't my influence working on Nif? Garum asked himself. *Perhaps my words weren't strong enough?*

"I have plenty of experience ignoring orders I don't want to obey," said Nif. He waved to the orc mages standing by the soldiers and simply said, "Silence." A few flicks of their wands later, everything went quiet. The omnipresent pounding of hammers on anvils ceased and Garum couldn't even hear his own lungs draw breath.

A clever trick that, thought Garum. *We should have tried it on Galena back in her office. Time for some misdirection.* He stared at the soldier holding Lark then raised his glance to look at a point a foot or more above the soldier's head. Garum let his eyes go wide as if some sort of giant monster was standing behind the soldier.

Instinctively, the soldier lowered her short sword a few inches before turning to see whatever threat Garum had seen. Garum threw the lead bullet he'd palmed directly at the soldier's helmet with enough force to make her head ring if the silence spell hadn't been in effect. As it was, the woman with the short sword toppled over, collapsing onto the cobblestones.

Lark leaped over to stand beside Hrefna while the troll mage spun her club-wand over her head and released a massive blast of percussive force at Nif, the squad of soldiers, and the orc mages standing with him. They joined the soldier who'd been threatening Lark on the cobbles.

Garum sensed movement at the other end of the alley and turned to see a sight that made him grin. Görthang was there with the remaining members of the combined Black and Golden Companies. They had apparently taken advantage of the silence spell to sneak up on the second squad of soldiers and mages. Prestyn's Cloak of Arms proved most effective in dealing with the second squad by wrapping tentacles around each soldiers' mouth and nose, keeping them in place until they all lost consciousness and joined their comrades on the alley's uneven stone surface.

A well-muscled ogre so short and with such broad shoulders his body seemed square, not rectangular, stepped out of the door below the hanging Wolf-Ram-Fess sign. He was obviously trying to shout, but the silence spell was canceling out his words. Hrefna made a gesture with her club-wand and suddenly everyone still conscious knew exactly what was on the ogre's mind.

"What in the sixteen keeps is going on here!" said the ogre. "Don't you know I have to *hear* my hammers strike metal to forge weapons and armor effectively? I'm an *artist!* How can I practice my art without sound." Not hearing an immediate reply, he looked both ways along the alley, took in all the soldiers in livery, and shook his head. "And what in the seventy flocks of Shepherd's Keep are *they* doing here?"

"There's a Shepherd's Keep?" Garum whispered to Sweetie.

"I think it's just a figure of speech," Sweetie replied.

"There are flocks of sheep on the hills beyond Dragon Keep," said Lark softly. "The dragons get the meat, and the shepherds get the wool." Lark turned away to enlist help from Arrex in dribbling small amounts of the liquid from the potion bottle into the mouths of Nif, the mages, and each of the liveried soldiers. Garum put his palms together then caught Lark's eye and rested his cheek on his conjoined palms as if he was taking a nap. Lark nodded.

One less thing to worry about, for now, thought Garum. *They should be asleep for an hour or so. But I'll want to have words with Nif when he wakes.*

"The reason the soldiers are here is probably not a topic to be discussed on a public street, or alley," said Blōgot.

"I negated the silence spell," said Hrefna. "You must be Fess, the master of this forge."

"Not just must be, but *am,*" said the ogre.

"We came to find you," said Hrefna. "You can pound away and ruin your hearing as much as you want, now."

"Clearly, you don't know the best smiths stuff their ears with beeswax," said the ogre. "And I *know* you and that orc archer beside you as well. Where's the duplicitous so-called *leader* of your Black Company?" Fess smacked one of his meaty fists into his palm hard enough that the sound of the impact echoed up and down the alley. "I'd like to put his head between my hammer and anvil to teach him to honor his agreements."

"I'm here, you over-muscled metal mangler," said Görthang as he quickly stepped over to stand beside Blōgot and Hrefna.

"Metal mangler, is it?" said Fess. "I'll extend my line of business to mangle your *bones* for you, you incompetent second-rate sell sword! Where's the backplate I commissioned you to bring me?"

"Still protecting the back of the flaméleon, I suppose," said Blōgot in a soothing voice Garum thought she was using to ratchet the tension level down a few notches.

"When you promised to deliver it to *me!*" said Fess.

"The flaméleon had other ideas," said Görthang.

"You knew *why* I wanted that backplate," said Fess. "Were you at least able to confirm if there were slots in it for wings?"

"We were," Görthang replied.

"Well, *were* there?" Fess bellowed.

"In return for showing us, the flaméleon swore us to never to disclose if there were or not," said Görthang.

"We had to sign a formal agreement about it," said Hrefna.

"In red ink," added Blōgot.

"But blood is thicker than ink," said Fess.

"What's he talking about?" asked Garum.

"Couldn't you tell from how they spoke to each other?" said Hrefna. "Fess and Görthang and brothers."

"Half-brothers!" Fess and Görthang shouted simultaneously.

"Fess's mother was an ogre," said Blōgot.

"That makes sense," said Sweetie.

"Can't you at least give me a hint about the flaméleon's backplate?" asked Fess. "I *really* want to know."

Blōgot made the same sort of butterfly with her outstretched fingers that Garum had made earlier and flapped her palms. Hrefna frowned and shook her head from side to side, leaving Garum—and Fess—still in the dark about the matter. Finally, Fess shrugged his massive shoulders.

"Looks like I won't get an answer today," he said. "But you said you had something to talk about that would be better discussed in private. Come in. I was just making dinner. You're all welcome to join me." Fess waved them through the door beneath the sign for his forge and closed it behind him. After a few words from Garum, Prestyn used his Cloak of Arms to carry Nif's sleeping body inside along with them.

* * * * *

The room Fess welcomed them into was long and wide enough to fit two magecoaches or a four-horse team side to side. Broad-bladed fans spun slowly near the ceiling and the space was comfortably cool even though they could hear the roar of the furnace blasting away on the other side of the left-hand wall. A table ran half the length of the room and comfortable-looking overstuffed armchairs and sofas lined the left and right walls. A massive desk stood a few feet out from the far wall, flanked by a pair of slate boards mounted on casters that were covered in designs for some sort of machine with several pairs of thick rollers.

Fess casually erased part of the drawing on the upper-left side of one of the slate boards, grabbed a piece of chalk, and called out to the members of the Black and Gold Companies. "I can make custom flatbreads for your dinners," he announced. "Let me know what you'd like on yours and I'll get started on making them."

"Won't that take a long time?" asked Sweetie.

"Not at all," said Fess. "There's an oven set into the left-hand wall that has an insulated connection to my wolfram furnace. Once it's spun out and topped, each one takes under a minute to bake."

"Let us help," said Crank.

"Many hands..." said Xarra.

"...make light work," added Yarra.

"Very good," said Fess. He opened a door behind his desk which turned out to be a wizard's cold box holding chopped vegetables, sliced meats, shredded cheeses, and minced garlic. Following his instructions Sweetie and Garum discovered an enclosure along the left-hand wall well-stocked with balls of dough kept there to rise. Below it, he found a rack packed tightly with thin metal plates. To the side of the enclosure was a small canvas bag of finely ground maize meal.

Blōgot suggested that she could write down individual flatbread orders while Fess managed the actual baking, since he had the most experience with the idiosyncrasies of his oven. Garum showed Drain and Sir Donal how to punch down and spin-flatten balls of dough with Drain using the Stone Prince's hammer-axe for the flattening and Sir Donal's augmented strength for the spinning.

Xarra, Yarra, and Crank assembled ingredients on top of each flatbread and Prestyn conveyed each one from the table to where Garum and Fess worked at the oven. Garum stood on a bench and used one wooden paddle to deal with the flatbreads in the front of the oven, while Fess focused his attention on the ones in the back, rotating them to the front every few seconds as their toppings began to bubble.

"It all smells *wonderful,*" said Sweetie. She checked with Fess and got several of the others busy with putting knives, forks, and napkins around the table, setting out mugs, and putting pitchers of ale, cider, and water in place at intervals.

As Garum worked side-by-side with Fess he asked the smith a question. "If it's hot enough to melt wolfram on the other side of this wall, why isn't *this* side as hot as a flatbread oven?"

"Magic," said Fess.

Garum bit back a snappy retort, remembering that he needed to stay on the smith's good side, trying a gentler response instead. "Like a mage's cold box?" he asked as he moved a flatbread from the the oven to one of Vip-vip's waiting hands.

"Sort of," said Fess. "There's a three-foot gap between the furnace and the office. I sealed it and pumped all the air out of it when I built the building." He shifted two flatbread rounds from the back of the oven to the front and nodded to Garum that they were now his responsibility.

"How did you manage to maintain a vacuum with masonry?" asked Garum.

"The hot side is lined with clay over thin sheets of wolfram," said Fess. He waited for Garum to pass another flatbread to Vip-vip. "And the other is lined with sheets of tempered glass scavenged from ancient ruins."

"Clever," said Garum as he transferred the last two flatbreads to Vip-vip and one of the arms of Prestyn's cloak. "That does it," he said.

"Let's eat," said Fess. "Then we can talk."

They joined the others at the long table with Fess pausing long enough to fill Garum's mug with ale. "You didn't need to wait for us before you started eating," he said. "I don't want your food to get cold."

"Cold?" said Sweetie from Garum's side. "Mine is still so hot I nearly burned my tongue trying to taste a stray mushroom."

"How hot is your oven, anyway?" asked Crank.

"Well," said Fess, "Wolfram melts at over six thousand degrees."

"Flatbreads would turn into charred smears in seconds in an oven that hot," said Drain.

"My flatbread oven is only eight hundred to a thousand degrees," said Fess. "You'll want to blow on it first to cool it before you bite into it—at least if you value your hard palate."

Púki put a bite of flatbread in his mouth and immediately made a face like he'd just kissed a flaméleon. He snatched up one of the water pitchers and poured its contents down his throat like he was trying to swallow a waterfall. Garum imagined he could see smoke coming out of Púki's ears.

"You should have waited," Xarra told him.

"You should have blown on it first," said Yarra.

Púki glared at the twins and reached for another water pitcher, ending up with ale instead. He poured the contents of that pitcher inside him as well. The twins shook their heads.

"It seems like we'll need to wait for a little while before enjoying our dinner," said Sweetie. "Maybe now would be a good time to talk?"

"Go ahead," said Fess. "You seem to be good people from the way you pitched in to help make dinner—my *half*-brother excepted. What can Fess's Forge do for you?"

"First," said Garum. "Is your furnace currently hot enough to melt wolfram?"

"I never let my furnace go cold," said Fess. "It takes too long to get it back to its full heat if I do."

"How long would it take you to get it back to full heat?" asked Garum.

"An hour or so," said Fess. "But I wasn't planning to melt wolfram tonight."

"We need to destroy something," said Garum.

"Disintegrate it, really," said Sweetie.

"Is this thing you need to destroy dangerous?" asked Fess.

"Very," said Lark. "Tens, maybe hundreds of thousands of lives are at stake."

"Is it valuable?" said Fess.

"Only to those who would commit mass murder," said Garum.

"That explains why all the soldiers were outside my forge," said Fess. "The Marshall obviously wants this thing of value. Death is his business."

"Soldiers skills are for protecting people," said Sir Donal. "Not murdering them."

"You must not know many soldiers," said Fess.

"I've served on many battlefields and commanded armies," said Sir Donal. Sweetie crossed to her grandfather and held his arm.

"Why shouldn't I just let the Marshall know you're here and let him pay me for news of whatever it is you carry?" asked Fess.

Görthang cleared his throat, stood, and stared down the table at Fess. "How much do you want, *brother?* What will convince you to do the right thing and help my friends?"

"You know what I want, *brother,*" said Fess. "Tell me about the flaméleon's wings. Does it have them or not?"

"Very well," said Görthang. "I'll break my word of honor and tell you—after you've destroyed what Garum carries."

"I'll stoke the forge," said Fess. "Enjoy your flatbread." The smith left through the front door, carrying his own round of flatbread with him.

Görthang sat down. All the others' eyes were on him. "It's necessary," he said.

From the sofa on the side wall, Nif groaned.

Chapter 35

Forging Friendships

"Give him more sleeping potion," Lark told Arrex in a healer's do-what-I-say voice that could rival any military commander's. "I should go with Garum to make sure the vials are incinerated properly." She followed Fess and Garum out the front door without a backward glance to confirm Arrex was obeying her 'orders' to keep Nif asleep.

Garum wondered why Fess didn't have a door directly from his office to his furnace, then shook his head. *It's because of the vacuum gap, idiot,* he told himself. *Though that makes me wonder why he didn't simply build his furnace building as a standalone structure fifty feet away from any other structures.*

The liveried soldiers and orc mages were still sleeping in the alley, though someone—Garum thought Forge Keep Town constables—had positioned them neatly against the walls on either side of the alley, leaving enough room for people and carts to pass.

"I need to be close at hand to monitor the furnace and the melting wolfram," Fess told Garum as he unlocked the door to the thick-walled building holding his forge and furnace. "It can be a challenge to maintain the high temperatures needed and to adjust things to keep the metal workable after it comes out."

By this time, Lark and Sweetie had caught up to them, with Görthang standing a few paces behind.

"They can come in, but not you," said Fess, waving his free hand at the women, but shaking his head at Görthang.

"What if you need someone with a strong back to work the bellows?" said Görthang.

"I have megapedes for that, as you should know," Fess told Görthang. "And I'm using high-speed fans, not bellows—as you should also know, if you were paying attention."

"We ran into megapedes in the Deeps," said Sweetie. "I didn't know they could be tamed and put to work."

"It was my half-brother's idea," said Fess. "They run on a big wooden wheel chasing a chunk of freshly butchered meat that's just out of reach. I gear down that motion to turn small fan wheels very fast, sending lots of air into the furnace."

"I can hold the meat in front of the megapedes for you," said Görthang. "Please. Let me help."

Fess sighed and reluctantly decided he wouldn't close the door to his furnace leaving Görthang on the outside. "Very well," Fess said. "If I didn't let you in, you'd just sit outside the door and complain all day, like you did as a child."

"The same way you used to sit outside and complain when I wouldn't let you in the room where I did my pell work when it was raining," said Görthang.

"What's a pell?" asked Lark.

"A wooden pole wrapped with cloth stuffed with wool," said Garum. "People practicing their swordplay strike a pell instead of another person or an animal."

"That seems sensible," said Lark.

"But it only takes you so far," said Garum.

"Because pells don't hit back," said Görthang. "You can practice your blows, but not your defense."

"Maybe you should have practiced with Fess," Lark suggested.

"I *like* her," said Fess. "And I would have liked practicing with *you*, brother."

"Peace," said Görthang. "What's passed is past. I'd be glad to spar with you, if you'd teach me some smithing."

"Let's get the furnace up to full heat before we hug," said Fess. Laugh lines appeared at the corners of his mouth. "Get the megapedes started."

The forge and furnace room was divided into two parts by a masonry wall with a small door in its center. On either side of the door were windows of a sort, made from what looked to be quartz blocks a yard square. The part where they were standing included cages, each holding an armored megapede with hundreds of chitin-covered legs. It was the size of an ox but twice as long. Beside the cages were huge steel wheels of the sort that might power a mill, except these didn't have paddles to catch water. Instead, they had smooth flooring on their inner surfaces where megapedes could run. Chains hooked over sprockets on the outer edge of the wheel disappeared into the rear of the building.

The furnace itself must be back there, thought Garum. *And the forge, so Fess can soften the wolfram while shaping it.*

Görthang rattled the bars of the left-hand megapede's cage, then raised the metal plate separating the cage from the wheel. With a scrabble of feet, the giant arthropod moved on to the wheel and lifted its front-most body segments in the air as if seeking a reward for its actions. Görthang spotted a wizard's cold box near the cage, removed an entire ham from one side of it, and carefully attached the ham to a hook before swinging it into the wheel above the megapede. As designed, the megapede began to run, chasing the meat that was, at least for now, out of reach.

Garum could hear fans whirring from the other side of the wall separating the front and back of the building. He watched Görthang repeat the process of moving a megapede to its wheel on the right side as well. The fan noise doubled.

"Don't you have to stoke the furnace?" asked Sweetie.

"That's next," said Fess. "Agní has been keeping it warm, so it's Ātar's turn to ramp of the heat."

"Agní?" said Sweetie.

"Ātar?" echoed Lark.

"My fire worms," said Fess. "Wingless dragons that breathe fire. Lots of smiths use them to heat their furnaces. I have two, since I don't dare let my furnace go out. Together, they can get the heat close to the temperature needed to melt wolfram and the high-speed fans take it from there to over six thousand degrees."

"Impressive," said Garum. "Do you have to instruct them to start heating?"

"No," said Fess. "They know to get on it as soon as the fans start turning. Fire worms aren't the brightest of dragons, but Agní and Ātar are plenty bright enough. It costs me a lot of gold to keep them in reading matter, but I don't begrudge them their books, since they're engraved on thin sheets of wolfram. Sales to the specialized fire worm publishers help keep my shop in business, since there are only so many wolfram shields needed in a given year. They're practically indestructible, you know."

Garum did know. One of the captains he'd served with carried a wolfram shield passed down from his great-great grandmother.

"What sorts of things do fire worms like to read?" asked Sweetie.

"Philosophy, history, travelers' tales, that sort of thing," said Fess. "At least that's what they'll admit to. The publishers tell a different story, though."

"Oh?" said Sweetie. "Tell me. What are fire worms *really* into?"

"Prurient romances," said Fess. "The spicier, the better."

"Now I want to meet them!" said Sweetie. "I like books like that, too, but printed on paper, not sheets of wolfram."

Fess smiled at Sweetie and his eyes flicked from her to Garum then back, as if asking what she saw in the halfling.

"He inspires me," Sweetie replied to Fess's unspoken question.

"It might be difficult for you to meet Agní and Ātar," said Fess. "When they're working, the temperature in their chambers is quite high. Unprotected, you'd be cooked in seconds."

"Good to know," said Sweetie. She winked at Garum because she knew he'd be thinking of her naked the way she liked to be in a hot steam room, though visiting the fire worms' quarters sounded like a different order of magnitude from a sauna. Soon, they could feel the room getting hotter.

Garum wiped droplets of sweat from his forehead. "How hot does it get in here?" he asked Fess as he started to feel like *he* was melting, not any sort of metal.

"Sorry!" said Fess. "I forgot to start the fans on *this* side of the barrier. I'm so used to the heat; I sometimes forget how others might respond." Fess pointed to a pair of chains leading up to the ceiling, one on the left side of the room, one on the right. "Pull on those," he said.

Lark grabbed the left chain and Sweetie took hold of the one on the right. They nodded to each other and pulled them simultaneously. Fans inset into the ceiling began turning rapidly, sucking hot air out of the room and lowering the overall temperature.

"More megapedes on the roof?" asked Sweetie.

"No," said Fess. "A dozen Megascuriuses."

Lark saw the confusion on Sweetie's face. "He means big squirrels," she said. "Probably running around in wire wheels to turn the fans that suck hot air out."

"Correct," said Fess. "The squirrels above the forge are efficient *and* economical."

"Let me guess," said Görthang. "They work for peanuts?"

"Walnuts," Fess corrected. "But close enough."

"I'm impressed," said Garum. "They appear to be doing a great job, despite the work being exhausting."

Sweetie gave Garum a look that told him he'd be *pun*-ished for that remark later, when she had him helpless in bed.

Fess shook his head and assumed a *what am I going to do with someone like Garum* expression. He crossed to the far wall next, the one separating their current room from the one where the furnace was located, and opened a deep cabinet, revealing a pair of long black gloves mounted a few inches below shoulder height.

"What are those?" asked Görthang.

"Odlaw's Hands," said Fess.

"Who's Odlaw?" asked Görthang.

"The wizard who created the spell," replied Fess.

"*What* spell?" said Görthang.

"Oh, I know. I know," said Lark as she bounced on the balls of her feet like a child waiting to be given a square of honey cake. "I've heard of this spell. Anything you do with your arms and hands in the gloves is duplicated by an equivalent construct a few feet away. Is that how you can work the wolfram without getting cooked like a rib roast in the furnace room?"

"Exactly," said Fess. He glanced from Lark to Sweetie to Garum. "Now I'm going to need whatever it is you want me to vaporize."

Garum looked at Lark and Sweetie. They both nodded, so he opened his belt pouch and carefully removed the vials he'd taken from Galena. He held them out to Lark for her to inspect.

"I can't say for sure," she said, "but they look like the standard vials where we healers keep dangerous animacules."

Fess frowned. "Are they dangerous even in sealed vials?"

"No," said Lark. "Unless you drop them or break the seal."

"I'm not going to do that," said Fess.

"And the vials won't be dangerous at all after you vaporize them in your furnace," said Görthang. "Just get on with it."

Garum checked to confirm his hands weren't shaking and was about to hand the vials to Fess. "How do you get them into the furnace room?" he asked.

Fess pointed to another cabinet beside the one with the Odlaw's Hands gloves. "This is a *very* well insulated pass-through," he said. "It's how I get wolfram ingots over to the furnace where I can work them."

"You won't need to do anything more to the vials than toss them in the furnace," said Garum. *I hope,* he thought. He turned to Lark looking for confirmation. "Right?" he asked her.

"Right," said Lark. "Six thousand degrees should turn the animacules into nothing more than a steaming cloud of chemicals and totally disrupt any *clarks* circling around them."

"Good," said Garum. "The sooner I'm not responsible for carrying something that could kill millions, the better."

"Let's eliminate the problem, then," said Fess. He held out his hands to receive the vials.

Before Garum could put the vials in the wolfram-smith's palm, the left-hand wall exploded inward and a large, smooth ball of heavy stone the size of a troll's skull flew across the room and smashed into the wheel on the far side where a megapede had been running.

"Down!" shouted Görthang.

That was a ball from a mangonel, thought Garum, drawing on his years of military experience as a slinger working side-by-side with artillery specialists. *Given its size, I can probably guess the exact model of catapult that threw it.* A second spherical projectile hit the wall between the furnace room and the one where they were standing—or crouching, depending on whether or not they'd had time to act on Görthang's recommendation. Narrow jets of superheated air shot out from the furnace room, raising the temperature far beyond the capabilities of even a thousand megasquirrels to lower it.

One of the megapedes had been hit by a ball and continued running on its wheel, but in two separate segments.

"Blast!" said Fess as he took in the gaps in the insulating wall.

"Run!" said Garum as he tucked the vials back into his belt pouch.

The others didn't need the power of Garum's influencer potion to see the wisdom in his words. Sweetie opened the door to the outside and stepped out, followed promptly by Lark, Garum, Görthang, and Fess. A third round ball smashed into the room and rolled across the floor where they'd been standing moments before, accompanied by chunks of masonry and mortar dust.

Garum spotted a squad of soldiers with swords and pikes standing close at hand, waiting for them to appear. "Hide us," he whispered to Sweetie. She nodded and used her wand of illusions to trick the soldiers into ignoring them. "We need to get the others and leave," said Garum softly.

Lark opened the door to Fess's office and studio and led them all inside. The rest of the combined Black and Golden Companies were on high alert, given the sounds of mangonel balls striking one of the walls of the room beside them.

A light haze of dust filled the space, but Garum could see they were all prepared to leave, except for Púki, who was shoving a piece of flatbread into his mouth instead of putting his pack on his back. Garum grabbed his own pack while Sweetie, Lark, and Görthang did the same. Nif, against one wall, was waking.

"Marshall Dylán's people?" Garum asked Görthang.

"Most likely," Görthang replied. "We're going to need to lie low for a while."

"Can Fess hide us?"

"That's not what I meant," said Görthang. "We're going to need to enter the Deeps and work our way *past* South Keep on a low level. There are too many troops at the Martial Academy for us to risk taking the ring road."

"And likely too many Academy people on the upper levels of the Deeps, too," said Hrefna. She put one of her massive hands on Fess's equally massive shoulder. "Is there any access to the Deeps here that *doesn't* require entering the Keep itself?"

"Indeed there is," said Fess.

"Take us there, please, brother," said Garum.

"Gladly, *brother*," said Fess. "But even with Sweetie's illusions it will help if we have a distraction."

"Ah," said Görthang. "A pair of unhappy fire worms."

"I'm sure Agní and Ātar are not all that happy about having boulders thrown at their home," said Fess. "Let me shout through my oven. I'm sure they'll hear me."

Garum and the others, led by Fess and disguised by Sweetie's illusions, made their way along the twisting passageways of Forge Keep Town, past the somewhat singed retreating soldiers.

No featherbed with Sweetie for me tonight, Garum grumbled. *But at least Marshall Dylán doesn't have the vials!*

Chapter 36

Rest Stop

The fire worms were more than adequate distractions, roaring and shooting pillars of superheated flame toward the sky like erupting volcanoes. A pair of red-hot stone balls also sped into the air to crash on the siege equipment that had tossed them originally, transforming the Martial Academy's *mangonels* into so many smoldering piles of kindling.

Garum was pleased that Sweetie's illusions effectively disguised Fess and the combined parties, making them look like squads of soldiers moving through the streets under orders only they were privy to. Hidden in plain sight, they covered perhaps a quarter of a mile of twisting alleyways, working their way closer to the town's central citadel and wherever Fess was leading them.

"Down these stairs," said Fess as he held open a disguised door in the wall of a building half a block from the tower of Forge Keep. The wall was made from riveted iron, steel, copper, brass, and bronze plates. "It's an annex to the smith's guild's headquarters," Fess informed them.

Drain led the combined parties down the dark stairs with Prestyn behind her. Two of the tentacles of the young mage's Cloak of Arms held glowing wizard globes to help light their way. Garum and Sweetie, along with Görthang and Hrefna, brought up the rear with Fess, who had just closed the heavy metal door behind him.

"Sometimes we need access to the Deeps without attention from the guards," Fess explained. "The Martial Academy controls the keep itself and the smiths constructed their own separate access."

"For which we're all grateful," said Görthang.

"It probably helps that so many smiths are dwarves, able to work stone and metal," said Drain.

"True," said Fess, "but gnomes and ogres—with training—can command the same magics."

"So long as we can get where we want to go without fighting an entire army from the Academy," said Sir Donal.

He makes a good point, thought Garum. *I wonder if Sweetie's grandfather had any Academy training? Or remembers any, if he did?* Garum shrugged and kept moving.

They all walked lightly down a long flight of stairs until they reached a broad, square chamber that nonetheless seemed crowded given their numbers.

"Where to now?" asked Hrefna.

"More stairs," said Fess as he waved toward the far side of the chamber. "At least two dozen flights until there's a cross-corridor leading to Forge Keep's main stairs."

"Which gets us well past the Academy's checkpoints closer to the top," mused Blōgot.

"You're a wise woman," said Fess. "Which makes me wonder why you're still with my half-brother."

"Hey!" said Görthang.

"Let it pass," said Hrefna, putting one of her massive hands on Görthang's shoulder. Görthang smiled, removed Hrefna's hand, and stepped close to Fess, his brother's teasing comment seemingly forgotten.

Fess and Görthang spoke quietly for a few seconds. Then the big smith hugged Görthang. When the hug ended, Fess waved the combined companies on their way and wished them well before heading back up and out. "Good luck!" he called.

"Thanks!" said Garum. *We'll need it.* He was very much aware of the weight of the two dangerous vials in his belt pouch as he trudged down the stairs. Everyone else in the combined parties had their heads down, watching their steps, except for Vip-vip, who seemed excited to be back underground. *Well,* thought Garum, *Vip-vip is from the Deeps and is effectively going home.* Garum smiled to himself. *And at least we're walking down, not up.*

The flights of stairs ended several stories down at a large chamber hewn from a fine-grained gray stone and lit by wizard lamps that began to glow when they entered. Swords, spears, halberds, helms, shields and other examples of smith's arts were mounted on the walls. A tall steel door with enough clearance for a giant or a sylviant was in the center of one of the walls. It was polished enough to shine and incised with intricate geometric designs.

When Garum looked closer, he saw the door's decorations also included some writing.

"Abandon all hope, ye who enter here?" asked Púki.

"Shut your face!" said Xarra.

"And keep it shut!" added Yarra.

"Probably *This Way to the Egress,*" said Crank.

"Close," Garum replied. "It says, 'Main Stairs to the Deeps.'"

"Let's take a short break before proceeding," Sweetie suggested. "We've had quite an afternoon."

"It's not every day soldiers try to drop boulders on you," said Kléppri the gnome, who was standing near Drain. He seemed glad to take Sweetie's suggestion and remove his helmet for a few minutes. The others did the same, sliding their packs off their shoulders and stretching.

"Any idea why we were attacked?" asked Prestyn.

"Probably because Marshall Dylán wants what I'm carrying," said Garum.

"But throwing rocks at us could have damaged the vials and released their contents," said Arrex.

"Which I expect is what he wants," said Lark. "Once the vials are open, the transformations will start."

"Making more orcs and ogres," said Arrex.

"Nothing wrong with that," said Gêrdun.

"Except that we don't know what the contents of the vials will do to those of us who are already orcs and ogres," said Blōgot. "I don't want to turn into something truly monstrous."

"I'd still love you," said Görthang with a grin that promptly turned into a solemn expression when faced with a withering glance from Blōgot.

"We still have to figure out what to do next," said Sweetie.

"The vials must still be destroyed," said Lark.

"How can we do that without the heat of a wolfram-melting furnace?" asked Drain.

"I have an idea about how to accomplish that," said Görthang.

"I thought you might," said Hrefna. "The Old Worm?" she asked.

"That's right," said Görthang.

"What's the Old Worm?" asked Sweetie.

"Not what, who," said Crank. "The Old Worm is the oldest, largest, and most powerful dragon in the Deep Lands, maybe in the world. I read about him growing up and my aunt even met him once—and lived to tell me about it. His fiery blasts are said to be hot enough to even melt wolfram."

"Good to know," said Garum. "I assume we can find him at Dragon Keep?"

"Correct," said Görthang.

"Which is *only* three keeps away," said Sweetie.

"Past South Keep with all the forces of the Martial Academy," said Sir Donal.

"And Iron Keep, the Academy's close ally," said Drain.

"Not to mention that dragons, particularly great *old* dragons, never do anything without compensation," said Flisk.

Garum looked at the elf, surprised to hear the normally taciturn archer string together so many words at one time. Other than the young scout dragons he'd served with—and occasionally fed meals to—while serving in various armies, he knew little of the species beyond the standard elements such as scales, bat-like wings, long, sharp teeth, and breathing fire. *I hope Görthang knows how to bargain with one,* thought Garum.

"What sorts of things do dragons want in return for their services?" asked Sweetie. "If it's virgins, I think we may be out of luck."

"I'll say," said Xarra.

"True enough, sister," added Yarra.

Crank laughed, giving Garum a sense that the young man was glad he could no longer be described by that label. On Crank's shoulder, Jelly waved a pair of pseudopods to attract everyone's attention, then changed shape to look like an unclothed human woman barely two feet tall. Jelly waggled one eyebrow and gave them all a look that was somehow both demure and *come hither.*

"I guess we've got that covered after all," said Sweetie.

"Somehow, I doubt the Old Worm will want something so pedestrian," said Görthang.

"No streetwalkers, got it," said Púki as he ducked to avoid slaps on the back of his head from Xarra and Yarra.

"Görthang means lacking in excitement or dull, not someone walking," said Crank. "He's using the word as an adjective, not as a noun."

"That's *bor-ing,*" said Púki.

"Exactly," said Crank.

"What *do* you expect the Old Worm to want in return for helping us?" asked Sweetie.

"That's hard to tell," said Görthang. "I've bargained with dragons in the past and they often want gold." He shook his head from side to side then tilted it, considering. "The Old Worm is reputed to have a huge hoard already, though. I expect he'll want something more valuable than mere gold."

"We won't know until we ask him," said Hrefna.

"And we won't be *able* to ask him until we get past South Keep and Iron Keep," said Drain. "We shouldn't count our tunnel snake eggs until they hatch."

"Tunnel snakes?" asked Lark.

"They're supposed to infest the southern keeps," said Blōgot. "The Martial Academy is always testing their trainees by sending out parties to eliminate them."

"How big are these tunnel snakes supposed to be?" asked Prestyn.

"About as big as your arm," said Blōgot.

"Garum's arm or Hrefna's arm?" asked Prestyn.

"Yes," said Blōgot.

"Got it," said Prestyn. "Small to frighteningly large. Thanks."

"No problem," said Blōgot.

"And how many tunnel snakes are we likely to encounter at one time?" asked Prestyn.

"That depends," said Blōgot.

"Depends on?" said Prestyn.

"How many eggs there are," said Blōgot.

"And if they've hatched," added Drain.

"Dozens, most likely," said Blōgot.

"Up to hundreds," said Drain. "But the newly hatched ones are tiny, not much bigger around than my finger."

Púki seemed ready to offer a comment, then saw the twins' hands raised to smack him and thought better of it.

"Wise move," said Xarra.

"For once," said Yarra.

"We can imagine something else about the size of Drain's finger…" said Xarra.

"Her *little* finger," added Yarra.

"How far down do you think we'll need to be to avoid Academy training parties?" Sweetie asked Görthang.

"We're already deep enough to be unlikely to encounter any of them," Görthang replied. "Unfortunately, training parties searching for tunnel snakes aren't what I'm worried about."

"You're thinking Marshall Dylán will send elite teams after us?" said Hrefna.

"I'm almost certain he will," said Görthang. "He wants those vials and would gladly have his soldiers kill us all to get them."

"I don't like the sound of that," said Garum. "What sorts of soldiers are on such teams and how do you recommend we avoid them? Can we go deeper than they expect?"

Hrefna answered. "They're mostly teams of highly trained warriors carrying multiple weapons types—swords, bows, spears, halberds, and maces, leavened with battle mages and a healer or two."

"Sounds like us," said Crank.

Hrefna laughed, sounding like the rumble of thunder after crack of lightning. "The Black Company is, effectively, and elite team. The current Golden Company may achieve that level of competence in half a decade."

"Understood," said Crank. Jelly, who had long since dropped his temporary semblance as a nubile female, melted his protoplasm into a frowning yellow sphere.

"Going deeper is one option," said Görthang, returning to one of Garum's original questions. "But there are also excellent trackers on the elite teams. If they come across our path, they'll find us whichever course we take."

"If it came to a fight, could we take out one of the teams?" asked Sweetie.

"Possibly," said Görthang.

"Probably," said Hrefna. "We're twice the size of one the Academy's elite units. The only problem is the noise of battle would likely attract any other units nearby—unless I cast another silence spell. Hmmm…"

"Would it make sense for me to take a shot at using my influencer abilities on an elite team?" asked Garum.

"That's worth trying," said Görthang.

"I won't cast a silence spell until after you've made such an attempt," Hrefna told Garum.

Sir Donal caught Garum's attention and spoke. "Soldiers are used to following orders," said the old knight. "Use your command voice and they should obey."

Garum nodded and moved to study the metal door in more detail. He gestured to Görthang, and the orc warrior joined him. "What did Fess tell you before he left?" Garum asked quietly.

"He told me about a transportation system connecting Iron Keep Town and Forge Keep Town," said Görthang. "Supposedly, the Martial Academy doesn't know about it."

"What sort of transportation system?" asked Garum.

"Large carriages and open hoppers for ores that float above metal rails by some strange magic," said Görthang.

"An underground rail road…" mused Garum. "That could be very useful. How do we find it?"

"I'll show you," said Görthang. "It's only another two dozen levels below us."

"Packs on, everyone," said Garum. "We're following Görthang down more stairs."

Chapter 37
Like Clockwork

Görthang pointed at the tall, highly polished steel door and Drain moved in front of it, ready to open it. Garum saw that the intricate geometric designs incised into the door included small, raised circles from floor to ceiling along its right-hand edge like the domed ends of planished rivets. Drain extended her arm and touched the circle closest to her fingers. The massive door swung open silently of its own accord.

Impressive, thought Garum. *Knobs or handles mounted at a height convenient for the average human would be inconvenient for giants—or halflings. I'd bet the door was the product of smithcraft, not magic, as well.*

With Görthang in the lead, they filed through the door and found themselves on a landing of what they assumed was the main staircase from South Keep providing access to the Deeps. The landing was empty and once the tall steel door had closed behind them, they realized its face on this side perfectly matched the stone of the stairwell, making it effectively invisible.

"I don't think we're going back that way," Sweetie whispered.

Garum nodded and followed Görthang and Hrefna down several more flights of stairs. Everyone was careful to make as little noise as possible, since sounds carried up the stairwell and they didn't want to alert any guards higher up to their presence.

Sweetie squeezed Garum's hand and leaned down to put her lips next to his ear. "I wonder how long it will be until we're back in a featherbed," she said softly.

Garum squeezed Sweetie's hand back and smiled then raised both eyebrows, sending a *Who knows?* message while trying hard to suppress his actual thoughts which were more like *I wonder if our next beds will be in South Keep prison cells?* He took a deep breath and forced himself to keep up Görthang's rate of descent—a challenge because Görthang's legs were longer than Garum was tall.

Drain seemed to be inspecting the stonework on the staircases as they went down each flight. To Garum's eyes, they looked identical to the stairs at North Keep, Rose Keep, and East Keep. *I wonder if the same group of dwarvish masons crafted all of them?* Garum mused.

After descending so many flights that Garum lost count, they reached a broad landing that included one of the metal doors that led into the Deeps. More steps continued down but Görthang held up a hand and motioned for everyone to stop. He stepped over to the metal door, put a finger to his lips to remind everyone to stay quiet, then lowered his hand and opened the door. He nodded to the rest of the combined companies and waved for them to follow him through.

Garum tried to stretch out his calf muscles as he moved across from the stone of the stairway to the metal floor of the Deeps. *I must be an experienced adventurer now,* he thought. *This room is like all the others I've seen next to entryway doors.* The chamber was perhaps twenty by twenty feet with slightly curved corridors going off to the left and right. Straight ahead, a wide passage led toward the center of the Deeps.

Sir Donal was the last person through. He shut the door carefully, so it wouldn't clang, and nodded to Görthang.

"Gather 'round," Görthang stage whispered. "We still need to be quiet, in case any elite teams or cadres of tunnel snake hunters are on this level, but I can at least brief everyone on what Fess told me."

The rest of the combined parties pressed into a close semicircle with three rows. The larger and taller individuals were in the back and the smaller and shorter ones in the front. Xarra and Yarra stood in the middle row, each gripping one of Púki's arms and holding him up so he could see over Drain and Kléppri while ensuring he couldn't cause any mischief. Garum and Sweetie were beside Drain and Kléppri in the front row.

Görthang cleared his throat, sounding like he was gargling rocks. "I have good news and bad news," he began.

"What's the good news?" asked Blōgot.

"We don't need to walk all the way to Dragon Keep," Görthang answered.

"And the bad news?" said Púki, earning glares from the twins.

"We *do* have to walk down more stairs to get to our ride."

"How many more stairs?" asked Garum.

"Another ten flights," said Görthang.

"I can manage that," said Garum. "Down is a lot easier than up."

"If you're tired, I can carry you," said Sir Donal. "My strength is as the strength of ten, because…"

"…you're wearing magic vambraces," said Sweetie, smiling at her grandfather.

Sir Donal's face fell.

"And because your heart is pure," Sweetie added.

Sir Donal's expression changed from a mask of tragedy to one of comedy in an instant. "Thank you, granddaughter," he said.

Sweetie's smile grew wider, and she curtsied.

"I think my dignity would prefer that I move myself under my own power," said Garum. *She's adorable,* he thought.

"Good," said Görthang. "Because I'd prefer to have Sir Donal unencumbered in case we run into an elite team from the Martial Academy…"

"Or a squad of soldiers hunting tunnel snakes," said Lark.

"Don't forget to listen for other sorts of threats, too," noted Görthang. "The Deeps are a dangerous place, and we don't want to let our guard down."

"Right," said Crank as Jelly split himself in two and formed a pair of giant ear trumpets for Crank. "I'll keep my ears peeled."

Garum, remembering all the skins he'd removed from potatoes as an army cook, didn't feel it necessary to correct Crank's usage by telling him it only applied to eyes, not ears. He suspected Crank knew that quite well and was simply trying to lighten everyone's spirits. *How do you specify sharpened hearing, anyway?* Garum wondered.

"I'll listen, too," said Flisk, cupping a hand beside one of his pointed ears.

Ah, thought Garum. *Elf-like hearing is probably a good choice.*

The stairs, made of the same gray metal as the corridors, were only a hundred paces to the left. Before they began their descent, Garum looked over his shoulder and saw Vip-vip was bringing up the rear. He watched the vixer wave to him, then touch something on a section of wall, causing a pair of hitherto unseen doors to slide open. They silently closed after Vip-vip stepped through them, causing Garum to shake his head. He considered alerting everyone to the vixer's disappearance but ended up going down the stairs instead. *I shouldn't worry about Vip-vip,* Garum realized. *He's more at home in the Deeps than any of us. I'm sure he can take care of himself.*

When they'd reached their designated level, Görthang led them into the curving corridor analogous to the one they'd left above that appeared to circle the outer circumference of the Deeps at every level.

Vip-vip was waiting for them. "ELLY!" he said by way of explanation for his appearance.

"There was a lift," grumbled Garum. "I didn't need to *walk* down more stairs at all." He frowned at Vip-vip. "You might have told me."

Vip-vip shrugged, an elaborate rippling process for a being with six arms and turned up the palms on all of his hands as if to say *Sorry.*

Garum realized Vip-vip probably would have told him if he'd stopped to listen instead of just following Görthang. He put his hands together and bowed to Vip-vip, offering an unspoken apology. *I'll have to remember to take Vip-vip's route back up,* he reminded himself. *My calves will appreciate it.*

"How far is this *ride* you mentioned?" asked Púki.

"Pipe down," said Xarra, leaning close to Púki's ear.

"Shhhh!" added Yarra.

Görthang moved his lips without actually speaking. "It's not far," he mouthed.

Garum struggled to keep from laughing when he read Lark's lips as she 'talked' to Arrex. "Watch out for tunnel snakes!" he thought she said, though it could have been, "I'll have some funnel cakes!" *Now I'm making myself hungry,* Garum realized. *I'd gladly deal with tunnel snakes if they're such minor threats the Martial Academy only sends out squads of trainees to eliminate them.*

Not far turned out to be not that close, either. They had been proceeding along the curving corridor for hundreds of yards when Garum's ears—not as sensitive as an elf's but more sensitive than a typical human's—detected a soft, rhythmically recurring sound. *Tick tick tick tick tick tick tick.*

Flisk cupped his ear and shook his head, then accelerated his pace to come up next to Garum. "Do you hear it, too?" he mouthed. Crank joined them a moment later. Garum read his lips: *What's ticking?*

The ticks grew louder and louder over the next few seconds. The sounds were coming from far down the corridor. Something out of sight around the curve was headed their way.

Vip-vip reacted to the sound like someone had goosed him with lightning bolt. All six of his arms began to wave and he ran frantically along the curving corridor away from the sounds until he found what he wanted. The vixer pushed a symbol on the corridor's wall and a door opened. Everyone except Crank, Flisk, and Garum—who'd been farthest away—crowded through the door, which closed leaving no visible seam in the smooth metal.

"That's not good," said Garum, no longer worried about speaking, given the volume of the rhythmic, high decibel ticking.

Motion-activated wizard lamps along the corridor's length activated and the human, elf, and halfling saw a massive flood of brown, pill-shaped creatures the size of full-grown boars inexorably heading their way. They were insectoids, with six legs and over-lapping plates of chitin. Their legs made the tick tick tick sound as they moved. Garum also noted how their huge, multi-faceted eyes had a short and a long line radiating out from their centers like the faces of the time trackers atop some of the towers in the ruins of the ancient's cities.

"Aiiii!" said Flisk. "Clockroaches!"

"I've heard of them," said Crank. "My aunt says they'll eat anything in their way, flesh, bones, and all."

"That's doubly not good," said Garum. "Can they fly?"

"I don't know," said Flisk.

"My aunt didn't say," said Crank. "They seem a bit heavy to manage it."

"Maybe we can get out of their way, then," said Garum.

"What are you thinking?" asked Flisk. "And whatever it is, think fast." The elf could see the wave of clockroaches fast approaching their position.

"Can Jelly make himself sticky?" Garum asked Crank.

"I think he has to concentrate *not* to be sticky," Crank replied.

Jelly understood what Garum wanted even faster than Crank did. He immediately fissioned into a dozen pieces and attached those pieces to Garum, Flisk, and Crank's hands and feet. Garum, using Jelly's stick-to-itiveness, began to climb up the wall of the corridor and flatten himself on the ceiling. Flisk and Crank did likewise, just before the wave of clockroaches swept by beneath them. They watched a nest of tunnel snakes with bad timing for hatching be completely consumed by the giant ticking insects.

"Quick thinking," Crank told Jelly.

Garum let it slide, realizing that Jelly really did deserve the credit for rescuing them. Then Jelly stretched out bits of his protoplasm and reduced his adhesion to gently lower the three adventurers to the floor of the corridor. Once that was accomplished, the twelve separate balls of protoplasm consolidated and reformed into Jelly's normal self. A heartbeat later, Jelly resumed his usual perch on Crank's shoulder.

"Thanks, Jelly," said Garum.

The blob of protoplasm stretched and bent to bow to Garum before slumping back into an undifferentiated mass like a bowl of thick pudding.

"That got my blood pumping," said Flisk.

"Mine, too," said Crank.

"I'd gladly never do that again," said Garum. The others nodded their agreement.

"I wonder why they came by when they did?" asked Flisk. "Could we have simply been in the wrong place?"

"They're *clock*roaches," said Crank. "It was more likely the wrong time."

"I'm just glad we got out of their way," said Garum. "I'll give the others the *all-clear* and we can get on with finding our ride."

"Suits me," said Crank. He looked down and noticed a tiny broken glass bottle on the corridor's metal floor. "Well, I may be wrong," said the young cook. "I think my tincture of teaberry fell out of my pack when we first passed this point. I wonder if that's what drew the clockroaches. There aren't any traces of the liquid left."

"That could be," said Garum. "I have more in my cooking kit if you need it."

"Thanks," said Crank.

"What *is* tincture of teaberry and what do you make with it?" asked Flisk.

"It's a delicate sort of mint," said Garum. "It grows wild in the mountains east of Confluence."

"I add it to rice pudding and use it to flavor candy," said Crank. "I'll make you some."

"After we're out of the Deeps," said Flisk.

Garum found the spot on the wall where he thought the door must be and rapped on it three times. Someone on the other side rapped back twice and before Garum could step back the door opened, and Sweetie was hugging him.

"I'm *so* sorry the door closed before you were inside," she said. "Vip-vip indicated that it was some sort of automatic function when danger was detected. I hope you weren't harmed by whatever it was."

"So far, I'm in one *time* piece," said Garum.

It took a few minutes for him to explain himself, but once that was done and they'd been congratulated by the other members of the party on their quick thinking, they followed Görthang once again. Five minutes later, they saw markings on the inner wall showing parallel lines with rounded rectangles between them.

"Here we are," said Görthang. "This is the *rail road* Fess told me about. I'll summon a carriage for us." The big orc pushed a section of wall and soon they heard soft chimes and a whoosh of air like the sound of a falcon's wings as it stooped on its prey.

Two adjacent segments of wall slid open, revealing a carriage like a luxurious oversized magecoach, complete with comfortable couches and chairs in an assortment of sizes. Everyone found suitable places to sit, with Garum and Sweetie occupying an overstuffed human-sized armchair that was more of a loveseat given their small statures.

"How does this *rail road* work?" asked Arrex.

"I think it levitates above a guide track," said Crank.

"By magic?" asked Prestyn.

"I expect so," said Crank.

"So, it's a *magelev* system?" said Prestyn.

"That's a reasonable name for it," said Crank.

Garum smiled. *I'm less interested in what it's called and more concerned with getting past South Keep without a fight.*

Görthang saw a circular diagram on the wall of the carriage near the doors and tapped on the third square clockwise from their current location. The doors of the carriage closed with a distinctive puff of air. Garum felt himself gently pressed back against the armchair's padding as the carriage moved smoothly, sliding like soft fluffy clouds scudding gently across a summer sky. He sighed and snuggled under Sweetie's arm, listening to her breathing. A dozen breaths later, he was asleep.

Chapter 38
Marshall Dylán

Pleasant dreams of cuddling Sweetie in a featherbed were interrupted when the part of Garum's mind that still retained some awareness of his surroundings even in sleep sensed that the carriage he was riding in was slowing down and coming to a stop. *Too soon?* the wary part of his brain asked. He was reluctant to wake up further but had that choice taken from him when he heard the distinctive puff of air that marked the doors of the carriage sliding open. Garum felt clawed hands pull him away from Sweetie. His eyes snapped open as one of those same hands covered his mouth and strong arms attached to the hands dragged him out of the carriage and into a large, gray-walled chamber much like the one they'd left from in the Deeps below Forge Keep.

"Put him down!" shouted Sweetie.

Garum heard a low-pitched rumbling laugh resonate in the chest his body was held against and saw his friends' faces flow into expressions of shock, fear, and horror. *This isn't good,* he thought. *Wake up, Garum,* he told himself. *Not good is clearly a massive understatement—probably as massive as the individual holding me.*

"Dylán," said Görthang.

Garum felt the head of the person holding him shift up and down in a nod.

"Welcome to South Keep Deeps," said Marshall Dylán. "Please step out of the magelev. If you don't, I might have an involuntary muscle spasm and break this bothersome halfling's neck."

"We'll get out," said Hrefna as she moved her considerable trollish frame out into the chamber, making room for the others to leave behind her.

"Your muscles haven't done anything involuntary since you last soiled yourself as a toddler," Görthang told Dylán.

"And you, Görthang," Dylán replied, "never understood the distinction between polite and overt threats."

"You weren't polite when you demanded we work for you," said Hrefna.

"Then again," said Dylán, "was it polite for the Black Company to leave South Keep in the middle of the night without giving me an answer to my request for you to be one of the Martial Academy's elite teams?"

"I thought you were smart enough to understand that our departure *was* an answer," said Görthang.

Garum saw Görthang's lips curl, revealing even more of his fangs. *These two have some history,* Garum's increasingly alert brain informed him. *And I'm a pawn in their chess game.* He tried to smile but couldn't, because the hand held tightly over his mouth gave him no room. As he had another second to consider his situation, Garum had a further insight. *Marshall Dylán knows about the influencer potion I drank and doesn't want to risk me speaking. I wonder who told him? Galena?* Garum would have slapped his forehead if he was capable of moving.

Görthang was staring at Garum—or rather, at Dylán, Garum realized, locking in some sort of battle for mental dominance. Garum had seen that sort of thing often enough serving in the army. It could end with one party backing down or with an explosion of violence. *I can't exactly offer to buy them both a drink at present,* thought Garum. That was one of his usual strategies to deescalate such confrontations. The part of Garum's brain responsible for answering the questions he'd asked himself finally responded.

No, he thought. *Not Galena. She's probably still feeding geese. More likely, the woman with blue highlights in her dark black hair who wore white healers' robes with a single wide red stripe—Galena's chief lieutenant.*

Görthang and Dylán continued their conversation.

"I must admit, you and your Black Company proved yourselves capable as independent operatives," said Dylán. "I've been following your exploits."

"While I haven't spared *you* a moment's thought," Görthang replied.

"Which was clearly a strategic oversight," said Dylán. "Get me the vials, woman, and no fast moves."

Garum watched Sweetie approach and slowly open his belt pouch. She removed a pair of vials and held them out to Marshall Dylán for his inspection.

"Good," said Dylán. "Put them on the deck in front of me and back away slowly."

Sweetie did as she was ordered and Garum could see her eyes pleading with Dylán not to hurt Garum. He tried to make his own gaze reassuring but just wasn't feeling it with Dylán's tight grip over his mouth.

"You've got what you wanted, O High and Mighty Marshall with two Ls," said Görthang. "Now let us get on about our travels."

"But I *don't* have what I wanted," said Dylán, "or not *all* that I wanted, at any rate. And marshall spelled the way I prefer is a usage that was ancient even to the ancients. I think it adds an element of *gravitas* to my title."

"I'd prefer to add *grave* instead of *gravitas* to your appellation," said Hrefna.

"Listen to you, sounding as erudite as one of the scholars at the University," said Dylán.

"What else do you want?" asked Görthang.

"What every marshal has always desired," said Dylán.

"The Golden Sword," said Crank.

Garum shifted his eyes to see Crank off to one side and watched as everyone else turned to face him as well.

"The young scholar is wise," said Dylán. "Your aunt trained you well."

"Not well enough," said Crank.

"What's the Golden Sword?" asked Sweetie.

"The ultimate symbol of command for the military leaders of the Keep Lands," said Crank. "The scholars took it half a century ago when Dylán's predecessor decided to ignore the advice of the Guild Master, the Provost, and the Dean."

"How do *you* know such things?" Hrefna asked Crank.

"My grandfather was the Dean who took the sword," said Crank.

"Oh," said Hrefna.

Garum saw Sweetie's eyes grow wide and remembered that Crank had worked with her at the inn where they'd all met. The young kitchen drudge who'd prepared boiled potatoes for a cook-off a few weeks ago was the closest thing to a prince of the University.

"This is convenient," said Dylán. "You shouldn't have any problem collecting the Golden Sword and returning it to me in a week's time."

"We're not leaving without Garum," said Sweetie.

"I thought you might say that," said Dylán.

Garum felt a gag being stuffed in his mouth and a wide leather strap fastened around his neck. It tightened, replacing the grip of Dylán's fingers.

"This enchanted band around the halfling's neck will contract every day until he will no longer be able to breathe," said Dylán. "It should be about a week, give or take. Perhaps that will provide an incentive for you to work expeditiously."

A gag was roughly shoved in Garum's mouth and he was pushed away from Dylán and into Sweetie, who hugged him close. Her embrace was much more welcome than Dylán's had been.

"We'll get you the sword if you'll remove the enchanted strangling band after we do," said Görthang. "But we're not going to be one of your elite teams."

"So long as you'll act as one long enough to get me the sword, I can accept that," said Dylán. "Remember, you only have a week before the band cuts off the halfling's air."

"We won't forget," said Sweetie.

"What about the inimical animacules in the vials?" asked Hrefna. "If you release them while we're seeking the sword, the ensuing chaos might hinder our quest."

"Don't worry," said Dylán. "I'm only planning small scale experiments to breed super soldier orcs while you're away. They'll be bigger, stronger, and smarter when I'm finished."

"So you're going to turn them into trolls, then?" said Hrefna.

Dylán chuckled. "But more tractable, willing to follow my orders."

"So dumber than trolls," said Hrefna.

"And orcs," added Blōgot.

"And ogres," said Gêrdun.

"Anyone else want to chime in and waste time?" asked Dylán. "Wait too long and the halfling's head will be rolling on the floor."

"Mmmmph!" said Garum.

"We're leaving," said Görthang.

"Good," said Dylán. "I held the magelev for you."

The doors to the waiting conveyance opened behind the Black and Gold Companies. Garum allowed himself to be pulled back aboard by his companions. The doors of the magelev slid closed and it started moving. Garum's muscles didn't stop twitching and tensing until Sweetie removed the gag from his mouth.

"That's better," she said after she gave him a quick kiss on his now liberated lips.

Garum rubbed his neck and tried to fit a finger under the leather band, to no avail. "Easy for you to say," he said with a grimace. "You're not the one being slowly strangled."

"True," said Sweetie. "But we'll figure out how to save you. If we *have* to, we'll find the Golden Sword for Marshall Dylán.

"I suppose so," said Garum. "It's a shame he managed to get the vials before we could destroy them, though."

"Did he?" said Sweetie. The grin on her face suggested otherwise. "Check your belt pouch."

Garum opened his pouch and reached inside, finding the vials he'd taken from Galena on the way to Horse Keep Town. "If I still have *these,* what did Dylán get?"

"Your condiment tubes of oil and vinegar," said Sweetie. "They should be useful next time he has a salad."

"Blast," said Garum.

"What?" said Sweetie.

"That vinegar was made from my favorite grapes, and the oil was..." began Garum.

"We'll get you more," she replied. "After we destroy the *dangerous* vials at Dragon Keep Town."

"If we can find a cooperative dragon with a hot enough fire, that is," said Garum.

"I have confidence in you," said Sweetie. "In the meantime, we should find a place to stop and get some sleep, so we're rested before we negotiate with dragons."

"That sounds wise," said Garum. He looked up at Görthang who was shaking his head and smiling.

"You two should get a room," said the orc warrior.

"That *is* what we'd concluded," said Sweetie. "Know any good inns around Iron Keep Town?"

"If he doesn't, I do," said Drain. "There are a lot of dwarves there."

"We'll need somewhere that has beds big enough for trolls, ogres, and sylviants, not just dwarves," said Hrefna. "I'm not interested in sleeping on the floor."

"I know just the place," said Drain.

"Does it have rooms with large bathing tubs as well?" asked Sweetie. "I have plans for this evening."

"Oh yes," said Drain. "I helped design the water flow for some of the suites."

"Good to know," said Garum, clearly referring back to Sweetie's plans, not Drain's designs. He rubbed the band around his neck again. "I hope this won't get in the way of what you've got in mind."

"What I have in mind is a scenario along the lines of *the princess and the prisoner*," said Sweetie.

"Which one of us will be the princess?" asked Garum.

Sweetie patted Garum on the head. "You'll figure it out," she said.

As the magelev accelerated away from the station, Garum's mind considered just what Sweetie's plan might include. *Yes,* he told himself, *I* will *figure it out and that can be enough for today. Destroying the vials and finding the Golden Sword can be our* next *adventure!*

Please visit

www.GuardianKeeps.com

for more information about
Garum, Sweetie, and their friends